Perfect Touch

ROMANCE

This Time Love

Eden Burning

Beautiful Dreamer

Remember Summer

To the Ends of the Earth

Where the Heart Is

Desert Rain

A Woman Without Lies

Lover in the Rough

Forget Me Not

HISTORICAL ROMANCE

Winter Fire

Autumn Lover

Only Love

Enchanted

Forbidden

Untamed

Only You

Only Mine

Only His

Perfect Touch

Elizabeth Lowell

HARPER **LUXE**

An Imprint of HarperCollins*Publishers*

PERFECT TOUCH. Copyright © 2015 by Two of a Kind, Inc. All rights reserved. Printed in the United States of America. No part of this book may be used or reproduced in any manner whatsoever without written permission except in the case of brief quotations embodied in critical articles and reviews. For information address HarperCollins Publishers, 195 Broadway, New York, NY 10007.

HarperCollins books may be purchased for educational, business, or sales promotional use. For information please e-mail the Special Markets Department at SPsales@harpercollins.com.

FIRST HARPERLUXE EDITION

HarperLuxe™ is a trademark of HarperCollins Publishers

Library of Congress Cataloging-in-Publication Data is available upon request.

ISBN: 978-0-06-236976-5

15 ID/RRD 10 9 8 7 6 5 4 3 2 1

To Emily Krump,
who makes all things editorial run so smoothly for me.
Much appreciation!

Perfect Touch

Chapter 1

The motel room door was ajar.

I locked it, Sara Anne Medina thought. *Didn't I?*

She pushed the door open with her big purse and froze. The room had been tossed ruthlessly. Her suitcase was upended and off the stand. Her clothes were strewn across the worn carpet, her toiletries scattered, her underwear and workout gear tumbled together. The lavender scent of her favorite shampoo filled the air.

I was only gone for five minutes.

The take-out coffee she had bought was hot against her suddenly chilled hands.

Some stranger went through my things. Did the tweaker get off on my underwear?

Is he still here?

The thought had her jerking back so quickly the coffee sloshed over her cold-numbed fingers. She looked around the hallway. No one in sight.

I don't have time for this drama. I have to be at the courthouse. I have to finally meet my mystery man, so I'll stop dreaming and get back to reality, where I belong.

Where I want to be, even with the damn tweakers.

Using her foot, she kicked the door all the way open until it slammed against the stop. No one was behind it. No one was in the room itself. The closet was open, no place inside to hide. The bathroom door showed a view of the toilet, shower, and sink. The mirror was smudged where she'd cleared the shower's steam with her hand just minutes ago.

Whoever had been here was gone.

The mess wasn't.

It will have to wait. Then, *They took my computer. It's all backed up on the cloud, but damn it!*

The cord dangled from the wall, over the chair that had held her overcoat. The coat, like the computer, had vanished.

Wonder how many pawnshops there are in Jackson, Wyoming? And why would they take a woman's coat? There aren't too many women my height who are a size six.

With a hand that trembled slightly, Sara set down her coffee, took a pen out of the bottomless bag that passed for her purse, and poked through the mess of clothes on the floor to the suitcase half hidden beneath. The inside pockets were still zipped closed.

They missed my little jewelry case. I'd rather they take the jewelry and leave the computer, but they didn't ask me, did they?

A glance at her watch told her she was out of time. Soon, a different stranger would be deciding the fate of her career in a Jackson courthouse. With a silent curse, she hurried to the front desk.

"I'm in room 101," Sara told the woman there. "My room has been robbed. Computer and coat missing. Tell the sheriff or whoever cares that I'll be at the courthouse."

Leaving the woman stuttering questions behind her, Sara strode out the front entrance into the chill streets of Jackson in the spring. Within ten steps she was regretting the loss of her coat.

And she had forgotten her coffee.

Quickly she walked down what had to be the coldest sidewalk in town. The wind rolled straight off the snow of the Tetons through the streets. The chill was made worse by the fact that the sun was shining bright and hard enough to look like summer.

An archway leading into a small park caught her eye. At first she thought the arch was made of the bones of cattle that she'd seen as a child. But these were different. They were more elegant and pointed, tapering out. They didn't feel like the finality of death, but more a symbol of life cycling through change.

Antlers, she realized. *Grown and shed each year in a cycle that isn't birth or death, but simply another way to be. Like Custer's paintings, a beautiful and eerie reminder that wilderness—wildness—isn't all that far away.*

Shivering, she hurried on.

I should be back in San Francisco, holding hot coffee from Murray's Cafe as I head up to the offices of Perfect Touch.

But then all I'd know about my mystery man is his voice.

So what? the practical part of her mind pointed out. *The last thing I need is a man.*

Sara liked living her life on her own terms, doing what she wanted whenever she wanted. As the only girl out of seven children, she'd had more than enough diapers, housework, and babysitting to last her a lifetime.

Wind with icy teeth bit at her black slacks and tugged at her red pullover sweater. The only thing that kept the wind from billowing up her sweater was the sleek black leather belt snugged at her waist. But it wasn't enough to keep her warm.

Damn that thief.

Then she reminded herself that it could be worse in so many ways. She could be back home on the dairy farm—a plain, rebellious teen hauling a feed cart through damp, drafty barns, then making the return trip leading a stubborn Holstein.

At least there aren't any holes in my boots forcing me to get up close and personal with fresh cow flops.

The phone in her pants pocket rang.

If it's the sheriff, he can wait.

Even as that irritated thought crossed her mind, she hesitated. The call could be from Jay Vermilion, the man who had dozens of fine art paintings that could kick her career up to the next level, paintings with the potential to be so valuable that they'd been the part of an ongoing hotly contested divorce settlement.

Maybe, just maybe, she thought, *one of those paintings is the fabled* Muse, *the only portrait painted by* Custer.

That would explain why the legal battle had outlived the original owner of the paintings, JD Vermilion. His much-younger ex-wife, Liza—who had begun suing JD's estate six years ago to gain access to the art her former husband had begun collecting before she'd even been a teenager in braces—had, with his passing, simply turned her lawyers loose on the primary heir to JD Vermilion's estate, his son, Jay.

Sara's mouth curved slightly as she continued walking. *I've never met the infamous Liza Neumann, once Vermilion. But with possession being nine-tenths of the law, I'd put money on Captain Jay Vermilion keeping his ex-stepmother's hands off the undiscovered Armstrong "Custer" Harris paintings in the future.*

The retired army veteran who had recently inherited the family ranch—the fruit of generations of his Vermilion ancestors—had a grit and determination to him that came right through the phone line.

You haven't even met the man, Sara reminded herself. She fished the cellular out of her tight front pocket at last, glanced at it, and saw the call had gone to voice mail. She palmed the phone and gave a mental shrug. It wasn't a Wyoming number calling, which meant it wasn't the sheriff.

Or Jay, damn it.

Think of the good captain like any other potential client who calls you during business hours to get advice on western art, she told herself firmly.

Impossible.

Jay Vermilion might be a potential client, but he was also the man she had been talking to half the nights for the past few months. At first it had been all business, but somehow the conversations had quickly evolved into . . . more.

I don't know how I could talk about myself and my work and my dreams like that with someone I've never met. And he talked to me, too, about the ranch and weather and the western woman he hoped to find and marry, the woman who would bear the seventh generation of Vermilions.

We have such different lives and goals, it's surprising we had so much to talk about in the first place.

Sara's phone chimed and vibrated in her hand. She looked down, saw her partner's phone number, and connected. For a few minutes Piper Embry would take Sara's mind off the cold and the man whose deep voice wove through her dreams.

"Bought any great rugs lately?" Sara asked.

"I've got my eye on some that have me checking Perfect Touch's bank balance."

"What happened to consignment?"

"I'm working on it," Piper said. "What's this message you left about Wyoming?"

"I wrapped up the Chens early and came to Jackson."

"I thought you were getting tired of flying all over the place."

"I am."

"But you're still lusting after those Custers? Or is it Jay Vermilion of the incredible voice?"

"Wait until—if—I get my hands on those paintings," Sara said, ignoring Piper's teasing. "They will wring the hearts and pocketbooks of at least five of my clients, and go a long way toward reducing my world travel." Chilly air swirled hard against her, blowing her hair into a nearly black cloud around her face.

"What's that sound?" Piper asked.

"Wind. Spring here is long on bluster and short on cherry petals."

Sara glanced around quickly, looking for shelter. All she saw was another odd arch leading into another part of the park. Or maybe out of it. Whichever, she opted to stay in the sun.

"You okay?" Piper asked. "Your voice is different. Kind of strained."

"You know me too well. My room was robbed. Computer and coat are gone. But I'm fine. Don't have time right now for some junkie's drama. In five minutes the judge is supposed to finally deliver the verdict on the Vermilion case."

There were a few moments of silence, then Piper asked softly, "Want me to come out?"

Sara hurried in the direction of the courthouse. "No need. I can handle the Vermilion paintings alone."

"Ah, yes, Jay Vermilion. He of the deep and delicious voice. Does he look half as good as he sounds?"

"Haven't seen him." Sara glanced both ways and trotted across the street against the light.

"Maybe he can warm up your . . . spring," Piper said.

"If I get to handle the sale of the Custer paintings, my spring will be just toasty. Yours, too. The Newcastle twins are dancing in place at the thought of owning paintings seen in *The Edge of Never*."

"The what?"

"Weepy contemporary movie about a young couple who doesn't know how to love and doesn't have the sense to separate."

"Ugh. If you have to be taught those things, you've got more problems than a movie can solve."

Sara laughed. "I hear you, but it rocked Sundance. That's where the Newcastle twins saw it and immediately huddled with the director, very hush-hush. The movie is probably going to rock Cannes just as hard."

"And Custer, the moderately well-known western artist, ties in how?"

"There's a painting of his, *Wyoming Spring*, that's featured prominently throughout the movie, including the heartrending scene where—"

"Spare me the details," Piper said quickly. "Merchant-Ivory movies make my butt numb."

"Because of it—the movie, not your butt—the market for Custer's works will heat up like Vegas in July."

"What about the big auction houses?"

"The Vermilion estate has probably half the Custers that were ever painted and nearly all of them that aren't yet in circulation," Sara said. "We may not need to go through a big public auction if we can act as the agents. No percentage sharing."

"Go for it. I'll get Lou to cover anything on this end for Perfect Touch. She's got some downtime."

"What happened? Couldn't Lou seal the deal with Najafi?"

"Lou's good, but Najafi would try God's patience," Piper said. "How long will you be gone?"

"If Jay Vermilion loses the paintings, I'll be home tomorrow."

"In that case, girlfriend, have a long stay in Wyoming."

"You'll nag me to come back after two weeks."

"Not if there's money involved. Bye. Go get those bucks!"

"Go get some yourself."

Smiling, Sara pocketed the phone, flipped her hair out of her face, and hurried along the sidewalk to meet her future.

With her fingers crossed in her pockets.

Chapter 2

Inside the wood-paneled hearing room, Jay Vermilion stretched against his borrowed jacket, trying to loosen the leather across his shoulders.

Never thought anything of JD's would be small on me.

But it was.

Henry Pederson said under his breath, "Quit twitching, boy. Remember what JD said and never show anyone fear."

Their attorney, sitting next to Henry, bit back a smile as he made last-minute notes.

Jay gave his shaggy ranch foreman a sideways look. "I learned about fear and stillness in places you've never seen."

"Yeah. When you reupped for 'Trashcanistan' I figured you'd never come back to the ranch."

"So did I. Then I got tired of unreal politics and real bullets."

"Good thing. Liza about bled the ranch dry," Henry said. He started to spit, remembered where he was, and swallowed instead. "Hope the judge doesn't finish the job."

"We'll survive without the paintings."

"Thought you wanted to meet Ms. Sara Medina," Henry said, rubbing his mustache. "She sounds like a pistol."

Jay hid the warmth that slid through him at her name, but he didn't bother to hide his grin. "Yes, she does. A lot of fire and intelligence, too. If we get the Custers, we'll owe her."

"Damned painter. Never was worth much but trouble. Ranch was better off without him."

But we'd be better off with his paintings, Jay thought. *There's so much the ranch needs. I finally could fix all the little things that were let go until it became a big, expensive, run-down mess.*

He didn't say anything aloud about the condition of the ranch. Henry was seventy-four and thin as a fence post. As tough, too. He had done the best he could to hold things together while Jay was gone and JD went into his long, slow decline.

With a glance at his watch, Jay settled back. "No matter what the judge finally decides, fence wire still needs tightening in the south pasture, mineral licks need to be put out, irrigation trenches kept up, and cattle moved to greener pastures. That's real. The rest is just dogs barking at the moon."

Henry rubbed his long, uneven mustache, more silver than black now, and nodded. "Your daddy taught you good."

"He must have. I'm alive."

The foreman smiled crookedly. "Chip off the old stubborn block."

"JD met his match with Liza Neumann."

A grunt was Henry's only answer. He had never thought much of JD's second wife and had seen no particular reason to hide it.

While the second hand crawled around the old hearing room clock, Jay thought of all the things he could be doing at the ranch. He wanted to grab his town Stetson off the table in front of him, walk out of the court, and get back to work. Then tonight, Sara Medina would call with a question, or he would call her, and they'd talk. He'd tell her about the hearing room and the judge and the verdict. She'd tell him about the sophisticated, pricey items she searched out and bought for wealthy, demanding clients.

Give me an ornery cow any day, he thought.

He looked over to the plaintiff's side of the courtroom. Liza's pair of attorneys waited as quiet as owls hunting for their next meal. He knew exactly what her lawyers were being paid, since the Vermilion estate had been footing their legal bill for the past six years.

Just like everything else in Liza's life, Jay thought wearily. *She spends. Vermilion Ranch pays and pays and pays.*

Not for the first time, Jay hoped the screwing his father got was worth the screwing he got.

The hall door opened with a hollow sound that bounced around the bare hearing room. Liza Neumann, formerly Vermilion, made her entrance on high heels that stretched her five feet, five inches to five feet ten. Her strawberry blond hair had turned to platinum, a finishing touch on the ice-queen sheen. JD's diamonds hung from her ears and glittered on her hands. Unlike the Custer paintings, the jewelry JD had showered on his then-young wife was an uncontested gift.

"Ma'am," Jay said, standing when she passed around the side of his table.

Henry didn't move.

Liza paused as she reached her seat. "Thank you, Jay," she said in a husky, smoky voice. "Whatever JD's many faults, he raised you polite."

Henry waited until she was seated at the plaintiff's table before he said to Jay, "Wish JD was here."

"Even if he was still alive, he wouldn't be here in any way but physical." As Jay sat back down, he gave the buckskin across his shoulders one last stretch. "He used to be okay most of the day. Then he started fading before sundown. Then it was the afternoon. Then . . ."

"Hell of a way for a strong man to die," Henry said, shaking his shaggy gray head. "I get like that, just shoot me and leave me for the bears."

The hall door opened again. Jay didn't have to turn around to recognize the quick sounds of his much younger half brother's leather shoes making an expensive tattoo down the aisle.

"That kid will be late to his own funeral," Henry muttered. "Ain't much of JD in him. A mama's boy through and through."

"JD didn't get much of a chance to raise him." *And I left for West Point long before Barton could shave.*

What's done is done. Now we have to live with it.

Barton paused near the end of the aisle separating the plaintiff's and defendant's tables. His delicate features and pale skin were blotchy and flushed, as if he'd just run all the way there. He took off his black overcoat, showing a lightweight cream suit beneath. Like everything else about him, his clothes had an expensive eastern cut. In this case, New York via Miami, where he had been trying to finalize a big real estate deal.

Or so people said.

Jay didn't much care for gossip, but he could see that something was eating on his brother from the inside out. Beneath the pink flush of exertion, his skin was white and his shoulders hunched like a man hefting a heavy load. His rust-red hair was barely tamed by the expensive razor cut. At twenty-four, his light blue eyes had a look of permanent anxiety in them.

When Barton's eyes darted toward the defendant's table, Jay used his boot to shove out a chair in silent invitation.

Barton looked toward Liza just as she turned to him and raised her eyebrows. With an apologetic glance at Jay, the younger man went to the plaintiff's table. He reached to pull out a chair, discovered it was heavy, solid wood, and had to put his back into the effort. A few moments later he flopped down next to Liza.

She didn't even look at him.

Jay shook his head slightly. *A winter wind is kinder than that woman, and JD was old enough to be Barton's grandfather. Lousy way to raise a kid.*

Money only fixed the things that money could. Barton's childhood wasn't one of them.

"Give it up," Henry said. "The boy knows which side his bread is buttered on."

"If he did, he'd be sitting next to me. I keep trying to give him a chance, to teach him about the ranch."

"Can't teach what a kid don't want to learn."

Jay didn't argue with the truth. "In one way, Barton is exactly like I was at his age. I wanted to be hell and gone from the ranch."

Henry's gnarled fingers fiddled with the brim of his going-to-town Stetson, started to put it on, then remembered why it was on the table. "You sure got what you wanted."

"I sure did," Jay said, and then turned his mind from the distant place that had been dubbed the Meatgrinder by the troops who survived. "I guess lawyers are more civilized than bullets. But being sued to death one inch at a time gets tiresome. Thank God Sara—Ms. Medina—helped us fight for JD's claim to the paintings. Don't know what we would have done without her. And you, of course, helping to find those receipts."

"Foolishness, sneezing through boxes of old stuff when the ranch needed tending."

"It was what JD wanted."

Henry sighed. "He was set on keeping those paintings. Never knew why. Pure cussedness, likely."

"It was the last thing he ever asked of me. If I can keep the Custers out of Liza's hands, I will," Jay said simply.

It was the same vow he'd made every night to JD, a vow his father had to hear before he slept. Then he would curl around the reassurance like a big diamond as he slept.

Some diamond. It felt like an unsheathed blade to me, a cut that he mistook for comfort.

Or maybe he liked pain.

It sure would explain Liza.

"The man loved what he loved," Henry said. "Wasn't real smart about it, though."

Jay hissed out a breath. "I'm not sure that love had much to do with it. Liza and JD fought to the death over these paintings. But custody of the child? Settled in an hour. When I got old enough and left, Barton was stuck with two parents who were too busy fighting to raise him."

"Don't feel bad for him," Henry said drily. "Either way, he can go with the winning side."

Jay looked at his brother in his pale Miami suit and knew that Vermilion Ranch wasn't ever going to be home for him. But it was home for Jay and all the hands who worked there. Now more than ever, it was his job to make the place thrive.

In seven years, Barton gets a chunk of the ranch or I buy him out. If I have the money.

A stir went through the room as Judge Flink was announced. Everyone rose while the judge entered from the side and took her seat on the bench. When people were seated again, she smacked the gavel sharply and began summarizing the high points of the long case.

Good thing the military taught me patience, Jay thought, settling in to listen to the facts he had long ago memorized.

Chapter 3

The echo of Sara's footsteps faded inside the courthouse as she stopped in surprise. A small crowd loitered in front of the door to hearing room 3, where she'd been told the final words on the Vermilion case would be spoken. Most of the people who were waiting seemed to know one another. They were chatting in knots of two and three.

And everyone kept glancing toward the hearing room, waiting.

Friends of either side? Reporters? Bill collectors?

Nothing happened to answer Sara's silent questions.

Two men stood near the door to the hearing room. One was a bailiff in a sharply pressed khaki uniform with a thick brown jacket on top of that. His bronze badge gleamed in the hall's fluorescent lights. Sara recognized the second man, who was tall, gaunt, and dressed in a blue seersucker suit that bunched at his joints. Though his back was turned to her, she knew he would be wearing his trademark fuchsia bow tie.

Guy Beck. How did that pompous con artist find out about the Custers?

"Sorry, sir," the bailiff said clearly. "The defendant requested and received a closed hearing to avoid a media circus. You may wait with the others. Please clear the doorway."

Beck hesitated for a second, then turned and sauntered toward the knots of conversation.

Didn't see me, thank God, Sara thought. *Hope it stays that way.*

A uniformed man came down the hallway from the other side, had a quick, low-voiced conversation with the bailiff, then turned to the people waiting for the hearing room doors to open.

The new man was tall, tanned beneath his hat brim, thick through the body but not slack. His dark, keen eyes took in everyone with a quick sweep. There was some belly beneath his uniform, but he made no effort to hide it behind his open jacket.

Sara decided that he was a confident man, in or out of uniform.

"Excuse me," he said clearly, "is Sara Anne Medina here?"

From the corner of her eye she saw Beck's head snap in her direction. She ignored him and walked forward.

"I'm Sara Medina."

"Sheriff Cooke, ma'am." He nodded slightly.

"Look who's in trouble with the authorities," Beck said, and laughed.

The sheriff flicked him a glance. "God bless bystanders." His tone said the opposite. Then he said to her, "This way, please. It shouldn't take long."

Grateful that Beck wouldn't be able to overhear, Sara followed the sheriff about twenty feet farther down the hall, into the interior of the building.

"I understand that you're here on Vermilion Ranch business?" he said.

That's half true, she thought wryly. *Wonder which half he's most interested in.*

"I submitted testimony on the ranch's behalf," she said, indicating the closed hearing room down the hall. "But this isn't an official visit. I was hoping to see the case concluded."

He nodded. "When I was informed about the break-in and your connection to Jay, I figured that I had a moment or two to spare for this incident."

Someone sure has friends in high places, Sara thought. *Must be nice.*

"Mind telling me about your morning?" he asked.

Quickly, Sara ticked off the events of the morning, finishing with, "Can you tell me anything about the robbery? I was thinking that it might have been someone with a master key, since the door wasn't marked up."

The sheriff rolled his head just a little. "I doubt that there was much planning in this one. Feels more like a crime of opportunity. You probably didn't pull the door shut all the way when you hurried out for coffee. Good luck for them and bad luck for you."

"That's not reassuring."

The sheriff smiled slightly. "Crime didn't give Jackson a pass just because we aren't a big city. There are restaurants here that won't leave the good hot sauce out on the tables because it's too easy to pocket."

"Really? Why would petty thieves bother with hot sauce?"

"I've learned that the only real petty thieves are kids looking for a thrill. The rest of them are just plain thieves."

"Well, whoever trashed my room wasn't much good. He, she, or they missed the jewelry case in my luggage."

"Good news. Careless thieves can be caught. The careful ones rarely see the inside of jails."

Sara managed not to roll her eyes. "I know my computer and coat are pretty small in the big scheme."

"They are," he agreed. "But we fill out forms anyway." Without looking away from her, he pulled out his phone and swiped out the passcode with his thumb. "Any other details you can add?"

She gave him the model and year of the computer, described her black coat, and knew it was a waste of breath. Briskly she added, "I have my computer backed up to the cloud. The security on it will baffle an ordinary hacker, if it matters."

For the first time, the sheriff looked interested. "Had trouble before?"

"No. I live in San Francisco, so I'm careful about security of all kinds. I'm really angry about having to replace and restore a tool I use daily—and nightly—in my business. And I won't sleep in that room again. But that's not the kind of detail that will help you."

"Have you got another room?"

"Not yet."

"It will be tough," the sheriff said matter-of-factly. "The Norwegians are in town."

"The who?"

"Norwegians. They're late this year. Big group of them comes every year and takes over the town. Svarstad."

"Svarstad?" Sara asked, feeling like she had stumbled into someone else's play.

Nodding, he jotted out some notes on the phone while he talked. "Some generations back, a whole bunch of their kids ended up here. It's a big, multifamily reunion. Like I said, late this year. Add to that the regular tourist traffic and you've got a lot of No Vacancy signs." He looked at her with a smile in his eyes. "And don't try to buy any cod or salmon at the local stores."

"No cod, no salmon, no rooms. So I'm stuck at that motel?"

"You could try out of town, but there's not a whole lot to choose from."

Sara thought about having to rent a car and wondered if they were all snapped up, too. And she still had to order a new computer. And buy a coat. And find a place to sleep tonight. And break Guy Beck's kneecaps so he couldn't swoop in on the Custers. And meet Jay Vermilion in the flesh.

So much to do, so little time.

"If you think of anything else that might help, please call the sheriff's office." He flipped the cover on his phone and pocketed it once more. "When you see Jay, tell him I said hello."

"He mentioned knowing you," Sara remembered from a late-night conversation.

"I've known him for some time, worked for his dad. I might still be, but JD said that I was cut out for bigger things. Helped put me on this road."

"The Vermilions seem to be everywhere out here," she said. "He has some buildings downtown, right? I remember seeing that name on at least one from the taxi."

Cooke nodded and pulled up the zipper on his uniform jacket. "They're not the Kennedys, but they get by. Good to know that someone's taking a strong hand back at that ranch after JD's illness. Place was getting way too run-down. Henry did what he could, but he's no spring chicken."

Sara nodded. Jay had talked about that, too. A lot. "Well, thanks for your time, Sheriff. Good luck catching those guys."

He tipped his hat and nodded just as the hearing room door flew open and cracked sharply against the doorstop. A woman who looked like an aging showgirl stormed out.

A hard, sharp heart of mean wrapped in cashmere and diamonds, Sara thought.

Long platinum hair framed a face made rigid by anger. Rage boiled out of her as she brushed past the bailiff. Then she turned her head and growled.

"Barty, come along." Her heels clicked down the hallway with an irritable sound.

A short, redheaded man in a cream suit with a black overcoat over one shoulder slouched along after her. He was four steps behind and obviously not in any hurry to catch up.

"Well," the sheriff drawled as the woman vanished into the street, "looks like the Wicked Bitch of the West lost. Bless her."

"Who?"

"Liza Neumann, once Vermilion."

Chapter 4

The rest of the courtroom emptied more slowly. Most of the people who had been waiting in the hall rushed off after Liza Neumann. The rest converged around two men dressed like lawyers. Questions fell in a hard, cold rain.

When another man came out of the courtroom, everything female in Sara came to attention. It wasn't just the man's height that made him stand out. It was the way he carried himself, a man completely at ease in his own body. He had a face that was too strong, too masculine to be called beautiful and too unusual to be handsome. Striking. His skin had the kind of weathering that came from working outdoors. His soft leather jacket couldn't conceal the male power beneath.

Dark, western-cut pants outlined long, powerful legs. A black Stetson and polished black western boots were perfectly at home in the Wyoming setting.

Hoo doggies, that is one hot man, she thought. *Bet there isn't a Big Mac's worth of fat on him.*

Sara knew she was staring and didn't care. On- or offscreen, that kind of sheer maleness was rare.

Maybe I should get out of the city more.

Yeah, yeah, go to the country where men are men and smell like sweat and cow flops and have more children than they can take care of. No thanks. I had a whole childhood of that.

But she still could enjoy the one hundred percent male standing only twenty feet away.

Wonder if he's smart enough to add three and two and get five, or if he just coasts along on his sheer presence.

Then she saw Guy Beck closing in on the man.

That can't be Jay Vermilion, she thought. *It wouldn't be fair if the rest of the package lived up to that deep voice.*

Flashing a big smile and an embossed business card, Beck slid like grease through the people who had gathered around the man.

But then, whoever said life was fair?

Sara eased through people, careful to stay behind Beck, where he couldn't see her. She wanted to learn more about what Jay was like when he wasn't a voice on the phone, telling her about Skunk the Wonder Dog and his buddy Lightfoot, or King Kobe, the Terror of the Pasture.

As she closed in, she saw that Jay had navy blue eyes that were as clear as gems. There were small lines on his cheeks and the corners of his eyes that didn't look like age. They looked like experience. The hard kind.

Jay's dark, arched eyebrows rose as he considered the city man waving a business card at him.

"Guy Beck, Mr. Vermilion. Masterworks Auction Agency."

Jay took the card and considered the fancy letters stamped into the heavy stock. "Mr. Beck. And it's Captain Vermilion."

"Forgive me, Captain," Beck said. "Since it's obvious you're a very busy man, I'll be brief. It's my understanding that you have a considerable body of paintings that will be up for sale."

As he spoke, his eyebrows and face made exaggerated gestures of both sympathy and avarice, as if he was sorry for the burden of selling someone else's belongings and taking a generous cut of the value on the way by.

Jay waited for the rest of the spiel like what he had once been, a soldier ready for the newest round of political wish-think masquerading as orders.

Opportunity knocking for so many folks on my behalf, he thought drily. *No wonder Henry took a side exit. He'll be back at the ranch long before I will.*

"Mr. Guy Beck," Jay said as he tipped up the brim of his hat slightly, revealing a band of hair as black as the Stetson. "Heard of you. Hollywood, right?"

"You flatter me. I had no idea my reputation had preceded me all the way out here to Jackson Hole."

"It's just Jackson," Jay said gently. "Jackson Hole is the entirety of the valley made up by the Tetons, all the way to the plains. Doubt if the elk and pronghorn out there have heard of you."

"Oh."

"Makes no difference to me," Jay continued, his voice as easy as his eyes were hard. "Just trying to save you looking ignorant if you plan to work with folks around here."

Beck took a quick breath. "Ah, thank you. About the Custers . . ."

Jay looked puzzled. "The what?"

Sara stifled a snort. If Jay poured it on much thicker, she'd need barn boots to wade through the stuff. Beck, however, didn't seem to notice the aroma.

"The paintings by Mr. Harris. Armstrong 'Custer' Harris," Beck said with a grim kind of patience.

"Oh, right, those. Sorry," Jay said with a smile. "I only ever called him Armstrong. It was the folks who hated him that called him Mr. Harris."

"Fascinating, I'm sure. Now that custody of the paintings is in your hands, I wondered if they might be for sale."

"The custody of the Vermilion estate, you mean."

"Well, of course." Beck's fingers folded themselves into uneasy origami.

Jay paused and held a finger up. "Just realized who you were."

"The owner of Masterworks Auction Agency, yes, I know," Beck said.

"You're the dealer who's working for Liza Neumann. Better hurry along, son. She's got anger and a good lead on you."

Sara bit back a cheer when Beck realized that he wasn't the smartest man in the conversation.

"There was no formal arrangement," Beck said finally. "Nothing signed and notarized, you understand."

"I understand that she lost and you dropped her like a dead skunk."

"I'm a businessman. There was no business to be done with Ms. Neumann. The decision was mutual."

Jay nodded. "Gotcha." He tucked the business card into Beck's breast pocket, right next to the polka-dot handkerchief. "You're a mercenary. Nothing wrong with that, man's got to make a living, but I don't do business with someone who only cares about getting paid. Good-bye, Mr. Guy Beck. Please don't call me. You've used up more than your share of my time and patience."

Beck hesitated, then turned and left so quickly he nearly ran over someone. Jay hadn't looked past the agent's loud clothing and attitude to see the slender woman who had been waiting patiently behind him.

As Jay watched she moved nimbly aside to avoid being run over by Beck. She was taller than most women, tall enough to dance with him and not have anyone strain anything bending over or standing on tiptoe. Her pale skin was a stark contrast to her mink-brown hair, which was worn loose and free, looking soft enough to make his fingers tingle. Her deep brown eyes were large, richly framed by long, dark lashes. Her sweater and slacks showed a body that was female without fuss or apology. Unlike Liza, there was no severity about this woman, no sense of hostile walls standing between her and the rest of the world.

That intrigued him.

Too bad I don't have time for the male-female dance, he thought. *But I don't.*

Before he could move to leave, the woman stepper closer and held out a hand out to him. Thin silver and crystal bracelets on her wrist made a sound like distant birdsong.

"Captain Vermilion, I'm Sara Medina from Perfect Touch," she said.

Jay took her hand and was surprised by the quiet strength of her. "Sara. Good to have a face to put with the voice. Or are we Ms. Medina and Mr. Vermilion during business hours?"

"Sara works for me."

"And I go by Jay," he said, smiling. "I only use captain when someone rubs me the wrong way."

She smiled wide enough to show a dimple on the right side of her mouth. "I'd apologize for Guy Beck, but I had nothing to do with how he turned out."

"Glad to hear it." As Jay spoke, he stepped aside, gently pulling her with him.

"Thank you, Mr. Vermilion," the bailiff said behind Jay, closing the hearing room door and locking it. "I'll clear the rest of the people out of here, but you take your time."

"Do you have eyes in the back of your head?" Sara asked too softly for the retreating bailiff to overhear. "I didn't even see him behind you."

"I don't have anything as useful as another set of eyes. Just real good hearing."

"Like a-pin-dropping-on-Mars good hearing." She realized that her hand was still wrapped in Jay's and reluctantly pulled free. "And congratulations on retaining custody of the Custers—sorry, the Harris paintings."

"You know I call them Custers. Something about that seersucker slicker just made me want to yank his chain. Small of me, but I've learned to take comfort where I find it."

This time Sara didn't bother to muffle her laugh. "Sign me up in the small column. Beck is . . . quite a performer. I'm impressed that you outslicked him. Relieved, too. He's a pump-and-dump sort of dealer."

Jay's intent navy eyes urged her to continue.

"Beck will pump what buzz he can from the paintings and the trial," she said, "then dump the paintings on the market without regard for the worth they could have had with careful handling."

"Commodities."

A few blocks over a siren wailed, then stopped almost immediately.

Sara frowned. "Everything has a price in the art market. I'm pragmatic enough to understand that."

"I'm hearing a 'but' . . ."

"The Custers are worth more than simply money. They represent some of the last great artistic interpretations of a western landscape that was vanishing even as he painted it. The past can't be recovered, but we can sense it in those paintings."

"It's probably easier to see greatness if you didn't know Custer personally," Jay said. "I was just a kid, but I thought he was a petty, vain son of a bitch. That's why he got the nickname Custer, after the general who didn't know better than to lead his soldiers into a death trap in the name of spit and pride."

Inwardly Sara winced. "I gathered from some of our conversations that Custer wasn't Mr. Personality. The painter, that is."

"People had a hard time understanding why JD carried him so long."

"Carried?"

"Didn't I tell you? Room, board, art supplies, and pocket money."

"That's not well known," she said, feeling excitement tickle through her. "Maybe your father believed in Custer's talent."

"Maybe. And maybe he just liked having someone to wipe his boots on."

"Ouch."

Jay smiled slightly, softening the hard lines of his face. "Guess I didn't tell you that JD was as ornery and hardheaded as they come."

"Er, no. Sounds like your father and Custer were well matched."

"More like my mother had a soft spot for Custer," Jay said, taking Sara's arm and heading for the doorway to the street. "She loved his paintings. JD loved her."

And I like the feeling of his son's big hand on my arm, Sara thought. *He's one interesting man in person as well as over the phone.*

Good thing I'm immune.

"You're cold," he said, opening the door to the street, then closing it behind them. "Did you leave your coat in your car?"

"No. It was stolen from my—"

Just then Barton Vermilion rushed up, drowning her words. He looked tired and drained and tight as a new-strung wire. The black coat was no longer slung over his shoulder, but wrapped around him.

"Jay, I need to talk to you. Now."

Sara felt the instinctive tightening of Jay's hand on her arm before his grip loosened with a reluctance that made her want to ooze closer.

Of course I want to be closer, she told herself briskly. *He's warm and the wind isn't.*

"Ms. Medina," Jay said, "have you met my brother, Barton?"

"A pleasure, Mr. Vermilion," she said.

Barton gave her a dismissive nod and turned back to Jay. "We have to talk." Then his head snapped back toward Sara. "You testified against us. The judge quoted your opinion as a deciding factor in her decision."

"I gave a deposition, which included the authenticity of the receipts for Custers sold to JD Vermilion," Sara said. "As your last name is Vermilion, you're a beneficiary of my opinion."

Jay bit back a smile at Sara's cool reply. "Point to the lady."

Barton swept his eyes up and down her like it was just before the bar closed on a Saturday night. "If you're so smart, why don't you have the sense to wear a coat?"

The reply she wanted to make was straight out of the barnyards of her childhood. Before she could frame it in polite words, Jay had shrugged out of his jacket and put it around her shoulders.

She almost groaned at the heat of it.

"Thank you," she said.

"My pleasure." He turned to Barton. "Don't blame Sara for Liza's unhappiness. Or me."

"Easy for you to say. I'm stuck between mother and you." Barton scowled. "Ask me how much fun that is."

"No need. I was there." Jay's expression softened as he thought of his half brother as a redheaded tyrant clutching for the world with both chubby hands.

"Remember when I carried you on my shoulders and you yelled 'Giddyup' all through the house?"

"So you were older than I was. So what? I've grown up since then," Barton said impatiently.

The pouting line of his mouth contradicted him, but Barton couldn't help it if he had inherited his mother's lips.

But he sure could help himself by acting his age, Jay thought. *The older he gets, the less adult he seems.*

Being Liza's son didn't do him any favors.

Irritation snaked through Jay. At some point, Barton had to become responsible for his own life, his own choices. As far as Jay was concerned, that point was overdue. And yet, every time he argued with Barton, Jay felt like he was kicking a puppy.

"Since you're all grown up, you know Liza doesn't have anyone to blame for her life but herself," Jay said evenly.

Sara knew she should fade into the sidewalk and leave them to what was obviously a long-standing family quarrel, but Jay's coat was draped around her and she had barely stopped shivering.

"You could have just given the damn paintings to her," Barton said.

"I followed JD's wishes. He was real clear about the paintings."

"So? He's dead."

"I gave my word," Jay said.

"How the hell would JD know? He's dead!"

Sara felt the tension in Jay's hand on her arm and waited for the explosion. But when he spoke, his deep voice was calm.

"It's done," he said to Barton. "Get over it and get on with your life."

"It takes money to live," Barton said in a rising voice.

"That's why people work. Any time you want it, you have a job on the ranch."

Barton looked down, visibly fighting not to lose his redheaded temper. "Look," he said finally, meeting Jay's waiting eyes. "I found a guy who could help us sell those paintings."

"Was he wearing seersucker and a purple tie?" Jay asked.

For a moment Barton visibly wondered if the answer should be yes or no. "Uh, I didn't notice."

"Did he give you a card?" Jay asked.

"Uh, yeah." Barton fished the card out of his suit pocket. "Masterwor—"

"No," Jay cut in. "He already approached me. I turned him down."

"But this guy's the real deal. Knows a lot of Hollywood types, closes big deals."

"Not with me."

Tension simmered for a long moment before Barton shrugged. "Okay, you don't want him. That's cool. How about I handle the paintings then?"

Jay studied his brother. Barton alternated between careless and relentless, yet Jay felt a stubborn obligation to help out the kid who had once shrieked with laughter while he rode Jay's shoulders through the rambling ranch house.

"You mean it?" Jay asked.

"Sure. I do big deals all the time."

Jay's gut told him to refuse. The perennial hope that Barton would turn out to be something more than hot air urged Jay to agree.

"I'll think about it," he said finally.

"I could totally handle it." Barton straightened for the first time. "You'll see. I'm good at business."

"Would you do an auction or a consignment?" Sara asked quietly. "Sotheby's or Christie's? Or would you choose an auction house that specialized in western genre painters?"

Barton blinked. "Huh?"

"I was just wondering what your experience in art sales was," she said. "If the Custers are going to be sold, they need to be handled properly."

"And you think I can't? I've got a degree in management, Harvard. I know business."

"Then you know that the art business is as idiosyncratic as they come. This isn't the same as finding angel investors for a start-up. Selling art is part show business, part poker game, and part craps."

"And you're just the gal to handle it?" Barton asked. "The only guy who knows those paintings better than me is dead now." He flushed and jabbed a finger at her. "I've got a *personal* connection."

"That will be very useful in selling the paintings if the time comes," she agreed, smiling professionally. "Collectors like to have a personal link to the history of a painting. It helps add a glow to the narrative, to the legend of a painter, and, of course, to the artistic taste of the owner."

"Can't pay bills with a legend," Barton said.

"No, but you can make it work to your advantage. That's a medium-long game if you want to play it right. Sellers like that seersucker guy just pump and dump, but don't give the audience enough time to really get into the work."

"Legends aren't built overnight," Jay said quietly.

"Overnight sensations brought on by years of work are a lot more common," she said, nodding.

"Years?" Barton laughed roughly. "Who has the time?"

"A professional willing to invest in the future has the time," she said. "If you have any interest, we can talk about the process and the kind of work it will take to properly market paintings such as the Custers."

"And you're just the professional to show me how, right?" Barton said sarcastically.

"Glad you realize that," Jay said, glancing at his watch. "When the paintings are sold, I suspect that Ms. Medina will be a big part of it. Assuming, of course, that she wants to be hired for the job."

Relief snaked through Sara. "Thank you. If you want, I'd be happy to help you sell the Custers. Did you have a time line in mind?"

"No guarantees on handling the sale," Jay said. "Not yet. I need to know someone—in person—before I trust them."

"Understood."

Liza's voice called impatiently, "Barty, come here!"

Barton grimaced. "A minute," he yelled.

Wind gusted, making Sara grab Jay's coat at the same time he did. Their fingers tangled. She admired the difference in texture and strength and heat between his fingers and hers. He had calluses, but the skin itself wasn't rough. She couldn't help wondering how those fingers would feel against her bare skin.

Then she wondered how he could stand around in his shirtsleeves in a cold Wyoming wind and have warmer hands than she did.

"Listen," Barton said, leaning in to Jay. "Did you look over the new plan I sent you?"

"Ms. Medina is getting cold standing around in the wind," Jay said. "I'll call you after—"

"You remember that guy I sent out to my quarter of the ranch last week?" Barton cut in hurriedly.

"The one who was three days late?"

Barton waved that away. "He's an important man. Got lots of irons in lots of fires. Anyway, the reports came back and it's looking good. But he wants to dig a few more holes to be sure before he offers a deal."

Sara felt Jay go absolutely still.

"This is the land along Lash Creek?" Jay asked.

"That's right."

"That creek feeds Crowfoot, which waters most of the ranch. That watershed is too valuable to risk mining activity."

"Gold is valuable too, bro. Lash Creek is part of my land. I get a say in how it's used."

"When you're thirty-one and meet the stipulations in JD's will, yes," Jay said. "I had to do the same."

"Hey, I'm trying to do this the nice way. I could sue."

"Barty!" Liza's voice was more distant. "I'm leaving!"

Both men ignored her.

"You'd lose," Jay said. "Liza already tried to have the land divided during the divorce. The judge didn't buy it then and won't buy it now. JD's will is clear. You have to be thirty-one to have any say in how the ranch is run."

"BARTY!" Liza screamed above the wind.

Sara felt like hiding in her borrowed coat. Her family was poor, but they had too much pride to make a public scene.

"Fine," Barton snarled. "Be like JD. Leave money on the table wherever you play. Millions hanging on the walls, millions in untapped mining rights, and nothing in the bank for the rest of us."

With that, he stalked off after his mother.

Wind gusted again, making trees whip and groan. The smell of snow was stronger now, but the sky was nearly clear.

"Sorry that you had to witness that," Jay said, watching Barton's retreat.

"No need to apologize," Sara said. "Nothing argues like families."

"The least I can do is take you back to your room. Where are you staying?"

The thought of her room put a hitch in her stride. "I was at the Lariat. I have to find another room."

"Bad service?"

"A break-in. My coat and computer were stolen. The sheriff holds out little hope that the thieves will be found."

Or another room, for that matter.

Jay's arm came around her shoulders. "You've had quite a morning, haven't you?" He led her toward a big silver pickup truck. "With the Norwegians in town, you won't find a decent place left to stay."

"I'll—"

"Come to the ranch," he suggested. "We have five bedrooms and only one of them is being used. Some of the Custers are there, and there are a lot more up at Fish Camp."

"You're tempting me."

He gave her a smile that warmed her as much as his coat.

"No temptation, just common sense," he said, opening the passenger side of the truck. "You need a room and the Custers. I need to know more about you than a sexy voice talking to me while I make dinner and sneak bites."

She laughed, remembering doing the same thing while listening to him on the phone. "You, too? Eating alone can suck."

Navy blue eyes met hers. "Henry lives at the ranch, so we'll have a chaperone, if that concerns you."

"Good." She was too attracted to Jay for her own comfort. Having sex with a client was bad business.

Stupid, too.

"As long as you understand that Beck's sales pitch about the Custers being worth millions is a great wad of baloney, I'll come," she said.

Jay smiled and squeezed her arm. "Never did like baloney, even when I was young enough to eat it."

"And Sheriff Cooke said for me to say hello to you," she remembered as she climbed up into the passenger seat before Jay could blink.

"So you figure I'm safe," he said.

Safe wasn't a word she would have applied to Jay Vermilion, but she nodded. "Besides, I've traveled in places where staying with strangers and hitchhiking were the only way to see the country. You learn to trust your instincts." *Plus a few really nasty moves my brothers taught me.*

Jay laughed softly. "I thought so."

"What?"

"You're the adventurous sort."

Sara smiled faintly. She was hoping that handling the sale of the Custers would get her out of the adventure travel business.

Chapter 5

While Sara watched Jay walk around the hood of the truck to reach the driver's side, part of her felt like she was fifteen, wearing fashionably ripped jeans, a midriff top, teased hair, and purple eye shadow, standing in the movie theater parking lot with someone blasting trash rock from their cassette deck.

Back before I learned that having a man wasn't as good as having my freedom to be and do what I want to do and be.

"That's an interesting smile," Jay said as he climbed in.

"Just remembering how young I once was."

"Bet the boys chased you."

"You'd lose. I was plain as a fence post."

The engine revved, an echo of his laughter. "You'll have to show me pictures before I believe that."

"I burned them."

Shaking his head, he drove her the few blocks to the Lariat motel. When he saw the mess that someone had made of her room, his enjoyment vanished.

"I hope Cooke catches whoever it was," Jay said.

"I'm not holding my breath." She handed his jacket back to him and got to work.

With the efficiency of someone who spent too much time traveling, she put clothes and toiletries back into her suitcase, packed up the orphaned computer plug, and gave the room a final check.

"Do you have an uplink on the ranch?" she asked.

"Hard to do business without one."

"Good. I'll download what I need of my records onto my tablet."

"You're lucky it wasn't stolen, too," Jay said.

"It's in my purse, along with my cell phone. Where I go, my purse goes."

"I've seen smaller rucksacks," he said, eyeing the big purse.

"Some people lift weights. I lift my purse."

He smiled.

She reminded herself not to stare.

"I'm out of here," she said.

Pulling her wheeled suitcase behind, Sara headed for the door, eager to see the last of the motel room. Jay caught up with her just by lengthening his stride.

"I'll take it," he said, reaching for her suitcase.

With an easy motion he stashed the suitcase behind the driver's seat of the truck.

"How far is it to the ranch?" Sara asked.

"Depends on which pass is open. Twenty miles if Wolf Pass is open, almost twice that if we have to take the long way."

"And the winner is?"

"Us," he said. "Wolf Pass is open. Or it was when I came in this morning. Around the Tetons, weather changes when you blink, especially in the high country."

"You can't scare me unless it's a bear."

"Usually we only get them at the outer edges of the ranch," he said, "on leased grazing lands. Or sometimes up at Fish Camp, if the garbage smells particularly tempting before we get around to burning it."

"You're joking."

"No, we burn garbage. Burying it just gives the bears something to dig up, and they're a lot better at digging than a man with a shovel."

"You really do have bears."

He looked at her big eyes. "Yes, city girl, we really do. Cougar, deer, antelope, elk, and Henry swore he saw wolf tracks during the melt. Does that change your mind about staying at the ranch?"

"Are the Custers there?"

"Yes."

"I'll let you know after I see them."

He smiled.

Sensation shivered up and down her spine.

Forget the bears, she thought. *He's lethal.*

Good thing I spent my childhood raising my younger siblings, washing the smell of cow crap and baby barf out of my hair, and cooking for nine. I'm inoculated against his brand of rough-and-ready charm. I worked too hard getting out of the country to want to go back again for more than a brief visit.

Very quickly, the streets of Jackson bled into a strip of commercial development on either side of the road. A few minutes later buildings stuttered out and mostly grass grew. Trees lined small creeks and sagebrush thrived on exposed slopes. Barbed wire fences marked off small ranches, while narrow asphalt or dirt roads snaked off up the shoulders of ridges dressed in grass or sage and aspen.

After some miles, the top of the highest grassy ridges sprouted giant mansions placed above old ranch structures farther down the slopes. The old homes were all but falling down now. The new homes were supersized, decked out in finery that was sometimes restrained and more often looked like a TV reality show in waiting. She'd bet that ninety percent of the mansions were uninhabited.

Sara would have expected this sort of growth in upstate New York or even outside Atlanta, where she'd been decorating and appointing the inside of a house not unlike these. But not here, in the middle of ranching country.

I probably shouldn't look at it this way, but are these new places really such an improvement on the landscape? Were the old ranch houses so bad that they had to be left to rot from neglect while empty mansions are built?

Nothing answered her question except the complex reality that life changed.

Below the ridgetops, the flat land was empty of all but ranch fencing, occasional cattle, and the grass that bent beneath the wind. Silver ripples gleamed in irrigation ditches.

"I don't see many cows," she said finally.

"It's been a hard winter and a late spring. Price of hay was so high a lot of the small ranchers had to sell off stock."

"Did you?"

"Vermilion Ranch has its own hay meadows. We weathered it better than most."

"You're lucky," she said, remembering. "My father had too much family and too few milk cows to make ends meet anywhere near the middle."

"Hard work and plenty of it," Jay agreed. "When I

was young, I couldn't wait to leave the ranch and see the world."

"And you did," she said, remembering fragments of previous conversations.

"Yes. I left when I was eighteen. Didn't come back until a few years ago. A long time."

"I'm still gone. Can't think of anything that would drag me back. What changed your mind?"

"Afghanistan."

She knew a conversation closer when she heard it, yet she said, "One of my younger brothers feels the same. He—Look out!"

Before the words left her mouth, Jay had braked and swerved to avoid the deer bounding across the road. He missed it by inches.

"Deer have to be the dumbest thing on hooves," he said, quickly guiding the truck back into the correct lane. "Wonder what ran it out of daytime cover."

"A bear?" Sara asked, her voice thinned with adrenaline.

"More likely stray dogs."

His voice hadn't changed. She had a feeling that it would take more than a kamikaze deer to lift his blood pressure.

She forced herself to look away from his compelling features to the scenery outside.

The road climbed, wound around, and climbed

some more. For a time there were aspen groves in every crease and sometimes on the ridgeline itself. High-end houses disappeared. Though ranch fences remained, the country looked wilder. Some of the fences were very old, made of wood that had turned pale gray beneath relentless weathering.

When they left the highway, the surface of the road went from asphalt to graded gravel.

"How far does this road go?" Sara asked.

"About thirty miles before it dead-ends at Mitchell's ranch gate. There are some nice moose bogs down in the bottoms along the way." Jay slowed. "Hang on, hard turn coming."

"More deer?"

"Narrow road and a tourist riding my bumper. Damn fool is in a city car. If he keeps going, he'll get stuck in the mud holes ahead."

Despite Jay's turn signal, the car kept riding his bumper. He said something under his breath as he turned sharply onto another gravel road. This one was posted as Vermilion Ranch, private property, no hunting, no trespassing, and no turnaround. A locked gate was set back just far enough to keep the pickup truck from blocking the larger dirt road where the tourist zoomed eagerly past, spraying gravel, unaware of the muddy bottomland and huge tow bill waiting a few miles farther on.

Jay swung down out of the truck cab, opened the combination lock, and pushed the gate wide.

"Want me to drive through?" Sara called.

"Thanks. Appreciate it."

She scrambled over the console into the driver's seat, took the truck through, and then slid back into the passenger seat.

"Agile lady," he said, giving her an appreciative glance as he got back in. "Don't tell me it's yoga."

Laughing, she shook her head. "I ride horseback in the Sierra Nevada every chance I get. BLM and national forest lands are full of gates."

"Hear they have bears, too."

"Not where I ride. My horse wouldn't put up with it." Then, "Why are all the big estates up on the grassy ridgelines? There was flat land closer to Jackson."

"City people like the view up there. When Liza hounded JD for more money, he leased off some of the more useless ridgeline pasturelands to rich folks. Resorts, condos, miniature estates, whatever."

"Leased, huh? That's smart."

"The only thing JD was stupid about was Liza. Every time I look at the fake rustic estates crouched on the heights, I see more proof that when an older man marries a much younger woman, money always changes hands. A lot of it."

Jay drove on down the road at a good clip, slowing

only when fence lines gave way to sunken cattle grates that worked as barriers for hoofed animals. Some dust rose behind the truck, but not much because it had rained the night before.

When Sara caught herself admiring his profile or lean, strong hands too often, she forced herself to look out at the land. She was here for the Custers, period.

Custer painted this land. What did he see that moved him to set up an easel? The shadows of aspens on a rough slope? The sharp angles of fence meeting fence? The racing line of the wind across the grass?

"Do you have many memories of Custer?" she asked after a time.

"Some. I was twelve when my mother died and JD married Liza. Custer took off about that time. He didn't like kids much, especially when I got taller than him, which happened when I was about ten. From what I learned after I grew up, Custer had an eye for the ladies and they returned the favor." Jay shook his head. "Never could understand it. Maybe it was the smell of oil paints and turpentine, or whatever the hell it was that he used for cologne. Or maybe he was hung like a prize bull." Then, "Sorry, don't mean to be coarse."

Sara bit her lip against a laugh. "When I was twelve years old, I spent more than a few hours up to my armpit in a cow's birth canal, trying to grab the second slippery little hoof so that dad could put a rope around both of them and pull. I know all about birds, bees, and how bulls hang."

He glanced away from the road and smiled. "You're one surprise after another. You sure you live in San Francisco?"

"Very sure. I love it there—the taste of so many different cuisines, the color of faces from white to black and every shade in between, fog like a cold cat winding around my ankles, the horns of cars and big ships, clothes and goods and art from all over the world. It's exciting, energizing. Always something new to discover. And the only cows are hanging in upscale butcher shops."

"Yeah, I used to feel that way." He shrugged. "I changed."

"Did Custer love the land?" she asked.

"Love, hate . . . there's a real fine line between. I don't know. He and JD fought like old marrieds. Custer always lost. He'd tear out and go painting and not be around for days. Sometimes I wonder if he didn't fight just to get his blood up to paint."

She tilted her head. "Another nugget from the personal history of an artist. You'll have to write down your memories."

"No time for it. The ranch is two full-time jobs and then some."

"Another thing I hate about cows. No time off for good behavior."

Jay gave Sara a glance that looked casual and missed nothing.

She is really something, he thought. *Strong hand-shake, slender female body, yet plenty tough. She didn't scream at the deer or leave town because of a small-time burglar. She's smart, too, or the rest wouldn't be nearly so appealing.*

Too bad she's a city girl and there's nothing left in the city for me. My roots are planted in Wyoming, and that will never change. The land is part of my DNA. How stupid I was to fight my roots most of my adult life, only to realize in the end that the ranch is exactly the challenge and peace that I need.

"I'm really eager to see those paintings," she said. "The only Custers I've seen in person were his later works, after his move to Roanoke."

"When I was old enough to think about adults being people like me," Jay said, "I wondered why he went that far away. Nobody knew him in Virginia, and Custer was a man who liked to be known."

"Maybe he got sick of the West. Whatever the reason, he was sure done with everything western, including landscapes. Odd, though. His later paintings were more technically polished, certainly more accessible, but they all lack the raw energy and emotion of his earlier ones."

"You want raw energy, look over there," Jay said, gesturing with his chin.

She looked to her right. The wind had stripped most of the clouds away from the Tetons. They thrust into the air, jagged and bright with ice on the north slopes. The south-facing slopes gleamed with water in patches where the snow had melted. The forest was a dark, dark emerald where trees grew, with ghostly streamers of naked aspen trees running up the ravines. At lower elevations the grass was fiercely green, supple as water beneath the wind.

"I always thought the coastal hills above our farm were as ghostly and wild as anything on earth," she said. "This is more. Much . . . bigger."

"Make you feel small?" he asked.

"No. Should it?"

"Not everyone likes this much openness."

"Then they'd hate the Pacific Ocean," she said. "Now *that* is one wild and restless place."

He smiled.

She looked at the mountains again. Clouds formed and re-formed as she watched, tossing like the manes of countless wild silver horses.

"Custer must have painted that," she said. "It's the kind of powerful collision of land and sky and cloud that he loved."

"We have a painting like this of his."

A chill snaked over Sara's skin at the thought of seeing Custer's earlier—and in her opinion—far superior works.

She watched the clouds and wind for a long time. They looked free as only things of the air could be. Below the arching sky, where the Tetons zigzagged down into tall hills and rolling hillocks, wind rushed over the pastures, green and grassy and rumpled like the back of an endless herd.

"Custer must have painted that, too," she said. "There are so many ghosts and echoes in his work. That's why it fascinates me."

"Plenty of ghosts and echoes in you, too," he said.

Startled, she looked away from the scenery to him. "What do you mean?"

"You're a city girl who rides horseback in the mountains for fun and you remember helping a cow give birth."

"That's why I'm a city girl. No cows."

"No horses, either."

"Nothing's perfect," she said.

"Except the name of your company."

She laughed. *He's quick. I really like that in a man. Or a woman, for that matter. Too many people just stumble through life, eyes fixed on the ground.*

Jay's cell phone made a sound like a bawling calf. Slowing down, he pulled the phone out of his pocket. As he moved, his pants pulled across his crotch tight enough to strike a match on.

A quick mind isn't all he has. I like that in a man, too. A lot. Sara felt like fanning herself and settled for blowing out a soft breath.

"What's up?" he said into the phone.

"Where the hell are you?" Henry demanded. "I got back to the ranch near an hour ago."

"I'm a few minutes out."

"Well, take your foot off the damn brake. Liza's here and she's mad as a skunk in a bubble bath."

Though the news of Liza made Jay want to turn the truck around and head back to town, he said, "On my way."

He shoved his phone back in his pocket and started driving like he was alone.

After a few hard bumps, Sara braced herself and hoped the ranch wasn't too many more miles away.

Chapter 6

Vermilion Ranch's main house was sheltered among huge old trees whose leaves were just past budding. They surrounded the second story of the house in a shimmer of faint green. Fenced pastures bigger than Sara's family farm spread lushly in every direction. Outbuildings were scattered at the back of the house. Pickup trucks of varying ages and upkeep were tucked close to a bunkhouse.

Though the exterior of the living quarters could have used some paint, the pasture fences were straight and tightly wired. Like the barns and outbuildings, sections of fence had been recently repaired.

Jay drove straight up to the big house and parked next to a red Mercedes that looked like a beauty queen in a construction yard.

"This could be ugly," he said.

"At least your family has stuff worth fighting over," Sara said, releasing her seat belt. "We always fought hard because we had close to nothing."

"Some folks never get enough."

"Then it's not money they're after."

"Liza doesn't understand that," Jay said, opening his door. "Too damn bad the ranch doesn't have enough money to fill the hole inside her. Never has. Never will."

The door shut hard behind him.

Two black-and-white dogs raced out from behind the house, barking as fast as they were running.

Jay gave a shrill whistle. "Skunk, Lightfoot, go back to the barn."

The dogs looked disappointed, but trotted off toward the barn.

Sara slid down out of the truck and nearly landed on Jay's big boots. When he steadied her, heat sizzled through her blood at the casual strength in his arms. She remembered his jeans stretching tight across his lap when he reached for his phone.

Think of something else.

Anything else.

Like having to live in the country again.

Her blood cooled immediately.

"I've had clients like Liza," Sara said. "Well off and able to do nearly all of what they want, but all they think about is what they don't have. It gnaws at them. They love buying things, because until the sale is closed they're in the spotlight. I think it's really the attention they crave."

"Once a showgirl, always a showgirl." Jay shut the passenger door and took Sara's arm.

"Was she really? Liza?"

"When JD met her, she was slinging drinks and dancing. Mom had just died, and Custer talked JD into a wild drunk weekend. JD and Liza were married about four months later."

"He must have been very lonely." *And vulnerable,* Sara thought.

"That's one explanation," Jay said neutrally.

The front door of the ranch house opened, revealing Liza.

"I've been waiting an hour," she said. "If you want to fuck your little friend, do it on your own time."

Sara felt the tension sweep through Jay's body. She remembered the arguments that her mother and father had had, fights both savage and bloodless, words and acid emotions from either side of the chipped paint on the kitchen table.

"Would it be better for you if I waited in the truck?" Sara asked in a voice too low for Liza to overhear.

"It would be better if Liza learned to keep a civil tongue in her head," he said, voice equally soft. "But if you want to lie low, I won't force you."

The sheer neutrality of his voice told her just how angry he was. And beneath that, she wondered if she was being tested somehow.

I wouldn't blame him. If I owned something like the Custers, I'd want to take the measure of anyone I was going to trust them with.

"Will this be about the Custers?" she asked.

"Can't think of any other reason she'd be here."

"Then I'll just pull on my big girl pants and come along."

He gave her a sideways glance and a smile. "If those aren't your big girl pants, my heart stops to think of what they would look like."

"Ah, the sweet smell of cowsh."

"Cowsh?"

"Cow shit."

He laughed and gave her a one-armed hug.

Liza stood on the porch, fists on her hips.

Jay took Sara by the arm and walked slowly toward the ranch house.

She noticed that despite Liza's obvious impatience to talk to Jay, she had taken the time to change from her courtroom clothes. Her oversized fur-collared jacket came up around her head, and her needle-heeled boots belonged in the city. So did the black leather pants. The fury etching her face made her features sharper and deeper, aging her fiercely.

She's afraid, Sara realized. *But why? Obviously she's not worried about her next meal or even her next pair of couture boots.*

Barton slouched in the doorway behind his mother, hands in the pockets of his loose slacks. He had changed, too. His slacks were brown, worn with a pale silk shirt and an equally pale, silky jacket thrown over his shoulders. His shoes were casually expensive brown leather. The expression on his face was amused.

Sara felt like she was walking in on the third act of a play.

"What happened today isn't any kind of justice and you know it," Liza said.

"It's a pleasure to see you, too," Jay drawled. "Good to know that you still remember how to get to the ranch. Barton, you're blocking the doorway."

Jay led Sara past his glaring stepmother and her amused child.

"Aren't you going to answer my question?" Liza started to point at him but stopped herself.

The harsh light on her skin made every worry line stand out.

"I will when you ask one," Jay said.

Sara felt both Liza and Barton staring at her like she was up for sale. Or rent. Red flared across her cheekbones. It wasn't shame. She had gotten over that useless emotion in high school. The burn on her cheeks was all anger. She wanted to get in Liza's face and tell her that unlike others, Sara wasn't the type to flat-back her way to success.

"I'm Sara Medina, art historian and design consultant," Sara said pleasantly. "So pleased to meet you." *Not.*

Liza flicked her eyes up and down in disapproval and then frowned at Jay. "So Beck is right. You're going to sell them all off instead of keeping this a private matter."

Without a word, Jay kept walking with Sara on his arm.

Liza and Barton gave way.

In that moment Sara understood that Jay's command presence hadn't come from a uniform and insignia. He had been born with it.

"Well? Are you?" Liza demanded as she followed them inside.

Sara felt the tension in Jay's body, but his pace, like his expression, didn't change.

"If you wanted it private," he said, "you shouldn't have been giving interviews to local news outlets and talking all about how you were finally going to get justice today. Which, according to the judge, you did. Sorry you don't care for the taste of it."

As Sara sat down on the leather couch, she watched Liza change tactics. A gleam of water softened the older woman's eyes, if not her mouth.

"JD wouldn't want family matters discussed in front of strangers," Liza said. "Send your little friend out and we can get down to family business."

"If you want to pretend to be family again," Jay said, settling next to Sara on the old leather couch, "sit down and be civil. I'm not JD. I don't argue for the sheer ornery hell of it."

"That woman isn't family," Liza said through her teeth, glaring at Sara.

"Legally, neither are you," Jay said, his voice calm and his eyes hard. "Sara is here to lend her expertise on the subject of Custer's paintings."

"Sure she is," Barton said with a wink and a pumping gesture of his hand.

"Do you need a time-out, Barty?" Jay asked.

If Sara had ever wondered if the two men were really brothers, she knew now. Only siblings could know all the hot buttons to push.

"Don't fight with your brother," Liza said to Jay.

"Half brother," Barton corrected, his voice tight.

"If he acts like a kid, he'll get treated like one," Jay said, letting his impatience show. "Sara is a guest of

Vermilion Ranch. If you're rude to her, you're rude to me."

Barton grimaced. "Fine. Whatever."

He flopped into a Stickley chair so old that the original fabric had been replaced by cowhide, which in turn had been worn down to bare leather at the arms and seat.

Liza took a matching chair and sat like a queen giving audience to peasants.

Silence.

Sara wished that she was free to roam and admire her surroundings. The main room of the ranch house was framed in timbers that looked strong enough to hold up the sky. There was safety and comfort in the wood-paneled walls, traceries and patterns in the grain that made the place feel warm. Nothing had been cut with machine precision, but instead was shaped by human hands. Any irregularities in the grain were clear in the light reflecting on the varnish. The house was real rather than architecturally perfect.

There is history here. So far from the glass and steel of my office, newly built on the rubble of old houses. And yet, both wood and steel architecture have their beauty—each in its own place, appropriate for the environment it was in.

Her eyes moved from the walls to what was on them. Her heart stuttered for a second when she realized what she was looking at.

Those are Custers on the walls! she thought.

The impulse to go to them, to study them, was so great that she had to fight to stay seated.

Henry stepped out of a darkened doorway that led to the back of the house. He nodded to Liza, ignored Barton, and focused on Jay.

"I sent Billy out to see to the stock in the northeast pasture," he said. "We're gonna have to move them up to summer pasture or start feeding hay."

"I'll move them tomorrow. How are the two new hands doing?"

"Told them not to drink Penny's homebrew," Henry said. "They're both puking their guts out in the bunkhouse. Can't pull wire for fences, much less ride herd on King Kobe all the way to Fish Camp. Oh, and the Stinson kids can't meet you partway to take the herd to summer pasture, either."

"I'll take care of it," Jay said. "Beats pulling wire."

"The summer pasture will be easy, but you can't wrangle those Angus up to the lake alone. Soon as you get to cougar country, they'll spook."

"Sara will help. She's eager to look at all the Custer stuff stored at Fish Camp." He looked at her with a challenge in his eyes. "Right?"

"As long as I'm on four feet rather than two for the trip," she said, rising to the bait. "This looks like great country for riding."

"The best," Jay said. "I'll provide the horse. Staying on it is your problem."

"You don't raise rodeo stock, do you?"

"No."

"Then I'll look forward to it."

He smiled and said too softly for the others to hear, "So will I."

Suddenly she felt light-headed. *Too much happening too soon. The robbery, the judge, Jay smiling at me like he wants to lick me from toes to forehead.*

And me really wanting to return the favor.

Deliberately she called up memories of cow shit and isolation. The memories were so clear and deep, she could almost smell the dairy barn—which cooled her off immediately. Country was fine for a week or two. Any more and she would go crazy.

"I didn't come here to talk about cows, drunken cowhands, and the state of whichever pasture it is," Liza said stiffly.

Jay nodded. "You never did care about the business that kept you in diamonds and couture."

Henry faded back into the darkness, a man who knew what was coming and wanted no part of it.

The sound of his retreating footsteps faded into silence.

"It was JD's money," Liza said. "He spent it the way he wanted to." Her voice, like her spine, was rigid.

"Yeah, family business," Barton added quickly.

"You both might have forgotten," Jay said, "but cows *are* the family business."

"Just a part of it, and an outsized one at that." Barton leaned forward. "If you'd just look at the plans I—"

"We had this discussion already," Jay cut in. "The answer hasn't changed. It's time to put money back into the ranch rather than pumping it into blue-sky get-rich plans and couture clothing. Any other 'family' business you want to discuss?"

"The Custers are mine," Liza said. "JD gave them to me."

"The judge didn't agree. Neither do I," Jay said. "The jewelry, furs, clothes, cars, condo, and stipulated generous allowance were all in your name. The paintings weren't."

Deliberately Sara concentrated on a large canvas over the cold fireplace. The painting depicted the ranch as seen from a place high on the less-famous back side of the Teton range. The painting was unmistakably Custer's work, bold strokes of color and energy visible from across the room. The art was calling to her, a siren song of discovery, but she didn't get up.

Beside her, Jay waited for Liza to get to the point. And he wondered why Barton was still in the fight.

It was unlike his half brother, who had always taken the easy path paved by the Vermilion name and wealth.

Something lit a fire under his tail, but I'm damned if I know what it is, Jay thought. *Probably another get-rich-now scheme that he can't wait to dump money into. Ranch money.*

Jay watched Liza squeeze Barton's hand.

Here it comes, Jay thought. *Finally.*

"I looked you up," Barton said, indicating Sara with a careless flick of his finger. "You sell junk. Hell, you don't even sell real paintings, but you're solid on wallpaper and kitsch."

Jay started to defend Sara but subsided after a slight shake of her head. He settled back on the couch and wished he had known her long enough to pull her onto his lap. She was intelligent, vibrant, and ready for round two.

As Henry said, she's a pistol. She won't be like a lot of people who Barton overwhelms with his rude mouth and air of entitlement. Or even his charm, when he bothers to use it.

"Kitsch. Really?" Sara's right eyebrow shot up. "Did Google or one of my competitors state that?"

"I've got connections that you don't even know about," Barton said, "in places you can't imagine."

Barty is bucking for a session in JD's punishment chair, Jay thought.

"Connections?" Sara asked. "I suppose you mean the big auction houses."

"You don't know," Barton said.

She shrugged. "If you want to jump in and let Christie's take twenty percent of the pie *before* you start paying out your agent—and remember, that's all installment payments to you, not lump sum—you're welcome to try to convince Jay. If he agrees, it will be the slowest fast money you'll ever make."

"Don't you dare take that tone with my son," Liza said. "Those paintings are much more valuable than someone like you can imagine."

Sara's expression showed just how impressed she wasn't.

"You don't know anything," Liza said, her voice rising. "I knew Armstrong personally and those paintings are priceless!"

"What else did Beck tell you?" Sara asked calmly. "Did he mention that half the money trading hands in art today is modern art?"

"He knows his business," Barton said quickly.

"Then he knows that everything painted after World War One isn't modern art." She leaned closer, her body crackling with restrained energy. "*Contemporary* modern art is making the big money. Custer isn't a modernist. If you can't understand that simple truth, Beck will smile all the way to the bank. Custer was a brilliant artist, but east of the Rockies, he's not an easy sell."

Beautiful, beautiful woman, Jay thought. *I'd love to have that fire warming my life. Sometimes I feel like I haven't been warm since Afghanistan.*

And that is an outstandingly stupid thought.

I'm not a San Francisco kind of man. She's not a ranch woman. But it would be good while it lasted. Really good.

"That's not what Beck says, and he's the expert," Barton said. "You're just a pretty wannabe who doesn't mind putting out to—"

"Beck knows the difference between genre and modern and contemporary," Sara said, cutting off the standard insult every successful woman heard. "Contemporary is what's selling now. Industrial buyers are driving up the prices on commercial fine art. But Custer won't raise an eyebrow in those big-money circles. They want Lucy Giallo and Damien Hirst."

"Who?" Jay asked before Barton could say anything.

Sara turned to him. "They're consortium artists. They get a 'vision' and then dictate it to a workshop. Highly conceptual and cold. Their work sells to emirs

and corporations. Installations, not traditional paintings or even sculptures."

Barton spoke up. "I've heard of Hirst. I saw *Beyond
Belief* when I was in London a couple years ago. Fifteen
million pounds sterling worth of diamonds stuck to a
human skull. Takes balls to do that."

"That piece sold for a hundred million pounds,"
Sara said without looking away from Jay. "The buyer
was a consortium of which Hirst himself was part.
That should tell you something about art business and
artistic scruples in some circles. The man doesn't even
execute his own designs. It's not traditional art, but it's
being eaten up as fast as he dishes it out."

"So he just collects the money after putting his name
on something someone else did," Barton said. "Sweet.
That's my kind of business. Smart, really smart."

"That isn't art. It's manufacturing," she said flatly.

"But people pay through the ass for it," Barton
said.

And there it is, Jay thought. *The meat of the matter.
Money.*

Sara leaned back. The leather couch sighed for her.

"To me," she said, "that kind of art is too often intel-
lectual masturbation. No sense of wonder or transcen-
dence or even simple humanity. The results are meant
to strike, not to engage. And yes, they are worth a lot of
money in today's market."

"That's what Beck said. About the money, anyway," Barton said. "You get a classy art handler and you get classy prices."

"Unfortunately, the Custers aren't even Edward Hopper," Sara said. "Anyone telling you different is just hoping to dazzle you into giving them a plump percentage."

"Those paintings aren't yours to sell," Liza said.

"And they're not yours, either," Jay said to Liza. "That's what the six years of legal drama we went through decided."

"It's not right," Liza insisted.

"I disagree," Jay said, "and isn't this where the conversation started?"

"Look," Sara said quickly. "I'm not interested in taking the Custers from anyone. The paintings are Jay's to sell or keep."

"You can't understand what they mean to me," Liza said through tight lips.

Jay saw the tears begin and wished he was out in a pasture pulling wire. *If Liza can't steamroller it, she floods it.*

"At the end of six years of paying everyone's legal bills," he said, "I'm flat out of sympathy and damn tired of arguments."

"All right," Liza said huskily. "All right. Just give me one of them to remember my younger years by. You have so many paintings. Surely you can spare one for the woman who was once your mother."

My God, Sara thought, biting her tongue. *The woman is relentless.*

"Peace for one painting, is that it?" Jay asked.

"Yes. I choose the painting."

"No."

"What?"

"No," Jay said. "It's time you learned that I'm not JD. I won't be wheedled, cajoled, or worn down by words."

Silence echoed in the room for several long breaths.

"So that's it?" Liza asked finally in a quavering voice.

Jay could see that she was like the tide going out in advance of a truly monster wave coming back and hammering down on the beach.

He really wasn't in the mood for one of her tantrums.

"You just give a royal no and expect everyone to accept it?" Liza's voice was as high as her color. "God damn you, Jay Vermilion, just like he saw fit to damn your father to—"

"That's enough," Jay cut in. "You've had your say, I've had mine. The judge had hers. We're done with the subject."

"I expected this kind of behavior from JD, but never from you." Suddenly Liza fell in on herself, shoulders rounded and slumped forward. Her words tumbled down to the floor, not to Jay. "I thought you were better than that."

"It's over, Liza." Jay's voice was flat. "You tried every trick, burned every bridge along the way, and you're still on the wrong side of the river. Get on with your life and leave me to get on with mine."

Her head snapped up. "It's not over. Not until *I* say it is. You'll learn, just like JD did. One of those paintings is *mine*."

"Good-bye, Liza," Jay said, and turned to Sara.

Barton stood to the fullest height he could manage. "Some of us like to live in the real world. The one where resources can be developed into something really worthwhile and not ignored just so you can play cowboy with everyone's money."

Jay turned to him. "You want reality? What do you think paid for your failed education in acting, your failed restaurant in Miami, your failed gallery in Boston, and your failed delivery service in Baltimore?"

"It's not my fault the economy tanked," Barton began.

"Vermilion Ranch money paid for all your bad bookkeeping, failed businesses, and back taxes," Jay said. "You want more money, earn it the way Vermilions have for six generations. Work on the ranch."

"Cow shit isn't my style," Barton said.

Finally, Sara thought. *Something we agree on.*

Liza stood. "Come, Barty. We have lawyers to talk to."

"Beck recommended some Boston attorneys who specialize in just our problem," Barton said, following her.

"You'll be paying them, not the ranch," Jay said. "Judge made that real clear, too."

"There are other judges," Liza said.

The front door slammed behind her and Barton, a loud period to the argument.

"I apologize for my relatives, ex and otherwise," Jay said.

Sara shrugged. "They're not the first ill-behaved adults I've ever dealt with. Won't be the last."

He just shook his head.

Impulsively she touched his shoulder. The heat and power of him through the cotton shirt startled her. "Don't let either of them manipulate you with guilt. Families are way too good at that. You're a good man. Don't let them drag you down."

Jay shuddered lightly at the feel of her hand's warmth sinking into his skin. "If you knew what I was thinking right now, you wouldn't call me a good man."

His voice dropped in tone, and the heat in his eyes was unmistakable.

"I didn't say you were a saint," she said, slowly lifting her hand away from his shoulder.

For a long moment he watched her watching him.

"They gone yet?" Henry called from the kitchen.

"Yeah," Jay said without looking away from Sara. "It's safe for you to slide off to your cabin."

"You cooking tonight?"

"Did you bring fresh stuff back from town?" Jay asked.

"Sure did."

"Then I'm cooking."

"See you in a few."

The door shut smartly after the foreman.

Jay stood up, pulling Sara lightly after him. "Let's get your luggage out of the truck. Do you have something you can wear on a horse? If not, I'll find something. Mother's clothes are still packed away. She was about your height and build. I want to leave for Fish Camp around dawn. We'll overnight there with the caretakers—Ivar and Inge Solvang—then push on to the summer pasture the next morning."

"I always pack something I can hike or ride or relax in. You said dawn?"

"Crack of. The calves are just old enough to be stubborn. The mamas are better, except when they aren't. It will take us some time to convince all of them to stay on the trail. It could be a long day. Cows like staying in one place."

"Stubborn beasts," she said, remembering. "At least my horse will be doing the work rather than my own feet."

"You sure you're used to riding?" he asked.

"I'm sure."

"Western saddle?"

"I didn't grow up in the East."

His half smile said they would find out for sure in the morning.

Chapter 7

Henry dried the last dinner plate and stacked it in the cupboard. "Since you're not paying lawyers anymore," he said, "you should have cash for a dish-washer that works."

Jay said, "It's on my list."

"How high?"

"Bottom of the top half."

Sara laughed softly. "I've heard that one before, only it was usually bottom of the bottom half. I made a religion out of 'gently used' whatever and grew a skin thick enough to ignore the snark at school when I wore some rich girl's castoffs."

"It would have done Barton good to be raised that way," Jay said.

"Maybe," Henry said. "But he still would have had the Wicked Bitch of the West as his mother. Everything she touches turns to shit. Pardon, Sara."

"We called it cowsh when we were growing up," she said. "Less punishment that way."

Henry snorted and set the last dish in the cupboard. "I'm turning in. Seems like dawn comes earlier every year."

With a slight frown, Jay watched Henry leave.

"What?" Sara asked.

"Henry's so active that I don't think about him aging. But he's years older than JD was when he died." Jay shook his head. "Time is a tricky thing. So long and so short at once." He drained the sink and dried his hands. "Now let's get some art education in me before we turn into cowhands in the morning."

"Now you're talking," Sara said, quickstepping out to the living room.

By the time Jay caught up with her, she was already lost in the painting that hung over the fireplace.

"What are you seeing?" Jay asked.

"Vast space," she said almost absently. "And maybe, just maybe, Custer's perverse sense of humor."

Jay made an encouraging noise.

"Do you know if JD commissioned this painting?" Sara asked.

"JD wanted him to paint the ranch, if that's what you mean."

"That's what I mean. But instead of painting the ranch house set against the lush pastures and rugged peaks of the Tetons, Custer chose to view the ranch from a location that diminishes everything to the point that the ranch looks like a tiny lifeboat all but lost at sea, the sky and land ready to swallow it whole, leaving no trace of the legendary cattlemen who carved Vermilion Ranch from the wilderness."

Silently Jay studied the painting that for him had always been part of his home life.

"And yet," she said, "at the same time the painting shows the immensity of the task awaiting every generation of Vermilions. One man overseeing the well-being of everyone and everything that goes into keeping the ranch alive. The land serves your needs, but the land doesn't need you."

"A fact I learn every dawn," he said. "I'm transient. The land is forever. That's why I came back home. I wanted to be a part of something that endures. Cities, cultures, empires—they all come and go. The land remains."

"Barton and Liza don't feel that way," Sara said. "To them, the ranch is just a stubborn ATM."

"Now they think the paintings are another ATM. Are they?"

"Properly handled, they're worth good to really good money."

"How much?" he asked bluntly.

"Undetermined short of an actual sale."

"They must have a hell of a value for Liza, considering how much time and effort—and ranch money—she burned up in a legal wrangle over paintings she once walked away from."

Sara's eyes widened. "She walked away from them? Before the divorce?"

His mouth flattened. "Think of this as divorce phase two. Evidently she had a change of heart several years back. Maybe she thought the Custers would be valuable today. Not that she ever has to worry about cash. As long as Vermilion Ranch makes money, she does."

"She would have needed a crystal ball to see this Custer buzz coming. Value comes from an audience. Custer's potentially widened audience came from luck as much as anything else."

"How?"

"Didn't I tell you about the movie?" Sara asked.

"Probably," he admitted, "but sometimes I got to dreaming while I listened to your voice."

She blinked.

"Sweetheart," he said, "you have a voice that makes a man think of tangled sheets and slow, hot sex."

She laughed even as heat flushed her core. "You're talking about your own voice. Midnight and velvet. Annnnd we're getting off track. Value versus money. Art in general, Custer in specific."

"I can multitask," Jay drawled.

"Excellent. Put your multitasking mind to work on what it feels like to see Custer's paintings for the first time. The impact."

A long pause, then, "No can do."

"Okay, try to imagine how it would feel to be in Custer's territory for the first time."

"South Dakota is that way," he said, pointing due east.

"You passed geography," she said, wide eyed. "Good for you."

"Let's try it this way," he said. "Why is Custer's world so different from yours?"

While Sara thought, she absently ran a hand through her hair and stretched her shoulders and torso, trying to shake off the long day.

He watched her through narrowed eyes. Even though she wasn't trying to turn him on, the tightness in his groin increased. Pretty soon he'd have to hang his hat off his belt buckle.

He forced himself to look at the painting rather than the woman.

"Custer's world is vast and quiet," she said slowly. "Cities have no reality in his early work. Neither do humans. The land is . . . everything. Godlike."

After a moment, Jay nodded. "Custer knew that cities are big to men, but small in the larger scheme. Full, but empty of the things I'm looking for. I guess Custer and I have that much in common."

"Value comes from cities," she said. "From having an audience. That's where I come in. Or any good art seller. I bring my understanding of Custer's work and his potential audience, add in everything I can learn about the man and his life, then I create a narrative around each painting for the audience I have identified."

Jay studied the painting that had been part of his life. "Are we talking art or legend or plain old hype?"

"Yes."

Silently he digested the unexpected aspects of selling art. "You're saying it's not just the painting."

"The paintings are the tree. Narrative is the leaves reaching out to the sun of the audience. The coincidence of an offbeat movie featuring Custer's art, and then the movie going mainstream, is pure luck."

He listened to fabric whisper as she stretched some more.

"What about finding a patron like JD?" Jay asked.

"Luck. I've known landscape painters who have to paint houses to pay for their modest lifestyles, and still they die mostly forgotten. Luck comes in two flavors."

"Good and bad," he agreed. "The difference between coming home on my feet or in a pine box. Got it. What about the part that has nothing to do with luck? What about the skill?"

She wanted to ask him about his time in Afghanistan, but that was personal. She was here as a professional.

"It's easier to show you," she said.

Jay felt her grab his sleeve, warm fingers brushing against his exposed wrist. She vibrated with a controlled energy, every motion urgent as she led him toward the south wall of the big room.

"By the way," she said, "you really need to move these if you're going to sell them. I can see they've gotten some sun, but not enough to damage their value yet."

"Sun?"

"Sunshine is the enemy. Given enough time it can bleach anything, even oil paints. Any watercolors hung on this wall would have been ruined by now, even with protective glass."

"We always just enjoyed them," he said. "Or ignored them."

"A crime."

"Does arrest involve handcuffs?"

She had an instant vision of him handcuffed for sensual play. Heat streaked through her. "Ask the sheriff."

Sara stopped Jay in front of a painting of the eastern face of the Tetons, the legendary side, where the land got more and more dry as the mountains gave way to evergreen forest and then to the low scrub of the plains. The rocky peaks looked like they had been clawed from the earth during a violent birth. The snow that dotted the peaks was almost blood-red in the sunset. The Tetons themselves were laid out with strokes of purple and indigo, a cold contrast. At the feet of the mountains, the forests looked like a frozen wave captured in near black and crimson. The foreground was ablaze with wildflowers in orange and yellow and gold like a river flooding.

"So what do you see in this?" she asked.

Jay was overwhelmed by her female scent, a heat so close that he could feel her breath. Against a wild surge of desire, he struggled for words. "I hadn't thought of it," he managed. "I've passed by this painting hundreds, thousands of times."

"Okay, don't pass it this time."

She leaned in even closer now, her elbow pressing in below his rib cage. She was half a step in front on him.

His arm was just behind and all but around her now. And the painting was her focus.

He tried to make it his.

"Color," he said finally. "Up close it's all color and brushstrokes and energy. Across the room, it's still color and energy, but the brushstrokes all add up to a view of the land."

"Good. Besides the incredibly bold use of color, Custer was a master at portraying space and making it real. Later on he did that with light, making it tangible. But this is an earlier piece, where he was making distance real."

"But the colors are wrong," Jay said. "Nothing ever looks like that."

"If you want exact representation, go to photography. And even that lies. This painting is Custer's impression of the land at the moment he painted it."

She leaned back a bit and studied the painting, not realizing that with every breath her body brushed his.

He wished he'd worn something that would conceal his reaction to her. *Maybe a kilt,* he thought. *Or not.*

"Photography lies?" Jay asked, grabbing onto anything that would get his mind above his belt.

"Sure. All art is about showing what the artist wants to show. But that's okay. These paintings are good lies.

Custer's art is as much about how he views the West as it is about the mountains themselves. Look at how magical he makes them."

"Even if it's a lie?"

Sara gave him a sideways look. "Surely you've looked at the mountains in this kind of light and felt something that you couldn't put into words."

"All the time," he said finally. "But they don't look like this to me."

"That's the beauty of it. Each painting is an individual vision." She swept her hand across the surface of the painting, inches from it, fingers spread. "But it's one that's being completely shared."

Jay looked at the painting. "Okay. I see what you mean. I've just always taken it for granted, like the beams in the ceiling."

She watched him looking at the painting. His profile was a series of angular shadows softened by dense eyelashes and the hint of sensuality in his lips. Then he turned and looked at her.

"What are you thinking?" he asked.

"I'm finally understanding the appeal of portraits. And again, you've taken me off topic."

He gave her a slow smile. "Is that bad?"

She shut her eyes for an instant, took a grip on her wandering attention, and turned back to the group of paintings on the wall.

"There have been generations of western art, but each new one brings a different meaning," she said. "Imagine looking at an unfamiliar landscape for the first time. You've been back east, right?"

"West Point," he said. "Can't get much more east and still be in the U.S."

"Imagine describing the Rocky Mountains to someone back east. Someone who's never seen a mountain bigger than the Adirondacks. Someone who's never known a night sky without it being blocked by skyscrapers and city lights."

"I've tried. None of them really believed me until later, when we trained in the Sierra Nevada for mountain fighting overseas."

"Custer would have helped with the believing," she said. "Training for war is another thing entirely. But looking at this painting, you know the feeling of being in the West, which for a very long time was an utterly alien part of America, one that many people couldn't really believe was on the same continent, much less a part of the same country."

"It's different when you've lived it all your life."

"Yet even for you, this painting shows a facet of the land, the feeling of being in it, *experiencing it,* that connects you to Custer's vision."

Jay looked at the painting, then nodded slowly. "Beautiful . . . and fierce at the same time. Not a gentle land, yet generous enough to anyone willing to accept its harsh edges."

"Exactly. Information, emotion, beauty. Art was, and sometimes still is, a vehicle of education and social unity."

"No diamond-studded skulls?"

"Modern art, especially in the past half century or so, reflects the dissonance of modern life. Because I don't feel that kind of anomie, the art of anomie simply doesn't speak to me in the way it speaks to academia. My loss, I'm sure. Just as the inability or unwillingness to engage in nonacademic art is academia's loss. And we are way off topic again."

"Not really." Jay smiled and ran a fingertip over one of Sara's high cheekbones. "I'm learning more about you. Art, too."

And I'm learning that he has a warm, slightly rough fingertip, a killer smile, and a way of touching me that is much too good, she thought rather grimly.

"I live in a world filled with art," she said, pleased that her voice was more even than her heartbeat. "Most of that art gets written off because it's not academic. I've fought to get too many artists respect and recognition, and most important, an audience so that the artist can earn an adequate living."

"So that's what Barton was going on about. You deal in artists who don't have a national reputation."

"Yes. Your brother is a bit of a bastard, by the way."

"His parents were married several months before his birth." Jay's smile was as cold as the wind searching around the eaves of the house.

"I've always believed that bastards are made, not born," she said.

"No argument there. Barton was pissed that you were the key to the ranch keeping the Custers."

"I'm surprised that I made that much of a difference, especially in a case that had gone on so long."

He shrugged, brushing against her warmth. "Liza never was any good at losing."

"Who is? From what I learned about the lawsuit, nobody much cared about hurrying it along until a few years ago. Is that when you came home and started kicking butt?"

"JD was sick and Henry had his hands full running a ranch that was being bled dry by Liza and lawyers." Jay shrugged. "I asked the judge what it would take to move things along. She said receipts would be good, but even better would be someone who knew something about art to give expert testimony."

"I'm glad you called Perfect Touch."

"I researched and kept running across your name attached to Custer's art. There were damn few experts on his work."

"Until *The Edge of Never* was made," she said drily, "when the scent of money brought expert cockroaches out of the woodwork. Finding an audience for an artist is hard work. Experts like Beck only do easy."

"Most people don't want to lead. Too much work, too much risk."

"Risk?"

"Yeah. The guy in the lead gets shot first."

Chapter 8

Silence stretched, underlining Jay's words. Sara knew without asking that he had been one of the men in the lead.

"Did you get shot?"

"Nothing permanent," he said.

She remembered his words about the difference between coming home in a pine box and on his feet. Then she remembered what he had said about Liza bleeding the ranch to death.

"Bet they were sorry you came back," she said without thinking.

"They?" He raised dark, winged eyebrows.

"Liza and Barton. He would have inherited the whole ranch."

Jay shrugged. "I dodged enough bullets to stay alive. It will take her some time to work off her mad, but she'll get over it. Paying her own legal bills will speed the process."

"What about Barton?"

"I'm hoping that he'll grow a pair and start supporting himself."

Sara tried not to laugh. "Well, at least Liza had good timing. Custer's paintings are worth more now than they were a few months ago."

"Because of the movie?"

Sara nodded.

"Hard to believe that Hollywood is setting art prices," he said.

"You take what you get. *The Edge of Never* may not be to my taste, but I'll hold my nose and use the movie for all it's worth. The full impact probably will take several months—maybe close to a year if the movie is in play for an Oscar—to percolate through the entire art market. The more hype the movie attracts, the better for your bottom line."

"Not mine. The ranch's."

She looked at the hard lines of his face and wanted to ask how much trouble the ranch was in.

"I want Vermilion Ranch to survive for my kids," he said evenly, "and for my grandkids. I want them to have more to anchor them than some movie about people who couldn't find their ass with two mirrors and printed directions."

"Did you watch *The Edge of Never?*" Sara didn't bother to hide her surprise.

"Enough to see where it was going."

"How long did that take?"

"About ten minutes." He shook his head. "Why would I waste my time watching people commit slow-motion suicide? I felt like sending my 'special preview' back to them in a box of bull crap—the real kind."

"I'm told the movie is a tearjerker," she said, but she couldn't help smiling.

"There was some jerking going on and it wasn't tears," he said. "I've seen tragedy. *The Edge of Never* was too self-absorbed to be anything but silly and faintly disgusting. Misery porn. Why would I pay good money to watch that?"

"Don't ask me. After the first ten minutes, I fast-forwarded through my complimentary copy to find the scenes that had Custer's art."

Jay slung his arm around her waist and gave her a fast, hard hug. "I knew there was a reason I liked you."

"Same goes," she said lightly, pretending that she didn't feel the heat of his muscular arm and body all the way to the soles of her feet.

Smiling, he slowly released her.

Sara wanted to lean in and track his smile with kisses. With a mental head slap, she brought her attention back to the only thing that should matter.

Custer.

"Just be glad that no matter what we think of the movie," she said, "it will bring Custer a lot of attention from the elite who can afford to pay for original paintings. It will also bring dealers who make Beck look like a fluffy little bunny."

"There are phone messages from several other dealers."

She wasn't surprised. "And the next ones will be ruder and more persistent. Believe me, I know these guys."

"One of them was a woman."

"Theresa Overland, right?" Sara's expression was unhappy.

"Good guess."

"Not a guess. I'm surprised"—*grateful, too*—"that she wasn't out here in person. She'll plug you right into Christie's if you want her to."

"Big money?" Jay asked.

"For them, certainly. Maybe even some for you after all the percentages are paid."

"How much?"

"Depends on who you ask. Everyone has different ideas."

"I'm asking you. You're the expert on Custer and art here. I'm just a simple rancher."

And I'm a fluffy bunny, she thought.

"I have clients who wouldn't look twice at this painting," Sara said. "I have others who wouldn't be able to look away. That's the personal aspect. Then there is the positional. Say you already have everything you need to survive a hundred times over. How else do you announce you have arrived? And, more important, that you are different from the crowd of wealthy people around you?"

"In the military they have bars and confetti to show rank," he said.

"A civilian has Versace and Gucci and more elite designers than you can wear in a lifetime. Plus he or she has all the cars anyone could drive. All the boats. Airplanes. Toy trains. Jewelry. Whatever. But everyone with real money already has those things. How do you stand out from that crowd, a first among equals?"

"Why would you care?" Jay muttered.

"Ask them. But I can assure you that they do care. They want to acquire something no one else has. So instead of another stable of cars, they want to buy the first Maserati 3500 GT Spyder. The prototype from 1959."

Jay watched Sara as she spoke, her mouth shaping words, her dark eyes radiant with energy and intelligence.

"That car is unique," she said. "A big deal. And thanks to *The Edge of Never,* Custer's paintings are a big deal. Each one handmade. Each one unique. Each one something that no one else has. Exclusive."

Jay shook his head. "You're as much a psychologist as an art dealer."

She smiled. "All good salespeople are. That's why I'm telling you that if you sell the Custers now, you will get a fraction of what you will get if the movie takes off. If that happens, and I'm betting it will, the paintings will be worth at least triple what they are now."

"What if the movie doesn't take off?"

"You're no worse for the wait."

"It would be easier if I hadn't known Custer. He was . . ." Jay tried to find polite words.

". . . vain and temperamental?"

"Kind of a cliché, right?"

Sara grinned. "No more than the rigid and unthinking officer."

"Ouch."

She touched his arm, then snatched back her hand as if burned.

"Sorry," she said. "My brother came back from Afghanistan and he was . . . not taking it well. He felt like he'd been used as a football in a game between two teams of tanks."

"Smart man. You think you're the elephants, but you always end up being the smashed-flat grass."

Outside the wind flexed again and again, searching among the eaves for anything that could be peeled away and sent flying.

"You said something about 'narrative.' What did you mean?" Jay asked.

She accepted the change of subject without comment. Business, not personal.

"Narrative is anything unique to the piece that adds to the appeal of the art," she said. "For example, my partner, Piper, specializes in fine rugs. If the rug comes from a celebrity's estate, it adds to the price. Or if a piece has a history—lovers separated by war or families or death—that also enhances the appeal. Whoever buys the rug can say more about their purchase than the dollar amount spent."

"What's to keep someone from making up a history?"

"Ethics."

"Gotcha," he said. "That's why I sent Beck back where he came from."

A dog barked from the direction of the barn. A voice called out. Silence returned.

"I can't prove that Beck would make up history to increase sales," Sara said carefully. "In this business all you have is your reputation."

"And all I have is my ability to judge character. I like yours. And I would have liked it if you were twice as old, ugly, and male. So come with me and I'll show you some genuine Custer history."

"Really? Now?"

"Unless you're ready for bed."

Heat snaked through Sara. She knew he hadn't meant anything sexual, but the idea of bed and him in it made her pulse stagger.

"History," she said, hoping that he didn't hear the huskiness in her voice.

"Then come with me."

His midnight, velvet voice stroked over her.

"Are you doing it on purpose?" Sara asked before she could stop herself.

His smiled slowly. "It?"

She took a grip on her mind and yanked it back where it should be. Business. "Lead me to the history."

He took her arm and guided her from the main room to the kitchen, then through the mudroom where everyone left wet or dirty gear.

Outside, cold rolled off the mountains like an invisible avalanche. A nearly full moon made the snowy peaks glow as if they were lit from within. Even the shadows had a polished gleam.

The night itself was vast beyond comprehension.

"He didn't paint them big enough," Sara said in a hushed voice.

"Custer?"

"Yes."

"He'd have needed a canvas the size of Wyoming," Jay said. "And God's own brush."

Two dogs came out of the night like spotted ghosts. Jay spoke to them and they vanished back into the darkness.

"Working dogs," she said, not a question.

"Everything on the ranch works. I kept trying to sneak dogs like them into the house when I was a kid. My mom explained that they wouldn't be happy for long in the house. They needed a ranch to look after to be happy."

A falling star blazed across the sky, then vanished behind the mountains.

For a long time Sara silently absorbed the beauty of the night and the mountains swathed in moonlight. The city was beautiful at night, but in a very different way.

"You're shivering," Jay said finally.

"It's cold. But I don't want to go in yet."

He pulled her against his back and wrapped his arms around her. The masculine warmth enfolding her made her shiver again. He tucked her closer.

"Vermilion Ranch is an extraordinary place," she said, sighing as she leaned against his heat. "It's utterly unique and packed with both national and personal history. If you're broke, I get that you can't eat scenery and can't feed it to a cow and would have to sell out."

"I'm not that broke," he said simply. "Not yet. It was touch-and-go for the first years after I got back. Lawyers were a cash drain. Ranches don't have a lot to spare. Liza damn near forced the ranch into bankruptcy."

"That would have been a shame. If you sell, all you'll have is . . . money." She laughed, puffs of breath that vanished on the wind. "That sounds silly. Money is important and I'm not so stupid or naive as to discount the value of cash. But this ranch is so much more."

"Sure you're a city girl?"

"Real sure. Just because I recognize that Vermilion Ranch is worth more than its cash value on the market doesn't mean I want to live in Wyoming. I can appreciate beauty without having to own it or turn it into a pile of money. But that's all that Barton or Liza wants. Money."

Jay looked at the mountains and weighed her words.

She tilted her head back and watched him, a man caught between moonlight and darkness. She wanted to touch him, to learn his features with her fingertips, and she wanted it so much she had to clench her hands to keep from reaching for him.

"Jury is still out on Barton," Jay said finally.

"I was a scholarship student at an exclusive school. I met enough guys like Barton to understand the type." She exhaled hard between clenched teeth. "He's spoiled. He wants money, but he doesn't have the desire, smarts, strength, or guts to build anything on his own."

"Can't argue that," Jay said. "I'm just hoping that he finds a train set for him to play with that isn't the ranch. Not much luck on that so far."

"Barton knows that working on his own is hard. Breaking up the ranch for cash looks easier."

"He might think so," Jay said. "He's wrong."

She felt the tension in him and put her hands over his. "Sorry. Just tell me to butt out. It's really none of my business."

The wind wrapped around them in a cold hug, then uncoiled and raced on through the darkness. Long, lavender-scented hair slid off Jay's face and back down around Sara's shoulders. Several strands stuck to the beard growing around his lips. He left the hair there, liking the connection.

"I hope to buy Barton out before he's old enough to have a say in the ranch," Jay said.

"How much does he want?"

"Whatever he can screw out of me. Millions, I'd guess."

"The Custers I've seen here are awesome, but millions? Maybe at auction, if the movie is a wild international success. Auctions are notorious for raising emotions and prices, but by the time everyone takes his percentage and you pay taxes . . ." She shrugged, rubbing her shoulders against Jay's hard, resilient chest.

"Go on. Say it," he said.

"Unless you can swap paintings for Barton's interest in the land and avoid paying anyone, including Uncle Sam, Custer's landscapes can't save your day. Wait— the buildings you own in town. What about them?"

"I've already taken out loans against them for ranch improvements."

She sighed. "It doesn't matter anyway. What Barton really wants is to prove that he's better than you. That's the black hole in his soul that he's throwing designer clothes at."

Jay was silent.

"And I've talked out of turn again," she said briskly. "In any case, I'll do everything I can to turn those landscapes into money. It would help if you had a portrait called *Muse* stashed away somewhere. But the painting is considered to be more legend than reality. There are no photos of such a work, no sketches, no letters describing it. Nothing."

"I don't remember Custer painting any portraits," Jay said. "Certainly JD never hung any portrait, though I think one might have been listed in the receipts I turned over to the court."

"If there is a history—especially a salacious one— attached to the portrait, you might have a real leg up on your millions. Wyeth's Helga paintings put wings on his prices."

"Educate my ignorance."

"Helga was a model Wyeth painted," Sara said. "He also had an affair with her. That narrative made the paintings much more valuable in the public eye."

"Can I be blunt?" Jay asked.

"Sure."

"Custer screwed anything that would hold still for it. When he was drunk, gender or species didn't much matter to him."

Sara blinked. "I'll leave the species bit out of the narrative. It's salacious, but appeals to only a very narrow audience."

There was a silence, then he threw back his head and laughed and laughed. "You're good for me," he said finally, letting his cheek rub lightly over her hair.

"I'd be even better if you knew anything about the Custer works that are rumored to be lost, including the portrait. Really early works. Anything that could be put in a narrative frame that would help people to understand how Custer developed as an artist. There is so damn little real information about him."

"JD had paintings stashed all over the ranch. Down here, up at Fish Camp—hell, maybe even in the out-buildings or some of the office buildings JD rented out. I don't know how many. We never kept track of the paintings. Never had a reason to."

She groaned. "Other than a potential receipt that doesn't name the painting, there's no direct evidence of a Custer portrait actually existing?"

"No."

"Even after Custer's move to Roanoke, he didn't keep many notes. It's believed that the only paintings he left behind from before Roanoke are the ones your family now owns. And the one that JD gave as a gift, which ended up in the movie."

"There are some papers and notebooks and such at Fish Camp," Jay said. "I saw them when I was looking for receipts."

For a few moments, Sara forgot to breathe. Then her breath came out in a silver plume. "Are you sure?"

"Yes."

"Oh. My. God. Why didn't you say so earlier? If the notes are any good at all, you've just doubled the price of the Custers. Using his own words, I can lay out the framework for a lovely coffee-table book that shows the trajectory of his early painting. We can get a quality printing job in Asia at a fraction of the cost here and—"

"Breathe before you pass out," Jay said wryly. Then, slightly louder, "You need something, Henry?"

Sara jerked. She hadn't heard anything to suggest that they weren't alone in the cold, radiant night.

"Forgot to set up the coffee for the morning," Henry said. "Getting old, I guess."

"I pulled wire with you a few days ago," Jay said. "You're a long way from old."

Henry gave a bark of laughter, then the mudroom door shut behind him.

"Before you get too breathless about finding old paintings," Jay said, "I have a story to tell you." As he spoke, he led her farther into the yard. "JD and Custer had been drinking. It was just before Custer left. Happened right here out between the house and the barn."

Sara studied the grass, dark beneath the moon, but for the vague silver ripples when the wind gusted really hard. Off to one side, there was a small island of flagstones set in the ground around a low rock ring. The stones were pale as ghosts.

"Imagine it's the middle of the night," Jay said, "with the only light coming from a roaring fire almost as tall as a man. And dancing around that fire is a very loud, very naked, and very drunk Armstrong Harris. Almost as loud, but not nearly as drunk, and fully dressed, is JD yelling at Custer to put out the fire and go to bed."

"It's a good thing I fell in love with the paintings before I knew the man," she muttered. "How old were you?"

"Almost thirteen. JD and Liza weren't married yet. They had just come back from a big party in town. Guess what Custer was burning?"

"I don't think I'm going to like the answer."

"Some old paintings of his. Probably a bunch of notes, too. The whole mess was burning like hell on fire."

Jay looked at her expression as she gazed at the fire pit. Her face told him everything he needed to know about how she saw Custer and his work. Her eyes gleamed silver with tears that made slow, cold trails down her cheeks.

"What a huge loss," she said finally.

"Custer didn't see it that way," Jay said. "He pissed on the fire, told JD to finish the job, and walked away. Custer was gone in the morning."

Sara gave a long sigh. "So much lost. That story didn't make the history books. And it's the kind of detail that makes Custer and his work come alive, beyond the paintings themselves."

"More dollar signs."

She wiped away the last of her tears. "What you've told me makes the artist more human, more accessible to people who can't paint but can appreciate art." She looked past the site of the burned paintings. "Where else did Custer live while he painted landscapes on the ranch?"

"He stayed in every building on the ranch, with the exception of the main house. Well, maybe he passed out here once or twice. JD, too." Jay smiled. "They were good friends until they stopped being good friends. Maybe they both outgrew each other. More likely they just got on each other's nerves."

"Tough for two legends to share the same space," Sara said.

"What do you mean?"

"I've seen the Vermilion name on more than a few places in Jackson. JD was a big wheel and a statewide legend."

Jay made a sound that could have been a laugh. "Tough for me to see it like that. One of the 'legends' was my father and the other was a prankster, a drunk, and JD's sidekick."

"Sounds like more stories."

"A whole childhood of them. But I'm not keeping us up all night jawing. Dawn comes early and cold at this time of year."

"Just a few minutes more. I can't believe it's real and I'm here. It's the difference between reading history and living it."

Sara looked at the barn and the outbuilding, ebony against the lambent sky. The buildings stopped and the land kept going and going, all the way to the mountains. It was big, so very big, and anything was possible in it.

I'll help Jay keep his ranch. The next generation of Vermilions? Well, a man like him will find a woman willing to spend her life out here and have his children.

And if I don't like that thought, tough.

I've worked too hard to end up like my mother.

Chapter 9

Jay and Sara were just finishing a big breakfast when Henry came in.

"A friend called me and said he'd heard some half-drunk gold hunters bragging about panning in our creeks," Henry said.

"Are the two new hands on their feet yet?"

"Not hardly. I sent Billy to check on Barton's quarter of the ranch."

Jay waited. Henry had run the ranch a long time. Jay hated to second-guess him, but he would.

"I don't trust Barton not to sneak some engineers or such up there," Henry said. "He knows we're not using the land for grazing because the fences have been cut so many times by trespassers and druggies."

All likely sent by Barton, Jay thought. *In his own way, he's as persistent as his mother. But what he doesn't know or won't admit is that the less grazing land on the ranch, the less money for everyone.*

"Does Billy have a radio?" Jay asked.

"He knows the rules."

"Anything else I should know?"

"Supposedly some crazy mountain man is roaming around the north forty, shooting at whatever takes his fancy."

"Have you told the sheriff?" Sara asked quickly.

Henry laughed. "Until someone is shot, the sheriff don't care much."

"Cooke has too few men to ride herd on our ranch problems," Jay said to her. "He'll write reports if we insist, but why waste his time and mine?" He looked at Henry and asked drily, "Any more good news?"

"Nope. Horses are loaded up and ready to go. Amble is saddled for you. I saddled Jezebel and Mooch. Sara can take her pick. Skunk and Lightfoot are waiting by the corral. Saddlebags are packed."

Jay said, "Sounds like you covered everything. Good work."

Henry grunted and went back outside.

Sara started collecting dishes.

"Leave them," Jay said. "Elena and her daughter will be here today to clean and cook meals for the week."

By the time they had gathered what they would need for the trail, the sun was just up, flooding over the mountains, making everything come alive. The green of the grassland was edged in gold, dew scattering the light. The hush was broken only by a horse snorting in the corral.

"Times like this, I feel like the richest, luckiest man alive," Jay said. "A whole day of riding ahead and a beautiful ranch waiting for me."

"You forgot your cowboy boots," she said.

He looked at the battered, comfortable lace-up boots he had worn through mountains half a world away. "These are just as good in the saddle and way more versatile on the ground. Sort of like your boots."

She smiled and stretched. "I love riding. The ranching . . ." She shrugged. "Not so much."

Despite her words, he enjoyed the sight of her stretching toward the dawn. She was wearing her own jeans and light hiking boots, one of his mother's flannel shirts and a going-to-town Stetson, plus a jacket that had once belonged to a much-younger Jay. None of it fully concealed Sara's female line. Watching her leaning against the top rail of the corral pleased him as much as the dawn.

The more he was with her, the more he liked her. Wanted her.

And knew it was a really bad idea.

I went all over the world and discovered the ranch is my home. She went all over the world and discovered the city is hers. I should be old enough not to start something that will end badly.

But I've never wanted anything like I want her.

Absently he petted Skunk and Lightfoot, who were watching him intently, waiting for their first orders. The instant Henry had started saddling horses, the dogs had known they would be working today. Except to the dogs, work was the finest kind of play.

Jay took the rifle he had brought from the gun safe in the house. He went to the big chestnut gelding called Amble and slid the rifle into its saddle sheath. Then he swung the saddlebags up onto the horse and tied them in place.

"The bay mare is Jezebel," he said while he worked. "The strawberry roan gelding is Mooch."

"Which one has the best cow sense?" Sara asked.

"Jezebel."

"What is Mooch's claim to fame?"

"He's as even-tempered as a rock."

Since Mooch was closer, she went to him. With calm, easy motions, she checked the gelding's feet. His shoes were well worn but secure on his hooves. No stones were caught between steel and hoof. Next she adjusted the length of the stirrups, tightened the saddle cinch, made sure that the buckles on the bridle were secure, gathered the reins, and stepped into the stirrup.

During the whole process, Mooch flicked one ear.

Every motion Sara made told Jay that she was used to horses. He concentrated on checking the tack on his own ride. The cinch was a bit loose and one stirrup was too long.

Henry's hands must have been sore from pulling wire, Jay thought as he tightened the cinch and adjusted the stirrup. *I should have insisted that he let me get the horses ready.*

But the foreman was a proud man. It was better if Jay checked everything than to point out that the foreman sometimes wasn't quite getting the job done.

Jay opened the saddle canteen. The water was fresh, as cold as the morning. A second big canteen held coffee hot and strong enough to float a horseshoe.

Henry still makes the best coffee around, Jay thought. *For that, I'll tighten a cinch or two without complaining.*

Across the corral Sara kicked Mooch into a trot and tested his response to the reins. After a minute or two she brought him back and tied him next to Jezebel.

Jay watched her change horses, repeat the inspection of animal and tack, mount with the grace of experience, and put Jezebel through her paces. Very quickly she came back to where he waited.

"I'll take Jezebel. Mooch is strong and willing, but his trot is worthy of a cement mixer," she said. "Jezebel is quick and easy to ride."

"For you, maybe. She doesn't much like men. But she's a good cow horse. She knows which critter is going to be trouble before the cow knows it. Trust her judgment over your own. And hang on. She's real sudden when she's going after a contrary calf."

Sara looked at the rifle stock gleaming in the shadowed dawn. "Is that normal trail gear in Wyoming?"

"What?"

"The rifle."

"For me it is." He didn't mention the Glock in one of the saddlebags or all the ammo.

So I'm paranoid after Afghanistan. Sue me.

He gathered Amble's reins and stepped into the stirrup even as he swung into the saddle. A short whistle brought the dogs up on their feet, quivering with eagerness. Skunk and Lightfoot went to the left of Amble. Jezebel fell in on the right as they walked quickly up a dirt road toward the north pasture.

"The cattle we're moving are for breeding, not eating," Jay said as the sunlight slowly strengthened. "Vermilion Ranch's bloodlines need upgrading. I started with ten head of expensive breeding cows. Sperm wasn't cheap, either. Now I have fifty cows and fifty calves. All pure-blooded Angus. We got lucky on sex this year. Only twelve males. We haven't cut three of them, the best little bulls I've seen. Their bloodlines are going to work for me. They're worth more as range bulls than as beef."

"Is King Kobe one of the uncut?" Sara asked, remembering past phone calls.

"Sure is." Jay shook his head. "If he lives up to his pedigree, he'll be worth all the trouble he causes."

"If he doesn't?"

"I'll sell him or turn him into burgers."

"Sounds like my childhood," she said. "Raise the boys for veal and the girls for milk, and pray that the stock stays healthy long enough to earn enough money to feed the family."

He glanced over and saw that her full mouth had thinned. *Jagged memories,* he thought. *Soldiers aren't the only ones who have them.*

"How many head of cattle are we moving?" Sara asked.

"Only thirty-five, and one of them is Queenie. She's an old Hereford and a born leader. Once the Angus cows settle, they'll follow her through hell. The calves—well, they'll learn."

"If they're as stubborn as dairy cattle, we'll have a lively hour or two ahead."

"That we will."

The quick flash of his grin said he was looking forward to it.

By the time the sun was up enough that Sara had unbuttoned her jacket to cool off, she knew exactly what Jay had meant about Jezebel being a good cow horse. Sudden, too.

She hadn't fallen the first time the horse had pivoted sharply on its heels to block King Kobe, but it had been close. But Jezebel wasn't trying to dump her rider. The animal was just doing what it did best—keeping cattle in line.

At first the trail they followed had been clearly defined. As the hours wore on, Queenie seemed to be the only cow that could find the way through the grass and scrub and encroaching trees. The old cow finally led the cattle into a natural meadow that was higher and rougher than the pasture at home. A burly stream appeared, rumbling to itself as it ran between banks of willow and rocks. The water was high and cloudy with runoff from the slowly thawing Tetons.

Jay reined his horse over to Sara.

"That's the Crowfoot," he said. "By the end of summer it will be about a third that size and clear as air. Right now it's busy deepening its bed as it runs down to the valley."

"Is it safe to drink?"

"Probably, but I have purifier tablets. You never know what has happened upstream."

"What about—"

A quick, two-note whistle from Jay sent Skunk after King Kobe.

"—wild animals?" Sara finished.

"They're here. Most of the time they keep to themselves. It's the people you have to watch out for. There's a lot of organized, illegal growing around here."

"Marijuana," she said.

"You don't sound surprised."

"It's a big problem in the Sierra Nevada. There are some trails I just don't ride anymore."

"Smart woman. Growing pot used to be a lone wolf operation, one person tending a few plants for his own use. Now it has been taken over by international gangs. They go out into the national forests and BLM lands, make a mess diverting streams to water the plants, guard the crop with automatic weapons, then fly out the harvest in helicopters to northern Montana. From there, it's taken in backpacks to Canada."

A three-note whistle sent Lightfoot racing to the right of the cattle, outflanking another bull calf that didn't want to stay with the small herd.

"Have you had a lot of trouble on the ranch?" Sara asked.

"It was bad the first year I was home. But the *campesinos* weren't used to someone who shot back and had better aim. The gangs found easier places to grow their pot real quick after that."

She glanced at the rifle holstered beneath Jay's powerful right leg. "The gangs aren't on Vermilion land anymore?"

He shrugged. "They don't divert our ranch creeks anymore. After that, it's pretty much live and let live. They don't get in my way and I don't get in their face. Unless it's a meth lab. I take those down where I find them. If they blow, they could burn up the mountain."

"What does Sheriff Cooke have to say about it?"

"Nothing fit for your ears. Every so often the feds and the locals will make a sweep, bag some meth labs or bales of weed and a handful of headlines, and then everything settles back to the status quo."

King Kobe bawled and lowered his head at Skunk. In a flash of black and white, the dog outmaneuvered the calf and sent him back to his mama to sulk.

Sara laughed. "You don't need me. The dogs could do everything on their own."

"Wait until we have to cross the Crowfoot."

"Looking forward to it." As she spoke, she peeled off her jacket. Without stopping her horse, she rolled up the jacket and tied it behind her saddle. "It's getting hot."

He grinned. "If you don't like the weather, wait a bit. It'll change."

She looked at the peaks of the Tetons, where a few clouds had begun to gather. That didn't matter at the lower elevations, where the sun was hot enough to make horses and humans sweat.

Jay had tied his own jacket to the saddle much earlier. He took off his hat, wiped his forehead on his arm, and wondered how anything as plain as an old rust-and-gold flannel shirt could be so sexy on Sara. He had to keep reminding himself that she wasn't the kind of woman he was looking for. He wanted a wife, a mother for his children, and most of all a woman who didn't balk at the demands of ranch living.

A movement caught his attention. He saw that the herd was fraying into clumps of five and six, spreading out to graze in the new grass. A two-note whistle sent Skunk and Lightfoot racing out to collect the herd. The dogs split, each taking a different side. Cows that were too slow got a show of teeth and a growl. Too many warnings and they got a nip. Very quickly the cows were bunched up again.

"I'm used to seeing people carry around purse-pets or have these oversize hulks that they can't even house-break," Sara said. "It's a pleasure to watch dogs doing what they were bred to do."

"Just like it's a pleasure to watch cows being cows."

"I'll get back to you on that," she muttered.

Jay's delighted laugh warmed her in ways it shouldn't have.

The two dogs stitched around the herd, moving with fierce speed and focus.

"Thirty-five head isn't much more than a snack for the dogs," he said. "But they love working so much I didn't want to leave one of them behind."

"Dad always talked about getting a good working dog," she said, "but there never was enough money. Trained dogs are seriously expensive."

Oblivious to the people watching them, the dogs continued their work herding the reluctant cattle through the mixed grass and willow toward the Crowfoot ford just ahead.

"I have to admit that the scenery is extraordinary," Sara said.

The foothills were like a green sea flowing up to the rocky Tetons. Shades of green on green, grass and willow and the silver-green mist gathered around aspens as their leaves got ready to unfurl. The sky shimmered with light and moisture.

The wind made the whole landscape breathe, giving it the pulse of life.

"I can't believe that I was freezing yesterday," she said.

"Believe it. You'll be freezing again tonight."

Jay watched as Sara finished unbuttoning her flannel shirt, revealing the scarlet glow of the sweater she wore beneath. The sweater wasn't painted on her by any means, but it distracted him every time she moved.

Sara never looked away from the mountains. They were imposing in a way that the man-made landscapes of San Francisco never could be.

"Dime for your thoughts," he said.

"I thought it was a penny."

"Everything is more expensive in the high country."

Her laugh mixed with the sunlight. "I was thinking of San Francisco and its man-made heights. It's useful to navigate off the Hyatt and know how many blocks you are to the next pho café, but there isn't the same sense of time, of being in a land that existed long before people set foot out here and will be here long after civilization is gone. The mountains are so *old*."

While the people studied the land, the dogs had kept the cattle walking toward the ford.

"How do they know where to go?" she asked.

"The cattle?"

"The dogs."

"It's not the first trip to summer pasture for anything but the calves," he said. "The dogs and the older cattle are used to working together. Skunk will keep them on this side of the ford until we catch up. Then we'll all have a lively time until the cows are convinced to cross."

"They don't like crossing?"

He gave her a sidelong look. "Would you like your, er, teats in ice water?"

She smothered a laugh. "Gotcha." Then, "I can't see the herd anymore."

"They're about a hundred yards ahead. Follow my lead. Cows aren't as dumb as deer, but a mama cow with a calf can be unpredictable. As sudden as your mount, Jezebel. Henry calls them 'notional.' I just think they're stubborn in unexpected directions. If we spring up on them, God only knows how they'll take it."

Jay lifted the reins, tightened his legs, and Amble shifted from a walk to an easy canter. Jezebel followed, tugging at the bit, wanting to race. From the corner of his eye, he watched while the mare and its rider fought a silent skirmish for control.

Sara won.

Wish she wasn't a city girl. But she is. Sure as hell she didn't buy that heart-stopping sweater in a small town.

When the cattle were in sight, he tightened the reins. Amble went from a canter to a trot, then to a walk. Jezebel followed without a struggle.

"You snookered me," Jay said.

"What?" Sara asked, thinking of the paintings.

"I've been taken. Rooked, for those of you who play chess. Suckered." He smiled slightly, almost reluctantly. "You ride, and handle yourself just fine while doing it. And you haven't made one complaint yet on this trip."

"Were you expecting me to?"

One of the calves bleated suddenly and balked. Lightfoot dashed in, nipped at a tender leg, and the calf hurtled back into the herd.

"You keep insisting you're a city woman."

"Just so long as I'm not an uptown girl," she said drily.

"You're too young to have heard that song."

"Pop music is eternal when your mother can only afford a few cassettes. I used to pray the tape would break, then I'd feel bad because there was so little that made Mama smile."

Again he heard the combination of sadness and determination in her voice. She wasn't going to have a life like her mother's. Period.

And here I am talking about kids and the ranch, he thought. *Dumb.*

But he couldn't stop wanting her more with every instant, every smile, every bit of her laughter curling around him like a caress.

Taken, indeed, he thought. *Hook, line, and sinker.*

Chapter 10

Skunk gave a sharp bark, jerking Jay out of his uncomfortable thoughts. The dog was standing—or racing around, when needed—between the cattle and the tumbling, frothing stream. The cows were moving uneasily, bawling. They knew what was coming and would try their best to avoid it.

But first they would drink.

Sara took her mare upstream of the cattle, where Jay was watering Amble. Jezebel immediately stretched her neck and sank her muzzle into the cold tumble of water.

"Where do you want me for the crossing?" Sara asked.

He looked at the sunlight reflecting off the stream, lighting her face under the wide brim of her hat. She looked eerily beautiful, like a dream.

"Just stay back and cross when the last of the herd is on the other side," he said. "The dogs and I will take care of everything. But if a cow gets past me, it's all yours."

"Are you sure I can't help more than that?"

"If a cow gets away, you'll help a lot. The problem is that Jezebel hates water unless she's drinking it. She may try to jump the stream, so hang on."

Sara looked at the water, which was at least twenty feet across and racing like an avalanche. And she was on a horse that didn't like water.

Hope I don't get an ice-water bath, she thought.

Jay gave an intricate whistle. Both dogs sprang into action. Skunk made a pass at the lead cow's heels, Lightfoot harried the right side of the herd, and Jay rode at the rear, cutting off cows that decided to head back to the ranch. When Jezebel spotted a calf trying to get away, she sprang forward so fast Sara had to grab the saddle horn. When the calf turned back to the herd, Jezebel stopped dead, snorting and shying from the water only six feet away.

"Oh, this will be fun," Sara said beneath her breath.

Lightfoot nipped the last, reluctant calf into the water. With Jay on the downstream side and Lightfoot bringing up the rear, Skunk kept the lead cow headed straight through the ford. On the far side, the cattle sloshed ashore and promptly headed for a lush patch of grass.

Sara had watched the cattle cross. She could see the water wasn't deep, and the bottom had good footing, making for a fine crossing. With that knowledge, she decided to take Jezebel by surprise. Simultaneously she tightened the reins and gave a hard kick. The startled mare leaped forward and was in the water before she knew it. She crossed the stream in great bounds. On the far side, she shook herself and snorted her displeasure.

Jay began breathing again. Seeing Sara cling to a mare that was acting like a show jumper on steroids had hit him hard.

"Thought you said you don't have any rodeo stock," she said, wiping stray drops off her cheeks.

He shouted with laughter, then abruptly leaned over in the saddle and gave her a hard kiss. "You scared the hell out of me, woman."

She felt as if the place he'd pressed his lips—somewhere between her cheek and her smile—had been warmed by fire. She swallowed, blaming her accelerated heartbeat on the wild ride, and tried to be as casual as his kiss had been.

"Me? All I did was stay on. I didn't want my teats—or any other parts—in that ice water," Sara said.

Before he could answer, Skunk gave a short bark. An instant later, Amble's ears shot forward and his nostrils expanded as the horse drank scents from the shifting wind. Jezebel did the same. Horses and dogs were all looking in the same direction.

"What—"

A sharp gesture from Jay cut off Sara's question. He watched the cattle. The old Hereford cow had her head up, staring in the same direction the horses were. After a minute, she lowered her head and began grazing again.

The wind shifted quickly, swirling around like a dancer, then fading into a sigh. Both horses snorted and started looking for grass.

Skunk stayed on alert.

So did Jay. He had taken small, powerful binoculars from one of his saddlebags and was scanning an evergreen-topped ridge that was perhaps a quarter of a mile ahead and to the right. He concentrated on the area where grass and low scrub met the tree line on the ridge.

While horses and cattle grazed, Sara watched him sweep the distant ridgeline with the binoculars. To her eye, nothing moved but a restive wind. The thought that every twitch and ripple of leaves might actually be a bear made her uneasy. She glanced at the rifle stock behind Jay's right thigh and felt better. When it came to bears, she didn't have much faith in her city pepper spray.

After a few minutes, he lowered the binoculars and looked at the animals again. The Hereford was grazing. The Angus were munching up tender grass at an extraordinary rate. Skunk's ears were relaxed, but he was looking at Jay for direction.

Whatever the dog had scented was either gone or downwind now. Jay put the binoculars back in the saddlebag.

"What was it?" Sara asked softly.

"I didn't see anything and Skunk can't talk, so I don't know why he alerted."

She noted the new tension around Jay's eyes and mouth. "A bear?"

"Doubt it. Bears don't hide. Could have been a cougar. They're real shy."

"Could it have been hikers?"

"That, too," he said. Then he decided that she would be safer, though less comfortable, if he told her the truth. "I'm ninety-five percent certain that Skunk alerted on a human scent. The cattle and horses wouldn't have started grazing again if they had scented bear or cougar. Probably it was hikers. If anyone had been on horseback, our horses would have whinnied a greeting."

Unlike the tough little ponies we rode in Afghanistan, he remembered. *Our feet might have brushed on the ground, but those ponies were wary as any wild animal. They didn't whinny to strangers.*

After a last look at empty land, Jay whistled up the dogs. They gathered the herd and got it headed toward Fish Camp again.

Jay kept his eye on the land where something had moved and then vanished.

There was nothing to see but the landscape and the sweep of the mountainside above them. The sun was near zenith. The shadows were minimal. Everything was green and black beneath the wide blue sky.

Sara strained her eyes and saw only a land without fences or buildings or signs of man.

Is this what my brother felt in Afghanistan? Only there, the shadows fired real bullets. She shivered at the thought.

The evergreens swayed just enough to shift the slender shadows and trick the eye into seeing things that very likely just weren't there. She fought against her imagination, which insisted on things that didn't exist.

There's nothing out there where tree shadows meet sunlight. If you don't believe yourself, look at the dogs. Their senses are much sharper.

Or watch Jay, who stayed alive in a land where shadows shot back.

The lead cow moved reluctantly forward, encouraged by Skunk. Lightfoot darted along the sides of the herd. The cattle walked slowly, snatching at grass. The calves were a lot quieter than they had been at the beginning. Even the very slow pace Jay had set had taken the bounce out of their little hooves.

It wasn't the calves that worried him. It was the trail ahead.

Too many places for an ambush, his old habits told him. *Too few defensible spaces.*

And I'm not at war anymore, so knock it off.

Without thinking, he touched the stock of the rifle again. The .30-30 was secure in the holster, and the saddlebags held more ammunition than a hunting party of twelve would use.

Sara watched him from the corner of her eye and told herself that he was only being cautious. Most of the time she even believed it. But every time his fingers unconsciously touched the rifle butt, her heartbeat shot up.

Skunk gave another short bark.

She gripped the reins tight in her left hand and kept herself from grabbing Jezebel too hard with her thighs. The last thing anyone needed was for her horse to bolt because the rider was nervous.

Jay unslung the rifle.

Adrenaline poured through Sara.

The wilderness around her became a lot bigger, dwarfing the riders and the cattle alike. The wind had stopped, but there were still a thousand sounds around them. The forest, the stream, the grass, even rocks shifting upslope. She held her breath and listened for what Jay was trying to hear.

I'd be happier out along Market Street, she thought. *At least there I know the terrain and the city danger signals.* On the heels of that thought came another. *Is this what it's like for some war veterans? Always on guard? Always on edge?*

How do they keep that up and still live their civilian lives?

Her younger brother managed, but it had been hard. Too much of the time he'd been like Jay was now. Very, very alert.

The change that had come over him was profound. He was another man in Jay's skin. The stranger was poised yet relaxed, vigilant yet calm. Like living radar, every bit of his being radiated outward. He held the rifle barrel up, his finger outside of the trigger guard.

Sara did the only thing she could. She kept her mouth shut and waited.

After some of the longest minutes of her life, Jay gave a low, long whistle. Skunk looked back at him.

"The horses and cattle aren't worried," Jay said to the dog. "So we won't be." *Much.* "We'll eat lunch a little farther up the trail." *In a pile of boulders with a view of the back trail.* "Ever shot a gun?"

Though the question was casual, for a moment her mind went blank. Then she said, "Piper and I both took pistol lessons when we were just starting up the business and basically lived in the warehouse that held most of our inventory."

"Were you any good?"

"The instructor said I'd probably hit a man at twenty feet and certainly would at ten. But frankly, I'd rather not put it to the test."

"Same here."

Jay handled the rifle with easy movements that spoke of long experience. A series of short whistles moved Skunk away from the lead cow and back along the left side of the herd. Lightfoot kept pace along the right. Sara and Jay brought up the rear. The rifle was across Amble's saddle rather than in its saddle holster.

Skunk didn't give his alarm bark.

When Sara looked at the sky again, the sun was well past its zenith, racing toward the time when shadows would lengthen and pool into moonlight and night.

The thought of night was unsettling, so she focused on the scenery, looking for inspiration of the kind that

Custer might have found. All she saw was the remoteness, the lack of human inroads. Even the route the Hereford followed was more a game trail than a welltrod path.

As the cattle walked slowly between stands of trees, a streamer of cloud passed over the face of the sun. The temperature dropped at a startling rate. Sara untied her flannel shirt, pulled it on, but left it half unbuttoned. Standing in the stirrups, she slowly flexed her body, stretching muscles that had tightened after many hours on the trail.

Jay watched her without seeming to. He couldn't help himself. Her curves and female strength attracted him more each time he noticed them. And nothing else required his attention. Trees now blocked the view of the ridge where shadows had concealed more than they revealed.

"See that pile of boulders up on the left?" he asked.

"Looks pretty much like every other pile of boulders I've seen so far."

A quick smile changed the lines of his face. "We'll eat lunch there. It has a good view of the land around. Custer painted there more than once. Said it was one of the best views on the whole ranch."

"I should have brought my iPad. I could take pictures to compare with Custer's paintings. I just didn't want to risk my only remaining computer."

"We can come back. If we use ATVs or the helicopter, it will take a lot less time. Be expensive in terms of fuel, though."

"Helicopter? ATVs?" Sara shook her head.

Jay lifted the worn, sweat-stained Stetson off his head and wiped his face on his forearm. "Most cattle ranching today is done with machines. Didn't you hear the helicopter earlier?"

"Er, no."

"It was far off. Probably one of the ranches to the northwest. A group of the smaller ranchers went in on a used chopper."

"Who flies it?"

"Whoever has a license. Quite a few of the younger men—and three women that I know of—are ex-military. Helicopter pilots are probably easier to come by in rural areas than in the city."

"Who knew?" Sara asked, looking at the land and the sleek black cattle.

"With lease lands spread all over, and terrain that would make a mountain goat look twice, a helicopter is the best way to check on herds. We can haul feed and mineral licks out to the range cattle if necessary. We can see if a cow is down or if a calf is orphaned. We can herd cattle out of the high country to places that are easier to reach with an ATV or a horse or even a truck."

He settled his hat back on with a snap of his wrist. Amble flicked an ear back. He stroked the gelding's neck with strong sweeps of his hand while his eyes searched the landscape for any movement.

"So we're riding herd the old-fashioned way because . . . ?" Sara asked.

"I love it. It's a break from bookkeeping and lawyers and pulling wire. I do too much of that and too little of this." Jay gave her a sideways look. "And it's a way to take the measure of a certain woman who wants to handle a part of my family history."

She wanted to ask how she was doing but didn't want to be too blunt. "I'm guessing I passed the riding part," she said.

"Beautifully."

"And I kind of passed the shooting part."

"Jury is out on that," he said. "And I'm hoping it won't be a problem."

"So am I."

He whistled a sharp series of notes. The dogs pushed the cattle to the left, urging them closer to a pile of boulders at the edge of a small meadow. Evergreens shaded half of the boulders. When he whistled again, the dogs backed off and let the cattle scatter. Soon the animals were grazing on new grass under the watchful eyes of the border collies.

"That's pretty amazing," Sara said.

"They're good dogs, especially for how young they are. I'm planning to buy a quality bitch, train her, breed her with Skunk, and raise more cow dogs."

"I was talking about you being amazing. Where did you learn all the whistle commands?"

"From JD," Jay said, dismounting. "He learned them from his father, who learned them from his father, and so on. But the dogs answer to standard hand signals, too."

She watched Jay reach for the cinch and asked hopefully, "Lunchtime?"

"Better late than never." He loosened Amble's cinch, took off the saddlebags, and led the horse to a spot about twenty feet away. "The 'facilities' are behind whichever rock you choose."

Sara dismounted and loosened the cinch. "Do we need to hobble the horses?"

"No. I'll tie them in the shade of those trees. It will be a quick lunch."

With a fast glance around, she oriented herself and headed off to a boulder that was big enough for a football team to crouch behind.

"We've had plenty of warm days at this altitude," he called after her. "Watch for snakes."

"Always," she said fervently.

He felt the same way, but it was the two-legged variety of reptile that kept him on the alert.

He would bet hard money he had heard at least one ATV behind them.

So what? A lot of ranchers and outdoor types use ATVs. We're on public land right now.

Druggies use public lands. They're like snakes, appearing when the ground warms. It's prime time for pot up here. The season is short and the crop is kick-ass.

He really hoped the *campesinos* and cartel types would stay out of his way. Hunting them on his own was one thing. Hunting men with Sara along was a different thing entirely.

That was the reason for the rocky picnic. If it all went to hell, the boulders would be good cover.

I'm being paranoid, he told himself.

It's called survival, himself shot back.

Ignoring both halves of his arguing mind, Jay carried the saddlebags, canteens, and his rifle toward a grassy patch hidden in the boulders. Rocks reflected the warmth of the sunlight, raising the temperature several degrees. With every gust of wind, lacy shade swept across the boulders like a lady's fan.

The wind had risen with the temperature. Air blew steadily, though from unpredictable directions, bringing scents and sounds along for the ride. With a last look at the dogs—relaxed, watching the cattle— Jay propped the rifle within reach and pulled out the Glock. He could tell by its weight that the pistol was fully loaded, but he checked the magazine anyway before putting the weapon next to the rifle.

By the time Sara returned, Jay had laid out sandwiches and fruit, using the saddlebags as a makeshift table. The itching at the back of his neck, caused by primitive nerves telling him that he was being watched, had subsided to an occasional twitch.

Sunlight filtering through the nearby branches kept Sara half in shadow, but the half in sun was looking at him. He wanted to ask her if she felt watched, but didn't.

"Help yourself," he said. "There's plenty of everything."

"You're back," she said.

He gave her an odd look. "I never went anywhere."

She sat cross-legged and reached for the nearest sandwich. "You changed back there when Skunk barked. If I didn't already know you, I wouldn't have recognized you. My brother is like that, two men wearing the same skin."

"Sorry." Jay took a drink from the coffee canteen. "Old reflexes and training kicked in real hard."

"I figured that. My brother is the same, but he never talks about it. I just observed it. Had to live with it." She drew a breath, remembering. "It's like he can't find the off switch or it's stuck halfway."

"You train so you don't have to think in a combat situation." Jay took a big bite of sandwich, then another.

She waited, hoping he would talk willingly.

"The feeling of being watched is a basic survival mechanism," he said after he chewed and swallowed. "Earlier, the back of my neck lit up like a Christmas tree."

The words were easy enough, but she saw the weight of Jay's experience in the tight slash of his mouth.

"Caught you by surprise this time?" she asked casually.

"Yes." He shifted his shoulders, a man readjusting an invisible load. "I don't get caught off guard much." Navy blue eyes locked with hers. "But sometimes it's a pleasant surprise. Like you."

She felt herself warm under the open appreciation in his eyes. "But sometimes it puts you on alert, makes you forget you're at home?"

"Like your brother?"

She nodded.

"Homecoming takes longer for some," Jay said. "You have to retrain your reflexes."

"How about you? Are you really back?"

He looked at her dark brown eyes, so clear, so aware. "Most times, yes. The wrong kind of people can set me off. And whether I like it or not, there are still plenty of *wrong* people."

"The West is still wild, is that it?"

"So are cities. Criminals are criminals wherever you find them."

A golden eagle's whistling cry rippled down from the sky.

"I'd like to have his wings and eyes," Jay said, his head tilted back, watching the bird's easy flight. "Then I'd never blindly stumble over a grow operation again. Gunfire sounds the same here as it does in the mountains of Afghanistan. Kills just as dead, too."

Her eyes widened. "The pot growers shot at you?"

He shrugged. "You don't carry guns unless you're going to use them." He finished off the sandwich. "I wasn't as settled back then. I told Cooke what I'd found and then I went back to the place. Quietly." He bit into an apple, savoring its crunch.

"And?" Sara asked, her eyes intent.

"Like most crooks, they were cowards. They blew out of there before I came back with more ammunition. Left me with a mess—garbage, a diverted stream, chunks of land dug up everywhere."

"They're lucky they ran, aren't they?"

"Do you really want to know?"

She looked at Jay and saw the truth. When it came to the ranch, he would do what he had to—and he had been trained by experts in the art of war.

"I withdraw my dumb question," she said. "Do you have to get rid of trespassers like that every year?"

"Pot and meth are the modern gold. A lot of fools think drugs are easy money."

She blew out a breath. "Stuff like that can't make homecoming any easier."

Normally Jay would have changed the subject long ago, but the knowledge that Sara had a younger brother who had gone through the same hell he had made it easier to talk about the past.

"To get through your time over there," he said, "you have to change into someone else. Changing back is harder than most want to admit, and you never really do it all the way. You can't. Knowledge gained in adrenaline and fear goes right to the bone."

"I have a few adrenaline-and-fear memories," she said. "Small-town nights and sneaking off the farm, doing stupid, reckless stuff in cars that makes me wonder how I survived. Two of my friends, Kelly and Jim, didn't." *Kelly and Jim and his crumpled Camaro that almost made that last curve. Two crosses and plastic flowers and signs handmade by teenagers who had just learned that shit really does happen.* She shook her head slowly. "I can't believe I was ever that young."

"You grew up real nice."

She smiled almost sadly. "So did you. I'm not going to run screaming just because someone taught you how to defend yourself and your ranch. I tried to get Kelly out of the wreck. I would have given anything to be able to reach her. But I couldn't. All I could do was touch her arm while she died." Memories darkened Sara's eyes and made her mouth turn down. "Sometimes I still dream about the blood and . . ." She shook her head.

Jay could accept his own nightmares, but seeing Sara's in her dark eyes ripped him up in ways he couldn't name.

"Come here," he said, gathering her into his arms.

She didn't protest. She just settled into his lap and put her arms around him, comforting him as much as he comforted her. Slowly, with small movements of her head, she pushed aside his open collar and breathed deeply of his living heat, grateful that he had survived to be with her now.

He felt the sweet rush of her breath against his neck and a different kind of tension slid through his blood, kicking up his heartbeat. He tilted her head up and brushed his mouth against hers . . . once, twice, again, savoring the plush warmth of her lips, outlining them with the tip of his tongue. He felt the tremor that went through her and knew he should stop.

But he didn't.

He had waited a lifetime for a woman like her to tremble in his arms.

With a slow movement he repeated the caress, felt her breath sigh through her parted lips, and sank into her, going deep, coming home in a way he couldn't explain, only feel.

King Kobe's distinctive bawl cut through the quiet.

Reluctantly Jay lifted his head in time to see Lightfoot harry the bull calf back toward his mama.

"If he didn't have prime bloodlines," Jay said in a husky voice, "I'd be having me some veal real soon."

"I'd be eating right alongside you."

He looked at her eyes, the elegant line of her nose, the flush along her high cheekbones.

"Custer was right," Jay said.

"About what?"

"The view up here *is* the best on the ranch."

Chapter 11

J ay had a hard time staying focused on the cattle and on searching for whatever had set off the feeling of being watched. Kissing Sara had scrambled his thoughts in a way he wouldn't have believed was possible. Though she and Lightfoot were currently pressuring an Angus mama to stay with the herd, he swore he could scent the light lavender smell of her hair and savor the shared apple taste of her mouth.

Heat streaked through his body like lightning.

JD's old mantra echoed in his head. *Let it go. Be a rock, motionless while life's troubles flow on by.*

Jay tried to let the sensual moments he and Sara had shared pass through him and vanish. The starkly remembered feel of her mouth opening under his made his groin tighten even more.

Think about something else, he told himself, shifting to find a more comfortable position in the saddle.

Lightfoot's bark brought Jay out of himself.

The collie was staring up at a small ridge that stood between the herd and Fish Camp an hour ahead. The dog was intent, ears and tail up, black nose sniffing the wind that flowed down from the ridge.

From the corner of Jay's eye, he saw Skunk come to a quivering point.

He pulled the rifle out of its sheath and waited.

From his vantage point, the land fell away in all directions, forever, shades of green punctuated by granite, patches of snow, and the silver exclamation marks of aspen whose leaves were only a dream. Off to the left, an invisible stream murmured to itself, dreaming of the distant sea. Boundaries disappeared. He was the land and the land was himself, indivisible.

The dogs shook like they were coming out of water and resumed harrying any laggards.

Jay took a deep breath and let go of the adrenaline, even though he couldn't let go of the moment when he had seen the land so vividly.

And it had seen him.

It had been the same when he kissed Sara. They had *seen* each other.

Then she rode up alongside him and he realized he no longer felt the chill of bloody memories that haunted his silences.

"How's your neck?" she asked.

"Fairly quiet. You?"

"I'm still trying to lift a nonexistent ruff," she admitted. "Did you see anything?"

"You."

She tried to say something but could only think what a dark, vivid blue his eyes were. Her lips tingled with the memory of his kiss.

"Beautiful, beautiful woman," he said.

"Sweet liar," she said, smiling.

"Pure truth."

Eyes dark with memories and desire, she watched his every movement. "I wish I could take this feeling and carry it around in my pocket forever."

She looked at his eyes watching her and she saw too much. His experiences, his burdens, his joy at riding across the land.

With her.

Then Skunk bolted toward the ridge where evergreens lifted shaggy heads to the sun. The dog was almost belly to the ground when he stopped as suddenly as he had started.

"There's a Glock in your right saddlebag," Jay said. "If you have to use it, pull hard on the trigger the first time. After that it will get easy. And be sure what you're shooting at."

"What is it?" she asked.

"I'm going to find out."

Amble trotted toward the place where Skunk lurked in the grass. With every step his horse took, Jay searched the land in front of the dog. The only movement he could see was the nervous flicking of Amble's ears. Like Skunk, the gelding had caught a scent he didn't like.

Skunk inched forward, tracking something with his nose in the wind. Though his ruff stood up visibly on his neck, the dog didn't make a sound.

Without looking away from the direction Skunk was watching, Jay reined Amble at an angle to the dog. Soon man and horse were in the cover of trees.

Skunk's nose twitched in the wind and he tilted his head up just a touch.

Jay studied the ridge where the dog's attention was focused. The face was steep granite that still wore white patches of snow. Bands and small stands of trees tumbled steeply down to the grass where the dog lay in wait.

Jay knew the foliage concealed game trails that people occasionally used. The ridge wasn't Vermilion land, although they had grazing rights and free passage. Parts of the ridge edged onto national parklands, which were open to anyone who enjoyed rough country and had the government's permission to play.

Something sure is out there, he thought. *Something Skunk doesn't like. Something that makes my neck itch almost as bad as it did this morning. Different from this morning but still a warning.*

His intent eyes searched for the telltale flashes of sunlight reflecting off glass or metal. He saw only the ripple of wind through grass and trees.

Skunk stood and trotted back to the cattle, which were slowly moving toward Fish Camp. Whatever scent had lured the dog was gone now.

Sure would like to know what's shadowing our trail.

But he knew that if Skunk had given up, there was no point in beating the bushes. With a final sweeping glance, he went back to the herd.

And Sara.

"Did you see anything?" she asked as he rode up.

"Just the mountain," he said finally. "It felt like we were being scoped out for a moment. But not like earlier."

"How was it different?"

"I can't explain. It just was."

She shaded her eyes against the sun, but their brown was still bright in the shadow of her hand. "I think my jumpiness is catching."

"It's not just you," he said.

"The dogs," she agreed.

He tilted his hat back and sighed. "I don't know whether the dogs are picking up cues from me or vice versa. Out here, sometimes your mind plays tricks on you. Like people who have gone deaf often hear sounds in their mind."

"You mean you're populating the empty space out there with your mind?"

"Close enough."

The cows walked slowly on, leaving the people behind. Sara and Jay reined their horses around and followed.

"The problem," he said, "is once you go on alert, your mind doesn't want to stop."

She looked at him. He was watching the ridge that the trail was slowly skirting.

Skunk gave a sharp bark and froze, looking at that same ridge.

"That's it," Jay said flatly, pulling out the rifle. "Skunk is convinced there's something up on the ridge." A low whistle sent Lightfoot running along the side of the herd that was closer to the ridge. "Get the Glock and stay with the herd," he said to her. "Keep an eye on the ridge where the scree slope is. Skunk and I are going hunting."

"How long will you—?"

But Amble was already cantering off, following an eager Skunk along an invisible scent trail on the wind. Sara stared after them for a moment, then reached back and pulled the pistol out of the saddlebag.

"Okay," she said to Jezebel. "It's just you and me and the Glock."

The mare flicked her ear and watched the side of the herd where there was no dog to keep the cows in line.

Sara watched Jay. She wasn't happy about being left alone with the cattle, but she understood why he had. Until they knew what was following them, they didn't know how serious it might be.

I wasn't on a horse when I was at target practice. Doubt if I can hit anything but the ground this way. But animals are wary of guns—the stink and the sound.

It will have to be enough.

She looked at the ridge above the trees, where broken rock cut a gray swath across the land. Light poured out from beneath clouds that had increased in size. They didn't look dark enough for rain just now, but they were too heavy to ignore entirely. Shadows lay in nooks and crannies and ravines, growing bigger as the sun slid down to the western horizon.

She felt Jezebel tightening beneath her and grabbed for the saddle horn with her free hand. The mare raced to cut off King Kobe before he reached a succulent patch of spring grass growing at the edge of dense forest. The calf gave an angry bawl, but turned back.

On the other side of the herd, Lightfoot was working hard. The cattle seemed to know that the herding staff had been cut in half. The calves, in particular, were intent on breaking away just because they could.

"These are the cows I know and hate," she said, keeping one hand locked around the saddle horn. "Contrary and stubborn to the bone. I wonder if there is any Holstein hidden in Angus bloodlines."

Jezebel didn't care what breed the cows were. She had her ears up as she danced and pivoted, cutting off any avenues away from the herd, convincing the calves that they were better off with their mamas. On the other side of the herd, Lightfoot fought a losing battle for control. The calves and their mamas seemed intent on heading off in every direction.

The trail the herd was following came closer and closer to the tree line. All that separated the cattle from the trees were scattered rocks that stuck out of the ground like a kid's abandoned construction set. The sun was shining on the boulders, picking out sparkly bits of quartz and mica in the granite.

Before Sara could enjoy the view—much less look for Jay—Jezebel was on King Kobe again.

Sara hung on and thought how good veal would taste.

Then she heard a rushing sound, as if a sudden burst of wind was combing over grass and scrub and trees. The herd came to a stop and milled uneasily, disturbed by something she couldn't see.

She held Jezebel still and looked toward the source of the sound.

There. In the tall grass where the forest can't grow.

Something was moving quickly, like water rolling downhill, swift and unstoppable. She saw that three calves had managed to confuse Lightfoot and head off for greener pastures away from the herd.

There was a tawny flash.

Abruptly she realized what was making the grass bend and ripple. She hadn't seen any nature shows since she was a kid, but the image of a lioness chasing down a gazelle was imprinted on her memory.

The distance was too far for a pistol shot. She'd be as likely to hit a calf as anything else. She glanced frantically around, looking for Jay. She saw him maybe sixty feet back, upslope from the herd, rifle at his shoulder, tracking the rippling grass. He was aiming parallel to the herd, but higher up. Unless there was a really bad ricochet, all the stock would be safe.

The cougar put on a final burst of speed to close the distance between itself and the calf that was farthest from the herd. Tawny shoulders bunched up with muscle, power rippling through its body as it broke into a surprisingly ragged run.

Jay's first shot sounded like it was right in Sara's ear. It was louder than anything she'd ever heard in the movies or on the practice range, where she wore sound protectors. There was a snap in the air as the retort washed over her.

Just in front of the cat, grass seemed to leap and swirl. The cat ignored the sound and the bullet that had thrown up a stinging burst of grit in its face. The prey calf was close now, and nothing would get in the way of a kill. The cougar bunched up for a leap.

A second and third shot echoed through the high valley.

The cat fell like a puppet without strings.

The cattle tried to break away from the small herd and run wherever their tiny little minds led them. Sara was too busy hanging on to the saddle horn to watch Jay approach the fallen cougar. Jezebel had a job and the mare was going to do it.

Skunk appeared out of the grass. Between the two dogs and Jezebel, the cattle were finally contained in a restive group. Jay rode slowly up to the herd, not wanting to spook them any more.

"I'll take the Glock," he said. "The cougar is dead."

Sara gave him the gun. Instead of putting it in the saddlebag, he pulled out a small holster and clipped it to the back of his belt. The Glock fit it perfectly.

She started to say something, but settled for, "I thought mountain lions didn't hunt cattle."

"Healthy ones don't," he said, watching the herd. "This cat was half starved and partly crippled from some kind of fight. Probably made a try for an elk or a moose calf and the mother took exception. Moose and elk have sharp hooves and the temperament to use them."

"Poor cougar. If it hadn't been for you, the animal would have died slow and hard."

He looked at her. "Thought you would be on the cat's side."

"I am. Mother Nature is not only a bitch, she's hardest of all on the predators. A sick or weak prey animal doesn't suffer for long in the wild. A predator in the same shape suffers a long, hard death."

A lazy wind ruffled the grass with cool fingers.

"You keep surprising me," Jay said.

"Why? I'm as transparent as glass."

He smiled slightly. "Whatever you say, sweetheart. Let's get these cows to Fish Camp."

"What about the cougar?"

"We're in a national forest. I'll let one of the rangers know by radio after the cattle settle into the trail again."

"Paperwork in the wilderness?"

"Is the land overseen by a bureaucracy?" Jay retorted.

She huffed out a breath. "If you need a witness, I saw you fire a warning shot even though it was clear the cat had veal on its mind."

"Thanks, but I won't need a witness. The carcass will tell a ranger all he or she needs to know." He looked at her closely. "I didn't think before I left you here alone. Are you all right?"

She gave him a puzzled look.

"You and me riding together out here is like you going swimming in a pool," he said. "You out here alone with an unknown threat is like you swimming way out beyond ocean breakers."

She smiled wryly. "Well, I did have an instant of *Yikes, what am I doing here?* Then Jezebel took off after a calf and I didn't have time to worry about anything but hanging on while riding with a Glock. Good thing you use roping reins. Otherwise Jezebel would have been stepping on leather."

"You held it all together. That's what counts."

Jay whistled to the dogs, and the herd began moving slowly toward Fish Camp once more.

"You're really okay?" he asked her.

"I . . . don't know how to put it," she said slowly, sorting through her thoughts. "Part of me was thrilled to be out in a place where I can't just call up a meal or connect to the entirety of human knowledge on my phone. And part of me thought I was flat-out crazy. Then wind rolled down from the pass and the air smelled like old stone and sweetgrass. I felt so alive and *real*. I could hear my heartbeat and feel the sun and the wind on my skin. And I wondered when I had stopped listening to my own body."

When she was silent, he made an encouraging sound, needing to know more about her.

"San Francisco is an extraordinary place, both exciting and secure," she said slowly. "There, I'm part of a huge, complicated system built by human beings. I'm one piece of a crowd that ignores all the other pieces that make up the whole. There are so many things to do, to see, to try."

"And you miss it."

She nodded. "And I discovered that out here I'm connected to a different whole that I had all but forgotten. That's why I ride when I can, to remind me there are many worlds. Different worlds. In my race to get away from my childhood, I forgot that. I forgot the part where I was a girl standing barefoot in tall grass on a bluff looking out over the Pacific Ocean, breathing air that hadn't touched anything since Japan."

Jay watched Sara's lips while an emotion he couldn't name twisted through him. "I feel like that, too. Different worlds. I just have to figure out how to live a barefoot child's life in at least one of them."

"What about the adult?"

"No worries," he said rather grimly. "The adult knows that each world reaches out and takes its toll in sweat and blood and dreams."

Her dark eyes searched his, finding little comfort. "No free lunches," she said. "Damn. I keep looking for one."

"Speaking of lunch," he said, "I have to call the Solvangs again. They didn't pick up a few hours ago."

While he unbuckled one of the saddlebags, Sara watched the dogs watching the cows. She had learned that the dogs would detect trouble long before she did. And they were fun to see in action.

Jay pulled out the radio, switched to Fish Camp frequency, and said, "Ivar? Inge? Pick up the radio."

He waited for someone to answer.

"Come on, Ivar," Jay said. "Even you can't fish all day. Pick up!"

He waited.

And waited.

"Damn it," Jay said, switching the radio back to standby mode. "They must still be out fishing or chopping wood or gardening or something. They're supposed to be within hearing of the radio at all times, but . . ." He shrugged. "They both are the independent kind. That's why they live at Fish Camp all year."

"You think they could be fishing for trout?" Sara asked, not bothering to hide her greed.

"They're the best eating we have, unless we get mad enough and grill King Kobe."

"Trout, veal, trout, veal. Who could decide?"

"If young Kobe doesn't clean up his act, we'll have both," Jay promised.

"How much farther to Fish Camp?"

"Getting hungry again?"

"You bet. Riding is a lot more exercise than sitting in a chair."

"We'll be able to see the lake part of Fish Camp from the top of the trail right up ahead," he said. "From there, it's about twenty minutes to the cabins."

"Trout. Veal. Trout. Veal."

He smiled, then whistled at the dogs to pick up the

pace. Soon they were up on the crest of the trail, look-ing down. The cabins were hidden among the trees, but the boathouse showed its weathered wood at the shore of a sapphire lake.

"You see any boat?" Sara asked, standing in the stir-rups as she searched.

"No." He tried the radio again.

No answer.

With a muttered word, he stowed the radio in the saddlebag.

"Is something wrong?" she asked.

"What?"

"You're looking like your neck itches. A lot."

Chapter 12

For a few minutes Jay concentrated on the dogs and the herd rather than Sara's question. Then he said, "It's not like the Solvangs to blow off my calls. One call, sure. Fish Camp is a pretty big place. Three cabins, a fenced pasture, a corral, a small barn, the boathouse, a little storage building Ivar turned into his tool shop and retreat. After winter, there are always lots of repairs to do."

"Sounds like a miniature ranch," she said, "but for fun, not work."

"Mom used to call it the play ranch. When she was alive, all of us spent a lot of time up here in the summer. After she died, I spent almost as much time at Fish Camp as I did at the ranch house."

"Stepmother problems?"

"Father problems, too. JD had a hard time adjusting to a son who was nearly as big as he was. Kept trying to treat me like I was in diapers. Ivar always accepted me as I was. And Inge"—he smiled—"Inge was always making cookies and pies and sneaking bits to me when I just couldn't wait for dinner." Then he said, "Lightfoot, get that calf!"

The dog was already on the calf, but it gave Jay a way to vent the tension that kept tightening his neck.

"If we show up unannounced, is it a problem?" Sara asked.

"No."

If contacting the caretakers didn't matter, she wanted to ask why he was worried. But she didn't. He was in an edgy mood and didn't need her questions picking at him. Instead of talking, she fell into the easy silence they had often shared throughout the long, lazy day riding through the mountains. Usually the sound of hoofbeats on the trail, the clean, shifting wind, and the easy rhythm of riding a good horse relaxed and renewed her.

But not today. Her mind careened between the starving cougar and the kiss she had shared with Jay, a kiss that kept reverberating through her.

Beautiful, beautiful woman.

Sweet liar.

She had been kissed many times, yet she had never shared a kiss like that, gentle and consuming, a need and an acceptance that seeped into her soul. She knew she should be much more wary of Jay. He was the wrong man for her, and she was the wrong woman for him.

Yet it had never felt so very right.

Fine. So be an adult about it. You want him. He wants you. We're both single. Go for it. Enjoy him. Be enjoyed. Savor it as long as it lasts.

Then go back to your real life.

A slow kind of heat filled her at the thought of an adult, no-strings and no-regrets affair with Jay. She watched him from the shadow of her hat brim, admiring his easy male grace as he rode. Sun glanced off the width of his shoulders and flowed down his back in a long caress.

Beautiful, beautiful man. I can't have you for long, but I can have some memories to warm up the cold San Francisco fog.

Lost in her thoughts, Sara didn't realize that the horses had crested the final ridge until Jezebel stopped and snorted out a long breath. Beside her, Jay had the field glasses out and was scanning the land below. Even without binoculars, she could see the general layout of Fish Camp.

The small lake was a ragged circle ringed with tall, shaggy evergreens, rocks, and pockets of grass. What she could see of the house and cabins, which were tucked away in the trees, was little more than a patch here and there of weathered wood. The barn appeared to be maybe a quarter the size of the home barn.

No wonder Jay spent all the time he could here, Sara thought. *Gorgeous, barely touched by people, with a lake to play in and a lot of land to roam and imagine all the things boys love to imagine.*

Fish Camp had the air of a Shangri-la where the worries of the outside world couldn't penetrate.

Yet Jay didn't seem like a man looking down at paradise. He was intent, concentrated as he scanned the land below, like the golden eagle looking for its dinner.

"Is everything all right?" she asked quietly.

He swept Fish Camp again with his binoculars, looking slowly, thoroughly. "No smoke, no boat, nothing moving but the wind." He lingered for several long breaths, searching the knee-high grass that grew in small openings between the lake and the house.

She looked and saw nothing out of the ordinary. The forest turned sunlight into green needles and shadows. Wind moved tree branches and grass. Solar collectors on the main house's roof flashed in the sun.

Rustic but not backward, she thought, eyeing the panels.

"Are we late?" she asked. "Maybe they're out looking for us."

"We could have been here hours earlier," he admitted, remembering the lazy ride. "But if they were worried, they would have used the radio."

What Jay didn't say was that he hadn't been up to Fish Camp much since he had become a freshly minted civilian. There hadn't been any time for casual visits. There had been too much work to be done at the ranch, where so much necessary upkeep had just been let go. And JD's illness had eaten away at everything, free time most of all.

Jay looked hard at the lake, searching for the telltale wake of a motorboat. Then he searched for someone walking on the tree-sheltered path to the boathouse, or the equally sheltered paths between cabins and the small barn.

Nothing.

"They could be fishing at First Pond," he said. "Granddad made a stone dam on the stream coming out of the lake and stocked the pond with native trout. I learned to fish there as a kid."

The memory of coming up here with JD and young Barton rippled through Jay. It had been so long ago, but the memories were fresh and sweet.

JD teaching Barton how to fish, to do something for himself. I used to give him my favorite lures. God, how Barton grinned when he caught a fish bigger than mine. And I grinned right along with him.

Good times.

Knowing that those times were gone and would never return was a heaviness Jay carried because he didn't know how to put it down. He kept thinking that he could have done something better, something that would have helped his little brother make different decisions as an adult.

You did all you could, Jay told himself.

It wasn't enough, was it?

And that was something that couldn't be changed, like his mother's slow death, or the first time he saw one of his soldiers die trying to breathe through a bullet wound in his chest.

"Hey, you okay?" Sara asked. "You look . . ." *Lost.*

But she wasn't going to say that aloud.

He lifted his hat and resettled it with a jerk. "Just remembering some things. Wondering where the road changed under my feet."

His eyes were bleak beneath the shadow of the hat brim. Though his mouth was in sunlight, it was equally forbidding. He lifted the gelding's reins and followed the small herd down the back way into Fish Camp. The tension in his body increased with every step closer they came.

Where in hell are the Solvangs?

The trail came in at the rear of Fish Camp, where there was a fenced pasture, corral, and small barn. The pasture was empty, because the caretakers had traded in their horses for ATVs.

Maybe they're off on a long ride.

Then they damn well should have taken the radio. They know the rules. And they would have to be hell and gone for me not to hear their ATVs.

"We're putting the herd in here," he said, gesturing toward the pasture.

Sara didn't say a word. The tension pouring off Jay had scuttled any thoughts of Shangri-la.

The dogs herded the cattle into the pasture. The water trough was full and there was plenty of grass to keep the cattle entertained. Jay took a battered tin bucket off its hook on the fence, filled it with water from the trough, and set it against a fence post for the dogs. Then he gave them the signal to guard the cattle. After a final look at the pasture, he shut the gate.

She wanted to ask questions, but held her tongue. If he knew any answers, he would have told her.

They headed for the small corral, which was close to the barn. The horses must have caught Jay's mood, because they minced and snorted and shied all the way to the weathered rails. He opened the gate for Jezebel to pass through, then closed it behind Amble.

"Loosen the cinch and take off the bridle," Jay said, working quickly over his horse. "The water trough is full. Feed can wait until I see what's going on."

It used to be good up here, he thought. *No matter how rocky things were with Liza, how bad things were with the family, up here was always a sanctuary.*

It didn't feel like a sanctuary anymore. He hesitated over the rifle, then left it in the saddle sheath. The Glock should be enough.

After Sara saw to her horse, she leaned against the corral fence and absorbed the silence. The sky between clouds and what she could see of the lake were a blue so brilliant it made her ache.

Jay walked toward her, then stopped.

"What?" she asked, turning.

He held a hand up, a signal for silence and stillness.

A single glance told her that the stranger was back in Jay's skin.

She couldn't see Fish Camp's calm and quiet anymore. Instead, she saw the motion in the wind-blown trees and occasional small patches of grass, and the cougar that had been desperate enough to try for calves and to hell with the people and the dogs on guard.

But there isn't a cougar lying in wait between the cabins and the main house.

Is there?

Get a grip. There's nothing but my overactive imagination out there.

She followed Jay as he walked around the back of the barn toward the main house, which was farther away, closer to the lake than either of the secondary cabins. As soon as the caretaker cabin was in sight, he reached behind his back for the Glock. He pulled out the pistol and held it down along his side. His left hand went from relaxed to a flat, open palm that silently told Sara to stay back.

She hesitated, then moved slowly backward, watching the cabin as she did. In the dappled shade of the surrounding trees, it looked like the back door was ajar. Or might be. It was hard to tell. At this distance it could have been her imagination.

"When I say go, we're going to move quickly and quietly into the trees on the far side of the larger cabin," Jay said. His words were barely audible, carrying no farther than her ears. "Go."

She was stunned that someone as big as he was could move so silently, so fast. She felt clumsy and noisy in his wake. It seemed like forever before she was under the trees on the other side of the caretakers' cabin.

With a signal for Sara to stay put, Jay carefully approached the side of the cabin.

I'm going to feel like a fool when nothing is wrong, he told himself.

Better a live fool.

He ignored the niggling voice of civilization and went with the paranoid, pragmatic side of his mind. He didn't know exactly what had put his hackles up. He only knew that every survival instinct he had was screaming that something was very wrong.

He held up his left hand, balled in a fist, and hoped that Sara knew enough about hand signals—or plain common sense—to stop forward movement.

"Wait here," he said, the words barely audible. "I'm going to check the cabin. I won't be long."

She started to say something, but he was already moving. If she hadn't been looking right at him, she wouldn't have associated the faint rustle of sound with a human being.

Like that cougar. Fast. Invisible until he went for the kill.

Jay slipped around the corner, still holding the Glock along his right leg. He didn't look back to see if she stayed in the relative safety of the trees. All his attention was focused on the cabin itself.

Slowly Sara worked her way through the trees until she could reach out and feel the planks of the caretakers' cabin, rough beneath her fingers. She shivered with the cold.

Nerves, she told herself. *It's not that cold.*

Or maybe it was simply that the wind off the lake was especially cutting. Her fingers ached.

Gradually she realized that she was gripping the wood so hard her hand was almost numb. Very carefully she eased the pressure on her fingers. Drawing slow, deep breaths, she waited for whatever happened next.

Jay stopped at the back of the house and listened. He heard nothing but his own heartbeat, even and steady. His body had been trained for stillness even when his mind screamed that he move and move fast. Up close, he could see what had set off his instincts. The door was ajar, leaking heat from the woodstove in the kitchen.

Not that there was a lot of heat. Barely different from the outside, in fact.

Inge will have a fit. She'll put up with a lot from her man, but messing with her kitchen isn't tolerated.

Jay stepped along the outside of the two stairs at the back door. They creaked, but no more than the cabin itself under the heavy caress of the wind. When the wind swirled, the door moved, showing him more of Inge's kitchen. The old wood floor gleamed with polish in the low light.

He nudged the door fully open and waited with his back to the outside wall.

If anyone was in the house, he or she didn't come to close the door. And Jay knew from experience that the draft from the open kitchen door could be felt in every room of the cabin.

He ghosted through the small mudroom and across the floor. A pot of pasta waited on the stove. The noodles had swollen to grotesque proportions. The stove beneath the pot was barely warm. An iron skillet full of crumbled, browned hamburger had congealed next to the pot. Whatever fire had been in the stove once was cooling ashes now.

Woodstove could have been running for hours, depending on how much fuel Inge put in and what position the damper was in. No way for me to know. Just another thing that is wrong, like the abandoned food and the door left open for the wind.

The comfortable living room was quiet but for the insistent rush of the wind and an occasional rattle of the front door, which hadn't been closed hard enough to latch. The compact hearth was cold.

Wherever they are, they've been gone for hours at least. Depends on whether the spaghetti was for last night or tonight.

There was no way to tell. When Inge and Ivar were alone, she cooked enough to last several days.

Swiftly Jay walked through the rest of the cabin. The Solvangs were tidy folks, but there was enough mess everywhere that he wondered if they were the only people who had been in the cabin.

When he went through the back door, he found Sara waiting. She looked pale, tight, and her eyes were almost black. He wanted to hold her, but he had another cabin and the main house to search. And the barn.

"What did you find?" she asked.

"Nothing definitive. Nobody home, no notes, nothing obviously missing or out of place." His tone was clipped, information only, no emotion.

"Have they ever left without telling someone before now?"

"No."

The word was like the man himself—remote.

"I wish I could shut down like you, but I can't," she said. "I'm edgy. Scared."

He holstered the pistol and took her hands in his own. Soldiers might be used to cold facts, but she wasn't.

"We're both okay," he said, stroking her hands gently. "We'll find out what happened. There's probably a simple explanation and I'll feel like an idiot. But until then, I have to check the barn and the guest cabin and the main house, just to be sure. I can do it faster alone. Okay?"

"No."

"No, as in you think I'll be faster with you?" he asked.

"I'll feel safer with you," she said bluntly.

As much as he wanted to, he couldn't argue that fact. "How about I whistle up Skunk for company?"

"Won't that give us away?"

"Anyone who was interested would have seen us coming down the ridge to the pasture. Hard to hide thirty-odd cows, two dogs, and two horses with riders."

"Then why are we sneaking—Oh, you think some-one might be hiding in one of the buildings."

"Possible, not real probable. But I'll feel better once the buildings are secured."

"So will I." She rubbed her arms. "Since we're working in possibilities, not probabilities, I want to stay with you. I'll do what you do, not ask questions, and in general not be the stupid blonde in the movie."

He hesitated, then half smiled. "I don't think you could be stupid if you tried."

"You should have seen me as a teenager," she said under her breath.

"I'll go from here to the barn," he said. "You wait to come until I signal. Clear?"

Her lips tightened, but she nodded. She knew better than to argue with him when he was in captain mode.

He watched the barn for a minute from the kitchen of the cabin. Then he walked among the widely spaced trees separating the cabins from the barn, keeping to cover when he could. The back of his neck was twitching before he got to the side door of the barn. He really hadn't liked coming across the open patches.

No bullets, so no sweat.

Inside, the barn was quiet, smelling more of machinery than horses or cows. Half the stalls had been converted to hold two ATVs, two snowmobiles, and the Jeep Scout that the caretakers used to go to town.

Either someone came to get them, or they walked out of here.

The vehicles were sitting oddly. Jay moved closer to investigate. The tires on the ATVs and the Scout were flat. A closer look told him that the air stems on the tires had been cut off. Easier than slashing tires and just as efficient. When he looked into the old tack room, it was uninhabited. Messy, too.

Either Ivar has been sick, or someone was looking for something in a hurry.

The hayloft had been taken out when the Solvangs converted to machines, so Jay didn't have to climb up to check for anyone hiding.

He left the barn, took the path through the trees to the guest cabin, circled it, and waited. Only the wind moved, herding clouds until they stacked up again the Tetons. He listened carefully, then signaled for Sara to come over.

She was out of the house and across the yard like a sprinter leaving the starting blocks. Even so, by the time she got to the front of the guest cabin, he had already been through its small rooms. Messy rooms.

The more he saw, the less he liked any of it.

And the less sense it made.

"Did you find anything?" she asked quietly.

"Messy rooms. Flat tires."

"What?"

"The ATVs and the Scout in the barn." Before she could ask another question, he said, "The main house is next. Stay behind me."

With every moment, he had become more and more certain that they were alone at Fish Camp. Even so, he approached the main house as cautiously as he had the caretakers' cabin, paying special attention to the small shed where the generator was kept.

Sara followed about ten feet behind him, not wanting to get in his way.

He went in the back door through the mudroom to the kitchen. The layout was similar to the caretakers' cabin, but more spacious. The woodstove in the kitchen was cold. The cupboards were open. So was the pantry.

Some of the canned goods were on the floor. A bag of beans had been cut open, sending the contents spilling out of the pantry into the kitchen.

A smashed shortwave radio lay on the floor.

Jay's mouth flattened into an even harder line. Everything he saw was adding up to something he didn't want to see at all.

Sara followed silently as he went through the main house. The living room and dining room were empty, furniture shoved here and there for no reason she could see. She followed him upstairs and saw the same—a mess. Winter gear on the floor, mattress askew, dresser lying on its face. The bathroom down the short hall was no better.

She felt like she was back in her motel room, putting together the wreckage of her suitcase, and each time she turned a corner things got worse. A cold that had nothing to do with the air made her clench her teeth to keep them from chattering. Slowly she became aware of Jay's hands running up and down her arms with gentle, steady sweeps that centered her.

"I'm okay," she said hoarsely. "Just reminds me of my motel room. I feel like trouble is following me." She took a deep breath, then another, and said again, "I'm okay."

He squeezed her arms gently, then slowly let go and headed downstairs. He heard her footsteps behind him.

"This looks like someone had a tantrum," she said.

"Yes."

"Disappointed meth heads?"

"Possible."

He headed down the stairs to the den, where JD had kept his papers and his poker cards and his booze. The rolltop desk was open. Another smashed shortwave radio lay on the floor near it.

That explains why Inge and Ivar didn't answer my call.

"I'm going to check the boathouse," Jay said. "Why don't you lock up and wait for me downstairs."

It wasn't a question. More like an order.

She surprised both of them by obeying.

He headed for the front door, the Glock once again in his hand.

Chapter 13

Jay walked through the trees down the well-used path to the boathouse. Memories fought for his attention with every step on the quarter-mile trail, but he pushed them aside to be dealt with later. He had to stay focused on what was happening now. The past could wait. Nothing in it could be changed anyway.

Thirty feet short of the boathouse, he stopped under cover of the trees and studied what was ahead. The lake was calm in sheltered areas. The open center of the water showed whitecaps from the playful wind. Marsh grass and plants grew in the shallows of the lake where leaves and soil covered the stony bottom.

The boathouse and short dock were weathered gray, looking almost velvety in the late-afternoon light. Clouds had expanded out from the Tetons, eating away at the sun. The first few drops of what could become real rain were falling now, bright in the broken sunlight.

Birds darted and sang in the bushes just back from the lake. Insects hummed and whirred wherever sunlight remained on the edge of the lake. Water was always a magnet for life. These small lives hadn't been disturbed recently.

As soon as Jay stepped out of cover, everything but the wind and lapping water fell silent. He pushed open the door to the boathouse. A patch of sunlight dappled the wide opening leading to the water and made bright reflections on the roof and rafters. The exposed beams and tight shadows between reminded him of the rib cage of a huge, long-dead animal.

The rows of neatly stored, oiled tools on the wall and a counter down the right side told him that whoever had searched the rest of the buildings hadn't bothered here. The only thing that caught his eye was the empty place, outlined in white paint, where a screwdriver in Ivar's tightly organized tool collection was missing. Smudge marks showed on the white, exactly where someone in a hurry would have grabbed the screwdriver.

"Ivar?" he called. "Come on out. It's Jay."

He held his breath as he waited.

Go ahead and tell yourself one more time that they just went out for a walk. You haven't believed it so far, have you?

Only the wind answered his call.

A small collection of dinghies lay overturned in a line, hulls facing the ceiling. Clean and well cared for, they waited in neat array for someone to use. One of the dinghies had been kicked or knocked out of place, with the barest smear of dirt accenting the disorder.

He lifted the boat aside and saw nothing beneath.

Without expecting to find anything different, he went outside. Nearby was the toolshed and fuel depot where Ivar had built a simple retreat, or "man cave" as Inge delighted in calling it. The old man had often said that the reason he was happily married was that each of them did just fine on their own.

Beyond the ramshackle retreat was a woodpile.

Nearly used up, like the one by their cabin. Long winter. There will be lots of wood to cut before the next winter.

Jay took two steps, then froze. His mind insisted he had seen something out of place in the groundcover. Motionless, he examined the grass and weeds and small shrubs encroaching on the buildings. The different heights and textures gave the ground a mosaic appearance.

Sitting on his heels, he searched for whatever was picking at his instincts. After a few minutes, he saw that the grass lay differently in places, suggesting someone had walked through, probably in the last several hours. He couldn't pick up where the trail started, but it became more noticeable toward Ivar's retreat.

He followed the trace and ended up losing it. He circled back to the front. There was a single door there, newer than the rest of the building. The wooden door had lightened to a fine silvery blond.

Locked.

No sign of forcing.

And there was blood on the threshold.

If anyone was waiting inside, they'd have shot at me or bailed out the back window by now.

Jay holstered his gun. In case he was guessing wrong, he stood to the side and worked the padlock without taking off his leather gloves. He tried the usual Vermilion Ranch combination first. It worked. Quietly he slid the padlock free, drew the Glock, and kicked the door open.

He stood to the side, out of the line of any fire. A beam of sunlight spread into the room, showing more blood tracked over the rag rug Inge had made. There was order to the marks, jagged and diagonal.

Boot tracks. Looks big for Ivar, much less Inge.

The room was dark but for a trapezoid of light falling in from the open door. The smell told him all he needed to know.

Too much.

As his eyes adjusted to the light, he saw a foot half covered by a slipper. The foot was bent at a wrong angle. Inge loved her warm slippers, but she never wore them outside the house. At least, she hadn't until now.

He stepped into the long, narrow room. Adrenaline morphed into rage.

Senseless. Meaningless. Wanton.

I thought I left this behind.

But here it was, at his feet, motionless, stinking of the aftermath of death. Without realizing it, Jay cursed with the savagery of the combat leader he had once been.

Slowly he went to kneel next to Inge. Her plump face was slack, her pale eyes open, seeing nothing. He closed them with a sweep of his fingers, surprised that his hands weren't shaking.

Later. I'll have time for rage and grief then.

And vengeance. I'll make certain of that.

He was glad Inge lay beyond the reach of the pitiless light. The wound in her chest was a bad one, T-shirt so bloodstained that it looked black. He had seen wounds like that before, too many of them.

Combat knife. Or a hunting knife.

Same thing, really.

He looked over to Ivar, who lay facedown, utterly still, a wide pool of dried blood beneath his head like a dark pillow. Careful not to get too close, Jay sat on his heels and studied the body.

Only a slit throat bleeds like that. If I really looked, I'd see splatter marks.

Jay hated that he recognized the cause of death, that he knew it so well. He hated that he was using knowledge gained in war to understand death in a place that had always meant peace.

Yet there Ivar lay on his stomach, his arms at his sides and his feet toed out at an angle that would have been painful for anyone still alive. He was in work clothes, a pair of jeans faded to robin-egg blue, topped by the green-and-black flannel shirt that he wore every day but the day Inge washed. Now the flannel was stained with blood that was so thick Jay could taste copper on his tongue.

With a grace and strength only the living had, he came to his feet and turned on a wall switch with his gloved hand. The old incandescent bulbs came on after a small hesitation.

Old room, old wiring.

Old people.

Only death is new.

A quick, visual inspection of the floor showed a scattering of boot prints.

Could have been three men. Probably only two. That will be for the sheriff to figure out.

For the first time Jay regretted Inge's one-woman war against dust and dirt. Dust would have helped distinguish the tracks, but even Ivar's man cave had a clean floor.

That's Cooke's problem. Mine is to disturb as little as possible.

The door to the minute bathroom lay open, as did the door to the tiny storeroom where Ivar kept whatever odds and ends of old stuff he thought might be useful some time in the future. Stuff Inge insisted had no place in her house.

Someone had been in the storeroom.

Avoiding the bloody tracks, Jay looked in. Surrounding the anonymous junk in the center of the room, large wooden crates were stacked along the walls like makeshift wainscoting. All the crates had been pried open, revealing unframed paintings by Custer. None of the crates had any empty space within.

Whatever the jackals were after, Custer wasn't it.

A gleam of metal lured Jay into the room. Ivar's big, missing screwdriver lay abandoned.

They used it to pry open the crates.

Later, he would be furious, grieving. Later he would hunt. Now he would gather what facts he could, though his eyes burned with unshed tears.

The sound of raindrops came on the parts of the roof that had been repaired with tin.

Real rain will make tracking anyone coming in or out of Fish Camp a lot more difficult.

The jackals who did this are gone.

Did they get what they wanted? Or will they be coming back?

Knowing the sheriff would disapprove but understand, Jay pulled a ragged tarp from the storeroom and covered Inge and Ivar.

God be with you, old friends.

Switching off the light, Jay stepped outside and locked the padlock behind him. There was nothing more he could do for the dead.

He walked back to the house in the growing drizzle. When he reached the yard, he called out and stood in plain sight, letting Sara know he was back. The door opened so quickly he knew that she had been watching for him.

"Did you find anything?" she asked.

He shut and locked the door behind him without answering.

She took a closer look at his face and felt her heart roll over. "Jay?"

"Ivar and Inge are in Ivar's special toolshed, next to the boathouse. Dead."

She put her arms around him and said, "I'm so sorry," again and again without even knowing it.

He accepted the embrace, returned it, then gently separated from her. "It's starting to rain. I'll get the tack under cover and bring in the saddlebags. And check the pantry. Inge kept dog food on hand for the summer. Then I'll call Cooke."

"Don't worry about the pantry," Sara said. "Are you bringing the dogs inside?"

He shook his head. "I'll leave Skunk with the cattle. Lightfoot will guard the toolshed from wildlife. If something is too big for him to handle, he'll make a racket."

The implication hit her like a bucket of cold water. To a wild animal, protein was protein.

Don't go there, she told herself fiercely. *It won't do any good. Jay needs someone he can count on, not a dumb blonde from a dumber movie, screaming and screaming.*

The sound of rain on the windows broke the silence.

"I'll help you with the tack," Sara said. "It will go faster that way."

Jay didn't argue.

With the two of them working, everything was quickly stowed in the barn. The rain was cold, refreshing.

Maybe it will wash everything clean, Sara thought, even though she knew that some things couldn't be made right, ever.

Jay turned the horses out to pasture with the cows, grabbed the rifle and saddlebags, and said, "Back to the main house."

It wasn't raining hard at all, more of a wind-swept sprinkle with fat, cold drops. Each drop was a separate sensation, reminding them that they were alive.

"Ever used a woodstove?" he asked when they were inside.

"Every day of my life until I was eighteen."

The grim line of his mouth shifted slightly. "You're a wonder, Sara Anne Medina."

"The only wonder is that I waited until I was eighteen to leave that farm behind."

She opened the door and took stock of the stove. A fire was laid, and there was no ash buildup that would need cleaning. Wood was stacked in a tub beside the stove. A box of matches waited on the built-up brick floor that surrounded the old stove. She opened the damper, set fire to the kindling, and watched little flames grow into big ones until she closed the door.

Keeping track of her from the corner of his eye, Jay set the saddlebags in the mudroom near a second wood bin and dug out the shortwave radio. Before the sheriff's office answered, he could smell the tang of fire biting into pine.

"This is Jay Vermilion. Who's on duty?"

"Afternoon, Jay," said the dispatcher. "Cooke just came in. Will he do?"

"Yes, thanks."

A moment later Cooke's voice came over the radio. "What's up?"

"Two murders. Inge and Ivar."

At the word *murders* Sara dropped the piece of wood she had just picked up to put in the stove. She looked at Jay, but all she could see was his back. It was tight, muscles bunched across his shoulders. Tension radiated from him.

While he relayed what he had found, she picked up the wood and tended the fire. After a few deep, slow breaths to steady herself, she went to the pantry. Plenty of canned goods. Dried beans, sugar, flour, ground coffee, dog food.

Plus two freshly baked loaves of bread and a lemon meringue pie.

Sara didn't know she was crying until she felt the tears on her face. Silently she went about making coffee, automatically feeding wood into the stove when needed, listening to Jay talk about bloody murder.

He watched her, wishing she didn't have to hear his words, yet glad that she was here with him.

"No blood or signs of a real struggle in any of the cabins," he said. "Either Inge gave up housekeeping or the buildings were searched in a half-assed way. ATVs and their Scout were disabled."

"Anything taken?"

"Not obviously. Could have taken money, booze, or guns. I haven't checked."

"How long ago?" Cooke asked. "Best estimate."

"Within the last twenty-four hours."

"How were they murdered?"

"With a combat or hunting knife. Inge's chest was sliced up, more than one blow. Ivar's throat was cut."

Sara fumbled with the stove, nearly burning her hand.

"Son of a bitch," Cooke said.

"Lightfoot is guarding the bodies."

"Hell of a thing," the sheriff said. "One sad hell of a thing."

Jay didn't think about it. Couldn't. There was too much to do. "I can't get out on my cell phone. Their kids and grandkids will have to be told. Henry has the contact numbers."

"I'll take care of it."

"Sara and I will stay until you can send someone up here tomorrow," he said, his voice neutral as it had been from the first word he had spoken. "We're in the main house. Don't know how the weather is in town, but it's raining pretty good up here. If the temperature drops much more, it will snow."

"I'll send someone up first thing in the morning, but it will be afternoon before they get there. Rain plays hell with that road."

"No hurry. They're not going anywhere."

"I'm sorry, Jay. The Solvangs were damn good people."

"Yes. And they were murdered just the same."

With savage restraint, he switched over to the home ranch frequency. Henry picked up immediately.

"Inge and Ivar are dead," Jay said. "Murdered. Tomorrow morning, send the new hands up in a four-wheel rig to . . ."

Sara did her best not to hear the sad details and regrets all over again. Instead, she concentrated on fixing food. The living had to eat in order to take care of the dead. Screaming and crying and cursing wouldn't do anything but waste energy that was necessary to take care of all the details for the dead. And for the survivors.

At least the cows don't have to be milked, with their scheming eyes and shit-covered tails waiting for a chance to smack me in the face.

She shook off the past and concentrated on what she could do in the present.

The rich smell of coffee began to fill the room. It was followed by the tang of gun oil as Jay began cleaning the rifle and the Glock. He knew the Glock wouldn't need it—he'd seen it take a mud bath and come out firing just fine. The rifle was different. It required more care.

In any case, he needed something to do with his hands. Part of him hoped that the murderers would return. He would enjoy getting up close and physical with the kind of cowards who murdered good people just because they could.

"Cleaning a pistol was part of my training," Sara said.

"I'll take care of this. But thanks."

She watched him for a moment—deft fingers, swift, experienced motions—and was glad she was cooking rather than fumbling her way through cleaning a weapon.

A closer survey of the pantry turned up onions, dried peppers, garlic, and cooking oil. The sink had running water. Cold. Apparently the solar panels were out or only generated enough electricity to run the lights. Gritting her teeth, she washed her fingers in well water so cold that it made her hands ache.

Very quickly the smell of chopped onions overcame that of gun oil and coffee. Jay finished with the Glock and set it aside, loaded and ready to go.

Sara handed him a mug of coffee.

"There's canned milk in the pantry," she said, "along with some sugar. Want either one?"

"No thanks. I'll take it straight up," he said, reaching for the mug. "Whoa, your hands are freezing. I'll turn on the generator. Water should be hot by the time we do dishes."

She breathed a sigh of relief. "That would be great. I was thinking of having to warm water for dishes and baths and . . ."

He smiled slightly. "Mom felt the same way. She said she'd put up with the racket a generator makes to have hot water at night."

"Your mother was a wise woman."

Moments after Jay went out the back door, a diesel generator sputtered, caught, and thundered happily to life. When he came back in, Sara was frying onions and chopping garlic. She opened a can of chili, looked over at the size of the man who was settling back in to clean the rifle, and opened four more cans, dumping their contents into the big frying pan with the onions.

"Do you want your canned green beans on the side or in the chili?" Sara asked.

"In it works for me. Fewer pans to wash."

"Good point."

She added more wood to the fire and went back to stirring. After a few minutes, she tasted and immediately went looking for cayenne pepper. It was in the pantry, along with some other spices she could use.

By the time Jay was done cleaning the pistol, the chili was simmering on the stove. He cleared away the cleaning materials and set out flatware on the small kitchen table where he had worked on the weapons.

Sara cut off thick slices of bread. "Grab a plate and fill it."

He came up behind her, slid his arms around her waist, and slowly, gently, kissed the side of her neck. "Thank you."

Her breath stopped. "Opening cans takes no particular talent."

"I was talking about being you, being what I need."

She leaned back against him with a long sigh. "I feel so useless."

"Looking at death, we all feel that way." He pulled her closer for a moment. "Keep my dinner warm. I'm going to feed the dogs and check that the storage room in Ivar's toolshed isn't leaking on anything important."

The knife hit the counter with a clang. "The Custers! How could I have forgotten them? We should bring them to the house."

"If necessary, I'll take care of it."

With another gentle squeeze, he released her. She turned quickly and hugged him back.

"I'll bank the fire and meet you at the toolshed," she said.

"You don't—"

"I need to check the paintings," she interrupted, looking up at him. "And I should be smacked for not doing it sooner."

"You'll have to walk past the bodies to get to the paintings," he said.

His eyes were dark and bleak and made her wish that she could put light back into them. But she couldn't. Only time could.

"Then I'll walk past them," she said evenly.

A single look at Sara's face told Jay that arguing was a waste of time. "There's a flashlight in the drawer to the right of the sink and cleaning rags under the sink. Soak them with the pine cleaner and throw in some ammonia. Stuff the rags in a covered pot and bring it with you."

She gave him an odd look.

"I put a tarp over the bodies," he said. "It takes chemicals to cover the smell."

She lifted her chin. *It can't smell worse than pulling that dead calf did.* "I'll be at the toolshed in five minutes."

Without a word he stepped away from her. He rummaged in the cupboard, found two bowls, and filled them with kibble from the pantry. Then he stepped out into the rainy twilight and shut the door behind him.

Chapter 14

It took Sara less than five minutes to get to the boat-house, but Jay was already there, waiting for her. Lightfoot waved his tail at her once, then returned to guarding the small outbuilding, watching from the open door of the boathouse. Rain came down steadily, coldly. She could see her breath between the drops.

The instant Jay opened the door to Ivar's retreat, she reached for the small pot she carried. The pungent smell made her cough and all but stunned her nose, covering the smell of death. She followed him inside, walking in his wet boot prints, fighting her gag reflex.

Throwing up doesn't help. It just makes you weaker, and the job still has to be done after you've cleaned up your own mess.

She kept repeating the words from her childhood as she followed Jay through the room that stank of death.

The overhead light showed only the ragged blue tarp draped over the bodies. Blood reached beyond the tarp. Quickly she looked away, fighting herself until her stomach stopped trying to crawl up her throat.

Ahead of her were walls and counters of neatly arranged tools. She concentrated on their patterns and was grateful she hadn't eaten recently.

"The junk room is over there," he said, pointing with the flashlight. "We'll go along the outside of the wall so if we leave any tracks, they won't be confused with any the killers left. Don't touch anything with bare fingers."

She swallowed hard again, took another sniff from the pot, and breathed through her mouth. And she carefully didn't think about the tarp. With quick steps she went through the door of the junk room, used her elbow to turn on the light, and stepped aside for him.

"May I look in the boxes?" she asked. "I can put on my mittens."

"Good idea." He tucked the flashlight under his arm, took his riding gloves out of his jacket, and pulled them on before he shut the door.

She breathed out in relief at having a closed door between her and the bodies. Carefully she circled the pile of odds and ends in the center of the floor in order to examine the first packing crate. It had been carelessly opened. The splintered boards and random nails looked like they had been wrenched out and thrown aside.

Though the overhead light was barely adequate, she could see that every slot in the first crate held an unframed painting on the original canvas stretcher or particleboard, whichever Custer had used. No sign of water damage on the wood or on the floor beneath.

"Can we take them to the house?" she asked.

"Not without messing up the death scene even more."

"Then I'll photograph each one, front and back," she said, taking her phone from her jacket. "If you hold them for me, it will go quicker."

He went to the box she had been working over and gently pulled out a painting. Her breath came in at the beauty and energy of the work emerging from the dusty crate. She took several images in succession.

And she tried very hard not to think about the incredible cultural treasure she was recording. There would be time later to exclaim and laugh and soak in the paintings, letting them soothe the ugliness of murder.

"Over, please," she said.

The back of the canvas held a few scribbled notes— time, place, title.

"Is this Custer's handwriting?" she asked.

"Think so."

"Okay. Next," she said.

He pulled out another painting for her to photograph.

Very quickly they worked out a rhythm of removing, digitizing front and back, replacing, and removing another painting. Not all of them were Custers. Apparently JD—or his wife—sometimes had purchased other painters.

Sara had to force herself not to linger over paintings only a few people had ever seen.

"How many paintings in that last carton?" she asked.

"Nine."

"Fifty-six paintings, total. Fifty of them Custers." *And not one of them a portrait.* She lifted the lid from the pot and breathed in a whiff. "Incredible."

He didn't ask if she was referring to the paintings.

She coughed and covered the pot. "What's in those cardboard cartons along the wall over there? Custer was careless with his work. He could have stacked smaller paintings in the cartons."

"I'll find out."

Jay went to the first carton and carefully slit the wide tape sealing the box. "Looks like papers." He reached in and flipped through random stacks. "Old records kept by Inge."

The next two boxes were the same.

"Keep going. Please," Sara said.

The fourth carton held Custer's papers. So did the fifth. The sixth one held field studies he had painted on everything from canvas to particleboard, with a few even painted on cardboard.

No portraits.

Beautiful plein air studies, yes.

People? No.

"Can we take these with us now?" Though her voice was even, her eyes pleaded.

"We have to walk out anyway. I don't see any harm in carrying three boxes that the jackals didn't even bother to open."

Breath rushed out of her. "Thank you. Papers in cardboard are much more vulnerable than oil paintings in special wooden crates. I know the cardboard boxes have been safe for however many years, but . . ." She shrugged, unable to explain.

"I understand. Too much has been lost as it is." He closed the three cartons of Custer's papers and paint-ings and picked them up, two under one arm and one under the other. "Take the lid off the pot and leave it. The deputy will thank us."

She put the open pot on top of a bench, switched on her flashlight, and led the way back to the main house.

The fresh air was staggeringly beautiful. The rain hadn't changed, except maybe to get colder. It certainly seemed frigid to her.

I'm just tired and . . . hungry.

Once the smell had vanished, Sara's normal healthy appetite had returned with a vengeance. She would have been embarrassed, but a farm girl learned young that death and hunger were a part of life.

The house mudroom was warmer than the outdoors, but not by much.

"I'll put the boxes in the den," Jay said, "and bring in some more wood. The bin here is nearly empty."

Sara shook the rain off her jacket and headed for the woodstove. The fact that it was barely warm told her how much time they had spent with the paintings. Her stomach was also registering a nearly continuous, rumbling complaint. A glance at her watch made her realize that it had been too long since they had last eaten. Quickly she went to work on the fire.

"Dinner will be hot in fifteen minutes or we can eat it cold now," she said as he headed back to the mudroom.

"Make it half an hour," he said, snagging his cold mug of coffee and downing it in three long gulps. "We need wood."

Even more, I need to pound on something.

But he didn't say anything about that. She had been a good partner. If she was managing to think of something besides murder, he didn't want to remind her.

The chili was bubbling fragrantly on the stove. The coffee was hot. Sara's stomach rumbled continuously. The rhythmic sound of chopping outside was like the sound of the generator. Relentless. She had heard Jay working even over the sounds of her meal preparation and the noisy generator.

Chop.

Chop.

Chop.

What is he, a machine?

Chop.

Chop.

Well, I'm not. I need food.

She poured a mug of coffee, put on her jacket, and headed out to lure him away from the woodpile. Rain and wood smoke from the stove blended in the cold air. Pulling her jacket closer, she turned the corner of the house.

And stopped.

Jay's back was to her, muscles bunching and releasing as the ax rose and fell, wood all but exploding apart.

He kicked pieces aside and lifted the next section of log into place.

He didn't have his jacket on, or even long sleeves. He didn't need them. Steam rose steadily from his white T-shirt, mixing with the rain. The work lantern he had hung on the eaves threw every line and curve of his body into sharp relief beneath the nearly transparent cotton.

Sara bobbled the coffee mug and barely held on to it. And she stared at him, compelled by his grace and his sheer, mesmerizing power.

I'd like to rub myself all over that fine male body.

The pile of split wood was knee deep around Jay before he stopped to wipe sweat from his eyes.

"Mind sharing that coffee?" he turned and asked.

She unstuck her tongue from the roof of her mouth and cleared her throat. "You can have anything you want."

Some of the hard lines on his face shifted into a crooked smile. "Anything, huh? I'll keep it in mind. But right now I'll settle for some coffee."

She tried not to stare at his body as she handed over the mug. Not looking wasn't really possible. The hair on his chest was like smoke against his soaked T-shirt. His jaw was highlighted by dark stubble.

He makes Michelangelo's David *look like a boy. It would take Rodin to capture Jay's raw male power.*

"Coffee?" he reminded her, but his eyes were gleaming with inner laughter.

"I spent years in art classes looking at the male form," she said, giving him the coffee. "Yours is—Oh my. I'm trying to think of words when all I want to do is . . . shut up. Yeah, that would be a really fine idea. Shutting up right now."

She turned to go back into the house.

He snagged her by her jacket collar, pulled her back, and gave her a coffee-flavored kiss.

"Thanks," he said when he lifted his head.

"For the coffee?"

"For taking my bad mood and turning it into something else."

"My pleasure. Dinner's ready."

He didn't point out that dinner wasn't all that was ready. "I'll have my knees under the table in ten minutes."

"Don't hurry on my account," she said, appreciating him with her eyes all over again.

"I've never taken a woman in a cold rain. Right now, taking you is sounding like a really good idea."

Her head snapped up so that she could see his face. "You mean it."

"Oh yeah."

"Try me on a warm night, rain optional," she said, then bolted for the house before he could stop her.

He was still laughing when she shut the door.

Feeling much better herself, she set plates out to warm on top of an upside-down frying pan on the stove. She stirred the chili, checked the fire again, and decided that she would do a quick survey of the contents of the boxes in the den. She poured herself a mug of coffee and sipped gingerly at the hot liquid as she walked to the den.

"Where to start?" she said under her breath, eyeing the cartons.

She went to the first carton of papers and rifled through, looking for intact notebooks or good sketch paper with drawings. She didn't find any. It looked like half the papers had been ripped from someone's notebook or torn off a writing pad. Most had doodles or sketches. Quite a few were caricatures.

Custer had a wicked, cruel eye. I doubt that anybody paid him for a caricature. Belted him with a fist wrapped around a roll of nickels, more likely.

The generator's background rumble stopped suddenly. The mudroom door opened and closed, followed by footsteps going up the stairway off the living room.

She wondered if Jay was wearing his soaked T-shirt or if he had already stripped it off.

Focus, she told herself sternly. *And not on sex.*

The shower came on. Her thoughts strayed—and stuck on what he must look like naked with hot water pouring over him. She shook herself. Hard.

Focus.

It had never been so difficult.

The next box held field studies and miscellaneous papers, often Custer's notes to himself on some aspect of the painting he had in mind.

Awesome.

People eat up this sort of personal history with a spoon. I'm really hoping a lot of these studies can be matched to the paintings Jay has. And if one of the field studies is of Wyoming Spring, *I'll dance naked in the snow.*

Alone, she added hastily. *No audience.*

With another mental smack to her wandering attention, she bent down to the third box. More papers, doodles, and sketches that could have been an end in themselves or a means to new paintings. There was no way to tell unless some of them matched up with existing paintings.

"Want to shower before you eat?" Jay asked.

Sara choked back a shriek. He was even quieter in his bare feet.

"Shower?" she asked blankly, staring at his feet.

She had never considered a man's feet one way or the other, but his looked strong and . . . edible.

"Maybe I should eat first," she said, dragging her gaze away from the floor and craning her head to meet his eyes. "I'm really hungry."

"Then let's eat," he said as she came out of her crouched position over the boxes.

"Don't get your hopes up. All but one can was vegetarian chili," she said, standing and stretching. "I considered going after King Kobe, but it was raining really hard."

"I thought about it, too. Decided to work out my mad on the wood, instead."

"Ah, well. I can always open the canned beef I found."

He shuddered. "No thanks. JD loved that crap, creamed on toast. I'd rather eat corral scrapings."

"Makes two of us. My grandfather used to call it SOS."

"Shit on a shingle?"

She nodded as they headed into the kitchen. "Somehow, it never sounded appealing to me, so I stuck with peanut butter on my toast."

Jay put the pot of chili on the table and held out her chair for her. "Smart girl."

She grinned up at him, then served him a heaping plate of chili. He sat and waited for her to pick up her fork.

"Eat," she said. "There's plenty for seconds, so I'm not worried about you getting a head start."

He grabbed his fork, shoveled in some chili, and muttered something that sounded like "Booyah!"

"Is that good or bad?"

"Best chili I ever had. Could have used more spice, though," he said teasingly.

She waved at the salt, pepper, and cayenne waiting on the table. "Help yourself. I made it fairly mild because I didn't know what you liked."

"I'm joking."

"I'm not," she said, adding more pepper—black and red—to her chili.

He slid his fork in for a taste of her chili and raised his eyebrows. "If we run out of wood, we can always use your chili to warm up the place."

"That's assuming there's any left."

For the next ten minutes there was no sound but the

rain and the occasional clink of flatware against heavy pottery plates. The thick slices of bread disappeared as fast as the chili in the big frying pan.

Sara stopped at two good helpings. Jay didn't stop until he saw the bottom of the chili pan.

"Should I warm up some more?" she asked, looking at his empty plate.

"No thanks. I'm saving room for pie. Inge makes the best . . ." His voice faded. *Damn those jackals to everlasting hell.* "She was a great baker. Ivar swore she could fatten up a fence post."

Sara put her hand over the fist that Jay had made and rubbed gently. Slowly his fingers uncurled and wrapped around hers.

"More coffee with your pie?" she asked quietly, but her eyes said she wished she could hug him and make it all go away.

He squeezed her hand. "That would be good, thanks."

Reluctantly she let her fingers slide away and pushed back from the table. When she reached for the empty dinner dishes, he was already picking them up.

"I'll take care of the kitchen and stack the wood while you shower," he said as he walked to the sink. "There are three bedrooms upstairs. Take your pick. The middle one is right over the kitchen stove. It's the warmest."

Sara found a pie knife in the utensil drawer and eyed the golden brown peaks of meringue as if there was an award for most even slicing.

"Which bedroom is yours?" she asked.

"The first one on the left."

She nodded and sliced the pie neatly. The meringue was fluffy, the lemon filling bright with promise, and the crust beautifully flaky beneath the knife.

"I don't know about a fence post," she said, "but I sure would get fat if this kind of dessert was part of my life."

"A few pounds wouldn't hurt you."

"Says the man who doesn't have an ounce of fat on him."

She hesitated, then gave in to temptation and ran her finger along the knife, picking up every sticky crumb. She licked her finger, closed her eyes, and made a sound of sensual appreciation.

"You make that sound again and I'm going to lick a lot more than your finger," he said.

Her eyes flew open. Jay was watching her lips and her tongue as she sucked her finger clean. She was tempted to do it all over again and see what happened. Then she caught a whiff of herself—onion and trail dust and wood smoke with an astringent note of pine cleaner—and decided that she needed a shower.

A cold one.

He saw her temptation, then her decision not to tease and test him. He told himself that it was better this way.

He didn't believe it.

To keep from grabbing her, he took two small plates from the cupboard and set them near the pie.

Automatically she started to serve the dessert, then remembered how many return trips her licked finger had made to the pie knife. She headed for the sink.

"You don't have to wash it on my account," he said.

She glanced sideways and saw the devilish light in his eyes. Pleased that she had done something to lift his mood, she ducked her head and smiled.

"My mother would faint," Sara said.

"She's not here."

"Behave."

"I am behaving. Like a man."

"One of us has to be sensible," she said.

"Why?"

"I don't have any condoms."

He smiled slowly. "I do."

Heat twisted through her. *This man is pure trouble. And God knows I've come to enjoy his particular kind of trouble.*

Barton has already trashed my professional repu-tation when it comes to having sex with a client. If I have to wear the name, why not enjoy the game? Life is short.

We just never know how short.

She served Jay a piece of pie with the freshly washed utensil.

"I'd rather have it tasting of you," he said.

"If you don't eat it, I will."

"Can I watch?"

Shaking her head, laughing softly, Sara served her own piece of pie while Jay topped off their coffee mugs. At the first bite of pie, she made a low sound of pleasure.

"Orgasmic," she said without thinking.

He gave her a heavy-lidded look.

"Well, it is," she said. She lifted her mug. "To Inge, who made the best pie I've ever tasted."

He hesitated, then clicked his mug against hers. "To Inge. God keep her and Ivar."

Chapter 15

Sara lay in the bedroom that was positioned over the kitchen. Despite the long, demanding day she was wide awake. It wasn't the coffee. She usually fell asleep with a half-full mug by her bed. In the morning, she would sip at cold coffee while she brewed fresh. Piper had scolded her endlessly until her partner finally gave up on converting Sara to the joys of green tea.

A branch knocked against the window.

Instantly she sat up, stifling a scream, her heart beating triple time.

Not the coffee.

Fear.

Every time she closed her eyes, mixed-up pieces of the day flashed behind her eyelids—Skunk alerting, the ragged blue tarp that couldn't hide the flow of blood, the stalking cougar falling limp, the smell of death so thick she could taste it, Jay's muscles flexing and sliding as he took out his anger chopping wood, the seething rustle of grass stirred by a predator.

Blood and death.

Don't be such a baby, she told herself. Again. *Go to sleep. Tomorrow is going to be a whole new experience in coping.*

She forced herself to lie down. Relaxation was impossible. Within seconds she was turning one way and another, trying to get comfortable, to not think.

I'm fine when I have something to do. Maybe I should just give up on sleep and work on Custer's papers.

Rain from the wind-swept clouds rattled distractingly, with no rhythm to soothe. A gust of wind scraped a branch against glass. It sounded like a muffled groan. She shot upright before she could stop herself.

To hell with it.

Throwing aside the covers, Sara put her feet on the floor. The surprisingly warm floor.

Jay was right. Sleeping above the stove is sweet.

If you happen to feel like sleeping.

She didn't.

Trying to move quietly so as not to disturb him, she covered her T-shirt and panties with her flannel shirt, which smelled of sunshine and rain and the time before she knew, really *knew*, how brutally life could be snuffed out.

Her bedroom door opened without a creak. Barefoot, she tiptoed down the hall toward the stairs. She was halfway past Jay's door when it opened. Light poured into the hallway.

"Can't sleep?" he asked, his voice husky.

"Don't start on my coffee habit."

He looked slowly from her flannel shirt to her bare thighs. "Coffee?" he asked absently. "Damn, woman, you make a flannel shirt look like Spanish lace."

She glanced down at her shirt. It looked like flannel to her.

"Sorry," she said. "I didn't mean to wake you up. I was just going to do . . . something. Lying awake is making me edgy."

"Me, too."

A branch slapped against the roof.

She flinched.

"Come here, sweetheart," he said, pulling her into a gentle hug. "It's been a hell of a day."

With a deep, breaking breath, Sara gave in to the embrace, wrapping herself in Jay's warmth and at the same time returning it.

"You're hotter than the stove," she said, brushing her cheek lightly against the neat mat of hair that covered the upper slopes of his bare chest. "Tickle more, too."

His muscles moved beneath her cheek in silent laughter. "Rub harder," he said. "Doesn't tickle that way."

"I'm not complaining." She breathed deeply and relaxed against him. "You smell of smoke."

He eased his fingers into the silky dark mass of her hair. "I must not have showered well enough."

Her soft laugh stirred the hair on his chest. "You showered just fine. You can't feed the stove without picking up the scent of fire and wood. I like it."

"Beats gun oil."

He felt her stiffen and silently cursed his unguarded tongue. With strong fingers he rubbed her scalp and the tension along her spine. Slowly her body loosened again.

"You must have washed your hair," he murmured. "It smells of lavender."

"And smoke from drying it near the stove."

"You have a thing for smoke."

"On you, yes. On me, not so much."

They held each other as the silence settled around them like another kind of embrace. Finally she rubbed her cheek against him slowly, breathing deeply of him before she loosened her arms.

"You must be cold," she said. She certainly was wherever she wasn't touching him.

His fingers—warm—tilted her chin up so that she met his eyes in the intimate twilight of the hallway. "You aren't used to the kind of day you had."

"And you are?"

"Not really. It just doesn't surprise me anymore. Come on, let's go to bed. And that's all it will be. Just let me hold you until your adrenaline fades and you fall asleep. Do you trust me that much?"

"You, yes. Myself, no."

He cocked his head slightly, looking at her.

"Oh, I won't jump you," she said wryly, "but curling up with you sounds way too good. I've wanted to get close to you for months. That's why I came to Wyoming instead of going back to San Francisco. I wanted to see if the rest of you matched your voice." Her sigh ruffled the springy male hair that tickled her lips so sweetly. "It did. Yowza, did it ever. And I'm babbling. Shut me up, Jay."

Slowly he bent and fitted his mouth to hers, giving her every chance to change her mind. She opened for him without hesitation, sharing the sweet heat inside her lips, touching the tip of her tongue to his, tasting him as he tasted her. Parts of her she hadn't even known were tight began to relax. Her body softened against his until they were so close that even breath couldn't get between them. They held each other, rocking slowly, letting the ugliness of murder slide away until there was only a man and a woman savoring the complex heat of life.

The kiss changed as gently as it had begun. Delicate tasting became a deeper seeking, a sensual duel with no losers. His arms hardened, pulling her closer and then closer still, until neither could breathe without the other. He ate at her mouth, wanting more. Her nails sank into his muscular shoulders as she tried to pull herself up his body, wanting to crawl under his skin. Needing to.

He lifted her until she was draped along his body, letting her know how much he shared her clawing need. When she felt the hard length of him, she made a sound of approval and . . . fleeting hesitation.

"Everything seems to come pretty big in Wyoming," she said, her voice low and shaky. "Are you licensed for that firearm, soldier?"

His laugh was also a groan. "Oh yeah. Are you?"

"I'm having a few doubts," she said half teasing, half not.

"We'll fit," he said, biting at her lips. "It's killing me to think about how hot it will be."

She let out a broken breath that was almost a laugh. "As long as you don't expect fireworks, we're good."

Slowly he eased her down his body until her feet touched the floor again.

"Define fireworks," he said against her lips.

"I'm, well, average. You aren't. I mean, I like sex as well as the next woman, but it's not a world shaker for—"

Her words were cut off by his tongue stroking deep and his hands rubbing down her back to her waist. His touch slipped under her panties until he could fill his hands with her sweet ass, fingertips sinking deep, opening her until she made a startled sound and shuddered at the lightning stroke of pleasure. The hot rush of her response spread between them.

"Average, huh?" He laughed. "Sweetheart, I can't wait to have an average night with you."

Without warning he shifted his grip, sliding one hand around to her front until he could sink a long finger into her.

"Wet," he said roughly. "Soft. So . . . damned . . . *hot.*"

He twisted his finger, rubbing against her deep inside. She gasped again and tightened around the sweet intrusion. The silky pulses of her pleasure made both of them groan.

"I want you to milk my cock like that when you come," he said hoarsely. "It won't happen the first time because you don't know how good it's going to be and I've been too long without anything except my hand for company. But it will happen, Sara. I promise you."

His hand moved again and suddenly there were two fingers pressing into her. They felt shockingly good, twisting and probing, scissoring until she shuddered and the air between them filled with the heady musk of her passion. Her body bowed into an arc of need, driving him even deeper into her body.

A groan ripped between his clenched teeth. "I could take you right here, right now, and you'd scream with pleasure. God knows I'd want to. In fact, I'd do anything to give you the release you're shaking for. But I don't trust myself not to part those plump, silky lips and push home while you're coming."

"Do it," she gasped.

"No condom."

She bit his shoulder in frustration.

"Christ, we're going to burn down the night," he said roughly.

With swift movements he shifted her until he could carry her against his chest. She inhaled sharply, unused to being carted around like a child. Before she could adjust, she was lying on her back in his bed, staring up at him with astonished eyes.

"Too fast?" he asked.

"No one has lifted me since . . . forever."

"I'll have to make you part of my regular workout." He smiled rather fiercely. "It sure would be more fun than the usual routine."

She watched him as he opened the drawer in the bedside table, removed some condoms, and threw them on top of the wooden surface. She reached for one of them, only to have him take her hand and kiss it hard enough that she felt teeth.

"Not yet," he said, looking into her beautiful dark eyes. "There's this little thing known as foreplay. I want to undress you, stroke you, feel your nipples rise against my tongue."

She felt her nipples draw up in an aching hunger that startled her.

"And I'd like to explore every inch of your body with my hands and teeth and tongue," she whispered, surprised at her hunger to taste him. "That's new for me."

A shudder ripped through him, hardening him even more. When he reached out to unbutton her flannel shirt, his fingers had a fine tremor. The fact that she was openly admiring his body—including the hard flesh that had shoved eagerly through the slit in his briefs—didn't help. And then her finger was touching his tip, lingering over the warm drops that had seeped out of his control. Curious, she licked her fingertip.

"You're not the only one this is new for," he said through his teeth. "I'm about to go off like a teenager."

Her smile was as old as Eve. "Then I won't tell you how much I like your taste."

"And you called yourself average. Sweet Jesus." He locked his teeth and fought for the control he had always taken for granted. "I've been waiting all my life for an *average* woman like you." He took a deep breath and counted to ten. Slowly. "Do you like sewing on buttons?"

She blinked. "Not particularly."

"Then you better finish opening your shirt. I'm about a breath away from tearing off everything you're wearing. With my teeth."

She looked at the burn of need riding his cheekbones and the stark lines of hard-won control on his face. Reluctantly she slid her hands away from his body and unfastened her shirt.

"All the way off," he said. "T-shirt, too."

Not giving herself time to feel shy, she reached back behind her neck, grabbed a handful of flannel and T-shirt, and pulled them off over her head in a single motion.

"Bossy, aren't—" Her voice broke off at the naked appreciation in his eyes.

"Perfect," he said, his voice husky.

"Hardly," she said.

"For me, you're perfect."

He lowered himself to the bed and took one dusky nipple into his mouth. After a few seconds, she forgot all about her imperfect body and began twisting slowly against the mouth that was turning her inside out. Other men had dutifully massaged her on the way to sex, their speed making clear that what they really wanted was between her legs. And theirs.

Jay wasn't dutiful. He quickly found what made her moan and writhe in wordless pleas for more. Then he settled in and drove her so wild she didn't even feel her panties being pulled down her restless legs. His hungry fingers parted her, twisting as she did, driving her higher and higher, and he savored her unknowing whimpers of pleasure. His thumb probed her slick folds, seeking the proud bud he had called up from her softness. First gentle, then demanding, he circled her flesh, pleasing, teasing, and above all avoiding the pressure that she demanded with each broken breath.

"Tease," she panted.

"Yes," he hissed between gritted teeth. "Something about you brings out the devil in me."

"Is that what you call it?" Her hand curled around his erection and squeezed.

"Ah, God," he said. Sweat broke out on him from forehead to heels. "Mercy, sweetheart."

"Why?"

"Condom," he said on a broken breath. He hugged her close with his free arm and rolled her across his body, massaging her butt cheek as he did. "On the table. My hands are busy."

Then so was his mouth.

She barely registered the words. The combined onslaught of his mouth and hands and the twisting flex of his body overwhelmed her. Between one second and the next, a savage ecstasy shook her. Despite her continued tremors of pleasure, she managed to snag a foil packet and blindly press it into one of Jay's hands.

In record time, he put on the condom. He rolled her over onto her back, lifted her knees over his arms, and sank into her pulsing core. He clenched his body and fought against his own release, wanting more, much more, than a few strokes on his way to orgasm.

But that was what he got before his body put paid to any idea of waiting. He had already waited a lifetime for a partner like Sara. He measured himself within her once, twice, three times and then ecstasy drew his body so tight he trembled. With a shout that was her name, he spent himself deep inside her.

When he could move again, he forced himself to separate from her. The hallway to the bathroom felt cold after her heat. He got rid of the condom quickly and went back to the room, not knowing whether to laugh or swear at the way she had described herself.

"Average," he said as he walked back in from the bathroom.

She opened her eyes for a second, then closed them and sank back into a boneless kind of languor. "I wasn't talking about you," she mumbled. "Hell, someone should bronze your dick and—" Her eyes flew open and she slapped a hand over her mouth.

He laughed a low, satisfied male kind of laugh. "Bronze, huh? Bet that would tickle something fierce."

She groaned. "I'd blush if I had the energy."

"Save your strength," he advised.

"For what?"

"Next time is your turn."

Her eyes opened. "I had my turn. Oh yeah, I had a really good turn."

"Who said you only get one?"

When dawn stroked gentle fingertips over Jay, he was lying on his stomach, his head turned toward the center of the bed.

No, not dawn. Sara.

He opened his eyes as he arched against the fingers sliding slowly down his spine, probing sensuously, caressing each vertebra.

"All there?" he asked, his voice husky with sleep and desire.

"Twenty-two . . . twenty-three . . . twenty-four," she murmured. "So far so good. The last nine are harder to count, even with the curtains open and the sun pouring in. Those are fused in two sections—your vertebrae, not the curtains. Five in the lower back"—her fingers probed less gently—"and four in the coccyx, also called the tailbone. Sometimes a light touch is better for counting there."

His body tensed as her fingertips slid to the crease in his buttocks and kept going.

"All thirty-three present and accounted for," she said. "Plus two, oh yeah, two really fine testicles, also called balls." Her hand massaged slowly as she admired the way his body tightened into clearly defined muscles. "And last but *really* not least"—her hand slid under his body—"we have one penis, which we've already established is truly a bronze-worthy work of art."

"I don't want to know how many ribs I have," he warned her, flexing and releasing his buttocks to rub against her fingers.

"Ticklish?"

"Are you?"

"Right. No ribs."

He rolled to his side, making it easier for her to stroke him—and for him to pet and tease her breasts.

"I could get used to waking up with you in the morning," he said, admiring the peak he drew from her breast.

"Same goes. I'm going to enjoy you to the max before I go back home."

His fingers paused, then resumed shaping her. "When do you have to go back?"

"I've been thinking about that since I woke up," she admitted.

"And?" He rolled her nipple.

Her breath caught. "I think the Custers will show best in Jackson. There's plenty of high-end traffic there, the kind that will be attracted to the paintings and can afford to buy. Of course, we won't be selling. We'll just be pumping up buzz before a future auction date. There was a space for rent across from the antler park that—"

"Antler park?"

"The place downtown that has antler arches leading to grass."

He smiled. "Antler park. I like it. There was an empty storefront?"

"Yes. If you rent it for, say, six months, I could set up a display space for the best of the Custers. I know it's hard to rent prime retail space for only six months, but some kind of deal could be worked out."

"No problem. If we're thinking of the same space," he said as his fingers probed between her legs, "Vermilion Properties owns the building. It used to be a modern art gallery."

"Handy," she said breathlessly.

"Very." His fingers slid into her. "God, I love the feel of you."

"We're supposed to be talking business."

"Multitask." He lifted her leg and rested it on his hip, opening her for his pleasure. And hers. "So assume that the space is rented. What then?"

"I know two of the best cleaners and"—she shuddered gently—"restorers west of the Mississippi. They—" Her voice broke. "I can't think when you do that."

"This?"

Fingers sleek with her passion plucked at her clitoris.

"Yes."

The liquid heat of her response licked over his hand.

"Just wanted to be sure." He moved his fingers up a bit to her dark, curly hair and began tugging gently. "Clean, restore, and I assume frame?"

She wanted to smack him. The devilish light in his eyes told her that he knew exactly how she felt. Deliberately she began tracing the thick vein on his penis with her fingernails.

"Yes, frame," she said. "It's very important to present the paintings in a way that states they are"—she squeezed gently—"museum quality."

His hand moved just enough to press his middle finger deep inside her. "Museum quality, definitely. How long will that take?"

She watched her fingers teasing the broad head of his erection. "As long as necessary." Her hand shifted until she could cup the warm weight of his balls. "Quality can't be rushed."

The gentle squeezing of her hand made his whole body flex.

"What next?" he asked hoarsely.

"Depends on how the movie does." Her hand moved upward, fingers wrapping eagerly around him. "By the time the Custers are buffed and polished, the movie should be generating a lot of buzz."

Jay closed his eyes, savoring the feminine touch that was making his body hum. "Buzz is good," he managed. "Really, really good."

Her thumb pressed against his tip and swirled, spreading moisture. "By then I'll have photos for a catalog and/or a book. Both would be better."

"Good idea," he said, sliding his wet fingers up and around her hard, eager bud. "Both at the same time."

"I can do a lot of the work from here," she said, bending down to sample with her tongue what her fingers had been caressing. "The atmosphere is"—she licked her lips—"awesome. So I'll shuttle back and forth."

He reached for a condom. "Back and forth is good. I can do that."

She took the condom and slid it on him with tormenting care. "You sure?"

"Oh yeah."

He fitted himself to her and pressed in slowly, deeply. He retreated the same way. And returned. Retreated.

"Incredible," she said, her breath breaking.

"Of course, there is more than one way to fly." He rolled onto his back, taking her with him.

She settled onto him, taking him so deep, so good. "Fly, ride. Either works."

"Then ride me," he said, plucking at her nipples. "Ride me hard."

She clenched around him and rose up, then slid down until she could go no farther. She swiveled her hips, seeking the perfect position, clenched, rose, fell, swiveled . . .

And then she rode him to the wild and sweet oblivion both of them wanted.

Chapter 16

The sound of distant helicopter rotors jerked Jay out of his sensual relaxation. He bolted out of bed.

"What's wrong?" Sara asked, half asleep.

"Incoming chopper."

Not bothering with underwear, he jerked his jeans on. Automatically he clipped the Glock into the belt harness at the small of his back. Boots came next, then he yanked on a dark T-shirt from a dresser drawer.

"What about the cows?" she asked, frantically untangling the T-shirt and flannel shirt she had thrown aside last night.

"I'll send Lightfoot to help Skunk. The dogs will crowd the cattle into a corner of the pasture away from the helo. It's not the first time the cows have seen a metal bird. The dogs know what to do."

Jay was out the door before Sara even had her T-shirt on.

"Where are you going?" she called out.

"To get the rifle. If it's some sightseeing yahoos, I'll give them something to talk about back home."

"What if . . . ?" Her voice died.

The thought of the murderers returning was terrifying.

His words came clearly from down the hallway. "I should be so lucky as to see those assholes over my rifle barrel."

The sound of the rotors came closer.

"Lucky," she said to herself. "Oh my God."

She was buttoning her flannel shirt when she heard Jay's piercing whistle giving the dogs new orders. By the time she raced to her room and found her jeans, the sound of the helicopter was shaking the cabin. She yanked on socks, laced her feet into her hiking boots, and ran downstairs.

Jay was in the mudroom, stuffing cartridge boxes from the saddlebags into his jacket pockets.

"What do you want me to do?" Sara asked.

"Make coffee."

"Excuse me?" From the grim expression on his face, she had expected to be told many things, none of them having to do with coffee.

"Coffee."

"Coffee," she said. "Right."

Automatically she adjusted the damper on the stove, raked the coals together, added kindling, and waited until it caught before she added larger wood.

The increasing racket from the helicopter made her want to scream.

Instead, she put water on to boil and set up the coffeepot.

"Stay inside until I say otherwise," Jay ordered.

And it was an order. No mistaking it for a polite request. The other Jay had taken over.

He was out the mudroom door and under cover before she could answer.

Outside it was fresh, crisp, beautiful but for the ominous sound of the helicopter that was circling Fish Camp. Jay waited back in the trees, concealing his presence while giving him a view of the possible landing areas for the helo. For now the helicopter was out of sight, finishing the last of its circle behind the trees.

A white Bell 429 came into view. JACKSON COUNTY was printed in bold black letters on the fuselage. The helo dropped down slowly, like a child getting in a pool for the first time. Dirt and pine needles flew up from behind the barn, more than a hundred yards from the pasture.

Jay relaxed a bit. He doubted the murderers would be considerate of any livestock. But he pulled binoculars from beneath his jacket and focused in on the aircraft just in case. The first person he recognized was Sheriff Cooke.

The second was Barton Vermilion.

Damn. My temper's already yanking at the leash, Jay thought. *I don't want to take it out on Barton just because he came at the wrong time.*

Jay had savored being alone with Sara. He knew it had to end sometime, but now was much too soon.

Cursing silently, he went to the mudroom door and called to her. "It's Sheriff Cooke. Come out if you want."

"I want," she said clearly.

Moments later she emerged, buttoning her jacket against the brisk morning.

He pulled her into his arms and kissed her hard. "I had other plans for the rest of the day," he said after he lifted his head.

"So did I." She nipped his jaw. "Mighty tasty sandpaper you're wearing."

Rubbing his lower face, he said, "Your fault. There I was, all innocent and sleeping—"

"Naked," she cut in.

"And the next thing I know you're having your wicked way with me."

Her smile widened, then slipped. "I don't want it to end this soon."

"Same here. But it has and the sooner we get through this, the sooner we can do other things." He gave her an intense, blue-eyed stare. "I have a list."

"Mmmm, so do I."

"Can't wait to compare."

Together, they walked toward the helicopter whose rotors were slowing to a lazy spin, *whap whap whap.* They stopped close enough to feel the rotor wash, but far enough away to avoid the worst of the debris kicked up by the landing.

Sheriff Cooke stepped off first, belly still plain beneath his open jacket. A deputy got out just behind him and so did someone else wearing crisp new blue jeans and a cream-colored jacket. His hair blazed like ruby sparks in the light.

"Barton," she said.

Jay didn't answer. He simply moved forward, taking her with him.

"Sheriff, Barton," Jay said, like it was the most natural thing in the world for all of them to be here at once.

Barton nodded, hands in pockets.

"Morning, Jay. How are you doing?" Cooke asked as he shook Jay's hand. "Losing people you've known all your life is hard. Murder makes it harder."

"I've seen worse," Jay said. "Sara has been a trooper."

Cooke nodded to her. "Good for you. The last thing anyone needs is a civilian puking all over the crime scene."

As he spoke, he motioned to the other men on board to climb out of the helicopter. The first two men were the newest of Vermilion Ranch's cowhands. The third was a crime scene tech.

Willets nodded at Jay as he disembarked. "Hey, boss. Rube and me got this," he said, pointing at the cows. "You worry about the rest."

"Glad to see you two on your feet again," Jay said. "We call it initiation by Penny. We warn everybody and they get sick just the same."

Willets gave a shamefaced smile.

So did Rube. "I thought my uncle had the best still going in the west. Shit, was I ever wrong."

"If you see more than thirty-five head of cattle," Jay said drily, "climb back in the helo and go."

"Seeing just fine," Willets said.

"Me, too," Rube said.

"Good. Whoever rides Jezebel, watch her at any stream crossings. Whoever rides Amble will have to stay alert, period." He turned to Barton as the cowhands headed toward the herd. "You need something?"

"I have a right to be here," Barton said.

"No question. But do you need something?"

Barton ducked his head. "I just . . . just wanted to pay my respects."

Jay put his hand on his half-brother's shoulder and squeezed gently. "Their bodies are in the old storage room off the boathouse, beneath a blue tarp."

"I'd appreciate it if you wait until we're finished," the sheriff said to Barton. "Davis won't be too long."

The crime tech nodded and chewed his gum.

The sheriff looked back at Jay. "I'd appreciate it if you came with us, too. You can fill me in on what you saw before the rains began."

Jay nodded. "Have to say, I wasn't expecting the helo, what with the rain ruining tracking and all."

"Barton insisted. And paid," Cooke added. "Another deputy will pick up the bodies in a truck and take them to the morgue." He looked at his watch. "In about two hours, give or take. Depends on how muddy the back road is. Davis will ride back down with the deputy if he isn't finished before we are."

"That was about how I expected the timing to work out, minus the helo," Jay said.

Sara looked at her boots to hide her smile. Like her, he was still chapped that their time together had been cut short.

Cooke glanced at Barton. "Well, since there were no lives at stake, the county wouldn't foot the bill, but your brother, bless him, said that Vermilion Ranch would pay for a tank and the pilot."

Jay's eyebrows went up. When the sheriff blessed someone, it wasn't a compliment. Barton must have been wearing on the sheriff's nerves.

"This is my land as much as it's yours," Barton said, his voice carrying. "Hell, part of Fish Camp is in my quarter of the ranch."

Jay pointed to the bird, rotors stilled now. "Our land," he agreed. "But the helicopter is a needless expense. It's not like there is a hot trail to follow."

"I didn't know that, did I? Nobody bothers to keep me informed. Like I'm invisible or something."

Sara was standing close enough to Jay to feel him tense. The last thing he needed right now was a useless family wrangle. But whatever she said would only make the situation worse, so she kept her mouth shut.

It was hard.

Why are so many small men defensive? Straight, gay, or undecided, it never fails. If they didn't try so hard, people wouldn't care either way about height or lack of it.

Be fair, she told herself. *No matter how tall Barton might have been, Jay is a very hard act to follow.*

Especially in bed.

She bit her lip and hoped nobody had read her mind or seen the small smile that kept slipping away from her control. A day at the spa had never left her feeling so buffed, polished, and just plain good.

Jay turned to the short, fresh-faced deputy with the tackle box full of crime scene gear. "Evidence trail is going to be cold. Had to cover and secure the scene from bears and check inventory."

The deputy shrugged and nodded. He chewed some strong, mint-scented gum. "From the report, cause of death isn't much of a mystery."

"Cause, maybe. The rest of it is wide open."

Davis nodded and popped his gum.

"So look, Jay," Barton said.

Sara wondered how anyone could take the man seriously in his new jeans and spotless cream sport coat and silk T-shirt. In San Francisco he wouldn't have drawn a second look. But this was a long way from the city by the sea.

"I'm just trying to take care of things," Barton said.

"Next time, talk to me," Jay said neutrally. "We'll save a lot of money that way."

"Money isn't my problem. I needed to know what was going on."

"You could have used the radio. Money makes or breaks a business. And that's what Vermilion Ranch is, a business."

"One quarter *my* business," Barton shot back.

"No question. Glad to see you're taking an interest in it."

Barton looked away. "I had to do something. Inge, Ivar, Fish Camp . . . no matter what came later, I have good memories."

Jay gave him a one-armed hug. "It's hard when life changes so fast. I'm glad you're here. Better that we get this thing done quickly."

"I remember this place, you know? Some good summers up here, and to suddenly find that they're both murdered . . ." Tears hung on his eyelids. "Who would do this kind of thing to them?"

"I'll find out," Jay promised.

Barton looked startled.

Cooke looked at Jay sharply but didn't say a word. The sheriff knew the reality: the Fish Camp murders already had cold case written all over them. If similar murders occurred, then money would be available for anything and everything up to a task force. If not . . . not.

But Jay Vermilion wouldn't stop until he had answers. They wouldn't bring back the dead, but they would comfort the living.

The sheriff looked at the helicopter pilot. "You want to wait here or in the house?"

"Here's good," she said, removing her helmet and revealing a luxurious fall of sun-streaked light brown hair. "I have coffee and a book."

Jay said quietly to Sara, "Do you want to come with us?"

"Four adults and two bodies is too much for that space. I'll be looking at the files."

"What files?" Barton asked.

"I found some cartons of old ranch files dating to my mother's time," Jay said before Sara could speak. "I'm having Sara look them over and give her opinion of whether there's enough for a family history."

You are? she thought.

But she didn't show her surprise, simply nodded and tried not to eat Jay up with her eyes.

"Back before Liza?" Barton demanded.

"Yes."

"Whatever." He turned to the sheriff. "Let's do this."

Sheriff Cooke gave Jay a sidelong glance, but said only, "Davis, you have everything you need?"

"Yes sir."

Cooke began talking to Jay as they started walking together toward the lake. "You say that the two of you were on the trail when the murders took place?"

"Unless Davis tells me different, that's what I believe."

As soon as the three men were out of hearing, Barton stepped toward Sara. "If you think you're going to milk ranch funds for some phony family history, think again. I won't allow—"

"Three quarters beats one quarter every single time." Her voice was cool.

"Listen, you—"

"I don't like you," Sara cut in. "You don't like me. Live with it."

She turned and headed back to the house.

"Bitch," he said.

"You better believe it."

Barton's face flushed red as he stared at her back and the walk that proclaimed her to be a female. Then he hurried after the other men.

". . . ate lunch on the trail, and we got here well after midday," Jay was saying when Barton caught up.

"You should wear a watch," the sheriff grumbled.

"When I got out of the military, the first thing I did was lose my watch."

"Lucky son of a bitch. So after you took care of the livestock, what did you do?"

"It took some time to get to the boathouse outbuilding," Jay said. "I had to clear the other buildings first."

"Something tip you off that there was a problem?" Cooke asked.

"What do you mean, 'clear the buildings'?" Barton cut in.

"Check to make sure that everything was okay," Jay said.

"I know what it means," Barton said, "but why? Did you see something wrong?"

"Other than not being able the reach the Solvangs by radio, and not being greeted as we arrived, nothing much tipped me off."

"Oh," Barton said. "Yeah. I'm not used to this sort of shit."

"Who is?" said the sheriff. "Now butt out. I'm asking the questions here." He turned to Jay. "Did you find anything with the search?"

Jay stopped outside the door that was newer than anything else in the old storage building.

"Their cabin had dinner on the stove," he said, "but only partially cooked. It could have been yesterday's dinner, but it has been warm up here and their bodies showed no sign of bloating."

Barton grimaced. "Gross."

Cooke gave him an impatient look. "Murders aren't pretty. Stay outside. I don't want my men having to clean up after you."

"It's my building and I'll—"

"Before you spend a lot of time inside," Jay interrupted, gesturing to the storage toolshed, "I moved cardboard cartons from the little room off the man cave. Didn't know if the place would leak in a good storm, and the boxes had important family papers."

"Piss-poor way to store them," Cooke said.

"JD wasn't much on history. I am."

"History is a waste of time," Barton said under his breath.

Cooke either didn't hear or ignored the words. He tapped at the door frame with his boot and said to Jay, "I can't blame you for preserving history, but this is part of a crime scene. Don't take out anything else until Davis is done."

Jay nodded. "Give yourself a few deep breaths out here," he warned as he put on his gloves to open the padlock. "It's not as fresh in there."

For a moment he weighed the padlock hanging on the hasp. A shard of memory stabbed him. The padlock had been closed the first time he went into the old storage room, too.

"Check to see if one of the windows has been forced," he said, slipping the padlock free.

"Any special reason?" Cooke asked.

"I found this locked. They had to get in somehow."

"They?" Barton asked. "We're talking about two old people. Hell, a kid could have done it."

"Boot tracks in the blood," Jay said. "At least two different treads. Man sized."

He opened the door.

"Davis," Cooke said. "Give me a piece of your gum."

Barton pressed forward as Jay walked in and carefully removed the tarp. Three seconds later Barton bolted for the door, knocking aside Davis in a rush for fresh air.

"Told him to stay out," Cooke said. "He doesn't listen worth a damn, bless him. Make that two pieces of gum, Davis."

The deputy handed over another piece, stuffed a fresh one in his own mouth, and followed the sheriff inside.

Jay went out and stood by Barton, waiting until he finished booting whatever he had eaten that day. His crisp jeans and jacket were spattered now.

GQ *meets reality.*

"I'm—I didn't expect it to be so—" Barton's stomach did another round-trip.

"Don't worry. Everyone does it the first time or two. Natural as breathing."

"You—didn't."

"Here? No. First few times I saw my men blown up? You bet I puked. But puking didn't help anyone and it wore me out. I learned to swallow whatever came my way and keep it down."

After a few more heaves, Barton straightened and wiped his mouth with his hand. And he watched the open door where slashed bodies were spotlighted by flash after flash of the deputy's camera.

"What kind of animal does that?" Barton asked.

"The human kind."

"But—"

"Somebody once said that civilization comes from the barrel of a gun," Jay cut in. "Smart man. The Solvangs didn't get to their guns first."

The sheriff came out for a fresh-air break. "Times like this I wish I still smoked," he said, pulling his phone from a pocket. "You're right about civilization. No enforcement, no law. Damn shame, but people are what they are."

"You're saying there's a lot of crime out here?" Barton asked, his voice hoarse.

"Meth cookers, runners, sellers. Same for pot and unlicensed liquor. Cigarettes. Indian reservations are a revolving door for smugglers of anything the feds tax off reservation or outright forbid. Hell, we even have rustlers, just like the bad old days." Cooke shook his head. "We have our share of snakes here, same as the city, but usually the crime is centered around money, not murder for the sheer bloody hell of it. There was nothing in Fish Camp to attract this kind of butchery."

Jay felt the rage bottled up inside shoving at him like a geyser getting ready to blow.

It never gets easier. First impulse is to find who did it and do the same to them. An eye for an eye.

And then some.

He choked the feeling back and spoke evenly. "There are fifty-six paintings, Custer plus a handful of other painters mixed in."

Cooke's thumbs danced across his phone.

"Any stolen?" Barton asked. Clammy skin aside, he was back on his game, and that game was money.

"All the slots in the crates were full," Jay said. "It's possible the jackals took an entire crate, but I can't prove it either way. Inge was a strict housekeeper. There wasn't a convenient clean space in any dust to point to a missing crate."

"If you had to bet, where would you put your money?" Cooke asked.

"That no crate is missing. Those crates are at least five by six feet and eighteen inches wide, solid wood. It will take a truck to get them out of here. Or a helicopter." He shifted his shoulders, trying to loosen some tension. "I didn't see any sign of fresh tire tracks coming in on the road. Same for horses. There were some ATV tracks, but Inge and Ivar both used ATVs. If a helicopter landed, it would have been at Fish Camp itself. I didn't see any marks."

The sheriff didn't ask any more questions. If anybody would know what marks a helicopter left on the land, it would be Jay.

"Who else knew you were coming up?" Cooke asked, taking notes as he spoke.

"Henry. The ranch hands. Sara. The Solvangs. Plus anybody who called looking for me and was told where I'd gone. I wasn't exactly on a black ops mission."

"Any chance you were being tracked?"

"I got a sense of being watched by humans, but it was earlier in the day. Skunk alerted."

"Why didn't you go after them?" Barton asked. "You're supposed to be hell on wheels tracking and shooting."

"Probably," Cooke drawled, "Jay didn't want to leave Sara and some really pricey cattle to fend for themselves while he chased what was ninety-nine percent sure to be harmless hikers." He turned back to Jay. "Anything else?"

"Later on, a cougar tracked us."

"How did you know it was a cat?" Barton asked. "Did you see it?"

"Once, when I shot it, just before it took a calf. Damn, I have to call it in to the rangers. The cougar was injured and half starved, but not part of any study that I could see. No tags, no collar."

"The rangers can wait," Cooke said drily. "Dead humans take priority here, no matter how much of a howl the animal rights folks put up. What about earlier? Was it the cat then, too?"

"No."

"How can you be sure?" Barton asked in disbelief.

"I've been hunted by men. It's different."

"*I've* been hunted by men," Barton said, "and I—"

"Dumb, hired muscle thumping on people who don't pay loans isn't the same as real hunting," Cooke said, never looking up from the notes he was taking on his phone.

Jay's eyebrows climbed. He hadn't heard about that incident in Barton's checkered past.

"That didn't happen here," Barton said. "It's none of your damn business."

"When Boston PD warns me that there might be some out-of-town talent headed my way, it's my business."

"I took care of it," Barton said.

"Bless you." Cooke glanced back over his shoulder to the open door. "What I'm seeing is a couple of men came across Fish Camp and thought they'd rob it. Then maybe Ivar jumped one of them. Things went to hell and two people ended up dead. You said the place looked like it had been searched?"

"Nothing thorough," Jay said. "Some drawers opened, cupboards, furniture pushed out of place, that sort of thing."

"Sounds like the kind of search frightened assholes might make before they run," Barton said.

"Lots of bad luck in this world to go around," Cooke said. "Looks like too much of it landed here."

Barton glanced at the open door. "Sure as hell did."

Cooke stuffed his phone back into his pocket and resettled his gun belt. "Okay, Jay, let's do some investigation. There's not much chance of finding something after the rain, but we have to try. Barton, stay here and wait for Davis while Jay and I go cut some sign."

"I can—" Barton began.

"How many deer, elk, cougar, and bear have you hunted?" Cooke asked.

"I eat game at high-end restaurants like a civilized man."

"Bless you," the sheriff said. "How many stray cows have you tracked? Search and rescue on hikers?"

Barton's face flushed.

"That's what I thought," Cooke said. "Stay here like I told you or I'll fine your civilized ass for interfering at a crime scene. Hear me?"

Barton kicked dirt, coming perilously close to the sheriff's boots. After a moment, the younger man deliberately lit a cigarette and walked stiff-legged toward the boathouse.

Cooke shook his head. "The best part of that boy ran down his mother's leg. Bless him."

Chapter 17

Sara was stirring hash at the stove and trying very hard not to think about what the gum-cracking crime scene tech might be doing. The sudden opening of the mudroom door made her jump. Three more cardboard cartons thumped onto the floor.

"Did you find anything?" she asked quickly.

Jay was too busy eating her up with his eyes to answer right away.

"If you count questions, we found a lot," Cooke said.

"Rain took out most of the trail," Jay said.

He removed his hat and whacked it across his thigh. Drops scattered. The trees were still wet from last night's rain.

Both men used the boot cleaner and shook out their jackets before entering the kitchen. The room was warm from the stove and fragrant with coffee and the pot of canned hash and freshly chopped onions bubbling on the stove.

"Smells like heaven," Cooke said.

"I didn't know when you had eaten," she said. "Not much here except canned stuff, but it will keep your stomach walls apart."

"Anything I don't cook is a good meal," the sheriff said. "Thank you. Mind if I pour some of that coffee?"

"I'll get it," Jay said. "Sit down, Sheriff. Your day started sooner than mine."

"Won't argue that." Cooke settled into one of the old wooden chairs, rubbed his face, and sighed.

Jay went to the stove where Sara was stirring some pepper into the hash. Her face was flushed with heat and something more, the same thing that had his heartbeat increasing just at the sight of her. He slid his arms around her from the back in a slow, gentle hug.

"You okay?" he asked softly.

She nodded.

The clean scent of lavender teased his nose. "You took another shower," he said, his voice too low to be overheard. "I must smell like a mountain goat."

She leaned back against him and murmured, "You smell good. Cold air, evergreens, and last night's rain."

"Sweet liar."

She laughed softly at his use of her phrase.

He brushed a kiss over her neck, felt her shiver of response, and knew he had to step away from her before he embarrassed both of them.

"You get the coffee," Sara said, her voice a bit husky. "I'll bring the mugs. Where's Barton?"

"With Davis," Jay said.

"Poor Davis," she said under her breath.

No sooner had she finished than a pounding came from the front door and Barton's voice called, "Let me in! It's cold out here."

"Come around to the mudroom," Jay called back as he lifted the heavy coffeepot.

"But—"

"Just do it," Jay said impatiently, "like everyone else."

"Bless him," the sheriff said. "He's trying. Very, very trying."

Sara covered the sound of her choked laughter by rattling the crockery mugs she was carrying. As she put one in front of the sheriff, he winked at her.

She winked back.

"I'll warm some plates," she said. "Then we can eat."

The mudroom door opened so hard it banged against the outside of the house before it bounced off and closed again. Like the self-absorbed child he was, Barton hurried toward the warmth of the kitchen.

"Boots," Jay said.

Barton looked up. "Huh?"

"Mud."

"Disgusting stuff. That's why I live in a city."

"Clean your boots," Jay said, pouring coffee.

"Hell, I always forget."

Barton scraped his boots before he rushed back toward the warm stove. "What's for lunch?"

"Corned beef hash," Sara said.

"I hate that shit."

"Warm up a can of chili," she suggested, turning to the cupboard for plates.

Cooke choked on a swallow of coffee.

Jay tried not to do the same. "Grab a mug from the cupboard. Coffee is hot."

"I don't drink brewed coffee," Barton said.

"At Fish Camp you do or you go without."

Barton got a cup, waited for Jay to fill it, took a sip, and grimaced. "Well, you sure aren't keeping her around for her talent in the kitchen."

Jay focused on his brother like a cougar sighting prey. "This hasn't been easy on anyone. Think about that before you run your mouth."

"Hey, I was just trying to lighten the atmosphere. Doesn't anyone around here have a sense of humor?"

"Say something funny and we'll see." Though not loud, Sara's voice was as clear as the mountain air. Cold, too.

The sheriff saluted her with his mug of coffee. "This is prime western coffee, ma'am. Just the thing for a working stiff like me."

"Thank you. The hash is ready when you are."

"That would be now," Cooke said. "Sit down. I can serve myself."

"Thanks, but it's no trouble." She smiled at him. "I haven't been doing anything more taxing than opening cans and making coffee."

Cooke smiled back, pure male appreciation in the curve of his lips.

"I went out to ask the pilot if she wanted to come in," Sara said, "but she was sleeping soundly."

"Reg had two emergency runs before she picked us up."

"Is she holding up all right?" Jay asked.

"As well as any girl—woman—who was dumped by her husband while she was overseas."

Barton pulled out a kitchen chair. "Maybe she should have stayed home."

Sara bit her lips and gave the hash a hard stir. The more she was around Barton, the more he grated. She grabbed the three warm plates and put one in front of everyone but Jay's brother.

"What about me?" he asked.

"You don't like hash."

She went back to the stove for the pot of hash. When she came back, her plate was in front of Barton. The condiments she had put neatly in the center of the table were scattered, along with the forks and napkins.

Jay pushed his plate into the empty spot in front of Sara's chair. It was an automatic gesture. After Barton could walk—and talk—Jay had spent too much of his time keeping his half brother from annoying JD.

As Jay started to stand, Sara's hand came down on his shoulder, holding him in place. "I don't mind getting another plate. Barton is doing the dishes."

"Like hell," Barton said.

Jay looked at his brother with hard blue eyes. "You'll do them, you'll do a good job, and you'll keep your mouth shut while you get it done."

Barton turned the color of a ripe tomato. Silently.

Jay flashed back to too many meals that had ended just like this, with Barton angry and everyone else impatient. Jay picked up his own coffee, swallowed, and said, "Thank you, Sara. That will get me through the rest of the day."

"You're welcome," she said. "Want more before I bring the hash?"

His stomach growled audibly.

She smiled. "Hash it is."

A few moments later, she put the pot of hash on the table and laid a big serving spoon beside it.

"Help yourself, Sheriff," she said. "Today it's boardinghouse rules. That means it's rude to ask anyone to pass something if you can reach it while still keeping one foot on the floor."

The sheriff dug in and passed the hash to Barton, who grimaced at the smell. But he served himself and passed the spoon to Jay, who filled Sara's plate before he served his own. She brought slices of bread and a quart of the home-canned peaches she had found in the pantry.

"Dessert or side dish, take your pick," she said, putting the sealed Mason jar and another spoon on the table.

Barton reached for the peaches. He gave the sealed top a twist. The only thing that moved was his hand on the lid. He made a few more passes and asked, "Where's the opener?"

"Sitting next to me," Sara said without looking up.

Jay took the jar, gave the lid ring a hard twist. Reluctantly the ring loosened and came free. He put his fingernail under the circular metal that remained behind, broke the suction, and set the two parts of the top aside.

Barton grabbed the jar and began forking succulent peach halves onto his plate. "Did you find anything out there?"

The sheriff looked at Jay, who shrugged and said, "Someone flew a helo to a landing zone in a small clearing just the other side of the ridge."

"The one toward town?" Barton asked around a chunk of peach.

Jay shook his head. "The other one. There's a landing mark and enough debris to tell me that the helo clipped a few branch tips on the way down. Real tight landing spot."

"But a great view of Fish Camp," Barton said. "You can damn near count blades of grass in the pasture."

"When were you up here?" Jay asked.

"I—" The second half of a peach slipped from Barton's fork and landed with a messy plop in the hash. He muttered something and speared it again. "I took a helicopter ride with one of the mining consortiums I told you about. Must have been late last summer."

The sheriff shoveled hash like a man used to being called away from meals.

"These skid tracks were a lot newer," Jay said. "Like yesterday. Faint signs of an ATV trail to Fish Camp. Or from it. Add in the two separate boot tracks, and it looks like someone landed a helo, off-loaded a two-man ATV, and butchered their way through Fish Camp."

Barton paused before forking in another peach half. "Graphic, bro. I just got some appetite back."

"Maybe an hour on the ground, max," the sheriff said, reaching for more hash. "No sign of torture or rape in the Solvang cabin."

"I'm eating," Barton said.

"Whatever they stole," Cooke continued, setting down his heaping plate, "if they stole anything, had to be small enough to take out on an ATV."

"ATVs make a racket," Sara said. "Wouldn't that have warned the Solvangs?"

"We get visitors up at Fish Camp after the melt," Jay said. "Not a lot of them, but enough. One of the problems of having an inholding on national forest land. Besides, the ATV could have been muffled or even electric. We had both in Afghanistan."

"Electric? Is that what hunters use?" Barton said.

"Hunters use a horse and their own two feet," Jay said.

"This wasn't a casual jaunt that ended badly, was it?" Sara asked.

Cooke breathed out a sigh that was also a curse. "It's coming down that way. Planned. And here I thought it was going to be simple. A messy kind of simple, but still simple."

"Wait, wait, wait," Barton said. "You're saying this was planned? Some kind of hit? Like in the movies?"

Sara wondered how he would look wearing hash along with his vomit. Her disgust must have shown on her face, because he stood and leaned over the table toward her.

"I used to live up here. I knew Inge and Ivar," he said in her face. "You're just a tourist."

Jay gave the top of Barton's head a shove, sending him back into his chair. "She saw a lot more of the mess than you did. Unless you want to go back and help move the bodies, zip it."

"But you're saying someone *planned* this." His voice broke. "Inge and . . . Damn it, that's crazy," he said, tears magnifying his eyes. "Why would anyone do that?"

"Because they could," Jay said evenly. "Now all that is left is to bury the dead and make sure the jackals don't run free to kill again."

"You still sure that you weren't followed?" Cooke asked. "This is looking less like a robbery and more like an ambush."

She looked at Jay with wide eyes that were too dark against her suddenly pale skin. Beneath the table he squeezed her thigh soothingly.

"I should have let you stay in town, away from all this," he said.

"How do you know I didn't bring it?" she asked.

"What do you mean?" Cooke asked.

"My room was robbed, remember?"

"And?" the sheriff pressed.

"Nothing. Just that." She took a deep breath. "I feel like some kind of Jonah, with trouble following me around."

"You could always go home," Barton said.

"I plan to, thanks."

"Barton," Jay began.

He held up his hands. "Just trying to help."

"Start on the dishes," Jay said. "That would help a lot."

"Whatever."

Barton sucked up another peach half before he took his plate to the sink.

"Just bag up anything that would attract a bear," Jay said to his brother. "We'll take it out with us. When the sheriff's done with Inge and Ivar's cabin, you can do the same there."

"Do I look like the garbageman?"

"Do I look like I care?"

A glance at Jay's expression shut Barton up.

Cooke saw Sara's pale face and sighed. It was always the innocents who were hurt, and sometimes it seemed like his job was to make sure they stayed alive to feel the pain.

"It could have been a setup to ambush you," the sheriff said again, watching Jay.

"If it was, they must have run out of patience."

"Did you take extra time on the trail?"

"Quite a bit," Jay admitted. "I was enjoying being on a horse on a beautiful spring day. I'd been cooped up way too long."

"Tired of paperwork?" Cooke asked sympathetically.

"All the way to my soul. Now that I'm not paying lawyers, I'm thinking of hiring an accountant."

How can they talk so casually? Sara asked herself. *If we had arrived hours earlier, we could have been murdered along with Ivar and Inge.*

"You make any enemies since you got back?" Cooke asked.

"Liza was mad enough after she lost in court," Jay began.

"Mother wouldn't—"

"Ease down. I know she's not a murderer. She reached for more lawyers, not a gun," Jay said. He turned to Cooke. "My enemies are all behind me and halfway around the world."

Sitting next to him, soaking in his strength, Sara wanted to believe him. She couldn't imagine being alive and knowing that there was some cold-blooded madman hiding out in the woods, waiting for a chance to murder her.

"What about the crazy mountain man?" she asked.

"Crazy doesn't mean killer," Cooke said. "The half-assed hermits out here run at the sight of people. How about your enemies? Did they follow you here?"

"I don't know of anyone in San Francisco who cares enough to cross the street to harass me, much less get on a plane."

"Figured, but I had to ask."

"Everybody finished eating?" Barton called from the sink.

A chorus of yeses went up from the table, with Sara in the lead.

Cooke looked at Jay. "Something eating at you besides lunch?" the sheriff asked.

"An idea just came to me. I don't like it, but I can't ignore it."

"I'm listening."

Jay hesitated and said, "In the last few months, I've had some personnel issues on the ranch. Henry said the two men were trouble after the first time I hauled them up short for drinking on the job. I kept them on anyway. They were good hands when they were sober, and one of them was supporting a kid. I fired them the second time I caught them drunk at work."

"According to JD, pity is a sucker's game," Barton said as he retrieved the empty pot of hash.

"He also said, 'Second chances often take first place.' JD had a hat full of sayings he'd pull out when he needed to."

The sheriff had his phone out again. "Names."

"Jimmy Duggan and Monty Valentine. They said they were Montanans, but hands like them drift a lot. They could have been from anywhere in the West that has cattle."

"What did they say when you fired them?" Cooke asked.

"A lot of trash. Then they went to town and started trouble at the Boot, ended up in jail."

"I remember that. Those boys had real foul mouths on them. We all hoped someone would bail them out."

"Not me," Jay said flatly.

"You think that's enough to make them want revenge?" Barton asked.

"Duggan and Valentine had a streak of mean between them. Good with livestock and hell on humans. If it hadn't been drinking, I probably would have had to fire them for fighting in the bunkhouse with the other hands."

"Where are these two now?" Cooke asked.

"Pretty sure they left Jackson," Jay said. "Maybe went to Cody. They didn't exactly leave a forwarding address for Christmas cards."

Sara listened and tried not to think they might be talking casually about murderers.

"I'll shake the record book and see what I can come up with," Cooke said.

"Do you have anyone who can check in Cody?" Jay asked.

Cooke nodded and made a note to himself. "What about your other cowhands?"

"They've been with us for years. No problems with them. Their wives and kids keep them too busy for that."

The sheriff grinned faintly. "I know how that works."

Jay looked out the window. The sun had passed its zenith. "When did you expect the deputy for the bodies?"

"An hour more, maybe two," Cooke said. "But even with Vermilion Ranch paying for the helicopter, I don't plan on wasting time here. I'll fly out soon."

"Do you have room for six cardboard cartons?" Jay asked.

"Should. That's a big machine."

"Are you flying out with him?" Jay asked Barton.

"So you and Sara can have some alone time? Chooka chooka," he said, with an accompanying hand gesture for the deaf.

Sara felt Jay go rigid.

Barton frowned at his brother's scowl. "What? You'd have to be blind not to see it, bro. And I'm happy for you. I mean, about time you got a little somethin'-somethin', right?"

"I know you mean well and you and I live in different worlds and all that happy horseshit," Jay said through his teeth. "But if you don't stop sharing your sophomoric insights, I'm going to take you to the woodshed in a way you won't forget. Got that, bro?"

"Yeah. Sure. Jesus, when did you get so touchy?"

Cooke shoved back his chair. "Show me where the cartons are."

"I'll help you load," Jay said. "Sara and I will fly out with you."

"Be a tight squeeze, with Barton and all," Cooke said doubtfully.

"He isn't coming," Jay said.

Barton jerked. "Hey, how will I get back?"

"Not my problem. Chooka chooka, bro."

Chapter 18

Henry stood with Jay and Sara, watching the helicopter lift off from the pasture that had recently held thirty-five cows and calves.

"We can go to the moon, but we can't make a quiet helicopter," Henry said, holding on to his hat while his salt-and-pepper hair flew up over his ears.

"We can make them pretty damn quiet," Jay said, remembering, "but it's expensive."

"Worth it," Henry muttered.

Sara sighed as the helicopter faded rapidly to a dot in the cloud-studded sky. "It was a beautiful ride. It reminded me of some of Custer's paintings. Did he go up in a helicopter or a small plane?"

"Probably," Jay said, picking up two of the cartons that had been dropped off with them. "Before mother got sick, JD loved to go up and look at the ranch. If he and Custer weren't fighting, likely they went together from time to time."

Sara whipped out her phone and started taking notes.

He looked at her intent face and her hair burning darkly beneath the sun. Smiling, he headed toward the truck Henry had driven to the pasture.

"What's all this?" the foreman asked, gesturing to the remaining boxes.

She started to tell him that they were Custer's papers, then remembered how Jay had answered when Barton had asked.

"Old ranch records, from his mother's time," Sara said, which was mostly true. "Jay mentioned something about doing a ranch history."

"Damn fool waste of time." The foreman picked up a box and headed for the truck.

She made a few more fast notes on her phone and reached for a box.

Jay was already there, scooping up the remaining boxes. She admired his easy strength and remembered some of the startling, sensual ways he used it.

After a glance to be sure no one else could hear, she said, "Henry asked what was in the boxes. I told him what you told Barton."

"Good."

"Why didn't you want him to know?"

"He's a gossip," Jay said softly. "We don't need to let the world know we found something that might be valuable and a lot smaller than the Custer paintings."

"Oh."

"I'll take one of those," Henry said a moment later. "Unless you're showing off for the pretty lady."

Jay handed one over.

During the short walk to the truck and even shorter ride home, the two men talked about ranch things—what had to be repaired first, which cows were too old to breed, and if the old bulls would be up to a few more breeding seasons. Sara did a fast review of the photos on her phone, mentally grouping the paintings under themes such as distance and space, sky and mountains. She was itching to get to her tablet and start listing paintings by date, title, subject, and her personal shorthand for okay, good, better, and best. Then she would—

"You want to work out here or in the house?"

Startled, she looked up into amused, navy-blue eyes. She glanced around. Henry was gone and Jay was leaning against the open door of the truck.

"Sorry," she said. "There's so much to do with the Custers, and the papers, and planning for a book and generating buzz and—"

He leaned in and took her mouth in a slow, devouring kiss. Reluctantly he lifted his head. "Save time for us, too."

She licked her lips. "Oh, yeah." Then, laughing, "When do we sleep?"

"When we can't stay awake any longer."

"That works."

"And don't answer a phone unless you know who is calling," he added.

"What?"

"Reporters. I can keep them off my land, but I can't do anything about phones. A double murder on Vermilion Ranch will have the newshounds slavering."

The reminder of sudden, bloody death made her flinch. "Right. No phones."

He put his hand on her cheek. "I'm sorry you had to be part of this."

"So am I. And we'll both live." She blew out a breath. "Work helps. So does making lo—sex."

"I've had sex," he said. "This was a lot better. Now come inside before I kiss you again and Henry decides to go all nanny on my ass."

She tried to visualize Henry as a nanny. She couldn't. "Where did you put the cartons?"

"In your bedroom."

"Good. I'll—"

"You want me to doctor that cow with the wire cuts?" Henry called from the back of the house.

"I'm on my way," Jay called.

"Nanny," she said. "Never would have guessed it. Did he fuss over JD like this?"

"Only toward the end. Despite my age and experience, Henry thinks of me as the kid who went to military school and didn't come back for too many years. It grates sometimes, but I owe Henry a lot. He kept the ranch afloat when JD was too sick to do it and I was overseas."

"Does that mean I sleep alone?"

"What do you think?"

"I think you're in for a lecture from Nanny Henry."

"As long as it doesn't include the words 'chooka chooka,' I'll take it with a straight face and memories of what it's like to lower you onto—"

The back door slammed again. The foreman was headed toward them.

"I'm out of here," she said. "Have fun with the cow."

She passed the foreman with a nod and headed upstairs to open the cartons. But first she downloaded the photos from the phone onto her tablet, along with the notes she had taken.

Then the savory smells of cooking registered on her senses. She shouldn't have been hungry, but suddenly she was. The cartons seemed less urgent than finding the source of the hungry-making scent. She followed it to the kitchen where a woman in jeans and a long-sleeved T-shirt was standing over the stove, adding ingredients to a huge, bubbling pot.

"Hi, I'm Sara. Will I be smacked with a wooden spoon if I steal a taste of whatever you're cooking?"

A rolling laugh came out of the woman's sturdy body. Smiling, she turned and pulled a tasting spoon from a nearby drawer. "I'm Elena. My daughter Ria is working upstairs."

"That's why my room looked so good," Sara said, accepting the spoon. She dipped it into the pot and blew across the savory contents. "I'll have to thank her."

"No need. It is what we do."

"A good job deserves thanks as well as money," Sara said and gingerly licked the spoon. "Oh, yum. Chili on really savory steroids. Beautiful, beautiful chili. I can't get a really good bowl of it in the city." She licked her lips and smiled at Elena. "When is dinner?"

"Lunch," Elena said, pointing toward the pot. "Dinner is Jay's favorite—prime rib roast, twice-baked potatoes, and fresh green beans. Since Inge, God keep her soul, always baked pie for Jay, dessert will be berry cobbler and ice cream."

"Comfort food of the first order. I really appreciate it. And in case you're wondering, I'm here to help

Jay handle Custer's paintings, for however long it takes."

"That's what I heard in town. Ah, that man Custer." Elena shook her head. "Always causing trouble when he wasn't painting."

"Do you remember Custer?"

"I was a girl, fourteen, and I made sure never to be alone in the same room with him after Virginia—Mrs. Vermilion—died. It was a relief when Custer left. He was always after Ms. Neumann, even though he knew she was engaged to JD."

"That was probably a lot of the attraction," Sara said drily. "From what I've learned, Custer was a court jester and world-class womanizer who resented the hand that fed him. And he never had a chance with Liza. That woman is all about money."

Elena gave her a sideways look. "You learn very quick."

"Where I come from, not learning fast meant getting stepped on twice by a dairy cow."

"Those cows," Elena said, making a face, "always waiting for a chance with that hard, smelly tail. I remember when I milked our cow as a girl."

"Nasty beasts. But the butter is almost worth it."

The mudroom door opened and then slammed on a gust of wind. Henry came into the kitchen a few moments afterward.

Sara was already on her way back upstairs. Unlike Jay, she didn't have years of fond memories to make nanny lectures go down more easily.

She opened the first carton she put her hands on and started pulling out papers. Surprisingly, some of what she had been thinking of as the Solvang cartons had papers mentioning Custer. She opened all six cartons and concentrated on the ones holding Custer's notes. Soon she was sorting papers on her freshly made bed. The stack that interested her most was the one containing Custer's thoughts about paintings he had done, wanted to do, and burned. His observations about the ranch went into another pile, his commentaries on people and politics made a third pile, and the rest went into a mound that she didn't know how to sort yet.

She scrounged in her big purse for paper clips and found enough to secure the most important piles.

The downstairs phone rang. And rang. And rang.

Either the ranch didn't have an answering system or someone had unplugged it. Knowing Jay, she would bet he had gagged the answering machine.

Wonder how he gets his calls.

Or if he cares.

"Probably he does what I do," she muttered, putting the papers back into a carton. "People who know me use my cell phone. The rest get frustrated."

As if summoned, her phone rang. Sara pulled it out of her pants pocket and started to answer it automatically. Then she saw that she didn't know the incoming number and let it go to voice mail. Very quickly she learned that someone in the sheriff's office was spreading around her cell number.

"This is Mr. Satler of the Jackson Gazette. *I would like to talk with you about the unfortunate death of—"*

She hit the delete button. Noting that the charge was low, she plugged the phone in before she opened another carton. This one held Custer's field studies. Though she longed to spread them out on her bed and see them in good light, she didn't. She folded the box top and put the carton aside. Once she got started on the paintings themselves, she wouldn't surface for weeks.

When will we get the rest of them from Fish Camp?

The thought of all those Custer paintings in such an insecure storage place haunted her.

They lasted there for decades. They'll hold until Jay and I pick them up tomorrow.

Jay's phone buzzed in his pocket. Cursing under his breath, he hauled it out and got ready to ignore one more message from the media. Then he saw the number and punched the answer button.

"What's up, Reg?"

"Barton says the ranch will pay me to pick him up. Since you're within reach, I thought I'd ask the man who signs the checks."

"My sweet, sainted brother can pay for any ride he can afford."

"That's what I thought."

"Thanks for checking. I owe you."

"No, you don't. This is my way of thanking your sweet, sainted brother for grabbing my thigh—way up—every time the chopper changed course or altitude."

"He groped you with the *sheriff* aboard?"

"Not quite groping, but enough that I'll enjoy leaving him stranded. Thanks, Jay. You're one of the good guys."

"Because I don't grope my pilot?"

"That, too. I've had three requests for a flyby of Fish Camp. I turned them down."

"Media?"

"Yes."

"Take them for a ride," Jay said. "Charge them double. Triple. Then go buy something you've wanted but couldn't afford."

"You sure?"

"Yeah. Someone's going to make a potful from the city boys and girls. Might as well be someone I like."

"Thanks, Jay. You really are one of the good ones."

"So are you."

He punched out and pocketed his phone. *I like hearing a smile in Reg's voice again. Her ex is a real dick. Thank God there weren't any kids to rip up.*

Jay went to his horse and swung up to the saddle, then wove through the scattered range cattle, looking for any that might need a round with his medical kit. He missed Amble's easy gait and on-your-toes personality, but the big, rawboned bay mare he was riding had good cow sense and an amiable nature. Very quickly the beef cattle in the area had been looked over and he was on his way back to the ranch.

And Sara.

Ease down, cowboy, he told himself. *You know there's nothing you can do to keep her here, any more than you could pray your mother better. Life is what it is and fair has nothing to do with it.*

As if to underline the point, his phone vibrated again.

"Judas Priest, you'd think aliens had landed here," he muttered, dragging out his phone.

It was Barton.

Sighing, Jay took the call. Before he could say a word, Barton was talking.

"The pilot said she was booked for the next three days."

"Hire someone else," Jay said. "There are a lot of helo operations between Jackson and Yellowstone."

"Do you know what a helicopter costs?" Barton asked in rising tones.

"To the penny. If you don't want to pay, catch a ride with the deputies."

"They laughed at my clothes."

"Lose the cream jacket and you'll do fine."

"But—"

Jay punched out.

Even as he told himself that he should be patient with his younger brother, part of Jay was just plain fed to the teeth with the spoiled child's demands. And yet, Jay's conscience still nagged.

It's not Barton's fault he's Liza's son.

So what's Liza's excuse? Was she born to lousy parents? And what's her parents' excuse? They were born to lousy parents? And so on and on all the way back to the Garden of Eden?

Where does the buck stop?

Look at Sara. Nothing she's said makes me believe she had a soft childhood, yet she pitches in and doesn't whine about life.

Reg was left holding the filthy end of more than one stick, but she's not complaining about how unfair life is.

I've had a gut full of excuses, Barton's most of all.

Jay trotted the mare back to the corral where the horses that would be ridden the next day were kept. Automatically he cared for the mare, then turned her loose in the corral and carried the tack to the barn before he headed to the house.

Sara is here.

He gave up trying to talk himself out of caring. Life was unexpected. Death was the same and utterly final. Sara was here and he would enjoy her for as long as it lasted. If it got under Henry's skin, he could take his meals in the bunkhouse the way he had when Liza lived on the ranch.

Within minutes, Jay was climbing the stairs to Sara's room. The door was ajar, so he pushed it open. She was sitting cross-legged on the bed, reading one of the papers from the carton open beside her. Other papers fanned across the bed in a pattern only she could make sense of.

"Can I help?" he asked.

"You know anything about Custer's shorthand?"

"As in old-fashioned bound steno notebooks?"

She picked up a paper. "As in 'GP. G's bad.'"

Jay held out his hand. Without hesitation, she turned over the paper. Frowning, he stared at the enigmatic letters. The date put the notes in the last months of his mother's long illness.

"Does GP appear in other papers?" he asked.

"Frequently. Often preceded by 'GDJD!!!' "

Jay closed his eyes, remembering his mother. Tall, dark, striking, with a laugh that lit up the world. Warm and gentle, yet demanding good manners and better grades, smiling as she checked his cheek for the stubble only a kid on the roller coaster of early puberty would long for.

He missed her still, an ache that would never leave because it had become a part of him.

"Let me see some more from around this date," he said, "and some from years earlier, if you have any."

Sara reached for one of the piles she had clipped together. "These are from before you were born to about five years after."

"How do you know when I was born?"

"It's in the papers you're holding."

He read through the papers quickly, efficiently, letting the words ignite memories long buried beneath passing years. He paused for the words that announced his birth. " 'GDJD over moon. LGDJD at last.' " He laughed. "That one is easy enough. JD was happy that they finally had a child."

"Really?" She leaned forward until she could read over his arm. "I didn't see that." She looked at the paper, frowned, and looked at Jay. "Translation, please."

"Remember that JD and Custer fought a lot."

She nodded.

"As a kid I often wondered why Custer muttered 'GDJD' all the time. I asked Mom what it meant and she laughed. She said Custer was calling on God to help him with JD."

"As in God damning JD?" Sara asked wryly.

"Like I said, they fought like two dogs over a bone, except that nobody ever figured out what the bone was."

"So LGDJD is . . . ?"

"Little GDJD."

"No wonder Custer used shorthand. So your mom and dad had trouble having children?"

"They never talked about it. From some of the things JD let drop, I figured that the problem was on her side. The fact that Barton was born so quick cinched it."

"Yet still Liza and JD had only one child," Sara said.

"It was the only thing Liza and JD argued about. He wanted more. She didn't."

"She'd already landed him. What did she need with more kids?" Sara heard her own words and winced. "That sounded awful. What I mean is—"

"You nailed it the first time," Jay said over her words. "She had a rich man bagged, tagged, and mounted on the bedroom wall. Now it was time for her to enjoy the results of all her hard work."

The ice and distance in his voice sent a chill down Sara's back. "You really don't like her at all, do you?"

"JD did. That's all that mattered."

"Was she a good wife to him?"

"She never got caught with another man, if that's what you mean. No surprise, really. She didn't have much use for the male of the species."

"Or the female, either," Sara said.

"Point to the pretty lady. All Liza ever needed was money and admirers. But that won't help us with these papers. Move over, would you?"

She scooted to the side, making room for him on the old double bed. Then she read over his arm, trying to see what he did with the papers covered with caricatures and a sprawling kind of writing revealing Custer's equally sprawling thoughts.

"So G is God," she said.

"Depends on the context. G also stands for Ginny, my mother, Virginia. Custer used to call her Saint Ginny for living with JD."

"He said that in front of your father?"

"Repeatedly, now that you mention it." He shook his head. "The things I have stored in my memory that I didn't know. G'mom, Mother's mother, called Custer and JD Mutt and Jeff. It fit. Custer certainly could have come from an insane asylum. JD was a lot smarter than

Jeff, except when he lost his temper. Then he was as dumb as any man."

Sara picked up her tablet and started entering in notes. "So SG can mean Saint Ginny. Any idea about GP?"

"Could be Gone Painting."

"Beats Going Postal, which was my best guess."

Jay smiled. "I think your slang is years out of date."

"Details." She leaned over his arm. "What's this about buying a kid?"

"Mother wanted to adopt. JD flatly refused. There's an old Vermilion saying, so old that it must have come over on the boat with the first Vermilions. 'Better one chicken than ten cuckoos.'"

"Meaning?"

"Better one child of your own blood than ten of another man's get."

"Good old patriarchy," she said. "Blood, not the child, is what matters."

"When property is tied to blood," he said, reaching for another paper, "things get real sticky. Apparently my great-great-great-grandfather found that two of his five children weren't actually his."

"Oops."

"He was furious. He wrote the first Vermilion will. Disowned his wife and her two kids. Every Vermilion male after that put the 'only blood inherits' clause into their wills. Of course, until genetic testing, no one was really sure either way."

"Were you tested?"

"Before I inherited, yes."

"Harsh," she said. "So a child only counts when it's your blood. Was JD into chastity belts?"

"Mom would have put it on *him*."

Sara laughed. "I would have liked your mother."

"She would have loved you. She always wanted a daughter to teach how to barrel race and cook and sing the old songs about love and broken hearts and death."

"Lots of new songs have those themes."

"People don't change much," he said. "That's the good and the bad news in one."

"I take it you don't believe in the perfectibility of man."

"If it could be done, it would have been done. It hasn't, so it can't." He set another paper down.

"No wonder you don't like cities," she said, reading over his shoulder. "People in cities tend to have a lot of rules designed to make everyone better than they would be otherwise."

"How's that working out?"

She laughed. "About like you'd expect."

"If it works at all, it's a tribute to the people, not to the rules. I've been in places where the only rule was survival. There were good people in those places. Rules had nothing to do with it."

"Did JD think like that?"

"No. Mom was the pragmatist. JD was JD. He was educated, but he wasn't bookish. Yet he read Mother poetry every day as she lay dying."

"Just when I think I understand the man," Sara grumbled, "I discover something that throws everything out the window."

Smiling, Jay stole a kiss. "My parents were people, sweetheart. They made mistakes, learned from them, fought, laughed, cried, made love—the whole human experience. Just because they were my parents didn't mean that they lived only for me. They had lives separate from their child. I didn't see it that way at the time, but that doesn't make it any less true."

Sara thought about her own parents, just people living each day as it came, coping as best they could.

Like her.

Except I made choices my mother never could, because the single choice of marrying a poor dairy farmer left her with too few choices after that.

Good for me. Now, am I going to let her choices continue to rule my life?

Motionless, Sara stared at the papers she was holding without seeing them, her mind playing Ping-Pong with the subject of choices.

"Yo?" Jay tugged gently at the papers in her hand. "Anybody home?"

"Sorry," she said absently, releasing the papers. "I was thinking."

"Nothing happy, from your expression."

"Not really unhappy, either. Just unexpected."

He stood and pulled her up with him. Before she could get her balance, he fitted her to his body and kissed her like she was water in the middle of a desert. By the time he lifted his head, she was clinging to him, taking from him, giving him her breath and her hunger.

"Come on," he said huskily. "Enough poking around in the past. It's been a long day. I don't know about you, but I'd like to take a nap before dinner."

"A nap?" She smiled. "I never heard it called that."

"Wait until you hear me snore."

"Remember how you didn't want your ribs counted?"

"Still don't."

"Then don't snore."

Sara didn't know when she had fallen asleep. She only knew that Jay's arms and warm male scent were wrapped around her. Or she was wrapped around him. Maybe they were just like the sheets, tangled together and warm. She was boneless, sated, utterly relaxed in the aftermath of slow, intense loving. Because she could, she licked the bulge of his bicep, enjoying the heat and salt on his skin.

Then she realized that his bicep was flexed, hard, as if his hand was fisted.

"Jay?"

"Go back to sleep, sweetheart. It's at least an hour until dinner."

"Is something else wrong?"

He knew she meant if anything other than the murders was bothering him. He hesitated, then showed her the text message that had just come in on his phone from Liza.

URGENT. MEET ME AT ROTH'S OUTSIDE JACKSON TOMORROW 9AM. YOU WANT TO HEAR WHAT I HAVE TO SAY BEFORE YOUR LAWYER DOES. BRING YOUR 'GUEST.'

"I thought the art community gossiped more than anyone else," Sara said. "Looks like the Wyoming grapevine is faster. Of course, Liza had an inside source. Is Barton getting even with you for the helicopter?"

Jay flicked the phone off and set it on the end table. "I'll know tomorrow."

"*We'll* know. She included me in the command performance."

"That doesn't mean I have to expose you to more of her poisonous tongue. Her choice of the meeting place tells me it's going to be a bad one."

"Why?"

"Roth's is a roadhouse Custer used to tear up with JD on a regular basis. The kind of place someone with Liza's mouth belongs in, quite frankly."

"I'm a big girl," Sara said. "I can do bitch with the best of them. But why the text? Why didn't she just call you?"

"She didn't want to hear what I had to say."

"That's what lawyers are for. Oh, right, now that she's paying, she may be doing a lot more of the leg-work herself."

He smiled rather grimly. "A minimum of two thousand dollars a week for her lawyers will cut into her pocket change."

"Two big ones per week? Whew. No wonder she's doing the meeting on her own."

Jay stretched, trying to release some of the tension Liza's text had caused.

Surprisingly strong fingers began massaging his shoulders as Sara said, "I could hate Liza just for the grief she causes you."

"Don't waste your energy," he said, flexing and turning beneath her probing fingers.

"Face down, soldier."

She worked her way down his back, admiring the line of his spine and the muscular bunch of his buttocks. Slowly his body loosened until she no longer felt like she was massaging rock. Smiling, she whispered a finger down his spine to the coccyx, then gently bit one of his cheeks.

"What was that for?"

"Just keeping you awake," she said.

He moved and suddenly she was on her back, knees spread, and he was teasing her so hotly that she could barely ask a question.

"What—about dinner?" she managed.

"In the flyover states, we eat dessert first."

Chapter 19

Roth's 24-Hour Roadhouse was crammed with hot-rod remnants, the debris of a hundred races gone wrong, pieces recovered and polished to a hard shine. A tangle of chromed exhaust pipes hung like a mass of silver snakes over the register, brilliant in the reflected light of morning. The waitresses were dressed like last night's party. Unlike the chromed wreckage, the daylight didn't do the people any favors. Televisions featuring various sports blared from every corner. Only the early—or late—drinkers at the long bar watched them.

"I bet there's a card room or two in the back," Sara said, fiddling with her coffee mug with one hand. The other was held by Jay.

"You win," he said.

"Are they legal?"

From the back of the main dining room came the clack of pool balls and the loud cursing of the loser. From the sound of her voice, she hadn't been home since yesterday.

"If things get too raucous, the sheriff notices," Jay said. "Otherwise, he waits for the good citizens to complain. A lot of the women are semipro, which, like the illegal gambling, is a big draw."

"Semipro as in part-time hookers?"

"Yeah. They do a big lunch trade with truckers," he said.

"And you say Liza belongs here, hmm?"

"JD and Custer met her in a place just like this down in Nevada." Jay glanced impatiently at his watch. "Three more minutes and we're gone."

Sara looked around again. Nothing had changed for the better. "Odd choice for a meeting. I can't imagine that returning here is very comfortable for Liza. Unless the food is better than the coffee."

"If she's here to chew on anything, it's us."

The front door opened, sending more unfriendly sunlight through the dark room. Sara looked at Liza. The older woman wore black jeans, a turquoise jacket, and matching turquoise sweater. Her needle-heeled black leather boots hit the stone floor with a tattoo that sounded like small bones snapping. She had left the diamonds at home, settling for some old, exquisite, and seriously expensive Indian jewelry. Her lips and nails were stoplight red.

Sara said quietly, "That outfit would support months of lawyers."

"I know. The ranch paid for every bit of it. The jewelry had been in the family for three generations. Mother loved it. Wore it every chance she got and talked about the granddaughter who would someday enjoy it." He shrugged. "Win some, lose some."

"I'm sorry," she whispered.

"So am I. Liza only wanted the 'Indian stuff' because JD's first wife had made it her trademark. She's wearing it today to remind me of who won that particular battle."

"Bitch."

"Oh yeah."

He watched as Vermilion Ranch's biggest enemy stopped in front of their table. He could smell the stale liquor on her breath and wondered if she had reached the stage where she sweat booze because her liver couldn't handle it anymore.

"Good morning, Jay," Liza said, glancing at his hand holding Sara's. "Ms. Medina."

He nodded—and didn't stand up.

Sara just watched Liza. If Jay had shelved his ingrained manners today, so would she.

After a brief hesitation, Liza sat down like she had built the place with her own two hands.

"Tomato juice," she said, without looking at the waitress who was a step behind her. "Nothing else."

The waitress looked uncertainly at Jay.

"We ate at home," he said to her. "Coffee is all we need."

The waitress smoothed her hands over the hips of her skintight short skirt, calling attention to an unusually nice ass. "Whatever you want, sir. No charge for the coffee . . . or anything else. Boss said it's been too long since he's seen a Vermilion in here."

"Bless him," Jay said blandly.

Sara choked back a laugh at his echo of the sheriff.

After a long look over her shoulder, the waitress sauntered off to get Liza's tomato juice.

"Well," Liza said brightly. "What should we talk about?"

Her eyes burned as she held herself absolutely still, waiting for a reaction.

"We don't have time to play games with you," he said evenly. "There's a ranch to be run."

"You called the meeting. Get to the point," Sara's cool voice did nothing to hide her dislike.

Liza let the silence grow until the waitress set down a tall glass of thick red fluid. The shock of living color with no artifice made Liza look like a bad reflection of life. Without the height of her heels, she was small, almost frail.

Don't fall for it, Sara silently advised Jay. *Like tears, it's the oldest trick in the female playbook.*

"This is the thanks I get for doing you a favor?" Liza asked, her voice raw.

She took a long drink, leaving a lipstick mark on the rim of the glass that was redder than the tomato juice. She dabbed at her mouth with a napkin, leaving another mark on the stark white paper.

He watched her like the venomous snake she was.

"No questions?" she asked. "How disappointing."

Silence answered her.

Liza fixed him with eyes that were somehow glassy, vague, and yet eerily intent. "My lawyers tell me we have a very good chance of vacating the previous judgment in the case of the Custers."

"On the basis of what evidence?" Jay asked, playing idly with his coffee spoon.

"Conflict of interest." Liza smiled like a child, but the gaze she turned on Sara was anything but innocent.

A chill moved over Sara's neck. "What conflict?"

"You. Obviously you lied in your assessment of the paintings in order to please your lover."

"Bullshit," he said. "We didn't even meet until after the judge decided the case."

"Barton talked to your last clients. The Chens," Liza said, her eyes avid on Sara's face. "They said you were in an awful hurry to get to Wyoming."

"I had been in Atlanta for months already. Get to the point." Sara's voice was calm, but what she saw in Liza's eyes made her want to run.

Does Jay know that his father's ex is more than fashionably insane?

"You were expected to be in Atlanta for two more weeks," Liza said in a rising voice. "But you rushed here to get some cock time with your client. Was that your payoff, or did you expect a crack at the Vermilion money, too?"

Sara's fingertips flexed on Jay's hand in a silent demand that he let her handle this.

"Don't judge me by what you would have done in my place," Sara said calmly.

"Does she hiss like a cat in bed, too?" Liza asked Jay.

"What do you want?" he asked, his voice calm and his eyes promising hell. "More money?"

"I want *everything*," Liza said, no longer hiding the vicious rage that animated her. "JD dumped me like yesterday's garbage."

"Wrapped in diamonds and couture? Try again."

"I want everything that JD loved more than he loved me. The ranch, the Custers, *everything*."

"And then what?" Sara asked. "You expect the black hole in your soul to be magically filled? News flash, sister. It doesn't work that way. You'd be no more happy—"

"Shut up! I don't need your whore's wisdom."

"If whores were wise, you wouldn't be here," Jay said to Liza. "But you aren't and here we are. You can spend the rest of your life trying to piss in my coffee or you can cut your losses and enjoy the good life you have."

"You'll learn," she said. "I promise you. Just like JD did."

"I already figured out why he divorced you," Jay said. "That's all the learning I have to do."

"I will be *respected*." Liza's shrill voice hung in the suddenly silent room.

"Not until you grow up," he said, his voice cold enough to burn. "Now, is there anything else you wanted to discuss?"

"You wipe that look off your face," she said, her hands trembling against the glass.

Jay smiled slowly. "Better?"

It wasn't.

Sara squeezed his hand lightly in warning. Baiting a crazy woman wasn't going to accomplish anything but a huge scene.

Maybe that's why she chose this roadhouse, Sara thought. *Anything short of knives won't be noticed.*

The thought of knives reminded her of the Solvangs, slashed and bloody, silently waiting for whatever justice there was.

Suddenly she was soul-deep tired of Liza and her constant search for a way to the bottom of the Vermilion pocketbook.

"You will increase my stipend by one hundred percent," Liza said.

"You already get more than the ranch can afford," he said.

"You can afford it. I've a good idea how much the ranch makes."

"Are you familiar with the Golden Goose whose owner killed it by demanding more and more eggs?" he asked sardonically.

Liza's hands gripped tightly around the juice glass.

For the first time Sara noticed that one of the older woman's thumbnails was bitten past the quick. The dried blood on the rim was darker than the nail polish.

"Barton will get control of his one quarter of the ranch right now," Liza said.

"No."

"And one more thing," she said.

Jay watched her with the eyes of the combat veteran he was. "Since all you're blowing is air, go ahead."

"I will have *Muse*."

"We can't prove it exists," Sara said. "Jay can't give you what doesn't exist."

"Custer painted it for a friend of mine," Liza said. "I watched him. I get that portrait or there is no deal."

"We've had this discussion and you've lost at every step of the way," Jay said, putting on his hat. "The answer hasn't changed. No."

"That was before Sara," Liza said quickly, harshly. "What do you think a new judge would make of the word of a so-called expert who is fucking you on her way to the Vermilion riches?"

"Not one word of the judge's verdict would change," he said. "It was based on law, not gossip."

"Perhaps. But," Liza added slyly, "can your whore's professional reputation survive the gossip?"

There it was, the reason Liza had brought them here. She thought she had a lever big enough to pry more money out of Jay.

"My reputation will do just fine," Sara said. "I've got a list of happy clients who keep me very busy."

"After Guy Beck gets through with you," Liza said, smiling like a death's head, "your clients won't call you."

"My clients know Guy. Whatever he says won't worry them," she lied without hesitation. *I'm damned if I'll be the cause of her ruining Vermilion Ranch.*

"The painting exists," Liza said to Jay. "It was mentioned in the receipts."

"Only a portrait was mentioned," he said. "No name attached."

"If you can't find *Muse,* it's because you're hiding it."

"Or Custer burned it before he left," Jay said.

"He wouldn't have done that! You have a week to cough up that painting. Then I'm going to hire lawyers and turn Guy Beck loose to destroy little Ms. Medina's reputation."

From the corner of Sara's eye, she saw the spoon between Jay's fingers flash as he fiddled with it, his big fingers turning it over and over in one hand.

"Your so-called conflict of interest is too thin a twig to hang a new case on," he said to Liza.

"No thinner than any of the other motions that kept dragging out the case for so many years," Liza said. "God, it was sweet knowing that you paid my lawyers to tie yours up in knots. Too bad I couldn't bleed you into selling the ranch."

"You've misread me from the jump," he said, his eyes gleaming from beneath his hat brim, the spoon flashing between his fingers.

"The hell I have. You want the ranch all to yourself, but your brother has his own ideas about what the ranch is worth and how best to extract it. He deserves his chance."

"He'll have it in seven years."

"No. Now!"

The spoon bent back on itself. Jay tossed it aside.

"I'm done," he said to Sara. "Let's go."

"Wait," Liza said urgently. "I can keep my son's focus off your precious ranch. He's a realist. You're a romantic. But since Barty *is* a realist, he can be redirected more easily than you." She crossed her arms on the table and leaned toward Jay. "Give me twice my stipend and *Muse*. I'll see that no more fences get cut or holes get dug in the creek and chemicals left behind. We won't ask any more of you. Ever."

Sara's lips pulled tight across her teeth. "Every boy loves his mother, right?"

"He may love me or hate me, but he listens to me if he wants money to spend."

"I'll require it in writing," Jay said, curious about how far Liza would go. "You get twice your stipend and *Muse*. I get an end to the engineering raids on the ranch, you make no more demands, and you give me your word that you won't trash Sara's professional reputation."

"No," Sara said angrily. "Don't let her use me against you!"

His fingers wrapped gently around hers beneath the table.

She looked at him and saw the faint negative movement of his head. "But—"

His fingers squeezed harder. With a muttered word,
she sat back silently.

"You get nothing in writing," Liza said. "You'd just
call it blackmail."

"Which it is. And that's why this isn't coming
through Mr. Abrahamson Esquire and Mr. Wilkie
Esquire, of Abrahamson and Wilkie Law Practice, two
of Wyoming's most expensive lawyers. This meeting
would have cost you about five thousand, coffee not
included."

"Did I mention that you will pay for any lawyers
involved?" Liza asked, wide-eyed.

"Unless you forget about me paying for your lawyers, we don't have anything in front of us but bad
coffee."

Liza waved her hand and her big engagement ring
flashed in the gloom. "I can afford to be gracious about
the lawyers."

"I'm not agreeing to anything right now," he said.

"Think about it for a day or two. You'll figure
out that lost causes aren't worth fighting for. Again.
No matter what you decide, the deadline is still two
weeks." She pushed herself away from the table and
stood. "Do let me know when you've found the portrait. Until then, all pieces remain in play."

She began walking away.

"Have you heard about Fish Camp?" he asked casually.

Liza stiffened and turned toward him. "Awful, just awful."

"You wouldn't know anything about that. Would you?"

"Surely you don't think I had anything to do with that sordid business? Shame on you."

"The painting you want so much could have been stolen from Fish Camp. Have you thought of that?"

"Barty said nothing was stolen."

Jay smiled grimly. "We don't *think* anything was stolen. We can't prove a negative."

"That's your problem."

"Like the murders?" Sara asked. "Nothing is your problem, is that it?"

"I don't need to kill anyone to get what I want," Liza said impatiently. "I just need to know other people's weakness. Then they'll do whatever I want. Like you, Jay Vermilion. You'll do what I want and you'll be damn glad for the opportunity." She turned her back again. "Let me know when you find the portrait."

Her heels bit across the room as she left the chrome and TVs and bad memories behind.

For the first time in her life, Sara understood why people wanted to kill.

"Keep a lid on it until we get to the truck," Jay said.

"I hate that she's using me to get at you," Sara said through clenched teeth. Her hands were trembling with anger, so she clenched them into fists. "If not for me, you'd have told her to eat sh—"

"Right," he said over her words, standing up, taking her with him. "We're leaving."

By the time they reached the truck, she had herself under control. Mostly.

He slid behind the wheel and started the truck as calmly as if he had just been to the hardware store.

"Slow down and think," he said as he backed out of the parking spot. "Liza is shooting blanks with her threats, but as long as she believes she has me by the balls, she'll go back in the woodwork for two weeks. We have to act like we're really worried."

"Shooting blanks?" Sara asked.

"An engagement ring on your finger would stop gossip quick enough."

Silently she chewed over that. Finally she asked, "Do you believe Liza about the Solvangs?"

"That woman is a lot of things, none of them to my taste. But murder for hire? You need connections to get to that kind of people. She doesn't have them. Blackmail? Hell, yes, she'll do that and laugh all the way to the bank."

Sara frowned. "Why does she want *Muse* enough to try extortion?"

He shrugged and drove out of the parking lot. "Remember what you said about the prototype Spyder?"

"Yes."

"Maybe that's what *Muse* is to Liza. It's also her way to shove the knife in me and twist it. I said no more and she gets the most expensive painting anyway."

"If she gets the chance, she'll bleed the ranch to death and laugh," Sara said. "And it would be my fault."

"Bullshit. I'll survive this skirmish. The Vermilion-Neumann war was being fought long before you came and it will likely be fought long after you leave."

Whatever she was going to say scattered in the face of that blunt truth.

She would leave.

He would stay.

Silence grew in the truck, broken only by the sound of the turn signal as he drove onto the main road.

"We'll have at least a week before Liza gets too impatient," he said. *I hope.* "There was a receipt for a five-foot-by-six-foot portrait, so we have to assume it's the one she wants."

Sara closed her eyes and struggled for the acceptance of losing that Jay had found on long-ago battlefields.

Even though he said they had to pretend to go along, she wondered if that was the whole truth, or even a part of it.

"Since I know that Custer didn't take any of his work to Roanoke," Jay began.

"How can you know that?" she asked quickly.

"Custer left behind paints, brushes, easels, everything but the clothes he walked out in. He hitchhiked his way to Roanoke. I can't see him doing that with a big painting under his arm."

"What happened to all his stuff?"

"It's probably packed up somewhere. Or burned. Custer wasn't the only one who knew how to start a fire. JD built plenty of his own." Jay glanced at Sara. Her face was set, flushed, and her jaw was tight. "Think about finding the portrait as a gain for the arts and your own career. Either one is reason enough to search. Forget about Liza."

"How has that worked out for you?" she asked.

"What do you mean?"

"Underneath that calm you're cold enough to burn." Silence again.

"It's not Liza alone," he said finally, his mouth grim. "I'd be a lot happier if I didn't feel like Fish Camp was tied up in all this."

"You said you didn't think Liza was involved."

"I don't." His hands flexed on the wheel. "But I feel like I'm fighting on too many fronts to win on any of them. So I'll spend a few days trying to eliminate the front called *Muse* and then get on to the important fight—finding the killers."

And, he thought savagely, *if this all tangles up with Fish Camp, I'll be that much closer to those murdering sons of bitches.*

"Blackmailers never go away," she said. "You know that, right?"

"Liza's pushing so hard now because she believes that once you leave, her leverage leaves with you."

That reality tasted as bad as the roadhouse coffee, but Sara accepted the sour truth. What she and Jay shared wasn't long term.

"I've called Liza a lot of names, but stupid isn't one of them," he said. "She thought she saw her time and her weapon and she struck. Why not? It's a win-win for her. More money, maybe a Custer painting, and sweet revenge to soothe whatever is gnawing at her. What more could she want?"

"I'm sure we'll find out."

Chapter 20

S ara hardly noticed the beauty of the cloud-dappled sunlight as Jay drove up to the front of the ranch house. She was too busy thinking of a lost painting and double murder.

"I'll leave," she said into the silence.

No!

But Jay kept his violent reaction to himself. "Liza will try to ruin your reputation just because she can."

"How do we know Beck hasn't lit up the gossip lines already?" Sara asked.

Jay turned off the truck. "Has anyone called?"

She didn't need to check her phone. She was still holding it in her hand from the last time she had checked her messages three minutes ago.

"No," she said.

"Then your reputation is intact. One of your competitors would have called to play 'oh, isn't it awful' with you."

She couldn't argue that. She was counting on human nature to let her know the moment gossip began.

Is that when Jay will hand me an engagement ring for Liza to choke on?

The idea disturbed Sara on too many levels to name.

He leaned over the console and gave her a nibbling kiss at the edge of her mouth. The thoughts that had made her frown scattered. She put her hand on his cheek, still smooth from his morning shave.

"Remember," Jay said, "we're just pretending to be worried."

"All right. I'll stop fretting." *For now.* She nipped his lower lip. "You distract me too easily."

"Sweetheart, you distract me every time you breathe. And if I don't get out of this truck right now, the proof of that will be in my pants for anyone to see."

"Have I mentioned how much I love your jeans?"

"You're not helping."

She was still smiling—and carefully not looking—when he opened the front door for her.

Henry was waiting just inside the house. "Well, how bad was it?"

The question reminded Sara of what Jay had said about the foreman being a gossip.

So I'll look worried. Because I am worried.

"Bad enough," Jay said. "Did you get the evidence box from the trial? With all the excitement yesterday I forgot to ask."

Henry started to ask another question, then looked at Jay's eyes and decided better of it. "It's in the den next to your desk. Sheriff Cooke called. Duggan and Valentine are in jail in Cody. Drunk and disorderly."

"How long they been there?" Jay asked.

"Too long for them to have murdered the Solvangs."

Jay took off his hat and tapped it against his thigh. "It was an outside chance, at best. Thanks, Henry. Stay close to the ranch house, would you? I may need your memories of Custer."

The foreman slapped a sweat-stained Stetson on his head. "I'll go check the horses we'll be using tomorrow. It's getting close to shoeing time."

"And some of the shoes are getting thin," Jay said, mentally adding the farrier to the list of chores in his mind.

"Yep." Henry stepped out of the front door and swiped long, graying hair behind his ears. "Rube and Willets are on their way back. Should be here by noon."

"They must be taking the steep way."

"Yep." Henry shut the door and vanished. His voice called back to them, "I'll check in when I've finished the horses."

"Steep way?" Sara asked.

"A shortcut," Jay said. "Too steep for cows but fine for good horses."

"Here I thought I was out in the wilderness. Turns out there are more trails here than in Central Park."

Smiling, he ran the back of his fingers over her cheek. "The idea of being untouched by man is just that. An idea. People had settled in the New World long, long before Columbus stumbled over it on his way to India. Wherever you go, people have been there before you."

"As long as they don't leave trash, I'm good with it."

"Speaking of trash, let's sort through that evidence box."

"Is it big enough to hold *Muse*?" she asked whimsically.

"Not unless it's folded down to the size of a legal document."

"Another dream dies."

He took her hand and interlaced their fingers. "You need tougher dreams."

She squeezed his hand. "Working on it."

Sara followed Jay into the room he had made his office. A bedraggled cardboard banker's box sat in the middle of his desk. Various stickers coded for the guardians of evidence decorated the cardboard.

When he opened the carton, pieces of paper popped up. The box was literally stuffed full of records.

"The stickers on the box led me to believe that the papers inside would be organized," she said.

"They scanned in what was important for the trial."

"And left the rest. Gotcha."

"There's a ledger in here somewhere," Jay said. He rummaged gently, found the ledger, and lifted it out. "Here you go."

She took it, sat, and began scanning lines and columns.

He went to get some coffee worth drinking and found he would have to make it himself. When he came back with two steaming mugs, Sara hadn't moved.

Out beyond the kitchen, the mudroom door opened and closed. Henry was back.

Her finger ran under a line that had been crossed out. "What's this one? May 5, 1993. Do you celebrate Cinco de Mayo?"

"Not when I was a kid."

She took his hand and urged him closer. "Well?"

"I won't know until you let me read it," he said.

"What's all the fuss about?" Henry said from the doorway. He was watching Jay the way Skunk watched King Kobe. "I thought you were done with digging around in dusty boxes. What in hell is that bitch Liza up to now?"

"We're in the extralegal part of the game," Jay said.

"This one," Sara said, reclaiming his attention. "It was written then crossed out real hard. Amount of five thousand dollars. Not a casual mistake."

Jay looked closely. "It's written to 'Cash.' "

"A lot of money," she said

"Not when you're buying livestock." Without looking up, he asked, "Any ideas, Henry?"

The older man leaned forward and pulled out a pair of wire-rimmed half spectacles, looking through them to the beaten page below. "Well, sure, I remember that date. It was right about the time Custer wore out his welcome here. JD got tired of him underfoot while he was courting that bitch. This might be what you'd call a parting gift."

"Or go-away money," Jay said.

"Same difference."

Sara exhaled sharply and tapped the line item with her fingernail. "But that's not what we're looking for."

"Not unless it was a payout for the painting," Jay said.

"Without some kind of note, there's no way to be sure," she said unhappily. "It's the same amount that JD paid for other Custer paintings, but that's not enough to convince me." *Much less Liza.*

Jay drummed his fingers on the table. The sound spread through the study and was absorbed by hundred-year-old books and hand-worked wooden bookshelves.

"That crossing out isn't like JD," she said, flipping back through the pages. "Every other line item is accounted for, business and personal alike. His record-keeping was idiosyncratic, but not chaotic."

"True," the foreman said. "He was particular about keeping these private records, probably so Ginny never figured out how much he spent on art."

"I thought she was the one who liked Custer's art," Sara said.

"Liking it and liking to pay hard cash for it are two separate things," Henry said.

Jay began sorting through the contents of the box, looking for a receipt for a portrait.

"What exactly is it you two are after?" the foreman asked after a minute. "I might be able to help."

Sara looked to Jay, who nodded.

"We're looking for a portrait that Custer painted, called *Muse*. As far as we can tell, it dates from before he and JD parted company."

"Which was about the time that JD married again," Jay added. "Which makes the two things stick together in my mind."

Henry nodded and thought about it. "A portrait? From the name, I'm guessing it's a woman. Unless they have male muses now."

"I haven't heard of one yet," Sara said.

Jay pinched the bridge of his nose to drive tension out of his skull. He wanted to be *doing* something rather than sitting around sifting through old records and pretending to be worried out of his mind.

"Man or woman," Jay said, "we need that portrait. There has to be some reason that Liza is hell-bent on getting it."

"She doesn't give up," Henry said, looking like he wanted to spit.

"Liza?" asked Sara.

Henry nodded.

"When all you have is eroded beauty and animal cunning," Sara said, "giving up isn't a choice." She went deeper into the carton and found a worn manila folder holding a sheaf of material. She opened it and flipped quickly through a few papers. "What are these?"

"Some of the junk Custer left behind," Henry said. "JD cussed up, down, and sideways over having to keep stuff until Custer sent his new address."

"Which he never did," Jay said. "We found a lot of the receipts in there. All but the portrait receipt said 'Gift to Ginny.'"

Sara set the folder down and read at random through the papers to get some idea of the contents. "Receipt, receipt . . . newspaper clippings . . . I didn't know that Custer rode broncos in the rodeo. Second place, bareback. My clients are going to lick this up like cream."

"He pressed flowers," Henry said, pointing to the dried petals that lay between pages. "Odd duck, that one."

"Any favorite kind of flowers?"

"Nothing from Ginny's garden," Henry said, chuckling. "She lit into him like a mama bear when she found him picking tulips one spring."

Sara paused, then went back to the folder. A wad of papers were stuck together, probably by the dried oil paints dotting them. She could imagine Custer interrupted while painting and being called to sign for receipt of something. The top paper was a bill for a shipment of oils and brushes. The amount was several thousand dollars.

JD had paid for it.

"Lots of information in here that will help in writing a book," she said. "Nothing about a painting called *Muse*."

With quick, impatient movements Sara tried to stuff everything back into the folder.

The wad of papers slid from her fingers and hit the desk with a crackling sound. Several of the papers came unstuck. Curious, she carefully pried at the rest of them. One of them was folded in half and stuck together among the larger papers.

When she unfolded it, she saw a pencil sketch of a face, drawn out in strokes that were both spiked and curved.

"Huh," Henry said. "Looks like a kid did it."

"A very, very talented kid," she said absently. "This is the start of a preliminary sketch. Almost a doodle, really. Look at the wild freedom in it. The main form is graceful, almost ethereal, but . . ."

"What?" Jay asked softly.

"Well, the main outlines are easy enough, but he's agonizing over the details. The eyes are barely there, yet they're the heart and soul of every portrait. He was having trouble *seeing* them. Or maybe he was just having difficulty translating what he saw."

The barest ghost of a woman's face stared from the page.

"Do you know her?" Sara asked Jay, eyes wide with wonder and hope.

"About all I can be sure of is that this isn't my mother," Jay said. "Eyebrows are wrong."

"Henry?" Sara asked.

He took out his half glasses and bent over the sketch. "Doesn't look like anyone I ever knew. Custer was probably too drunk or stoned to do the job right."

"Stoned?" She looked at Jay.

"Stoned," he agreed. "I always thought it was the paints that made his cabin smell funny. By the time I hit junior high, I'd learned better."

"JD didn't mind Custer's love of herb? At the time pot was seriously illegal."

"Still is," Jay said.

"JD told Custer he'd tan his bare backside if he ever caught the painter smoking anything but tobacco," Henry said. "After the first time in the woodshed, Custer believed him."

"JD spanked Custer?" Sara asked in disbelief.

"It ain't spanking when it involves a leather belt," the foreman said. "It was a downright ass whuppin'."

"Remind me to sit you down with a digital recorder," she said. "You know more about Custer than anyone alive."

Henry shrugged. "What a foreman don't personally see, he hears about in bunkhouse gossip quick enough."

She turned the paper over, hoping to find a notation on the back. Instead she found out how the sketch had ended up in a box of receipts. Custer's crabbed, small script was written on the back. The ink had faded but could still be read.

Jay bent over her so close that she could feel his heat. His breath stirred against her cheek while he read aloud. " 'Official receipt for the sale of *Emerald Solitude,* my last awful piece of shit landscape painting to the fool JD Vermilion who hid it so I couldn't burn it on this date May 1993.' " He laughed softly. "Custer sounds well and truly pissed off. Probably drunk, too. And look down here. 'Gift to Ginny' in JD's handwriting."

Sara turned the page back over and looked at the unfinished face.

"The odds are very good that this is a study for *Muse,*" she said, "but it's not proof that he actually created a finished painting. A study is just that—a beginning, not an end."

Jay rubbed his cheek against hers. "It's a start, sweetheart. That's more than we had." He stood and looked at Henry. "From the sound of all that barking, Rube and Willets must be back with the dogs."

"I'll take care of it. Want me to send them back up to Fish Camp to truck out those paintings tomorrow?"

"No," Sara said instantly. Then to Jay, "I'd like to oversee their repacking, if that's all right. Every bit of damage is a ding on the potential sale price."

"So you're selling them?" Henry asked.

"Thinking real hard about it," Jay said.

The foreman nodded, put on his hat, and headed for the back door.

"Why didn't you tell him the rest of it?" she asked in a low voice.

"The rest of what?"

"That the future of the ranch is riding on these paintings. Especially *Muse*."

"There's nothing he can do about it," Jay said, "so why add to his load? Liza is a loose cannon rolling around on the deck. Sooner or later something will get crushed."

Is that what happened at Fish Camp? Liza lost control?

He shook his head at his own thought. Liza couldn't use a knife for cutting anything but steak.

"This is all my fault," Sara said, her voice thinned to breaking.

Jay listened. He couldn't tell if Henry had left. *So I keep to the worried act.*

"Even if you and I had never met, Liza would have found something else," Jay said, "some bit of the past she could use as blackmail, and Barton would still try to sell the land to anyone willing to cut fences to look at it. And none of that matters anyway."

"What do you mean?"

"Even if I knew all this was coming because we'd met, I'd still go running toward you. Hell, I'd have run even faster if I'd known what was waiting."

She put her arms around him and hugged him hard. "I—" She shook her head and tried again. "I—"

"Don't cry," he murmured. "I thought I'd survived everything intact, and then you walked into my life and I realized how much of myself I'd left overseas. Liza can sue me and blackmail me until hell freezes over, and I'll never regret meeting you."

Holding on, feeling like she was wrapped in living sunlight, Sara finally sighed, accepting what he said. "You're a good man, Jay Vermilion. So good. God, what I wouldn't give to strangle that bitch."

"She's not worth going to jail for, which is why she's still running around loose."

Something in his tone made Sara's eyes widen. "You've thought about it, too."

"When I first got back, yeah. The lawyers were taking so much money that the ranch was failing. And I know a lot of ways to kill."

They held each other for a long time before he let go enough to tip up her chin.

"I can tell you're thinking," he said.

"Maybe it's just Henry burning the trash."

Jay laughed. "Damn, woman, you're good for me. Until you, I'd pretty much forgotten how to laugh."

She touched the dimple in his chin with her tongue. "I like the sound of your laugh. Maybe I should tickle you."

"Remember payback is a bitch."

She sighed. "Do you suppose it's in the attic?"

"Payback?"

"*Muse.*"

"If we had an attic," he said, "I'd look. I searched the ranch when Liza was first on the warpath. If *Muse* was here, I'd have found it. Same for Fish Camp. But we can look again when we go back to pack up the paintings."

"And if it isn't at Fish Camp . . . ?" She bit her lip.

"Don't worry." He lowered his voice. "I'm only going to waste a few days on Liza's silliness. I'll start on the buildings the ranch owns in town, which weren't mentioned in Liza's suit so I never searched them. In the ranch house, JD hung Custers everywhere but the bathrooms. When he got tired of looking at paintings on the ranch, he'd put them in buildings in Jackson or rotate them to Fish Camp for storage."

"Do you think there are more Custers in town?"

"Custer was living on the ranch for a decade before I was born and he didn't leave until I was close to thirteen. That's enough time to paint a lot of land-scapes. And burn them."

"Some of them probably deserved it," she said. "No artist gets it right every time, or even a lot of the time. There are paintings hanging in private collections that have a world-class pedigree and very ordinary results."

Jay looked at the watch he hated wearing unless he was going to town. With an impatient motion he stripped it off and dumped it on the desk. "Let's get Fish Camp wrapped up."

Sara froze. A single thought had kept haunting her, but she didn't want to bother Jay with it.

"What is it?" he asked softly.

"Sheriff Cooke talked about an ambush," she said reluctantly. "What if they . . . what if . . ."

"It's possible they'll make another try," Jay said, "at the ranch, at Fish Camp, in town. Anywhere."

She shuddered. "I'm not used to being hunted."

"I am. That's why I'm always armed."

Chapter 21

The late-afternoon landscape was both desolate and beautiful against the hammered-silver sky. Clouds coiled darkly but moved by too fast to leave much rain or snow behind. Clinging to the edge of the mountain, the big Ford truck hauled a closed black trailer and crept slowly down the rough road.

"It's a lot scarier going down than up," Sara said, eyeing the drop-off on her side.

"On the way back, you're on the outside looking down," Jay said, handling the truck and double horse trailer with experienced ease.

"Way down," she said. "Who built this—well, I guess it's a road?"

"The Weiss brothers blazed it on behalf of the Vermilions around two hundred years back. Can't imagine running cows over it, but trucks do just fine."

"Trucks don't have vertigo," she said, glancing down a slope of tumbled stones that looked like pulled teeth.

His phone bawled like King Kobe. Jay fished for it in one of the many pockets he had in his work pants, which were really army fatigues that he'd grown to prefer over jeans when he wasn't riding. The sound of Velcro being torn open as he searched was almost lost in the road bumps and the bawling phone.

Sara steadied the wheel for him with her left hand.

"Thanks," he said, and finally came up with the phone. "Yeah, Henry. What's up?"

"God damn it, Jay, I've been calling and calling and—"

"Hello, Barton. Try the radio next time. Cell coverage is spotty unless you're on a ridgeline, which you'd know if you spent any time working the ranch."

"Where the hell are you?"

"On the old Weiss road. What's the problem?"

"Someone broke into the storage facility in Jackson!" Barton shouted.

"What?" Jay lifted his foot and braked gently, coming to a halt while Barton talked.

"They cut the lock and rolled in pretty as you please. Then they went through the place and took whatever they liked."

"What did they get? And when did it happen?"

"Early this morning," Barton said loudly. "And we don't know yet what was stolen. Sheriff wants you to come down and check it out, get an inventory."

"I'm on a dirt track a long way from town. You deal with Cooke."

"Fish Camp again, huh? Getting a little somethin'-somethin'?"

"Get some of your own and you won't be so interested in mine," Jay said. "Now put Henry on before I forget we're related."

"He's getting the car warmed up so we can do some actual work. Maybe you ought to think about doing some, too. Don't hurry back."

The line went dead. Jay hissed a word under his breath and put the phone back in his pocket.

"That was Barton," Jay said.

"I heard. Didn't that boy come with a volume control?"

"None that I've found. Our storage facility in Jackson was robbed."

"I heard," she said unhappily. "Bad luck all around." *Or bad people.* But she didn't say it aloud. Jay had enough troubles already.

"That's why you're not going anywhere without me," he said.

She could tell from the sound of his voice that the captain was back in charge. "Is that an order?"

"Until I know better what's going on, it is."

She leaned across the bench seat of Jay's old, rough-country truck. Closer to him now, as close as the seat belt would let her be, she slid her left hand between his jacket and work shirt, savoring his warmth.

"The storage robbery isn't a coincidence, is it?" she asked.

"Twice might be coincidence," he said. "Third time is war."

What really bothered him was that this kind of war was waged by amateurs. Unpredictable as spring avalanches and just as likely to kill. The way the Solvangs had been killed, with no need other than cruelty, the blood-filled certainty that life was fragile and death was final.

Jay lifted his foot from the brake. The heavy-duty truck began crawling over the rough road again. On the ridgetop, with land falling away on all sides, he felt like he was driving over the stony remains of an animal that had died when the world was born.

After uncounted, bumpy miles, he hit the button and sent his window down. Cold air rolled in like thunder.

Sara gave him a sideways look and pulled her collar higher.

"I'm going to check the hitch," he said as he stopped and turned off the engine. "Something sounds odd."

"Can I help?"

"Just sit tight and stay warm. It won't take me a minute."

Before he got out, he unlocked the rifle, but left it in its rear window rack with just the snaps holding it in place.

She went very still, so tight she vibrated. Then she forced herself to breathe. *He carried the rifle at Fish Camp, too, and nothing happened to us. Fish Camp is behind us now. Custer's paintings are all tightly packed and bumping along behind us in the horse trailer.*

Everything is fine.

Jay got back in the truck and started up again. He left his window down as they bumped along the road.

"Is the hitch okay?" she asked.

"It's good." He hesitated, then said, "I thought I heard a helicopter. But with the wind swirling around and all the rattling on the road, it's hard to be sure. Could be just my imagination."

She tried not to shiver in the cold wind. The words he had spoken were uninflected. Information only. No emotion.

Captain Vermilion was back and in charge.

"But you don't think it's imaginary," she said.

He didn't answer. His face looked the same, but that internal radar had flicked on, reaching out all around, trying to sense the enemy. His navy blue eyes were both restless and probing.

Suddenly he tilted his head, listening intently.

She could only hear the trailer rattling and the wind outside trying to talk the clouds into a stormy party.

"You'd have to be crazy or desperate to be in a helo up here on a day like this," he said. "Gusty winds and cold air pockets are deadly when you're flying the nap."

"Nap?"

"Down close to the ground, below any radar. Plays hell with sound direction, bouncing off ridgelines and echoing through canyons."

"Maybe the helicopter is in trouble." She leaned closer to her window and looked up.

"Possible. Let me know if you spot it before I do."

The road twisted down, and the landscape around them began to change, giving way from a rocky ridgeline to a steeply sloping meadow with scattered stands of aspen and evergreens. The clouds were sullen steel turning to deep blue black along their bottoms. The wind bent grass and trees with equal ease.

She sat up straight and opened her window. "I can hear—" she began.

"I hear it, too," he cut in. "Rotors. Which way do you hear the sound from?"

She paused, frowned. "Behind, maybe more on my right side. I can't tell. It sounds odd, not quite like the sheriff's helicopter."

"It's the echo," Jay replied. "Sound slaps right off the mountainside. But it's low, coming in fast."

As he spoke his eyes were searching the area for cover. Nothing big enough to hide in but a thick stand of trees, and it was at least a mile away. At the speed they were going, those trees might as well have been on the moon.

They would never be able to reach them before the chopper caught up.

Slowly, evenly, he accelerated. The road fought him every foot of the way, sending the truck lurching and grinding from side to side of the dirt track. And still he increased the speed until Sara was hanging on to anything she could grab to stay in one place.

The sound was overtaking them.

"Maybe it's a medical flight," she said. "Just because it's a sound you associate with bad news doesn't mean—"

"A medevac chopper saved the lives of a lot of my men," he said. "Mine, too."

He glanced at the passenger-side mirror for an instant. Green and white flashed over the big rect-angular mirror. A buzzing sound rolled over them.

Bullets stitched into the ground near the road. One tore through a corner of the side mirror, shattering it.

"Get down!"

Sara stared at him and started to lie across the seat.

"All the way into the foot well," he said. "Move, move, *move!*"

She unclipped her seat belt and threw herself below the dashboard. "What about you?"

"*Stay down.* It will be rough," he said. "Moving targets are harder to hit."

"But—"

"My phone is in my right pocket," he cut in.

She reached for the pocket along his leg.

"Call 911," he said. "If that doesn't work, use the radio."

"Why not use it now?" she asked as she yanked out his cell phone.

"Cooke's office tracks cell phones using 911."

As he spoke, the helicopter roared overhead with shattering speed and noise. Jay cranked hard left, then right, sending the truck forward in an erratic zigzagging motion.

Despite being shaken like dice in a box, Sara managed to stab out the three numbers.

The helicopter pulled up and around, away from the mountainside, arcing slowly into the air.

Jay figured the trajectory as fast as the pilot did. He turned hard left, barely holding the bucking wheel.

"We're going off road," he warned as he fought the wheel. "Did you get through?"

"Once, but it dropped. I'm trying again."

The truck bounced over the uneven terrain so hard, Jay's butt barely touched the seat. Sara braced herself as best she could. The phone flew out of her hand just as the 911 operator picked up. When she made a try for the phone, she was jerked away from it as the truck hit a rock.

"Is it safe to sit up?" she asked, her voice like her body. Too tight.

"Stay down there," he said. "Sounded like a .22 Uzi pistol, full automatic."

"What does that mean?"

"It burns through ammo fast, and they'll have to come closer to kill us."

She wondered if that was good or bad, but instead of asking she searched around on the dark, bouncing floorboard for the phone.

"We have to get under cover," he said. "They have the advantage until we can make those rocks."

"Do you recognize the helicopter?"

"No. But I'll bet we crossed its trail at Fish Camp."

Jay spun the wheel and swiftly worked the brakes and accelerator to keep the truck right side up while moving as fast as possible over the rough ground.

The sound of the chopper hammered down on them.

"Get as close to me as you can without getting in the way," he said.

Sara inched along the foot well. She could feel as much as hear the helicopter now, the sound an assault on her senses that made her want to scream. Frantically she scrambled to brace herself in the pitching truck.

"Get ready," Jay shouted over the noise. "We're going hard right."

The helicopter grew louder still, its relentless noise swallowing the rattle of the truck, rotors screaming the end of the world.

Heart racing, palms slippery with sweat, Sara watched Jay's face for a cue as to what might come next. For all the emotion he showed, he could have been cut from the granite itself. The truck careened over a small boulder, sending the phone sliding within her reach. Grabbing it, she braced herself with her feet and elbows as she punched in the three numbers again.

The phone made a connection but dropped it just as quickly.

She tried again.

"Now!" Jay yelled as he cranked the wheel hard, not letting up on the speed one bit.

Bullets stitched in a deadly silence that became a sharp metallic tattoo on the back of the truck bed. The downdraft pushed against the truck like a giant hand mashing them into the ground.

"Can we outrun it?" she shouted, watching his face.

"Not even if we could ditch the trailer," he said. "This truck was built for bad roads, not speed."

The truck groaned as the trailer pulled at the hitch and the back end swayed. The helo pulled up hard, tail down and cutting its turn just short of the mountainside.

"This guy's more likely to kill himself than us," he said.

"That's good, right?" She punched in the three numbers again.

"Only if he hurries up about it. Or his gunner runs out of ammo."

With a fast glance Jay checked the position of the .30-30, kept in place by just one strap now.

"I don't want to depend on them screwing up to save us," Sara said. Then, "*Damn it.* The connection keeps dropping. How far are we from cover?"

"Good news is they're taking a very long time to make this turn. Bad news is it won't be long enough for us to make it to the trees."

She stabbed the numbers again and prayed that the connection would hold.

It didn't.

WHAM! A bone-cracking sound rang through the truck, centered right under Sara's ear. It jolted her so hard that the phone went flying. She snatched at it and got lucky. She looked at Jay.

"You okay?" he asked without looking away from the rocky terrain. "Too many rocks to miss all of them."

"Can't we run faster than this?" she asked, her voice sounding odd to her abused ears.

"No. And the truck is better armor than your jacket. You okay? You sound funny."

"Whatever you hit was right by my head."

"Sorry." His eyes swept the landscape and found little joy. The laws of physics hadn't been suspended. They weren't going to get to the trees. "We have to split up. The helo will stick to me. You take the phone and hide in the rocks."

"I'm not leaving you, remember?" The phone in her hand shook. She gripped it tighter, so tight that her bones ached.

"They're finishing their turn now," Jay said. "The pilot has gone cautious all of a sudden."

She thumb-dialed 911 and pressed it to her ear.

He watched the chopper dart around as though expecting an ambush.

Something in that last turn spooked them. Or they're not really trying to kill us, but just want to freak us out.

Or maybe they're playing with us before the kill.

He caught the chopper in the rearview mirror. The bird was lower than it had been before.

Within pistol range. But a rifle would do the job better.

While he balanced the efficiency of rifle versus pistol, he listened to Sara relay information to the 911 operator.

"Where are we?" she yelled at him over the increasing rotor noise.

"Tell them to grab our coordinates off the phone."

The roar of the helicopter covered whatever she was yelling into the phone.

He looked at the helo and knew what they were doing as well as if he had been inside it. They were low and slow, lining up their shots more carefully.

Automatic gunfire ripped across the front of the truck bed and caromed off the hitch. The fusillade stopped as quickly as it had begun.

"What happened?" Sara asked.

"Maybe they didn't like the shot they were getting."

"The trailer! Is it—"

"It's safer than we are," he cut in. "Any fire it gets is accidental, which is odd, because the shooter got his training watching television."

"The paintings. They must know."

The helicopter passed overhead, pacing the truck. Wind kicked up hard as the helo dodged over to her side.

"Get up here enough to hold the wheel," he said. "*Move*."

She responded to the command in his voice before she was even aware of shifting position. The wheel bucked and jumped in her hand like a wild steer.

How did he manage to drive? Sara thought, fighting to hold on to the wheel.

The truck slowed and he opened the door.

"What are you—" she began.

The helicopter gunner opened fire again, taking aim at the front end of the truck. The first shots raked the bottom edge of the front windshield, turning it into a wild web of cracks. An uneven series of holes opened across the hood. Steam erupted from some of them.

"Up here!" Jay shouted.

She came all the way up and out of the foot well onto the seat, holding the wheel with one hand and bracing against the dashboard.

Before she could ask what he was doing, he was already out the door, standing on the running board, Glock out and aimed up toward the sky. He took a firm pull on the trigger and waited. The helicopter hovered about a hundred feet off, just pacing the truck.

The helo itself is a pretty big target, Jay thought, *but picking out anything specific on it is a fast way to failure.*

He squeezed off three shots from his .45. The slugs were big enough that they would pierce any interior walls and probably the side doors as well if they were closed. He was sure that the first shot was true. The other two were fast, a screaming double tap telling the attackers that their quarry was armed.

The gunner had been reloading his Uzi when the first bullet hit. He almost dropped his weapon at the sound of incoming fire.

Not used to it, are you, you chickenshit son of a bitch, Jay thought with satisfaction.

The helo reeled away like a dog smacked across the nose, breaking hard and peeling wide to the right.

Overreacting. Amateur mistake that could kill everyone aboard. And wouldn't that be sweet—if they don't crash on top of us.

"Jay! We're losing power!" Sara yelled over the noise.

He had already felt the change in the truck. Something more vital than the radiator had been hit.

"We have to bail," he shouted.

With a swift motion he holstered the pistol and held a hand out to her. Their momentum had slowed to a human running pace.

"You're going first," he said in a voice loud enough to carry over the dying truck and all-too-lively helicopter. "The second you hit the ground, roll. Then run for the rocks and find a place to get under cover from the front and above."

"You're crazy!" she yelled. "We're still moving!"

"Roll and then run for the hillside. *Go.*"

As he spoke, he pulled hard on her, lifting her out of the seat. Then he released her.

Sara shot past him with a stifled shriek. Still in the air, she curled into an awkward ball and landed hard, well away from the truck.

"Go, go, *GO*," Jay shouted at her, falling back into his military training.

She scrambled to her feet, oriented herself, and began a lurching run toward the cover of rocks.

The truck was at a walking pace now, as each bump bled off a little more momentum. Jay pulled the pistol again and tracked the helo. It was making a slow, cautious return, wary now that its prey had demonstrated an ability to shoot back.

Not much cover for me if the helo hovers in place. But if Sara is right, they've been avoiding the trailer.

He weighed the risks and yanked the rifle loose. *They won't come as close to a .30-30.*

The sound of the chopper increased suddenly. Somebody had decided on a fast, roaring run. Jay felt a hard push of wind in his face and smiled. That helo had a vicious headwind buffeting it.

He looked over in the direction Sara had run. There was a hint of green and gold before her flannel shirt was yanked up and out of sight beneath a tall outcropping of weathered granite.

Good. Now stay there and don't stick your head out.

The helo was pulling closer, nose down, hanging like a deadly ornament from its whirling rotors. Jay didn't have both cover and room to use the rifle. He laid it on the seat of the truck and jerked the Glock from its holster. Standing in the door frame, covering as much of his body as possible behind the door, he took aim and waited. He wanted a shot that did more than make noise. Even with his pants pockets loaded with extra clips and ammo, he wasn't wasting any more bullets.

Gunfire from the helo ripped an uneven string of bullets into the grass and then across the top of the truck, right through the roof and into the passenger compartment.

Jay returned fire with a one-two, one-two rhythm of shots. The first shots were wide. He corrected and heard pings as his own shots went home. Before he could take better aim, rotor wash and the smell of exhaust hit him hard, along with anything loose on the ground that had been sucked up by the rotors.

As he cleared his vision, the helo roared past. He saw the machine come around, shuddering in the head-wind. Mentally he measured his chances of running for cover with Sara.

No way. Helo is coming in again. All I'd do is lead them right to her.

He grabbed the rifle and hugged the outside of the truck bed as he moved back to get the trailer between himself and the helo.

Mighty valuable paintings here. You didn't shoot at them. Not even with me and my .45 lighting you up.

The wind roared hard, laying the grass down flat. He hoped Sara would think to tie her hair back and control the flapping tails of her flannel shirt so that they didn't give her away. But it was too late to tell her, too late for anything but the helo coming right at him.

Come on. Come on, you son of a bitch.

Then he realized the bird was turning, banking toward the mountainside. It began to quarter the area like a dog looking for a scent. The helo was on a hunting run.

But not for him.

Sara!

Chapter 22

The hammering roar of the helicopter came closer and closer with every pass across the mountainside. When the wind from the rotors slammed down at Sara, she tried to crawl inside the granite itself. She felt the edge of her borrowed flannel shirt tugged free by the rotor wash and wind, whipping against her body. Debris and grit choked her. The sound echoing inside her boulder hideout was so loud she felt like screaming along with it.

But for all the noise, she couldn't fix on the direction of the helicopter.

Where are they?

Which way should I run?

She edged forward until she could see through a hole just beyond the rim of the rocky overhang she had flung herself into. The natural hollow wasn't deep enough to protect her fully, but it was the best she could find. It was littered with small bits of rock that pelted her when the rotor wash hit just right.

But what really worried her was that she hadn't heard any more shots. The fear of Jay lying wounded—or worse—on the cold mountainside was a screaming inside her greater than any mechanical noise could drown out.

He probably found cover, like me, she told herself savagely. *Don't freak out. It won't do any good. You screamed yourself raw when the Camaro crashed and Kelly died so slowly—and what good did screaming do, anyway?*

Do what Jay said.

Stay put.

The roar grew louder and then louder still.

The helicopter isn't going after the truck. Why?

She didn't think about Jay anymore. She couldn't. If she did, she would run screaming down the mountain.

She peered over the edge and saw that the helicopter was heading right at her. Suddenly her cover seemed too small, too flimsy. The urge to break and run for somewhere safer almost strangled her as she fought it down. There was no time to get a better hiding spot. All she could do was press herself farther into the shallow trench and pray that the overhanging slab of granite concealed enough of her.

Cold wind whipped up in advance of the helicopter. The sky went hollow and black, sound echoing. She tried to make herself smaller, thinner. Invisible. But if her head was under cover, her boots stuck out. The opening was too narrow for her to fold up, much less to bring her knees under her chest.

The thumping of the rotor blades was like an alien heartbeat taking over her body, shaking her. Rock bit into her fingertips as she tried to claw closer to safety. She didn't think. She couldn't. The noise consumed her. She barely noticed the swirling grit biting into exposed skin.

The helicopter hovered, slamming small rocks and sticks around. A violent storm raged through her hiding place.

Gunfire stitched through the storm. It was almost random, searching.

They're trying to flush me out like some screaming bimbo in a bad movie.

The flapping of her flannel shirt made sunlight stutter through the opening near her feet. She had no protection from a ricochet. She grit her teeth together so she couldn't scream and pulled her feet in as much as she could, wanting to leave nothing exposed.

But there just wasn't enough room.

Come on, come on, *give me a human target,* Jay thought savagely.

Shooting the tail rotor out could too easily swerve the helo right into Sara. He kept on tracking the helicopter with his .30-30 but didn't have a shot. The bird was hovering low over the scree and shrubs jumbled at the base of the steep slope, working the land, spraying occasional shots.

Don't move, sweetheart. Please don't move. The noise won't kill you—but bullets will.

He knew her instinct would be to run from the threat. No matter how brave she was, everybody had a breaking point.

I've got to get them off her.

Suddenly the helicopter dropped and was eclipsed by the trailer's bulk, which had been shielding Jay. His former shelter was now in the way. He had to get in the open to shoot the chopper down.

He ducked away from the trailer's cover and stood, feet apart, steady as if he had roots in the land. He didn't notice the rifle's weight any more than he would notice the hot shells ejecting when he worked the lever. Breathing out, he gently brought the trigger back.

The shooting from the helicopter stopped.

Reloading, Jay thought. *Now if the helo would just get its ass out of my face I could—*

Wind buffeted the helicopter, swinging its tail.

He pulled the trigger.

One.

The shot boomed out of the barrel and went right through the open passenger compartment, starboard side. Through the scope, he saw the pilot jump and the helo lurch to the left.

Two.

He settled against the recoil and followed, taking aim at the pilot again. A spark arced off the metal skin near the back of the open side door. He didn't wait to fire again.

Three.

The helicopter turned in place, but not quickly enough to change its profile in time. Over the booming shots of his rifle, Jay heard a long and wild chatter of the Uzi firing, the whole clip going off, finger down. But it wasn't aimed near anyone at all.

Four.

He'd dropped the barrel just a little bit to follow the open door as best he could. He couldn't see the gunman anymore. The next shot hit farther back along the passenger compartment. Through a gap in the clouds, the sun flashed hard on the helo's enameled skin as the pilot turned the machine to reorient it.

Jay let the last shots go.

Five.

Six.

As the helo spun toward him, he slung the strap of the empty rifle over his head and drew the Glock. At the rate the helo was coming, the pistol was the better choice.

More bullets, faster to reload.

The chopper was nearly head-on to him now, and less than sixty feet away. Grit and small rocks and debris scoured his face as the helo closed in. He shot furiously. A cloudy spot formed on the glass of the cockpit window in the instant before the shock wave of the bullet turned the windshield into an opaque mass of cracks.

Jay couldn't see anything through it—but then, neither could the attackers. He hit the ground and lay flat as the helo skids passed over him close enough to touch. When the bird lifted and spun away at a sharp angle, he was on his feet, pistol ready.

No more shots came.

Chickenshit bastard's probably sucking on the deck rather than shooting out the door.

Jay turned and ran hard, angling away from where he'd last seen Sara. If there was any fight left in the attackers, he didn't want to point out her hiding place. As he ran, he changed the magazine in his Glock. If he had time, reloading the rifle would be next.

Roaring past him, the helicopter wobbled as it turned to intersect his path. Then it swung away again. A thin stream of smoke washed into a corkscrew pattern as the helo retreated.

There was no more gunfire.

Jay kept running, but he changed his angle, each step now bringing him closer to Sara's hiding place.

The helicopter's sound shifted as it turned and headed back in the direction it had originally come from.

Keep down, sweetheart. Don't assume they won't make another pass.

Dodging boulders and scrub, he ran flat out, then dived behind a knucklebone of rock that was too high to jump over. He twisted before he hit the ground, landing in a controlled roll. Before he could blink his eyes clear of grit and see the retreat for himself, his ears told him that the helo had had enough and was leaving at full throttle.

It wasn't a pretty retreat. The pilot and the wind were wrestling for control of the airship.

Die, you bastards. Just put it in the mountain and fucking die.

"Sara! Can you hear me?" he yelled.

Nothing answered but the fading drone of the helo.

"SARA!"

An indistinct sound came back to him.

His name.

Instantly he was clawing his way over rocks to more even ground where he could run toward the sound. He heard his name again, called to Sara again, and ran toward her hiding place. When he reached it, he slid to his knees, reaching inside to pull her out.

And felt blood.

"J-Jay . . . ?"

"Don't move, sweetheart. I've got you."

God, let me change places with her. Let me be the one hurt and have her be whole.

But it hadn't happened in Afghanistan and it wouldn't happen here.

"Where does it hurt?" he asked, his voice sounding a lot calmer than he felt.

"I—" The word ended in a sound of pain as she tried to sit up.

"Easy, love. Easy. Talk to me. Where do you hurt? Can you move your arms and legs?"

"Yes. There's just no *room.*"

"I'm going to put my hands under your shoulders and ease you out of there. Tell me if it hurts."

"Do it," she said hoarsely. "Get me out of this coffin."

His thighs and shoulders flexed as he inched her far enough out from under the overhang to see where she was wounded. A gash in her neck bled way too freely.

Without even being aware of it, he shucked off the rifle and his jacket and tore his left shirtsleeve away from his shoulder.

"Get me—out," she said, struggling to move.

"Easy, love. Let me bandage your neck first." He tore off his other sleeve for a compress and bound her neck as much as he could. "Now, one good pull and— What the hell is that?"

She was so relieved to see sky beyond his face that she almost passed out. Instead she took several deep breaths and tried to figure out what he was talking about.

". . . nature of the emergency. Repeat. What is the nature of the emergency?"

In disbelief Jay pried her fingers away from the phone she had hung on to like life itself.

"Is this 911?" he demanded.

"What is the nature of the emergency?" The woman's voice was maddeningly calm.

"A woman has been shot. Bleeding is controlled but not stopped."

His hand pressed on the bandage as he spoke, trying to stem the red tide. The shirtsleeve was already saturated with blood.

Keep a steady pressure. Don't worry about the dirt. They'll clean her up at the hospital.

"Understood. What is your location?"

"I'm on the old Weiss road at the base of Satler Ridge. We need a medical chopper scrambled to our location." He spoke clearly, calmly. "Fast. Or she'll bleed out."

And inside himself he screamed.

"Could you be more precise about the location, please?" the woman asked.

"We're in the wilderness. Fix on the damned phone!"

"Working on it. There it is. Medevac is getting ready to dust off."

Relief went through him at the familiar term. "You served?"

"Half a tour. Injured. Do you want me to stay on the line until the helo gets there?"

"Not necessary. Thanks for your help."

He left the connection open and focused on his bloody fingers, keeping the pressure even. Sara was breathing steadily, but too shallow.

Distant thunder rolled up the slope.

Bloody hell. Medevac just loves flying in thunderstorms.

But fly they would if there was a real chance of saving a life.

Gently Jay touched Sara's cheek. It was too cool.

He wrapped his jacket around her, propped up her feet on a handy rock, and waited.

"Look on the bright side, sweetheart," he said, pillowing her head with his left hand. "I'm not having to hold down the LZ—landing zone to you—by myself while trying to bandage what few men survived. That's how I got to be called captain. I was the last man standing."

He heard his wild laugh and throttled it. Keeping pressure on her wound, he memorized the lines of her face, touching her gently, keeping his savage rage bottled up inside.

Listening to her breathe.

Chapter 23

Sara awoke in a hospital room under a paper gown. The room was mint green, too bright. One look and she felt like she'd been there for a week.

"Jay?" Her voice came out as a dry croak.

"Easy, sweetheart. I'm right here."

She felt his hand press against her right shoulder. Her neck hurt, and there was a nagging tug from an IV setup in her left hand.

"Thirsty," she said, trying to sit up.

"Juice or water?" As he spoke, he raised the bed to a more upright position. "Doctor said for you to drink as much as you want and then drink some more. You were a pint or two low by the time we got here."

Suddenly it all came back to her, the relentless helicopter and shots and hideous noise, Jay pulling her out from beneath a rock overhang she'd thought would be her grave.

"Are you all right?" she asked as her dark eyes searched him for signs of injury.

"Not a scratch. Wish I could say the same for you."

She took the juice he handed her and drank every drop. "Why am I in the hospital? Other than being thirsty and wanting to rip out that IV, I feel fine."

"You were wounded."

"Where?"

"Left side of your neck. Ricochet. You had bled a lot by the time the chopper got you out."

"The same bastards who shot at us rescued me?"

"No," he said, urging water on her. "Medevac. We're in Jackson now."

"What happened to the first helicopter?" she asked before she drank.

"It preferred targets that didn't shoot back." He smiled thinly as he remembered the helo's ragged retreat. "More water?"

"No. I have to pee."

"That's good," Jay said. "Means that you're rehydrating."

The curtain surrounding her bed opened and a man about her own age appeared. His skin was a chocolate almost as beautiful as his smile.

"I'm Dr. Burnham," he said. "How do you feel? Besides wanting to pee."

"Hungry."

"Excellent. I'll have food sent in."

"I'd rather eat out," she said. "Not that I'm not grateful, but—"

"You want to leave," Burnham said. "Are you sure? You weren't in great shape when you came in. A bullet fragment ripped into your neck and nicked the occipital vein, not your carotid or jugular. But still lots of blood, big mess, easy to panic. Fortunately Mr. Vermilion knew what to do to slow the bleeding until you got here."

"He's a very good man to have around," Sara said, touching Jay's hand on her shoulder. "But however messy I was when I arrived, I feel fine now, except that you've pumped so much fluid into me that I really have to pee."

"Bedpan?" Burnham offered, watching her bedside monitors.

"Toilet." A statement, not a question.

Burnham looked at her expression, eyed the depleted IV bag, and removed the needle from the back of her hand, talking as he worked. "Other than blood loss, you're very healthy. Wish we saw more like you. Now, let's see if you feel as good as you think you do." He took off the blood pressure cuff. "Move slowly."

"I'll help her," Jay said.

"Only as far as the door," she said.

"We'll discuss it when we get there."

Burnham hid a smile. "Let her do as much as she can alone."

"That would be all of it," she said firmly.

She put her legs over the side of the bed and sat fully upright. There was a moment of light-headedness, but it passed quickly.

Jay watched her intently. "Easy, sweetheart. You have four stitches along the side of your neck."

"I know. It feels like they left the needle in."

"Let me see," Burnham said.

He lifted the dressing and ran his finger very gently just outside the wound, but Sara still flinched. The whole area was tender.

"No needle," Burnham said. "It's just raw. Ricochets make the worst wounds, but we cleaned you up real nice."

"You have a lot of experience with bullet wounds?" Jay asked.

"I worked ER in Chicago for four years. Discovered I like Jackson better." Burnham pressed the dressing into place. "If you still feel up to it, the bathroom is about twelve feet away."

She eased down onto her feet and walked with increasing steadiness toward the bathroom. Though

Jay didn't touch her, he was never more than inches away.

The door shut firmly in his face.

"That's a determined lady," Burnham said. "Don't let her overdo once she's out."

"I'll brush up on my calf-roping skills," Jay said drily.

"I'd like to see that. Change the dressing every couple of days and come back in a week and a half to have the stitches taken out. I'm going to put her on a course of antibiotics as a precaution. If she's using oral birth control, you'll need to take other precautions as well. You'll get the antibiotics along with the discharge instructions. Make sure she takes it easy. Bed rest or some sitting at a desk. No more for the next twenty-four hours. After that, take it day to day."

"Thank you, Doc. We owe you."

"If you hadn't stemmed the bleeding, I doubt she'd have made it. She's very determined, but that only goes so far. Then gravity takes over and down you go."

The bathroom door opened and closed.

"I've buzzed for the nurse," Burnham said. "Hospital rules require that you be wheeled to your transportation."

"I can go?" Sara asked eagerly. "And here I was expecting a week in a private room complete with cabana boys."

Burnham laughed softly. "These days a transfusion is treated like an oil change. An outpatient procedure." His surgical gloves snapped as he pulled them off. "If you change your mind in the next few minutes, we're having meatloaf tonight."

"Pass," she said. "But thank you, Doctor."

"You can thank me by not showing up again."

He was out the door before she could say any more.

"Busy man," Jay said. "Good, too. Your stitches could have been done by a plastic surgeon."

"I hope you know where my clothes are. And why are your sleeves torn off?"

"Instant bandages." As she turned toward the bed, he tried not to look at all the places the paper gown didn't cover.

She had really sweet cheeks.

"Henry sent one of the hands down here with some clothes for both of us, and that rucksack you call a purse," Jay said. "We'll stay here."

"Here?" She looked at the hospital room in dismay.

"Town. We'll spend a few days in civilization while you recover."

"What about the Norwegian reunion?" she asked.

"They left yesterday."

"Oh." Still a little light-headed, Sara decided to sit on the bed.

Her stomach growled. Loudly.

Jay stuck a straw in another box of juice and handed it to her. "Drink this while I get the clothes."

She all but inhaled the juice. "Who would have thought that being shot makes you hungry."

"Your body is handing out marching orders. Eat, eat, and eat until you've replaced all your blood. Drink, too. A lot."

"I thought the transfusion took care of that."

"It kept you alive. Staying that way is up to you."

"Lovely bedside manner," she muttered.

"You're welcome."

She glanced up at him. For the first time she noticed that he looked tired and grim. Grim most of all.

"I'm sorry," she said, pulling his face down to hers. "Thank you for saving my life."

"For nearly getting you killed, you mean."

"That's on the shooter, not you." She kissed him gently, then less gently.

It was Jay who broke the kiss. "Any more and I'll be inside you when the checkout nurse comes calling. I nearly lost you, sweetheart. And now I want you like hell burning."

"Same goes," she said, reaching for him.

He held her back. "Do you need help dressing?"

She looked at the bloodstained fatigues he still wore. They did nothing to disguise his blunt hunger.

"I think I can handle it." Then she realized where she was looking and added hastily, "Getting dressed, I mean."

He gave a crack of laughter and dumped her clothes on the bed. "You're going to be the death of me, Sara." *Or the saving.*

She reached for the clothes on the bed. A woman's ranch clothes—jeans, a shirt, a pullover sweater, a jacket, and a scarf she wanted nowhere near her neck at the moment.

"Everything is out of fashion, but a lot warmer than paper." He turned his back on the temptation of her undressing.

"As long as these weren't Liza's," Sara said.

"Dad burned hers. These were my mother's."

"Thank God for that," Sara muttered. She shivered as the cotton shirt hit her bare, hardened nipples. A bra hadn't been included in the pile of clothes, but panties were. She pulled them on and quickly began to button her shirt.

"How are we getting out of here?" she asked. "I didn't notice a lot of taxis when I landed here."

"I rented a truck."

"Of course," she said. "Next stupid question. Has the sheriff tracked the helicopter? And is it safe to turn around now?"

He turned and was treated to a vision of long, long legs, sleek and warm and vibrant against the stark white sheets.

Safe? God, woman, you're killing me.

"Nothing yet on the helo," he said, his voice unusually deep.

She had buttoned her shirt wrong. When she noticed it, her fingers fumbled and she gave up in disgust.

"You want me to button it again?" he asked.

"I sh-should be able to do it myself."

She was crying.

He crouched down so they were at eye level. "Sweetheart?"

"I d-don't know why I'm c-crying." Her voice broke and her arms wrapped around his shoulders.

"Last of the adrenaline," he said, gathering her close, savoring the hot, living feel of her breath against his neck. "Don't ever scare me like that again. I don't think I could take it."

She heard the strain in his voice, and realization hit her like an avalanche. His strong arms around her were hard and yet trembling. He was getting strength from her just as much as she was getting it from him. They were linked beyond skin, deeper than their own flesh, deeper than anything she had ever felt.

Tears kept coming, washing away the fear that had lurked beneath her determination. What was left behind was stronger for it.

For both of them.

The café was small, the kind that tourists overlooked and locals loved. It was late for a weekday dinner in a working town, so there were few patrons. Despite that, Jay had chosen a table at the back and watched every person as if he or she was a potential attacker.

"Tell me you aren't armed," Sara said.

"Okay, I'm not armed."

"Is it legal?"

"To be unarmed?" he asked blandly.

She gave him a lopsided smile and put her hand on his thigh underneath the table. "What am I going to do with you?"

"You could move your hand up and to the right and then—"

"Evening, Jay. What brings you to town?" the server asked.

"Hello, John. How are Millie and the kids?"

"Right now, Millie's screaming at the sous chef"— John winked at Sara—"who is also our oldest son."

Jay shook his head. "Same as always. But she's a hell of a chef."

"That she is. The special tonight is scallops with vanilla bean sauce or ono with a vodka reduction on a bed of lemon grass. The seafood was flown in today."

Sara felt like she had been whipsawed into an alternate reality. Except for the decor, the café and its specials could have been in San Francisco.

Yet I almost died in a wilderness where the most terrifying animal was human.

"Would you care for something to drink while you decide on your choice?" John asked.

"Sara?" Jay asked.

She shook her head. "I'm muzzy enough already, thanks. Iced tea with lemon will do for me."

"I'll have the same," Jay said. "I'm ready to order if Sara is."

She grabbed the menu and saw that it was brief. "Lamb chops, medium rare. No salad. I'm too hungry for rabbit food."

Jay smiled. "Porterhouse for me. Rare. Nobody seasons it like Millie."

"Salad?" John asked.

"No thanks. I'm not going to stand between a hungry woman and her dinner."

John nodded and headed for the kitchen.

"Are you okay?" Jay asked. "You look a little . . . stunned."

"Like Alice, I just discovered that every looking glass has two sides and both are unexpected."

"What do you mean?"

"Hawaiian fish in Jackson? Fresh scallops?" She shook her head. "I should have dressed up for dinner."

"This is the kind of place where the food dresses for you, not vice versa." He brushed the back of his hand down her cheekbone. "Beautiful woman."

She kissed his fingertips. "Sweet liar."

A few tables away, sleet rattled loudly against the window.

"Are you warm enough? Would you like my jacket?" he asked. "Blood loss makes you cold."

"I'm fine. Stop worrying."

"Not likely. It will take a while for the picture of your blood soaking through my shirtsleeves to fade."

Her breath came in sharply, then went out in a sigh. "I'll be having a few memories, too. You standing in the open, firing at that damned helicopter. Talk about David and Goliath . . ."

Jay's phone buzzed with an incoming text. He pulled out the phone, looked, and put the phone away.

"News?" Sara asked.

"Liza. Said she wasn't giving us one minute of extra time because we had a 'problem.'"

"What a bitch."

"You're too nice. The word I'm thinking of has more bite."

They were silent for several minutes while he held her hand against his thigh, both of them needing the contact.

"We made it," he said finally. "That's what counts. Let me know if you need any pain meds. I brought some in with me."

"No thanks. Like my *unarmed* companion, I prefer to stay sharp." Images of Jay standing and firing at the helicopter swept over Sara in waves, unsettling her heartbeat. She shook it off and told herself to stay in the present. "What does Sheriff Cooke think of all this?"

"I gave him the helo's registration numbers. They came back null."

"Null?"

"Phony. Now he's looking for a rented helo, beginning at the local airport. The bird had to come from somewhere and be piloted by someone. The names on the records will be false, but it's a place to start. Flight plans have to be filed before anything leaves the ground. There are a finite number of chopper pilots around. It's a game of elimination."

"If I'd been flying that helicopter, I'd be on my way to Mexico right now," she said.

"So would I."

"If the pilot and his murderous friend have fled, why are you sitting in a lovely café *unarmed?*"

"Paranoia," he said, feeling the weight of extra magazines in the clean fatigues Henry had sent. "I'm hoping the helo flew into the mountainside. The weather was headed downhill when we left, and the pilot was nothing special." *Wish I'd killed the bastards.*

"What about the paintings?"

"Henry and Billy took a second truck up. They should be halfway to town by now. I told Henry to leave the paintings in the back room of the gallery."

"What gallery?"

"The one I rented to you," Jay said.

She blinked. "Oh. Thanks. With that and the hospital bill, how much do I owe you?"

"The ranch paid your hospital bill—and save your breath, you won't talk me out of this one. We can wrangle over the rent after the dust settles. If it settles."

"You expect more trouble," she said flatly.

"I doubt that the helo pilot and his Uzi-toting friend broke into the storage yard before they came to have a try at us. That means someone else spray-painted the security cameras, sheared off the locks, and took whatever they wanted. Only the Vermilion storage unit was hit."

"Paintings?" she asked instantly.

"No. Just stuff we didn't want to store in the barn and didn't want to give away at the time."

"We're running out of places that JD could have stored a full-size painting like *Muse*," Sara said. "Assuming Liza's right and JD had it. Big if. And here comes John. Does he have a replicator back there?"

"Just Millie," Jay said. "Outside the tourist district— and this is outside—the time is late and they want to close."

John served them and vanished.

Jay's steak knife gleamed in the candlelight. His face was lit from below, throwing shadows that moved as the flame did, making him look as dangerous as the day had been.

"There are still the offices to search," he said, slicing into the beef. "JD left a bunch of personal papers in his downtown office that I haven't had time or need to go through. Maybe there's something in there."

"We can check before we go to the hotel or motel or wherever we're staying," she said, diving into the meal as eagerly as he had. "Wow," she said after the first bite. "The seasonings are incredibly sophisticated. Millie could have a job in any restaurant in San Francisco."

He smiled. "That's where they came from. They like the hours here better. As for where we're staying, the ranch keeps an apartment in town at the top of one of the Vermilion buildings. I called while we were still at the hospital, so the place is ready for us. We're going straight there."

"What about JD's papers?"

"Forget the papers. The only thing you're going to be checking out tonight is me."

"Puts a new spin on the idea of bed rest," she said, smiling.

"It's a two-bedroom suite."

"Waste of a good room."

Jay decided it was easier to eat than to argue.

Shivering despite the old shearling jacket she wore, Sara waited for Jay to sort out the Vermilion building key from the others he carried. The passing storm had dragged winter out of an all-too-shallow grave and left everything covered by snow that was a chilling mixture of icy bits and slush that froze when it hit the still-cold ground. The sky was a rumpled steel gray that reflected the town's lights. Stars appeared occasionally between the wind-torn clouds.

The door opened, breathing warmth into the outdoors. Unfamiliar suitcases were stacked just inside the room.

"Ours?" she asked.

"Yes. Get inside. It's just cracking the teens out here. Worse, with the wind."

"I thought winter was over," she said with her nose buried in the jacket's woolly lining.

"We've got four seasons here," he said, shutting and locking the door behind himself. "Three of them have 'winter' in the name. We're in 'still winter,' right on the edge of 'construction season.' Last week's sun? That was a little tease. Not that we wait for good weather to build things around here. The ground thaws enough, building begins."

As he talked, he led her to the elevator just off the lobby. In the light from the overhead fluorescent bulbs, her skin looked too pale. Yet even in the harsh light, her beauty caught at his heart. Her features were a woman's still holding the sweet memory of youth.

How can I let her go?

On the heels of that inner cry came the answer. *She's not yours to keep. Remember that. Enjoy what we have. Sometimes tomorrow never comes.*

"Mark Twain said he never had a winter so cold as summer in San Francisco," Sara said as the elevator slid smoothly upward.

"I don't think Twain spent too much time butted up against the Tetons in still-winter-should-be-spring."

He walked her to the door of the suite. Nobody was in sight. The hall carpet had been freshly vacuumed. Their footprints were the only ones that showed. Even so, once the door was unlocked, he and the Glock made a fast tour of the suite.

Empty.

He holstered the Glock and went back to the hall.

"Clear?" Sara asked.

"Clear. Pick your bedroom."

"The one with you in it."

He locked the hallway door and turned back to her. "You need sleep."

"I need you."

He pulled her close, holding her, rocking gently. "I'm here."

For now.

The phone in his shirt pocket buzzed. He held Sara firmly against him for a moment longer, breasts soft against his chest, before reaching for his cell.

She felt his muscles flex as he pulled the phone out and looked at it.

"It's Cooke." He hit the answer button. "Hello, Sheriff. Anything new?"

She nestled in again, hearing his voice rumbling through his chest against her face. He slid his fingers into her hair and rubbed her scalp.

"Unless you feel like taking a drive right now," Cooke said, "I'll be sending you some pictures."

"Send them. It's damned cold outside."

"Don't I know it," Cooke said. "I'm ankle deep in icy mush, looking at a wrecked helicopter."

"Our shooters crashed?"

"Somebody did. White with a diagonal green stripe, null registration numbers, and seven bullet holes that we've found so far. You know where the weaknesses in a chopper are."

"The biggest one is the pilot," Jay said.

"You got him, too. Helicopter went in hard."

"What about the shooter?"

"He packed it in with the bird," Cooke said. "No need for another medevac run. These boys are one hundred percent dead. Cut and dried, at least as helicopter drive-by shootings go. Which I think is a first for Jackson County. Congratulations."

"Am I in trouble?" Jay asked.

"We'll need a statement, but that's it. Personally, I think you did the county a favor."

"The only favor I was looking for was survival. Is there anything beyond circumstantial to tie this to Fish Camp?"

"A Paul Basal Shadow—fourteen inches of knife for the man who's afraid his dick is too short."

"He won't need to worry about that now," Jay said.

Cooke laughed darkly. "No, he surely won't. Serrated top on the knife. Should make a distinctive mark on flesh. I'll let you know when we make the match. And if I don't hear from you right away, I'll assume that the pictures I send are of the same helicopter that shot at you."

"I'll check as soon as you hang up."

"You two get some rest now. I'll see you tomorrow and—Oh, wait. Almost forgot. My gum-chewing crime tech sorted out three tread patterns at the death scene. The pilot and the shooter are good for two of them. The third one was in some spilled paint and was probably made earlier than the others. Didn't match any boots the Solvangs owned, though. Henry never wears anything but cowboy boots, and the tread wasn't anything like your old combat boots."

"I guess it's a good thing I'm armed," Jay said.

"Stay that way. I don't have a spare deputy to watch over you. You two sleep good, now."

Chapter 24

"Don't look so discouraged," Jay said to Sara the following morning. "The weather is mostly sunny, we have another whole building to search, and more receptionists to terrorize. The day is young." He yawned. "A lot younger than I am. Not that I'm complaining."

"Your fault. You decided that I was so fragile that you had to take your time. Hoo-hah! No complaints here."

He laughed so hard he had to lean on the building.

"What?" she asked.

"I think you meant 'booyah.'" He snickered.

"Isn't that what I said?"

"Not quite. Military slang can be tricky."

"What did I say?" she asked.

"I'll tell you when we aren't in public." He swallowed a laugh. "But now that I think of it, you were accurate. For me, it was the best part of the night. Snug and hot and—"

"I'm getting the message," she cut in. "Part of the female anatomy, right?"

"Oh yeah. Very female."

She just shook her head and wished she could laugh, too. But the Vermilion building where they had stayed the night, and searched after breakfast, was empty of any portraits. There had been other landscapes—a few quite valuable—by various artists, but nothing that resembled *Muse*.

The second building to be searched was three stories of red-yellow brickwork and modest yet extensive concrete façade work that was a century old. Morning light slanted across it. The word *VERMILION* stood out in an arc of capital letters.

"Office manager said there's a master key in his office waiting for us," Jay said.

He took her up the stairs slowly, one at a time, his arm around her waist in case she needed help.

And his eyes searched every shadow for someone lying in wait.

"You're being ridiculous," she said as he practically lifted her to the next step. "Sweet, but ridiculous."

"I'm not taking any chances." *I don't want either of us to end up in the sheriff's photos, smashed and bloody, wearing a look of terror.* "Talk to me about exactly what we're looking for. There was a portrait in that other building that you didn't look at twice."

"Custer used hard edges, bold strokes, lots of contrast, especially in his color choices. But he also said in one of the notes I found that for 'her' he painted like Monet. Impressionistic, softer lines, romantic."

"Custer as a romantic. I'll believe it when I see it."

The interior of the building was sturdy and austere, grudgingly acknowledging modernity with its clean lines and lack of ornamentation. The hallways were lit with suspended lamps still burning incandescent bulbs.

There was art between every doorway, on every wall, and in every hallway.

"Good Lord," Sara said, and checked the charge on her phone. Three quarters full.

"I'm told the people who work here refer to it as the museum," he said.

"Better than the 'mausoleum,' which was what I called the first office I worked in."

Jay picked up the key at the reception desk and they began searching. Sara tried to do justice to each painting, taking photographs and brief notes, but after the first hour they all ran together into one category: not *Muse.*

She leaned against a wall and sighed.

"You okay?" he asked.

"Tired."

"I knew that this was overdoing it."

"It has to be done. By me," she added firmly.

"But you don't have to be on your feet, do you?"

He went back to an empty office and returned with a rolling desk chair. He nudged it against the back of her knees in silent command.

Relieved, she sat down.

"Only another two rooms on this floor," he said. "The good news is that most of the art is on the main floor for the public to see. The local schools tour every year."

"The bad news," Sara said, "is we're flat running out of places to look. You sure JD didn't have any paintings in the storage unit?"

"If he did, they weren't listed on the inventory sheet he kept at the ranch."

The final two rooms yielded two Custers each.

Landscapes.

"Right," she said. "Wheel me down to the elevator and we'll check the other floors."

He looked at her face. It was grim and set, a person nerving up for the last of a grueling hike.

"Let's rest and then—" he began.

"I won't walk anymore," she cut in. "Let's just do this."

After a few minutes, the elevator door opened like the antique it was. Sara eyed the threshold of the cage, which was nearly an inch higher than the hallway. A normal wheelchair would have had no problem. The office chair would send her flying at the first hard bump.

She started to stand up, only to find herself lifted, chair and all, into the elevator.

"Maybe you're not David," she said. "Maybe you're Goliath."

"Too many eyes."

She smiled faintly and touched his cheek. "You're thinking of ogres."

Jay kissed her gently and punched in the second floor. The cage lurched upward. When the doors opened, it was the hallway that was higher than the cage. He had to lift the chair out.

The second floor seemed to specialize in historic photographs plus a few paintings of historical events. It didn't take long to search before they were back in the hallway. When the elevator door opened, the feeling of being lifted no longer surprised her, but it did give her an acute understanding of Jay's strength.

He's always so careful with me, I forget how power-ful he is.

The cage lurched upward.

"Historical photographs are enjoying a revival," she said. "Some of those were of quite high quality. That DiMaggio painting of Hoover Dam under construction would make some collector very happy. If you want to sell, I could recommend appropriate experts."

"I'll keep it in mind when the fire sale kicks in." He watched her from the corner of his eye. She looked drawn, pale, but he didn't know how much of it was a hangover from yesterday and how much was disappointment. "Only one office to search up here. JD used it until he was too sick to care. Then he went back to the ranch to die. The other offices are held by tenants who do their own decorating."

Just one room? Sara thought, horrified that the search was all but over. Her hand fisted on the arm of the chair.

Saying nothing, he loosened her fingers and kissed her palm.

The elevator was level this time. He rolled her to an office door, unlocked it, and rolled her through.

The wall opposite the desk was dominated by a beautiful canvas of Jackson Hole, a muscular sunset study in pink and magenta and violet. It was signed by Weekly.

"That's stunning," she said. "I never understood why Weekly didn't become a bigger name."

"Maybe his art was bought by people who weren't interested in the critics."

She half smiled. "I think you're right."

The other walls were filled with Custer's work.

Landscapes.

"More empty land with a huge sky looming above," she said. Then, "Listen to me. Not long ago I couldn't get enough of his work and now I'm disappointed because these aren't the mythical portrait."

"I'll bet Ahab felt the same," Jay said. "Just another damn whale."

He parked her near JD's immense desk. Idly she ran a hand over its spotless surface.

"You could land a helicopter on this," she said, then grimaced. "Sorry. I guess I still feel kind of hunted."

"So do I," he said, thinking of the third pair of boot prints.

"Probably because we've been hunted."

He shrugged and returned to the topic of the desk. "Roomy underneath, too." He tapped it with a knuckle and laughed. "When I was a kid and Mother was too sick to watch me, JD would bring me here and park me under the desk with some comics. Then he would pace around talking on the phone, not even seeing the paintings on the walls."

"There's no *Muse*," Sara said starkly. "Odds are, it never existed. Why is Liza so convinced it's real? She was acting like she was there to see it and hold it."

"She acts like that about everything. It's her world and we're just tenants who don't pay enough rent." Jay ran through the desk drawers one at a time, flipping through their contents. "There's some old paperwork here, too. Maybe I really will do a family history."

She scanned some of the papers. "That's all about ranch land and head counts and not about the paintings." She chewed on her lip and stared at something only she could see.

He took her hand and placed it between his. She was hot. Not fever-hot, just alive-hot. "Relax, sweetheart. We have six more days."

"To do what?" she asked. "Rent a van, go picking in old houses, hit swap meets and galleries for two hundred miles around? Maybe we can sell the reality show."

He laughed.

She put both hands on the chair as if to brace herself to stand.

"What do you think you're doing?" he asked.

"I saw a restroom sign down the hall."

"Good idea. I could use one myself."

He rolled her out the door and down the hall, stopping at a door marked LADIES. The one marked GENTS was across the hall.

"Easy does it," he said, bracing her with his arm as she stood.

"I'm not made of spun sugar," she grumbled.

He licked his lips. "Could have fooled me."

Ignoring him, she opened the door and shut it pointedly in his face. "Go find your own."

Naturally the room was dark. Sara began patting down the wall for the light switch.

Welcome to Wyoming. Set the clocks back before motion-sensor lights were invented.

Yet the meal last night was as sophisticated as any I've eaten.

She found the switch and snapped it on. Light flooded the room. She went through the small vanity anteroom and into the restroom itself. When she turned down the aisle between the stalls, Sara stopped in disbelief.

From the far wall, a woman stared back at her. She was icy, cast in pale pinks and purples, with green undertones to the shadows.

Muse.

In a bathroom.

Stunned, she could only shake her head in disbelief.

Muse wasn't what she'd imagined at all. If this was a romantic portrait, it was the dark side of romanticism. Enigmatic, moody, vibrating with distance and emotions that were as difficult as the portrait itself. Though the rendering and technique were different from what Sara was used to seeing from Custer, there were enough echoes of his more familiar work that she had no doubt as to who had painted it.

The woman herself was pleased, almost exultant. Sara could see it around her eyes and enigmatic smile. There was triumph, but no warmth to it, no generosity, nothing shared. It was the woman's victory alone.

Sara stood and stared at the painting, the female face almost lost in the shadows of the cabin backdrop, which was dusky gray and pale but for the indigo and violet of the starless sky pouring through the window. The painting wasn't comforting at all, and in that it was unmistakably Custer.

Studying *Muse,* Sara felt a sense of lost dreams and desperate longing.

She also sensed that the painting itself was maddeningly incomplete, even at odds with itself. The dissonance in the canvas set her teeth on edge.

Jay's voice yanked her out of the painting. "Sara? Are you all right? I know women take longer, but seven minutes?"

"Come here," she called. "Hurry."

Before she finished speaking he was in the door, through the powder room, and striding toward her.

"Look," she said. "*Muse.*"

He stopped and stared at the painting, motionless, emotions cycling through his expression from confusion to wonder to relief to something else, something much more difficult to name.

"In the ladies' room," he said. "So JD would never have to look at it. Son of a bitch."

"We found it!"

She threw her arms around him, hugging him hard enough to make her stitches protest. He lifted her off her feet and spun her around before he put her down carefully.

"Take *Muse* down," she said. "I'll help you carry it."

"I can—"

"It's not safe for just one person to carry. This painting isn't leaving my sight until we can get it secured."

"Somewhere that Liza won't know about it. Or Barton. Or—"

"You're not telling her?" Sara cut in.

"No hurry. We're holding the trump card now." He looked at it, jaw set, studying the woman's face. "But who the hell is this muse, and why would Liza care?"

Chapter 25

When Jay tiptoed back into their bedroom, the afternoon sun had gone over closer to sunset than to dawn. Moments later he was stripping.

"You're cold," Sara mumbled as she pulled the blankets higher around her.

"You're warm," he said as he slid naked into bed. He nuzzled beneath the blankets until he found a breast against his lips. "I sense real possibilities."

She stretched sensuously against him. "Where were you?"

"Checking on things—the ranch, the paintings, talking to the Solvang family about funeral arrangements."

In a flash she was fully awake. "What time is it?"

"After four."

"You should have gotten me up," she said, horrified that a simple nap had stretched into hours.

"You needed the sleep. Besides, I was looking forward to waking you up from the inside out."

"Oh, well, in that case."

She pulled the covers up over both of them. In the
sensuous twilight, they loved each other until they were
a languid, sated tangle of flesh and bone.

A cell phone on the bedside table buzzed.

"It's yours," she said.

"Yeah." He emerged from the blankets, swiped his
phone off the table, hit the answer button. "What?"

"Hello to you, too," Cooke said. "When did you
turn into a daytime sleeper?"

"When there was something worth staying in bed
for." He put the phone on speaker and pulled Sara back
into his arms. "What's up?"

"We found a cell phone that we missed in our first
pass through the wreckage of the helicopter. Pilot's
phone. The shooter's was in too many pieces to put
back together. Direct hit from what looked like a .45.
But this phone was in a fancy case so the guts are mostly
intact."

"Anything good on it?"

"Velma, our resident tech-head, is working on it.
I've seen her resurrect worse phones than this, but it
takes as long as it takes."

"I'll hope for short."

"Hope is a good thing," the sheriff said, "so long as you don't confuse it with reality."

Jay scratched his chest and tried not to yawn in the sheriff's ear.

"Anything else?" Jay asked.

"They were freelancers."

"Local?"

"In the way that Wyoming, Idaho, and Montana are local," Cooke said. "Their street names—Sky High and Hilo—"

"Hilo?" Jay asked, startled.

"Surfer dude. Anyway, their names have come up before. Little bit of everything, but mostly the easy money in smuggling and delivery of drugs. Links to some pretty ugly acts, but that's hearsay from cons who are trying to buy their way out of jail early."

"So they were kind of local, thanks to the drug trade." Jay rubbed his head. "That explains the who and the how, but not the why. Don't suppose you have a line on that?"

"Nope. Just more on the who and the how. Of the two corpses, the pilot was the heavy hitter. His name has come up in the past as kind of a criminal fixer, getting crews together, moving stolen goods, that sort of thing. Which is why we're interested in his phone in particular."

"Can you give me odds on something useful coming out of it?"

"Define useful."

"The why of it."

Sara watched Jay closely, fingertips tracing her stitches as she remembered the horror of the Solvangs' bodies, the terror of being pursued by a helicopter, and the feel of her own blood hot against her chilled skin.

Why?

For what?

"Sorry, I have nothing about who hired them," the sheriff said. "Unless something else happens, the D.A. wants to close this case and bury it deep. Fresh, unsolved murders aren't a tourist attraction."

"What about the third set of boot prints?"

"Crime tech can't guarantee they were made at the same time as the other two, so the D.A. isn't interested. Frankly, I can see his point. That set could be anywhere from recent to three months old."

"You need us to sign a statement for all this?" Jay asked.

"Yeah, we can take an affidavit down here when you're ready. Today would be a good time for you to be ready."

Jay's eyes went to Sara and she nodded.

"And then we'll do some work at the gallery," she said softly.

"Call to let me know when you're on the way," the sheriff said. "Take care."

"You too, Cooke." Jay punched out, looked at Sara, and rumbled, "Gallery?"

"Don't worry, you'll be with me every minute. You'll be the guy with the big claw hammer opening all those wooden crates."

Well, that didn't take long," Sara said as they left the sheriff's office. "They really are in a hurry to bury this case."

"Cooke will keep working on it when he has time."

"And so will you," she said.

"Until I have answers, I won't stop."

"I wouldn't expect you to. Just—be careful. If the D.A.'s wrong and the third set of boot prints is related somehow, then it isn't over."

"Cooke knows what I'm going to do. He'll give me all the help he can without losing his job."

"Good to have the sheriff on your side." She checked for traffic, stepped off the curb, and nearly slipped on a patch of black ice.

"The suite is that way," he said, pointing.

"The soon-to-be-Custer gallery is this way. And don't tell me I should rest. I'm on to your sexy tricks."

"What if I said I'm tired?"

"I wouldn't believe you."

He followed her to the storefront. From several blocks over came the clang and bustle of a building site. It was away from the tourism, yet probably related to it. Tourism was the only growth industry in Jackson.

"This building is on the wrong side of your 'antler park,'" he said, looking at the empty display windows. "This block isn't nearly as trendy. In fact, there's talk of building a parking garage a few blocks over. Gotta have a place to stash all those fancy tourist cars while the owners leave Jackson richer than they found it."

"This building is in transition," she said, "but it still has the bones of the frontier West beneath. Like Jackson itself."

"Wait until you see the back entrance, where we're going in. It's old, all right."

He stopped and fished in his pockets. Instead of the gloves she expected, he pulled out some no-skid tracks and pulled them over the soles of his boots.

"I haven't seen those since I lived in Chicago one winter."

"Except in summer, people around here carry them all the time. Like gloves. We'll have to get you some tomorrow."

He led her down a paved alley where snow lurked in dark corners and trash bins waited to be picked up. No matter how spiffy and well cleared the street front was, the back of the brick or wooden buildings hadn't changed much in one hundred years. Dirty piles of snow lay beneath fresh. The smell of cooking food and hot oil wafted across the alley. Susie's Kitchen was painted over the back door opposite from where they stood.

The gallery's back door was locked, but hardly secure. It wouldn't take two seconds and a crowbar to open the padlock and hasp. *One more thing on the to-do list,* Jay thought. *Way too much went to hell while I was gone and JD was sick.*

In the failing late-afternoon light, Sara looked at the padlock, remembering another one in Fish Camp. She could still see Jay unlocking it: 9, 2, 7, 0.

He went through the motions again. Exactly.

"This one is the same as the one in Fish Camp?" she asked, watching him work.

"When JD's memory began to go, he had all the Vermilion locks changed to the same code." He yanked down on the padlock to open it. "I've been meaning to fix that, but had no reason to put it at the top of my work list."

She inhaled deeply and said, surprised, "That's minestrone."

"Susie's is a good place to eat when you're in a hurry," Jay said. "The soup doesn't come out of a can. The hours are iffy, though. If there aren't enough customers, they close." He flipped on an interior light. "Watch your step in here. I left a mess when I opened the crates earlier. The crate tops—with their nails sticking out—are propped against the workroom walls."

"Are the paintings all right?" she asked quickly.

"Nothing damaged that I saw. A minor miracle, all things considered."

She pushed at his waist impatiently and felt the Glock beneath his jacket. "Let me see them."

He stepped aside. "Have at it. I'll get the other lights."

"Where is *Muse*?"

"In one of the empty crates."

She laughed. "Hide in plain sight."

"Pretty much. Until I figure out why Liza's stuck on that painting, I don't want it 'disappearing' again."

Jay strode between the long, sheet-covered tables, the pegboards, and the empty easels that had been left behind by the previous tenant. One of the tables held the big claw hammer he had used to pry open the crates. He'd swept off that sheet and left it heaped on the table, out of his way.

"Watch the sheets," he said. "They're easy to trip over."

Sara stayed behind while more lights came on in the

front room. She thought of protesting at working in a fishbowl until she remembered that the display windows out front were walled in at the sides and back to give more walls for showing the previous tenant's art in the main room. Humming under her breath, she pulled clean white gloves from her big purse and began removing paintings from cartons.

Some of the paintings were still framed. Most weren't. None of the frames were elaborate. In fact, they were cheap.

"Were all of these framed once?" she asked.

"Mostly. When JD crated them and took them to Fish Camp, he left the frames behind in the storage yard here or in the ranch barn. We used them for kindling. Does it matter?"

"Only if the artist personally made or approved of the frames."

"Custer didn't give a damn."

"I could have guessed that," she said, placing a painting against the wall.

She tried not to notice how the brushstrokes all but leaped off the canvas, demanding attention and underlining the power of the mountains at the same time. No matter what Custer had been as a person, he was a fine artist.

Jay helped her lay out the paintings, kicking sheets

out of the way as he arranged and rearranged the paintings according to some logic that Sara didn't share. That didn't bother him. It was enough to see her humming and smiling over aspects of various paintings that he probably would never appreciate in the same way.

But he appreciated *her* in so many ways.

"Okay," she said finally, looking at all the paintings. "Would you get *Muse*? I want to see it in the context of his other early work. I'll set up an easel in the workroom. The light is better there."

"For a kiss."

"What?"

"I'll get *Muse* for a kiss," he said.

"Three kisses, and that's my final offer."

Smiling, he pulled her close and claimed his payment before he went to get the painting. As soon as he put *Muse* on an easel, the overhead lights made the woman's eyes the center of the painting's reality. There was something in them, something both ordinary and yet out of reach. Her eyes were haunted by something that he'd seen before but didn't expect to find caught within a cheap frame.

Desperation.

Jay's phone went off, singing *It's the end of the world as we know it.*

"Kill it," she said.

"Can't. It's the sheriff. I gave him a special ring-tone." He pulled out his phone. "What's up? Did we forget to initial something?"

The implication that Jay and Cooke would be calling each other so often that a special ring was needed made Sara frown.

I want it to be over.

But it wasn't.

She knew it deep inside, where primitive instincts whispered of ambush and bloody death. Even if she had been able to fool herself that everything was all right, there was Jay, relaxed yet fully alert, automatically checking the Glock at his back as he listened to Sheriff Cooke.

Cooke's voice was gravel rough. "You sitting down?"

Jay leaned his hip against a nearby worktable.

"Close enough," he said. "Go."

"The good news is that we got Velma to lay on hands and bring that pilot's cell phone back from the dead. For a little while, anyway."

"Good. Now give me the bad."

"We have not one but two calls coming in from a number in town." Cooke read it off, including the area code.

"Don't know it," Jay said.

"It's listed to Liza Neumann."

Jay sucked in his breath and went cold as disbelief and certainty fought in his head.

How could I have misjudged her so badly?

"Are you positive?" he asked.

"It's good enough for phone company billing, so, yes, I'm positive. I'm going to roll over to Liza's address and see what she has to say. You want to meet me there?"

"Give me a ten-minute head start."

"Can I trust you?" Cooke asked bluntly.

"For ten minutes? Yes."

"Are you taking Sara with you?"

"No," he said. *Even without a drop of blood spilled, it's going to be ugly.*

"Then stash her somewhere public. Safe."

"What aren't you telling me?"

"The D.A. might not be worried, but that third set of boot prints is keeping me up at night."

"I hear you."

Jay shut down the call and walked to the back where Sara was studying *Muse* with a hand-sized magnifying glass and a small flashlight pulled from her bottomless purse. He thought of the larger belt flashlight he always wore and wondered if he should leave it for her.

"Jay," she said, "I think there is—"

"Sorry," he interrupted. "I've got to run."

"Are you meeting Cooke?"

"He has a hot lead. You're going to Susie's for soup. I'll meet you there when I get back. It shouldn't be long."

"Then I'll stay here."

"No," he said. "Not alone. You'll have company at Susie's."

"I'd rather stay and study *Muse*," she said. "I think I've—"

"When I get back, you can study until your eyes cross," he cut in, picking up her shearling jacket. "Hell, we can sleep in the gallery if you want."

"What about the lights?" she asked as they marched out of the work area to the back door.

"Later," he said, moving fast.

After he hustled her outside, he closed and locked the door in a few swift motions.

She planted her feet stubbornly in the twilight alley where intermittent storm cells spat rain or snow. "What is this red-hot new lead that can't wait another minute?"

He thought about picking her up, opening the back door of Susie's Kitchen, and carrying her into the café. Instead he took her arm and began walking out of the alley and around to the front of the building.

"The shooter's phone had received two calls from a number in Jackson," he said.

She looked around suddenly, feeling hunted again. "Where in Jackson?"

"A listing billed to Liza Neumann. That's why you're going to hang out at Susie's Kitchen. Liza will make this talk as ugly as possible. I don't want you there."

"That makes two of us."

Sara wrapped her jacket more closely as she quick-stepped to keep up with Jay's long strides. Despite wearing her hiking boots, she slid a few times on new patches of ice left by clouds that wanted to snow but ended up spitting icy slush. They were spitting now, stinging pellets that raked bare skin.

"You say Susie's has good soup?" she asked.

"Nothing fancy, but it's good."

"Soup it is." Then, "Wait. I left *Muse* in plain sight."

"Nobody can see into the store. Everything will hold until I get back."

"Don't dawdle," she said, wanting to be back at the gallery so much she all but vibrated. "*Muse* is calling to me. I think I found a way to reveal her secrets. I took a picture and—"

"Good," he said over her excited words, his mind on Liza and what she might say. "I'll look at it when I get back. Half an hour, tops."

Jay opened the door to the eatery, pulled Sara inside, and spotted a booth at the rear. "Here you go." He tucked her into the booth, threw a twenty on the table, and kissed her swiftly. "The condo is about a mile away. I'll call if I'm going to be more than half an hour."

He was gone before she could tell him again that she would rather be studying *Muse*. As she watched him leave, she felt like she had been dropped by a whirlwind into a place with cozy booths and the muted chatter of a handful of people enjoying their meals.

A server appeared. Sara ordered the first thing that came to her mind. Then she settled back and tried to gather her scattered thoughts.

No point in wasting time. I'll study the pictures of Muse *I took.*

Sara reached into her bag for her telephone, only to discover that both telephone and bag had been left behind in Jay's rush to leave the gallery. The phone was on a table in the back room where she had photographed *Muse*. Her purse was in a corner somewhere.

At least Jay had remembered what was left behind. He'd given her enough cash to pay for her food.

Damn it, she thought. *He was in such a tearing rush to dump me here and I was so involved in* Muse *that I didn't even think about what I was leaving behind.*

Her thoughts were still churning, harder than ever now that she didn't have the painting to distract her.

How can he call me if my phone is in the gallery?

Did Liza really know the pilot? And why would she know someone like that?

If Jay died, Liza wouldn't inherit, Barton would. That's a motive of sorts. Although I'd hate to depend on his generosity for survival.

But why murder the Solvangs?

And most of all, why now? Why not years ago when JD was sick and Jay was half a world away?

Sara drummed her fingers on the table, barely noticing when the server put soup in front of her.

What a bloody, murderous tangle.

Still crackling with unanswered questions, she lifted a steaming spoonful of minestrone and blew gently. A glance at her watch told her she had been in the restaurant less than ten minutes.

At least fifteen minutes before Jay will call.

She could eat and still have plenty of time to get her phone from the gallery.

Chapter 26

The moon was playing tag with shreds of a storm cell. When the moon was free of clouds, light from its crescent came shining through the naked branches of trees. They looked like black veins sketched onto the blue-white light.

A single look at the sky told Jay it was cold and was getting colder fast. He slammed the door on the rental truck he'd parked illegally and went up the steps to the condo lobby. It was only a few miles from the gallery, but still in the sprawl of town that had grown up along the highway out of town, away from the national park.

Another piece of the modern built on the bones of the old, he thought.

If something is alive, it changes, the critic in his mind pointed out. *That's how you know it's alive.*

Don't have to like it, though.

Patches of ice gleamed sullenly in the shadows, waiting for an unwary foot.

He tried the lobby door, just in case.

Locked.

Will she let me in?

The pragmatic part of his mind laughed. If he mentioned *Muse*, she'd run to let him in.

"Yes?" came Liza's voice, tentative and hoarse.

"It's Jay. Let me in."

"Jesus, what next," she said dully, resignation in every syllable.

The intercom went silent.

He counted the seconds until he heard the door buzz, letting him in.

Fourteen seconds.

A lifetime.

Ignoring the elevator, he raced up the stairs to Liza's second-floor corner unit and knocked on the door.

"It's still me," he said when the peephole darkened.

She opened the locks reluctantly, dragging it out, telling him without words just how glad she was to see him. The door opened in slow motion. He didn't wait for a verbal invitation. He was inside and closing the door behind him before she could blink.

The room was as hot as a tropical beach. The air smelled of floral perfume, burned food, and stale alcohol.

He opened his jacket while he measured the once-young woman his already-old father had married. Liza was wearing a red satin wrapper that was more suited to morning in bed than to evening anywhere. The fluffy red mules she wore might have been sexy at one time but were simply ratty now. Her hair was uncombed except for a long platinum sweep on the right side falling forward to conceal that side of her face. She was swaying slightly in place.

All in all, she looked like a bad day in hell.

"Blackmail keeping you up nights?" Jay asked.

"Fuck you."

"No thanks."

Liza turned her back and went to a chair where a glass of gin or vodka or water waited on the end table.

"Are you drunk?" he asked.

"What do you want?" she asked, ignoring his question.

"Remember the helicopter crash?"

"The one you went Rambo on? Hard to forget." She took a deep swallow from the glass, as though it would help her forget. "It crashed. So what?"

A sense of futility and anger went through him, but he kept on anyhow. "Turns out the pilot was a seriously bad dude."

She shrugged.

"The sheriff's men found the pilot's phone," Jay said. "Your number was on the call record."

She took another swallow. For all the comprehension she showed, he could have been speaking Swahili.

I have to make it simple, he realized. *Something in her either isn't home or has broken.*

"I can help you or I can hurt you," Jay said. "Choose."

Liza stared at him blankly. "What on earth are you chattering about? I never called anyone in a helicopter. Why would I? They wear earmuffs or whatever."

He couldn't believe what he was hearing. "Listen to me, Liza. It's done. Over. Finished."

Starting past him, she chewed on a fingernail that was already bloody. Her hand was shaking.

He swallowed his anger. Badgering a broken old lady wasn't going to help him get closer to the answers he needed.

"Cooke knows you were in contact with the men who shot at Sara and me," he said evenly, "the same men who left boot prints in the Solvangs' fresh blood."

She blinked at him like a sleepy child, waiting for him to say something that she understood.

"Why, Liza? What made you hate me so much?"

For a long moment, she stared at him like she was putting puzzle pieces of reality together, all but moving her fingers to mimic the act. Then her hands went limply to her lap.

"It wasn't ever about you," she said finally. "You were just in the way."

She didn't cry, but her lips were quivering. When she absently brushed the hair away from her face, Jay saw a livid bruise there, running from her temple to below her swollen eye.

Who hit her? Jay thought. *That's a really fresh bruise.*

"And maybe he's right," she whispered. "Maybe it was all my idea and he was just doing what I was too weak to do." She sucked in a shuddering breath.

"He? Who are you talking about?" Jay crouched before her and touched her chin gently, tilting her face until she met his eyes. "Are you in some kind of trouble?"

"You have the painting and you didn't give it to me," she said.

"Why do you want *Muse*?"

"It wasn't for you. It's not yours." Liza clenched her body and tried to lunge to her feet.

Running into Jay was like hitting a wall.

She fell back into her chair and grabbed one of his hands. "You don't understand. I have to get *Muse* back. If you give it to me, this can all end."

He treated her like the child she had become, stroking her hair gently, avoiding the bruise that was still spreading, consuming her face.

"It already has ended," he said. "Your hired hit men are dead. I have *Muse* and I'm keeping it."

"Sara's reputation," Liza said, an echo of her old determination returning.

"An engagement ring will take the sting out of any gossip."

"No." She shook her head so that her hair swirled wildly.

"It's over, Liza. If you try to hurt Sara, I'll hound you out of Jackson. I can do it and we both know it. You'll have to live in a place where no one knows your name and no one cares."

"No. No. No." She shook her head emphatically. "It wasn't supposed to be like this. I told him but he laughed and called me names and threatened to . . ."

Her voice died and silence filled the room until it was as suffocating as the tropical heat.

"Who is murdering people and blaming you?" Jay asked.

The question came out of nowhere, blindsiding her, sending her back into her childlike hiding.

"No," she said.

"Do you owe some thug money because of another of Barton's screwups?"

"No. No. No. No."

It wasn't an answer. It was a denial that this could be happening to her.

"Why, Liza? *Why?*" Jay's voice, like his hand holding on to her arm, was gentle. And relentless.

She felt frail, vibrating so hard she might shake apart at any second. Eyes a darker blue than her son's filled and overflowed, sending more tears streaking through yesterday's makeup.

"He owes me everything, but even that isn't enough. More, more, more. He always wants more."

"Barton?" Jay asked. "He did this to you? He *hit* you?"

Tears flowing from her swollen eyes were her only answer.

"Where is he now?" Jay asked.

More tears came.

The intercom buzzed. "Ms. Neumann, this is Sheriff Cooke. You can talk to me in the privacy of your home or in the official interview room at my office."

Only the tears flowing down her face answered. Only they were alive.

Jay found the intercom near the door. "Cooke, it's Jay. Come up. Liza's in shock."

"On my way."

Jay opened the door and waited impatiently for the elevator to arrive.

"Talk to me," Cooke said as soon as he saw Jay.

"I think Barton is the one who backhanded her. Bruise is less than an hour old. Still developing."

The sheriff's eyebrows went up.

"I know Barton's the one pushing Liza for more and more money," Jay said. "I don't know how the Solvang murders meant cash for Barton, but it's all tied up somehow. And the *Muse* painting, too. But none of it makes sense. Barton's just a spoiled kid. How could he be capable of this? What a bloody clusterf—"

"Where's Barton?" Cooke interrupted.

"He has a downstairs condo. I'll start there."

"Leave him to me. Go get Sara and have dinner. I'll call you."

"I can't just—" Jay began.

"Leave it to the law. That's an order."

Jay's jaw muscles worked, but he nodded once before he turned and strode to the stairwell. He went down the stairs fast, the grip tracks on his boots scraping in the silence.

Sara was so eager to see *Muse* again that she fumbled the combination twice. The third time the ice-cold lock opened grudgingly. Before she went inside the gallery, she looked over her shoulder again to make sure she was alone.

There was nothing in the alley but the eerie gleam of ice buried in the thin shadows cast by the moon. A careless wind blew through the narrow lane, searching for something loose to play with.

She slipped inside the gallery just before the wind found her. The door creaked as it settled back into place. Her purse was where she'd left it in the corner. Her phone was with the magnifying glass and the small flashlight. She took off her shearling jacket and put it on top of her purse.

Just a few minutes with Muse. *I have to be sure.*

She checked her watch.

Five minutes. Then I'll go back to the café and wait for Jay.

With eager steps she went to the painting on its easel. She nearly tripped over the white sheets the previous owners had draped everywhere for their final art installation, a celebration of the ordinary.

As always, *Muse's* haunting and haunted eyes were the first thing to reach out to Sara.

The second thing was the fact that she was sure the face—and maybe the rest of the nude figure—had been painted on top of something else.

It could be just a redo. Even the greatest painters don't always get it right the first time, and we have x-ray photographs to prove it.

But a do-over gave a lot of insight into the artistic process.

She shoved her phone in her back pocket and went to work with the magnifying glass and the light. The more she looked, the more certain she was that everything within the frame of the window was a redo, including the model.

"Awesome," she said to herself. "Once I have this x-rayed, I'll know what's beneath. If it's more than just a correction of a mistake, I'll make a giclee print of this version, restore the original, and show them side by side. It could be a real showstopper, a rare glimpse into the process of creation."

Then she sighed.

"Or it could be nothing but a mess underneath, the usual reason for a redo. But I'll—"

The creak of the back door opening sent her pulse over the moon. Without even thinking about it, Sara whipped the phone out of her back pocket and punched in the three numbers she had come to know all too well. Holding the phone behind her back, her thumb on the call button, she waited.

It's just Jay.

Or the wind.

Or—

"Barton! What are you doing here?"

Chapter 27

Barton stepped out of the shadows, his red hair wild from the wind and studded with snow. "Since you were too selfish to show *Muse* to my mother, I thought I'd see it for myself."

Sara didn't know what was wrong, but she knew something was. Barton was flushed with more than the cold outside. His glance skittered from place to place, never quite fixing anywhere.

Drugs? she wondered. *Alcohol?*

Both?

One of his hands was bruised across the back. The other was in his pocket.

And then it wasn't.

The instant she saw the gun, she punched the call button and shoved the phone into her back pocket.

"What are you doing?" he demanded.

"With the painting? You can see for yourself. It's right here."

Muffled words came from her back pocket. *"911 operator. What is your emergency?"*

She prayed he didn't hear.

"Why do you have a gun, Barton Vermilion?" she asked, speaking loudly and very clearly. "Is it some new fashion statement?"

He looked at her like she was crazy.

"A gun, Barton Vermilion? Really? What kind of pistol is it? It looks small. Is your gun a .22? Point that gun somewhere else. This is an art gallery in downtown Jackson, not a shooting gallery."

Muffled words came from her back pocket. She coughed loudly to cover them.

Can the operator hear me?

Does he or she understand?

"Shut up!" Barton shouted. "You talk too much! Just like my mother, yammering and yammering and never getting anything done. Well, I'm in charge now. It's my ass that's going to get kissed from now on."

The only response that occurred to Sara would likely get her shot, so she asked loudly, "What do you want, Barton Vermilion? Why are you pointing a gun at me in an art gallery in downtown Jackson?"

Come on, operator, she thought frantically. *You have a name and a location and the type of emergency. What the hell else do you need?*

The muffled voice came louder, asking her questions she couldn't answer without getting shot.

"I said to SHUT UP," Barton shouted. "I know my name and where I am and—Shit, were you talking to someone before I came in? Where's your phone?"

"I left it in my room," she lied.

Jay, where are you? Barton's skittering, pale eyes are looking more than a little crazy.

"Come here," he said, glancing around jerkily. "Now. Make it quick."

Her back pocket was silent.

Is that good or bad or does it matter at all? Sara thought.

She followed Barton's directions, but she was looking for anything she could use as a weapon. The discarded boards with nails sticking out appealed to her, but she didn't see a way to get her hands on one without getting shot.

The claw hammer. It's on the table only a few feet from Barton.

Has he noticed it?

"Barton, why are you doing this? Why are you threatening—"

"Shut up and get over here or I'll shoot you right now!"

She began walking toward him. Slowly. She made sure that her steps took her close to the table and the butt of a hammer sticking out from beneath the sheet.

"Faster or I'll shoot you."

"I hurt my foot running from a helicopter," she lied. "I can't do fast."

"So that was why Jay was wheeling you around. Stupid bastards," he said, shaking his head jerkily. "Charge me fifty big ones and end up getting killed. Waste all those bullets and they didn't even nick Rambo after they killed the Solvangs just because they got bored waiting for you, what a nasty mess that was and all because my dear mother was too stupid to win a court case from a hick judge because if we'd had the damned *Muse* we'd have been safe and nobody would have ever known, but that's okay now because I'll burn the bitch after I burn you."

Sara couldn't make sense of his ravings, except for a few words she'd understood very clearly. Her heart staggered, then raced.

Barton sent the helicopter after Jay.

Louder and louder with each second, the thought ricocheted around her mind.

And following it was the certainty that Barton had had some kind of psychotic break.

I'm alone with a madman holding a pistol.

She inched closer to the claw hammer.

Jay, hurry. I could use a little help here.

"It's Jay's fault," Barton said, watching her through eyes that were almost entirely pupil.

Sara jerked, wondering if she had spoken her thoughts aloud.

"All of this is his fault," Barton said, waving the pistol around. "He wouldn't give me what was mine so what am I supposed to do, kiss his ass for another seven years and then take a DNA test with his blood?"

Barton answered his own ravings with a stream of profanity that assured him he was a man, as good as any other man, especially Jay.

Warily Sara eyed Barton as she inched forward. She was almost within reach of the claw hammer. One more step . . .

Her right hand snapped out and wrapped around the butt of the claw hammer. The top of it caught on the sheet, dragging it behind like a big flag as she swung the unwieldy tangle at Barton.

"What are you—Oof!" He gasped as the hammer thudded into his gut.

The sheeted billowed up and over him like a cloud, then deflated, blinding him.

She thought of trying for his gun, then did the sensible thing and ran to the back door, yanking tables and chairs askew behind her to slow down his pursuit.

"I'm going to kill you!" Barton screamed as he fought the sheet shrouding him.

You'll have to catch me first, she thought grimly.

She skidded to a stop, thumped against the back door, and yanked the handle. It moved, but the door didn't open.

The bolt. He locked it behind him.

She clawed at the bolt until it opened. A second later she hurled herself out the door, skidded on fresh snow, spun, and fell on her butt so hard her phone bounced out of her pocket and skated away into the shadows. She scrambled to her feet, got traction, and ran.

The night air broke around her like shards of ice, slicing straight through her light cotton shirt. Snow was intermittent, the latest storm coming apart and fraying into patches of stars.

At first Sara barely felt the cold. She was too busy sprinting down the alley and praying that she wouldn't slip on other hidden patches of ice. She thought she was heading back to the café, then realized she had turned the wrong way after she came out of her fall.

The soup place is behind me. Are any other businesses open down this way?

No lights showed in the alley in front of her and she knew Barton wasn't very far behind her. She had heard the sound of tables and chairs crashing around in the gallery, the slap of his leather soles, and his cursing when he finally fought his way clear to the alley.

Maybe he'll break his neck on the ice.

She heard the sound of him falling and smiled. But she didn't count on him staying down.

Moments later she reached the end of the alley, turned left, ran down one block, and then another and another, sensing her pursuer every step of the way. The buildings around her were dark. She had run to a part of Jackson where tourists rarely came and the businesses closed at five. There was no place to hide.

And Barton was still behind her.

He wasn't cursing anymore, but his shoes made plenty of noise. They had an odd metallic sound now that they hadn't had in the gallery.

He must have put on some skid-proof grippers after he fell.

She wished she had some for herself. Her boots were better than heels, but they didn't have metal teeth. Skidding on a glaze of ice halfway through another block, she ran by a doorway with a single yellow security light above it. Her shadow went crazy and long in it.

Everything glittered with fresh snow.

The next block across the street was dark except for a few powerful construction lights at the center, slicing night into crazy pieces. The half-formed skeleton of a building loomed ahead. Piles of materials—or dirt-covered snow—were heaped randomly, along with construction debris and sheets of ice where shallow puddles had been. Trenches for plumbing and drainage ditches to protect the worksite cut through the construction area, making a weird kind of obstacle course.

Maybe I can hide somewhere.

And freeze to death.

She had no illusions about how long she would last when she stopped moving and sweat froze on her skin, leaching heat from her body.

Beyond the construction site rose a new three-story apartment structure. The lights surrounding it were silent cries of welcome. The building couldn't be more than a block or two away.

Somebody will be there.

The sound of Barton's hoarse breaths coming closer told Sara that she didn't have time to skirt the construction zone. The cold was already working on her body. Her breath came out in bursts of white warmth and came in with searing cold. She ignored that and the burning in her neck where the stitches were stabbing in protest of her fall.

Ignoring the numbing cold eating her alive was harder, but she didn't have a choice.

She ran toward the apartment building like it was home. She managed to avoid most of the obstacles in the construction zone until she came to a dark area where dirt and snow were heaped up on either side of a large drainage ditch.

Can't jump it, she realized. *Can't trust the moonlight for judging distance.*

The sound of Barton's breathing was closer.

Why haven't his damn grips come off? she thought in despair. *In Chicago, they fell off my shoes all the time.*

Sara scrambled up the berm and over the top. Keeping her footing on the downward slope was impossible. She half slid, half rolled into the ditch. What looked like snow at the bottom was a thin skim of ice over running water. She fell hard on her left side into the ditch. The running water was only a few inches deep and it was the coldest thing she had ever felt.

Wherever she was wet, her skin registered the flash chill for only an instant before going numb. At the edge of numbness, she felt burning where cold mixed with the warmth of life. The cold was winning. Above her was only a patch of darkness lit with the Cheshire grin of the quarter moon.

Snow spun down from the sky in graceful silence.

"Shit!" Barton screamed.

His curse and the sound of his fall focused Sara. Awkwardly she forced herself to her feet. Her left ankle was numb, but it reluctantly responded to her demands. The only warm part of her body was a spot on her neck.

The stitches. Bleeding again.

It means I'm still alive. Move!

Scrambling, clawing, she pulled herself out of the ditch and over the heaped-up dirt and snow. Now the gold lights of the apartment seemed too far away, impossible to reach with her half-numb body.

But there was nowhere else to go.

"She left about twenty minutes ago," the waitress said.

Jay looked at the almost empty restaurant and then at the swinging door leading to the kitchen. Without a word he went toward that door, his long legs eating up the distance.

"Sir, you can't—"

He was already through the door. Ignoring the startled looks, he strode through the kitchen and out the back door into the alley. The first thing he noticed was that the gallery door was partly open. He started to call out to Sara, but hard-learned lessons ordered him to go across the alley fast and silent, gun in hand.

He went through the gallery the same way, quick and hard. The upended tables and chairs turned his mouth into a grim line. No one was here now, but she had been here earlier.

The only good news was that he didn't see any blood or spent shells.

She couldn't leave Muse *alone,* he thought savagely, *and I couldn't give her five minutes with the damn painting before I hustled her into the café so I could talk to Liza.*

If he could have done it again, he would have given Sara as much time as she wanted. But Afghanistan had taught him that do-overs were a fool's wish.

The claw hammer and sheet tangled on the floor made him pause. But it was *Muse* that made him stop. The eyes watched him in mute condemnation.

Jay went out into the alley and called Sara's name.

Nothing answered but an echo.

He really hadn't expected anything else. He grabbed his belt flashlight and switched it on. He moved the hard, surprisingly bright beam around the alley, looking for signs of a struggle or blood or anything other than emptiness.

A rectangular gleam caught his eye.

He bent down and picked up a cell phone and recognized the case.

Sara.

He thumbed to recent calls and his heart staggered when he saw 911. He pocketed her phone and reached for his own. A single number speed-dialed Sheriff Cooke. As the phone rang, Jay swept the flashlight's beam methodically over the alley, searching for tracks in the fall of fresh snow. The temperature and icy flakes of snow bit into exposed skin.

"Cooke," the sheriff said.

"This is Jay. Do you have Barton yet?"

"No. His place was empty and his car was gone. Black BMW coupe according to his registration. I put out a BOLO."

Jay pushed aside his emotions and spoke in clipped phrases. "Sara's missing. I'm in back of Susie's Kitchen, which is right across the alley from an empty gallery where we're storing Custer's paintings. Sara wasn't in the café and she isn't in the gallery. I found her phone in the alley. The last number she called was 911."

"Hold."

While Jay waited, he carefully went over the alley, searching for tracks that were recent enough to break the newly fallen snow and sleet. He saw a place farther away from the gallery where someone had skidded and fallen, and before that a print in the snow left by a leather-soled shoe that could have belonged to a woman or a small man.

Barton?

Wearing leather soles in this weather is the kind of damn-fool thing he would do. But it's good news for me.

The end of the alley closest to the gallery had a small parking area across the street. The only car in the lot was a black BMW.

He trotted across the street and put his hand on the hood of the car.

Warm.

"Jay?" Cooke asked.

"Here," he said curtly, staring into every shadow for a sign of Barton.

Nothing moved but the wind.

"A woman called 911 about five, six minutes ago. The message is indistinct, but it's Sara's voice and something about a gallery, a gun, and a name that sounded like Barton."

Jay said something savage. Then, "I found a black BMW coupe parked across the street from the alley. Hood was warm."

"Did Sara drive to the restaurant?"

"No. Both of them have to be on foot. I'm going out the other end of the alley, away from the BMW. If Barton had been able to get to his car, he would have."

"You think Sara got away from him?"

"Yes. No blood in the gallery and the route to the alley door is littered with chairs and an upended table. I think Sara's out there, running for her life."

"I'll put every man I have on it."

"Tell them I'm out there and I'm armed."

"No. Just stay—"

Jay cut off the call and ran in earnest. When he reached the end of the alley, he hesitated, then his flashlight picked out a fresh boot print in the crunchy slush next to a building on the left. He went left and tracked at a run, his flashlight easily picking out the prints on a sidewalk few people had used since the last snow shower.

He had gone almost three blocks when he saw the construction zone. Two sets of prints headed into the area. One of them now showed metal teeth.

Must be Barton. Sara doesn't have any grip-treads.

Jay snapped off the light and stood in the deep shadows surrounding the open street. Letting out his breath, he listened.

Nothing came to him but the wind at his back and his own heartbeat, deep, rhythmic, alert, his body responding to commands from a man who for too many years had hunted and been hunted by other men.

Working only by the thin light of the moon shining between fraying clouds, he followed the two trails of tracks, one nearly on top of the other. The prints were punched through the crust of frozen ice and snow in the construction area, leaving shadows that were easy to follow.

He loped alongside them like a wolf, silent and intent.

Around him, the night glittered beneath the moon. He saw where the grips on the second trail tripped, skidded, and fell, leaving an ungainly snow angel behind. Thirty feet away there was another ragged angel, its fresh edges sparkling beneath the quarter moon.

Good for you, Sara. Even without metal teeth, you're staying on your feet better than Barton.

The moonlight dimmed, and snow began swirling down as the wind pushed a new storm cell overhead.

The fading light revealed a small berm of snow-covered dirt, a place where even good boots and better reflexes lost traction. Jay could see the signs of her slip-ping, falling, flailing her arms to slow her descent.

He skidded down the side of the ditch. Shielding his flashlight with his fingers across the lens, he searched the bottom. The first thing he saw was the black streak where someone had broken a thin crust of ice and gone into the water. The second thing he saw was that there were two sets of tracks leading out and over the far side of the ditch.

The third thing he saw was bright drops of blood frozen between the tracks.

"Sara!"

He didn't know he had shouted her name aloud until he heard his voice echoing emptily through the night.

Then a sound came back on the wind, a man's voice promising death.

Chapter 28

Sara skated over a hidden puddle, jumped a stack of boards, and skidded wildly on landing. Finally she was free of the construction area. The yellow lights around the apartment building made everything look flat, almost one-dimensional, fooling human eyes. Her boot treads were packed with snow and ice from the construction zone, turning the sidewalk into a skating rink for her.

Breath sawing in and out, she went spinning, no traction, nothing to keep her upright. Her hands slammed into the icy sidewalk. She rolled with the momentum and smacked into a snowbank. At least the footing was better in the snow. She was on her feet and running.

Then her head snapped back and she went down again.

"Got you," Barton panted, his bare hand buried in her hair, twisting as he yanked her back to her feet. "Told you not to run or I—"

Her elbow missed his diaphragm but hit him hard in the ribs. Then her foot came down on the top of his knee, raking the shin through his slacks and slamming into the arch of his foot.

He snarled in surprise and pain as he reeled backward. He tripped over one of the wires holding up a newly planted, barren tree. The buttons on his long overcoat ripped open as he fell, but he kept a grip on her hair.

Barton might have been shorter than she was, but he was stronger simply because he was male. Sara twisted around, using the momentum of his yank to propel herself even faster toward him, remembering the dirty tricks her brothers had taught her.

"What the—" Barton began.

She slammed her fist up and between his legs.

His grip went weak as he gave a strangled cry.

Using his torso and legs for traction, she scrambled to her feet, delivering a few hard kicks along the way.

Then she ran. Vaguely she realized that the moon had gone and the sky had turned to wet snow. Despite her pace, her body was too cold to feel snow on her skin.

Breathing hard and fast and still not getting enough air, she bolted toward the building wreathed in yellow lights. She risked one quick glance over her shoulder and saw that Barton was slowly getting to his feet, cradling his crotch in his hand. His coat flapped in the wind like it was trying to get away from him.

"I'll kill you!" he screamed.

The wind ripped apart his words, but she didn't need them to know that he was crazy mad. Or just plain crazy.

It didn't matter to her. She was both burning and freezing, her back rigid and her lungs filled with fire stoked by her every tearing breath. Her neck bled slowly, a stubborn weeping. She pressed her fingers there, trying to stop the flow, but her skin was too cold for her to know if she was succeeding.

Something scraped behind her, not shoes, but something metallic.

Barton's grip-tracks, she thought wearily.

She felt like she didn't have skin or muscles any longer, that it had all cracked off and been replaced with plastic that was stiff and unresponsive. Only the fingers touching her neck wound could actually feel anything now—the sticky cold of freeze-dried blood.

In her mind she was running, but in reality her feet were clumsy, slow. The world was getting darker. She couldn't get enough air. She looked at the yellow lights around the apartment entrance, the lights that had become her talisman.

It's not that far.

Only a million miles.

Stop whining and run!

Then for the first time she noticed that it was snowing in earnest. The fat wet flakes were piling up on the cars and running down her cheeks like cold tears. Everything looked like frozen Halloween, all yellow lit and black with the eerie hush of snow drifting down.

How much snow does it take to track someone over a sidewalk? Or to cover tracks? And how quickly?

Her life depended on answers she didn't have.

The wind gusted, clawing over her face, bringing tears and tugging some of her wet hair free. Through squinted eyes, she saw Barton claw at his wildly flapping coat as he pursued her.

Cold, she realized, as she ran. *I'm freezing to death out here.*

Clumsily she ran toward the apartment entrance.

Following the blue-white cone of his flashlight, Jay left the construction zone at a run. He no longer cared if Barton saw him coming.

Better me than Sara.

He scanned the asphalt of the street, but found nothing. Snow hadn't built up enough to show tracks. It was different on the sidewalk and in the small heaps of snow both old and new that the wind had piled up against any barrier. There he easily could see tracks.

Sara's boot treads no longer showed. Instead, there was just a rumpled area in the occasional wind-piled snow.

Barton's grip-tracks showed up with deadly clarity.

So did frequent drops of frozen blood.

Jay tracked at a run while the snow intensified, ice-toothed wind raking over his face. Squinting against it, he looked at the newly planted trees and occasional streetlights.

Ahead and off to his right, a coat snapped in the wind, looking like a loose sail.

Barton, Jay thought, grinning savagely.

He ran harder toward the awkward figure, until his left foot hit a patch of ice that even grip-tracks couldn't defeat. The world tumbled around him as he landed hard on his shoulder, then rolled and came back to his feet. In the crazy, reeling illumination of his flashlight, he had seen more blood, bright proof of life.

He ran toward the streetlight again, then saw its yellow circle was empty.

A woman's scream shredded the night.

Sara didn't even know that she had screamed when she discovered Barton was only steps away from her now. Laughing. He could have caught her if he wanted to. He was enjoying watching her run.

The yellow lights of the apartment entrance were finally close enough for her to make out the intercom waiting on the outside of the freshly landscaped entrance.

"Give it up," Barton panted. "I've got—you now."

His breaths sounded like they were right in her ear. Her left foot landed hard. The ankle buckled, but she stayed upright. Snow raked her eyes as she ran, stinging like needles. She felt the swipe of his fingers grasping at the hair she had tucked beneath her collar.

Her whole being focused on the call box in front of the apartment. She could see a handset like an old-fashioned phone booth hanging up. She threw herself at it. Her numb fingers fumbled, but she got the receiver into her hand.

"Hello? Hello?" she gasped into the speaker. "Help me!"

Then she saw the banner across the recessed front doors.

OPENING THIS MAY—WINDSOR
LOFTS AT JACKSON

LUXURY CONDOMINIUMS MINUTES FROM THE ARTS DISTRICT

She dropped the phone and bolted toward the nearest patch of darkness, not knowing or caring where it would take her.

Barton moved to cut her off, but he was too winded to do more than keep her in sight. Holding his hand against the stitch in his side, he followed her around the empty apartment building. Sara angled across a vacant lot and into the inky darkness that surrounded the construction zone's core of security lights.

He thought of the icy ditches that would cross her path and smiled. Wrapping his warm coat around his body, he trotted after her. The farther she ran, the less distance he would have to drag her.

Then he realized that she was outpacing him and might get away. He cursed her viciously.

Sara heard Barton's savage words and didn't care. She simply, doggedly, ran through the darkness and stinging snow, alone as she had never been before in her life. She tried to scream, but only had enough breath for a hoarse groan.

A hand clamped onto one of her pumping arms, spinning her around. Barton kicked out at her, knocking her feet out from under her. She was on her back, unable to see his face, but she could smell the mint and alcohol on his breath. His voice was as ugly as any sneer. She tried to scream again, and again could only moan.

He dropped her foot and grabbed at her bare hand, yanking her toward him. Before she could counter the move, he had his hand in the hair at her scalp and was dragging her over the frozen lot. Snow scraped and gathered beneath her thin cotton shirt.

She clawed feebly at the hand buried in her hair and tried to lift her legs to kick him, but all she managed was a useless flopping around. Between the noise of his shoes crunching through icy snow, she heard the sound of running water.

Suddenly Barton yanked her upright and simultaneously shoved her forward so hard her feet left the ground.

And then she was falling down, down.

The shallow, deadly cold water waited for her below.

Chapter 29

Childlike, the wind played with falling snow, throwing curtains here and there, revealing and concealing the streetlights and two figures running. Breathing hard, Jay stared where he thought he'd seen movement.

There. Off to the right.

The pale blur of Sara's blouse was headed back into the darkness at the edges of the construction zone. He thought about using the flashlight on his belt to light the way but didn't do it. The moon appeared often enough between storm cells that he didn't want to ruin his night vision.

Besides, when it came to a fight, he wanted both hands free.

He lengthened his stride, leaping over small obstacles and watching for the treacherous drainage ditches.

Slipping, sliding, heart pumping, he closed the distance between himself and the two figures that had vanished into snow flurries less than a block away.

Then wind gusted, revealing only one person with a wildly flapping coat.

Barton.

Where's Sara?

Despite the fear clawing at him like another kind of cold, Jay knew he would have heard a shot.

She must have slipped and gone down.

He increased his speed, desperate to get to Barton before he could hurt Sara any more. As he pounded closer, he saw an indigo outline and a pale face. The features were small, delicate as a girl's, and twisted with hate. Then Barton turned and ran back in the direction of the gallery, pursued instead of the pursuer.

Jay tackled his brother hard, bone crunching on bone, making certain that Barton hit the ground first. Then he lifted his fist and flipped Barton over.

"Go ahead," Barton panted. "You've always wanted to do it. Beat me while she freezes to death in the ditch."

With a harsh curse and a hard kick, Jay shoved off Barton and ran back to the place he had last seen Sara.

Two hundred feet and a lifetime later, he was on top of a berm. The water below was an ugly black gash promising an icy death. He went down the slope in long, leaping strides until his right foot caught on a hidden obstacle. The ankle gave way, throwing him to the right. Twisting, he broke his fall with his shoulder, stopping just short of the water.

Sitting up, he yanked the flashlight from his belt and turned it on. For long, terrifying moments, the bright LED found nothing but blinding white snow and empty black water. Then a different color of white caught the light.

Sara.

She was sprawled on her back, her head and shoulders in the water. At the edge of the flashlight beam, the seeping blood on her neck was like a trickle of dark paint. It was the most beautiful thing he had ever seen.

Dead people didn't bleed.

In a blur of motion, he pulled her away from the water and stripped off her soaked blouse. She would have fought him if she'd had the strength, but the best she could do was a kind of reflexive twitching away from him.

"Easy, sweetheart. It's Jay."

He stripped off his shearling coat and stuffed her into it, yanking it up and over her head to keep her soaked hair out of the wind. Then he stood and pulled her up into a fireman's carry around his shoulders. Holding her with one arm, he fished in his pocket for his phone.

It was gone.

Shit. Must have happened during one of my falls.

He checked the Glock. Still in place. Wet, cold, waiting.

Too bad I can't make a phone call on it.

Using the flashlight to avoid obstacles, Jay began moving at a ground-eating trot toward warmth. Restaurant, gallery, his truck—he didn't care. All that mattered was getting Sara warm again.

As he double-timed it, he kept looking for Barton. Either his brother was still down or he had managed to get out of sight while Jay found Sara.

I'll find you again, little brother. Count on it.

"J-J-Jay?" The muffled word came from the depths of his coat.

"It's me. Can you feel your hands and toes?"

"C-C-Cold."

He felt the violent shivers racking her. Relief swept through him at the sign that her body was returning to life.

Two blocks later she said, "B-Burns."

"Good. That's circulation coming back," he explained as he stepped into the street. "Hurts like a bitch."

Not a single car was in sight.

Jay kicked the worst of the ice and snow from his grip-tracks and trotted toward the gallery. Burning hot streaks shot up from his ankle every time it met the hard cement of the sidewalk. He ignored the pain. He'd been injured worse and carried a wounded soldier back to camp. The experience had taught him that sometimes pain was a message without meaning.

"I c-can w-walk," Sara said as her head bounced against him.

"It's faster this way."

"B-But—"

"Save your breath for warming up."

By the time he reached the block with Susie's Kitchen in it, the sign in the window told him they had shut down and gone home.

"Gallery," Sara said.

"The truck will be more comfortable."

"G-Gallery," she insisted.

Remembering the last time he had run roughshod over her wishes, Jay turned toward the gallery. At least the phone there would be working. He was sure of it. He had started the utilities himself.

"Gallery it is. Hang on, sweetheart. We're almost there."

He passed the parking lot and noted that the black BMW was still there. Wherever Barton had gone, he hadn't taken his car.

"*Muse*," she said clearly.

The first word that came to Jay was savage, so he bit it back.

Sara gripped the arm holding her in place across his shoulders. Her head was spinning, but something Barton had said made awful sense to her now.

"The painting," she said carefully. "Barton wants to burn it."

For two cents, I'd help him, Jay thought bitterly.

"There's a secret in the painting," she said as he swung into the alley.

"I'm glad you're coming around, but you're not making a whole lot of sense. Easy now, I'm going to put you down."

He bent over by the gallery door and gently put her on her feet, steadying her with his hands. As he did, his instincts hammered at him, yelling that he had overlooked something.

Footprints.

Leading into the gallery.

Suddenly the door opened and a man's hand grabbed Sara, yanking her into the gallery.

"Get in here or I'll kill her."

"Henry? What in hell are you doing here?"

And then Jay was afraid that he knew.

The foreman backed up until he and Sara were beyond Jay's reach.

"Shut the door behind you," Henry said. "There are police cruisers all over the place."

Wish I'd seen one, Jay thought as he shut the door and watched Henry's every breath.

"As for what I'm doing, I'm cleaning up after Barton." His voice, like his expression, was heavy with contempt. "That boy can't take a piss without wetting himself."

Barton's voice came from behind Henry and off to the right. His voice was different, hard where it had been whiny. "I've done a lot more than you, old man. Two months ago, I tried to get the paintings out of Fish Camp alone, but the old man got mad when I kicked over an open can of paint. He told me not to come back without Jay."

Henry looked bored.

"I even robbed Sara's room to make her go home," Barton finished. "Now give me back my gun."

"Any idiot could walk through an open door. As for the gun you stole from Liza . . ." Henry flicked a glance at the gun he was holding against Sara's head. "A .22 purse pistol. Girly gun for a girly boy. But if you get close enough, it works okay. I'm close enough."

When Henry looked up an instant later, it was into the muzzle of another, bigger pistol, Jay's .45 coming around to draw a bead on Henry's head.

"Jesus, you're fast," Henry said. "Faster than JD, and he was lightning."

"Let her go," Jay said flatly. *Or look away again.* "There's nothing in this for you."

"Put your gun down," Henry said, pressing the muzzle of his pistol harder into Sara's pale cheek.

"Don't give up your gun, Jay," Sara said hoarsely, pleading with her beautiful, dark eyes. "He'll kill you and then he'll kill me."

"Nobody has to die," Jay said. *An amateur hiding behind a hostage always makes a mistake. The only question is when.*

And if the hostage gets shot first.

Henry looked into Jay's cold navy eyes and wished Sara was tall enough to hide more of him.

"You shouldn't have come back," Barton said to Jay. "We had a good thing. Meth labs, pot growing. Our cut was more than the stingy allowance you gave Mother, but she didn't know. She never knew. Then you had to go all Rambo on the grow operations and I had to take her orders again."

"Shut up," Henry snarled.

"Why?" Barton asked. "Jay won't do anything as long as you have a gun to that bitch's head. You call me stupid, but he's the one who fell in love. It makes him weak."

Sara looked frantically from Jay to Barton, who was holding a bloody cloth to one side of his face.

Jay's eyes never wavered from Henry. All it would take was another moment of inattention on the foreman's part and the standoff would be over.

"You can tell a man by his partners," Jay said. "You think about that, Henry?"

"Barton isn't my partner. Not like that."

"The hell I'm not," Barton said coolly. "I'm the one who made the deal with the local growers and cookers. I'm the one who picked up the money every month and passed it out."

"And you're the one who got cheated every month," Henry said.

"No, old man. That was you. I kept two-thirds. I pulled the strings, and everyone thought they were pulling mine. Those acting lessons Jay paid for were worth every penny. I fooled—"

"Shut up!" Henry said again.

"Why? You're going to kill both of them, I'll inherit, and—"

"You won't inherit," Sara said, clamping her jaw so her teeth wouldn't chatter. "You're not JD's blood son."

Jay felt shock waves move through him, but his aim never shifted by a millimeter.

It explains so much, he thought. *Too much.*

"So you figured it out," Henry said wearily. "I was afraid you would, but I thought it would take longer."

"Underneath all that do-over paint is a portrait of Liza," Sara said, her voice certain.

"Custer's damned muse," Henry said bitterly. "His lover. But Liza loves money and Custer was broke. She married JD, who was rich. Barton is Custer's get."

"Sweet, isn't it?" Barton said. He had shifted in his chair, leaning so far forward that his face almost touched his knees. He was holding the cloth awkwardly with his left hand on the right side of his face. "I would have been screwed out of my inheritance, but now Jay will be screwed out of his."

"That's crazy," Jay said calmly. "Blood or not, you're my brother. It's the raising that counts, the living together as a family."

"Saint Jay," mocked Barton coldly. "And you'd do it, too. You'd give me a quarter of the ranch."

"You're my brother."

"You're a schmuck," Barton said. "*Look at me, schmuck.*"

Jay's attention never shifted from Henry and the gun at Sara's head.

She watched Jay, only him. She thought about going limp to break Henry's concentration but was afraid that she would get shot the second she moved.

I never got to tell you that I love you, Jay.

"Henry," Jay said. "If you think Barton will give you one cent of whatever he gets his hands on, you're crazier than he is."

"You should have read JD's will," Henry said. "If I'm foreman when the ranch is sold, I get four percent."

Jay just listened and waited for Henry to make a mistake.

"Get the damned painting, Barton," Henry said. "I couldn't keep JD from getting in bed with Liza then, but I can protect my percentage now."

"What do you mean about Liza?" Sara asked, doing anything she could to get his attention away from the gun pressed hard into her cheek.

"JD told Liza he wouldn't marry her until he got her pregnant," Henry said. "He said Ginny was all but barren. He wouldn't have a barren second wife."

"Mother got knocked up real quick, but not by JD," Barton said, his smile as cold as the person he had always been beneath the act. "She fooled him but good."

"JD figured it out after years went by with no more kids," Henry retorted. "He divorced her. Then he held Barton's quarter of the ranch over her head to make sure she never told anyone that Ginny hadn't been the sterile half of the Vermilion marriage." Without looking away from Jay, he asked, "You have that canvas set up yet, Barton?"

"Ease down, old man," Barton said. "Wouldn't want you to throw a big clot and die before the fun begins."

While he talked, Barton finished dragging over and levering onto a nearby table a canvas taller than he was. Smiling, savoring every moment of power, he took a can of lighter fluid from his overcoat pocket and squirted liquid randomly over the painting. He was laughing when he tossed the can on top of the canvas.

"No," Sara said hoarsely. "*Muse* is priceless."

Barton laughed at her. "I only wish this was my mother. She could nag a statue to its knees."

Sara made a mute sound of protest, and the gun barrel dug deeper into her cheek.

Barton lit a cigarette with his pocket lighter, then grinned down at the painting.

"Do it," Henry said impatiently.

"What's the rush? I've waited years to see my older brother helpless. He's such a schmuck. All he has to do is shoot through the bitch and kill you, but he's too weak to do it. How's it feel to be the weakling, bro?"

"Love isn't a weakness," Jay said. "It's the greatest strength there is."

"And you call *me* crazy." Barton flicked the lighter to life and held it to a corner of the canvas where fluid dripped down to the floor.

"No," Sara said. "No! You're burning something that can never—"

With a soft whoosh, a cloud of fire billowed up into Barton's face. He leaped back, sending a chair crashing into Henry, who looked reflexively to see what had happened.

Two shots rang out like one. Henry was dead between one breath and the next.

The instant the grip in her hair loosened, Sara leaped away, grabbed a sheet from the floor, and ran to the painting. Hurriedly she began snuffing out the fire.

Jay bent to pick up Henry's pistol.

When he straightened again, he found himself looking at a gun held by the smiling stranger who had once been his younger brother.

"This isn't a pussy gun," Barton said. "It's bigger than yours. I just wanted to use Mother's for any killing." He shrugged. "Now I'll have to think of another story."

"Give it up," Jay said.

"Not a chance. You're too weak to shoot your little brother, but I'm not too weak to shoot you. Chooka-chooka, bro."

Two more shots snapped out as one.

"Jay!" she screamed, running toward him.

But it was Barton who fell to the floor, a surprised look on his face.

With movements too swift for Sara to follow, Jay kicked the gun out of his brother's hand and tested his neck for a pulse.

"Is he . . ." Her voice faded.

"Dead. Like Henry. The army didn't teach me to miss." Jay closed his brother's eyes with a sweep of his hand and looked up.

Sara saw the tears streaming down his face and held out her arms to him.

The gallery door slammed open. "Nobody move!"

She choked off a scream. *Will it ever be done?*

"Easy, Cooke," Jay said, his back to the sheriff. "It's over."

Three deputies piled in behind Cooke, guns drawn.

"Any weapons?" the sheriff asked.

"Three that I know of," Jay said. "I'll put mine down if you tell your deputies not to shoot."

Cooke looked at his deputies. "Stand down. Go ahead, Jay."

He put his pistol on the floor and turned around slowly.

The sheriff looked at Jay's face and sighed. "Damn, son, I hoped you wouldn't have to be the one."

Jay didn't say anything.

"It's not his fault," Sara said quickly. "Barton was going to kill me and then Henry was going to kill me and then Barton was going to kill Jay and—" Her voice broke into a sob.

Jay pulled her close and held her, just held her.

With a low curse, Cooke swept off his hat and then resettled it with a snap. "Benson, you protect the scene. It will be a while before Davis gets here. He has to wait for the ambulance to pick up Liza."

"Liza?" Jay asked. "Her bruise didn't look that bad."

"It was the bullet in her gut that killed her, but not before she talked."

"Henry," Jay said bleakly, remembering what his foreman had said about *cleaning up after Barton*.

"That's what she said, along with enough other stuff to make me want to kick some sociopathic ass. What the hell happened, Jay?"

"It's a long story," he said. "I'd just as soon only tell it once."

"M-Me too," Sara said.

Shivers wrought havoc on her equilibrium, but they had little to do with cold.

"Adrenaline overload," Jay said softly against her ear. "Hold on to me."

He lifted his head and said to Cooke, "Can we take care of the formalities at the Vermilion suite? Sara spent too long running through the snow wearing only a blouse and jeans and was dunked in ice water twice along the way. She needs a warm bath, hot soup, and a chance to come down from the terror of being hunted like an animal and then having a gun held to her head. Send a deputy along with us if you have to."

"After what Liza said, you're the last one I'm looking to arrest," Cooke said, glancing at Henry. "Son of a bitch. I wouldn't have expected it from him."

"They were going to sell the ranch after Barton inherited, using my blood for the DNA test."

"Barton isn't a Vermilion?" Cooke asked, startled.

Behind him, his deputies talked in excited whispers.

"No," Sara said. "Custer was Barton's sperm donor."

"I'll be damned," Cooke said. "Liza didn't say anything about that. Now it makes more sense, in a twisted up kind of way."

Jay closed his eyes for a moment, thinking about the irretrievable past. Then he tilted Sara's face up and kissed her gently.

"Come on, sweetheart," he said. "Let's go home."

He only wished it was her home, too.

Chapter 30

Six Months Later

The Jackson gallery was filled with swirls of well-dressed people holding champagne glasses and munching canapés. Beautiful color catalogs of previously unknown paintings by Armstrong "Custer" Harris were stacked on an elegant table. For those who actually had bought a painting at the auction earlier, there was also a complimentary, and very expensive, illustrated coffee-table book describing Custer's life and paintings. Studded throughout the text were anecdotes of his life on Vermilion Ranch.

Sara circulated through the crowd wearing a black sheath and the antique Indian jewelry that Vermilion women had worn for well over a century. In an irony that still burned as much as it amused, Jay had inherited Liza's and Barton's "material goods."

In addition to the jewelry, Sara wore a professional smile over the turmoil churning in her mind. *The Edge of Never* had become one of the most talked-about and nominated movies of the year. That, and the buzz around the newly discovered Custers—to say nothing of the scandal of JD's ex-wife and her child by Custer—had driven the price of the paintings higher than Sara had expected.

Once the press began to breathlessly report on stories of murder and mayhem in the well-heeled Wyoming resort town of Jackson, the resulting perfect storm of publicity meeting notoriety had made the furor around Wyeth's Helga paintings look like the kind of teenage hair-pulling that might occur when two girls wore the same dress to their small-town junior prom.

The effects of all of those factors combined had seen the restored *Muse* sell for over a million dollars.

Every one of the other Custers Jay had chosen to liquidate at auction had a sold sticker beside it. The cheapest painting, a small study of intersecting wooden fences that had once been stored in a cardboard box, brought seventy thousand dollars.

Nothing like a hot auction to wring out wallets, Sara thought.

Despite the unqualified success of the last six

months, leading up to the gala evening, she felt like she was being torn apart. Though she and Jay had alternated flying between Wyoming and San Francisco, saying good-bye had become harder each time—for both of them.

Tomorrow it would be the same.

Suddenly needing to touch Jay, she looked around the room, searching for a man with black hair and the muscular ease of an athlete or a predator. She spotted him trapped between two svelte matrons in designer clothes.

They reminded her of Liza. From the tension beneath his polite veneer of interest, Sara knew that Jay felt the same.

Even now, sometimes she woke up at night with her heart beating too fast and screams throttled in her throat. When Jay was with her, she curled into his heat and held on until the worst was past. When he wasn't with her, she got up and worked until she was tired enough to sleep again.

Get over it, she told herself. *It's past. Nobody is hunting us now.*

"You put together a first-class auction," someone said to her.

"Thank you. Custer is a first-class painter," she said automatically, smiling and moving on.

Only belatedly did she realize she had all but snubbed

the man who was her newest client, a man who had bought three Custers—all of them among the artist's best works. She thought about going back, but the lure of standing next to Jay was greater than any client, no matter how wealthy.

"Excuse me," she said to the designer matrons. "There's a call for you, Jay."

"Ladies," he said, nodding to the disappointed women.

He followed Sara as she wove expertly through the crowd, greeting half the people without inviting anyone to linger.

She's good at this, Jay realized anew. *Really good. She handled all the endless details and never lost patience or interest. Now she's getting calls to do the same thing all over the country.*

The realization that they would once again be saying good-bye tomorrow was a cold heaviness in him that had grown greater each time they separated, no matter how brief the trip.

Each time it became harder, tearing up both of them.

This has to end, he thought starkly. *It's costing too much.*

For both of us.

Sara unlocked her office door at the back of the

gallery. Moments later she locked it again behind herself, a new habit she saw no point in breaking.

"Is it about the ranch?" he asked.

"No. I just needed to hold you."

He gathered her against him carefully, completely, letting her female warmth and fragrance drive away the sinking cold that thinking about tomorrow had brought.

"I love you," he said against her cheek.

She brushed her lips over his neck and tightened her arms. "I love you so much it's tearing me apart," she admitted, her voice hoarse with pain at the thought of yet another separation.

"It's the same with me." The muscles in his arms flexed as he held her even closer. "I didn't want to say anything until I knew for sure, but this week I talked to a big corporate cattle operation. They offered me a good price for the ranch."

She pulled back to look into his navy blue eyes. "Do you want to sell?"

"I want a life with you," he said simply.

"Don't sell," she said, pressing her face into his neck. "The city isn't a place I want to be more than I need to be with you. San Francisco is lonelier than I ever imagined it could be when you're at Vermilion Ranch."

Sara felt his arms wrap around her until she could

hardly breathe—or maybe it was fear of the unknown that made her breathing unsteady. When she heard Jay repeat her name and his love against her ear, it gave her the strength to meet him more than halfway.

She turned her head to brush Jay's lips repeatedly with her own, breathing in his words and returning them with her own between hungry kisses. "Can I take over a room or two at the main ranch house for an office? The way my business is going now, I'll have to hire an assistant."

"You can have the whole damn house for an office," he said roughly.

She smiled. "We have to leave room for our children."

He put his cheek against her hair while emotion shook him. "You don't have to have kids. I know you don't want—"

She put her fingers over his mouth. "I didn't want to be like my mother. I'm not. I want children, Jay. Your children."

"Marry me."

The raw need in his voice made her eyes sting. "Yes. Oh, yes."

Jay lifted Sara into a kiss that sent heat racing through them, a fire that would grow through the months and years together, the future they would share.

And that fire was love.

Author's Note

As always, the landscape of my novel is real, but within that reality, I create something wholly fictional. Thus, Jackson and the Tetons exist in all their glory, but to my knowledge, Vermilion Ranch exists only in my mind. It is the same for the characters, alive only in my mind.

And now in yours.

About the Author

New York Times bestselling author Elizabeth Lowell has more than eighty titles published to date with over twenty-four million copies of her books in print. She lives in the Sierra Nevada Mountains with her husband, with whom she writes novels under a pseudonym. Her favorite activity is exploring the Western United States to find the landscapes that speak to her soul and inspire her writing.

THE NEW LUXURY IN READING

We hope you enjoyed reading
our new, comfortable print size and found it
an experience you would like to repeat.

Well – you're in luck!

HarperLuxe offers the finest in fiction and
nonfiction books in this same larger print size and
paperback format. Light and easy to read, HarperLuxe
paperbacks are for book lovers who want to see
what they are reading without the strain.

For a full listing of titles and
new releases to come, please visit our website:

www.HarperLuxe.com